MASTER CONTROL

a novel

Hugh Hanafi Hayes

Cover Design and Text copyright © 2007 Hugh Hanafi Hayes

This first edition published in Great Britain in 2007 by
four o' clock press - a discovered authors' imprint

ISBN13 978-1-906146-51-1

The right of Hugh Hanafi Hayes to be identified as the Author of the
Work has been asserted by him in accordance with the Copyright,
Designs and Patent Act 1988

All rights reserved.
No part of this publication may be reproduced, stored in a retrieval system, or
transmitted, in any form or by any means without the prior written permission of the
Author

All the characters but one in this book are fictitious and
any likeness to anyone living or dead is purely coincidental.

Printed in the UK by BookForceUK. (BFUK)
BFUK's policy is to use papers that are natural, renewable and recyclable products and
made from wood grown in sustainable forests where ever possible

discovered authors
50 Albemarle Street
London W1S 4BD
www.bookforce.co.uk

Also by the same author:

Hayes over New Zealand
(Non-Fiction)

MASTER CONTROL

Acknowledgements:

Thanks to my wife Ardilah for reading and checking at least four of my drafts and to my friend Dairobi who abandoned his family and business to read and enjoy the last one.

There are more things in heaven and earth, Horatio,
Than are dreamt of in your philosophy.
Shakespeare's
Hamlet

1

The light was flashing insistently. Master Control was empty. Well, apparently so. But suddenly a white flare darted across the space, momentarily illuminating a massive bank of monitors, each with its own light, glowing in the darkness. It was a space without doors, without walls, without any suggestion of size. Pure space. Suddenly, as if from nowhere, a presence manifested into a shape. An indeterminate shape. Immediately it was at the board, pressing a button below the flashing light.
"Yes?"
"I need some help."
It was a male voice and the words were scrambled, re-assembled and received in the control room simultaneously in hundreds of different languages, dialects and communication sounds.
As more lights started flashing, the shape spoke to the enquirer in the appropriate language.
"Could you hold the line please? Your call is important to us."

He pressed a button marked celestial music. Then he passed along the lines of monitors, pressing and repeating his message and tuning everyone in to the soothing sounds. A minute later, he had returned to his original call.

"How can I help you?"

"Is that Bapak…?"

"Nope."

"…Jesus…?"

"Nope."

"… Muhammed…?"

"Nope, again…"

"… er… actually, I was hoping to speak to the Almighty… through a Messenger of course."

"Who?"

"The Almighty. Well, you know, one of His Messengers, really, perhaps Bapak?… you see, I've been a diligent devotee of the spiritual way through the *latihan* for many, many years and tried always to follow His guidance, well nearly always." The voice was now supplemented by a face on the monitor.

"He's busy. So are Ibrohim or Abraham, whatever your faith, er… Adam and, well… look, all the Messengers are in a meeting. In fact, we're pretty well flat out just now up here, but I can take a message. I am Calisthene, by the way, I'm an Intergalactic Helper. I've seen you before, haven't I?"

"Well, no, not really I did try to get in touch before about the unsatisfactory results I've been getting from testing… even with others, but I didn't make it. I didn't get to ask my question. So this is me again and it seems that I've got through, and I really do have something I must resolve and I'm not at all clear what course I should pursue… I…"

"Actually, you did get through before and we were aware of your dilemma, but we decided at the time to let you continue with your life as it was for a while."

Calisthene was almost serene in his state as he talked to the man in need. In fact, his whole being seemed to change constantly. His countenance reflected exactly the mood necessary to deal with whatever was required of him.

"Now, here's the drill brother, tell me the question you want answered, I'll record it and we'll make contact with everyone on our residents' data base that you've had contact with in your life so far, so that they can all make their comments and assessments. We'll then have an Intergalactic Helpers' council meeting to make our recommendations. Probably won't need to bother the Messengers. Then we'll be in touch. Consensus is binding though, don't forget." A beatific smile left his face momentarily.

"Well, there are a few people I wouldn't bother, if I were you", the man tried to insist, "I mean …"

"Now, now, no choosy choosies." The smile was back. "How else are we to assess what quality of advice to give? How you've treated people during your life is of paramount importance to the Almighty and although He does of course know everything about everything, being omniscient and all, we can't be bothering him all the time, can we? And he does like us to double check. So, your behaviour and attitude to others is our principle gauge. Just have faith brother." Now, Calisthene was businesslike.

"What was your name again, Henry, wasn't it?"

"Yes, that's right, Henry Pild."

"And the problem that is so important?"

"Well, as you might know, I was a successful doctor at one time… that is until… well the fact is that although it's a little while since I practised medicine, pure medicine, I am experiencing strong feelings that I should return to that profession. Unfortunately, I did some testing with the local helpers in my group and I got a mixed bag of answers, so… well, then I tried the national helpers and the international ones and it was just the same thing… nothing very clear. I think they were all using their minds and they were clouded by, well, by things in my recent past."

"OK, that's lovely. Say no more, I've got it. Gotta rush now, talk to you later, Henry. Tootle pip!"

The face on the monitor disappeared and Calisthene, was now joined by several other flares of light that manifested into shapes of both men, women and a variety of other beings, all busy pressing buttons and parroting the standard: "Could you hold the line please, your call is important to us." in a vast collection of languages.

Calisthene was now at a computer calling up Henry Pild's data file.

Subject: PILD, H, R or P, he typed. *STILL ACTIVE.* Then the message: *Anyone who had any connection or dealings with this man please contact Master Control, ASAP, to make comment and assessment. Subject wishes to confirm or deny validity of feelings he is experiencing regarding changing professions, i.e., returning to the medical profession.*

Meanwhile Henry considered his position. He quietened his heart and mind and consulted his inner, asking it: "How should I behave in this situation?" *Calm and patient, in a state of submission* was the answer he received. It always seemed easy to seek and get spiritual guidance…but practical matters appeared to defy this source of help. Mind you, folks had told him, he could always use common sense. But that was no longer Henry's strong suit. He'd changed. Oh, how he had changed over the last few years.

In fact, Henry Pild was not really Henry Pild at all. Not in the world he now inhabited most of the time. Henry was a name given to him by his spiritual guide, because it was *received* as being more in tune with his inner, his soul, than the one his dear parents, Sam and Kerrin had landed him with. He was Christened "Rufus, Grenville, Pild". Rufus, after a dearly loved and sadly grieved cocker spaniel the parents had owned, before his arrival. Well, actually almost right up to the time of his birth. Sadly though, the dog had been the victim of a car accident. A tragic affair.

A handsome, but gently ageing animal, Rufus had been lying asleep just under the front wheel of the family car, when Sam got the call from the hospital that his wife was about to deliver. Not even stopping to put on a coat, the man had rushed from the house, leapt into the car and roared forward at considerable speed, crushing the unseen pet. The driver had felt a bump, and through the blurred rear mirror seen something stretched out. But, perhaps remembering the old adage: "Let sleeping dogs lie", he'd sped on to be at his wife's side for the big moment.

Regrets came later of course, but they were softened by the new arrival in the family. However, Sam and Kerrin felt the least they could do to pay their respects and keep the memory of their late "best friend" alive, was to name their son after him, particularly as it had also been the name of Sam's father.

The boy was never really comfortable with his given name, and was relieved when he acquired the new name of Henry. However, although he was recognized only as Henry amongst his spiritual family – he was a member of a group, which was part of an international brotherhood – Rufus was also to be known publicly, but for a very short period, by an altogether different name: "Paisley". Paisley Rathbone, in fact.

So, anyway, Rufus or Henry, or "Paisley" trained and qualified to become one of the country's most brilliant microsurgeons. Certainly one of the youngest. His remarkable dexterity and authority with the accoutrements of his profession soon built an amazing reputation for him, making him famous. Then, almost before he knew it, he was embarked on a new career.

It all started with a reality series on television called **Through the Microscope**. He was asked if he would take part as the surgeon-in-charge of a microsurgery unit. Each week different aspects of microvascular, microneural, and microtubular surgery techniques were illustrated and explained by Rufus Pild, MD, as he was then known. The series was so successful that the young doctor was asked if he would do a second series, in which he would train other would-be microsurgeons. However, as he was mulling over the prospect and, as his *alter ego*, Henry, *testing* for some inner guidance as to whether or not he should agree to do it, another much more exciting offer came. When that happened, Rufus didn't consult "Henry" and he certainly didn't bother *testing*.

The fact is that after just that first series, Rufus Pild had become a household name. So well constructed were the television programs and so eloquently did Rufus explain the sensitive and complex surgery on view that **Through the Microscope** surged to the top of the ratings after the first three episodes. It was popular amongst people of all ages, but particularly amongst teenage girls and gay men. Oh, yes, Rufus was very handsome, very tall and very well built and as he did his presentation usually in a tight tee shirt, it was sometimes hard for some viewers to take their eyes off him and concentrate on the bubbling arteries or crimson nerve ends as they were being tended to. Indeed it was his personal exposure in the program that brought the offer, the exciting offer, that really changed his life.

Rufus was visiting his parents when he got a call on his bleeper. He rang the hospital and was told a woman was trying to contact him. Her name was Mercy Cryer and she had said it was very important that he should get in touch with her as soon as possible.

Rufus wrote the number down in his diary and thought little more about it. Because of the program, he had more than his share of "calls" from interested young women and in fact he'd followed up on some of them. But at this stage not too seriously. At 29, he wasn't ready to settle down.

In fact, Rufus was a fairly naïve young man in the ways of the world – the material world. From the age of seventeen, when he was opened to the spiritual brotherhood to which his parents belonged, as 'Henry', his focus had been almost entirely on his medical training and his dedication to his work and the

Almighty. Like his parents and all the other adherents that he met, he believed that by diligently following a particular spiritual exercise, he would be purified and guided by a higher force than the animal, vegetable and material forces that dominated and influenced the actions of most folk. He might even get an insight if not an actual experience of what it's like to exist on the true human level. Beyond that he understood that there were spiritual levels he could only dream of. He was considered something of an oddball by his colleagues. Particularly, if he ever tried to explain his philosophy. But that apart, he didn't drink or smoke anything and the only thing he stuck up his nose was his finger on the odd private moment.

Mum and Dad Pild were, understandably, very proud of their son. They felt that their own search and discovery of life's true values had paid off big time. They both felt blessed that their quest for spiritual enlightenment had not only been successful in influencing and guiding their lives, but, also future generations of Pilds. However, contributing any further to the Pild dynasty was not on the young doctor's agenda just now. For one thing he hadn't met anyone so far that he felt was his soul mate; that special person with whom he could procreate and share his destiny. Oh, there was that nurse at the King Abdullah Free Hospital where most of his operations were carried out. But although there certainly was some electricity that seemed to pass between them when they were in the theatre together, Rufus always assumed it was the nerve-end cauterizer and the principal laser instrument that she passed to him hand to hand that was the cause of the little zing he experienced. Always, however, above her mask, Veronica, the most experienced and most attractive nurse in microsurgery, watched his every move with a love that knew no bounds.

At any rate, a few days after her initial call, Mercy rang again. This time Rufus Pild was at the hospital, fresh from an operation, changing from his theatre outfit to his civilian tee shirt and jeans.

"Yes, Pild here, who is this?"

"My name is Mercy, Mercy Cryer, I'm an agent, I have something I want to discuss with you… can we meet?"

"Are you with… look, I told Richard that I wanted a little time to think it over… that idea for a second series, if that's what you…"

"No, No, I'm not with those people. Not reality television. I'm an agent. You know I represent clients – only a very select or elite group of clients and I just know I can do wonderful things for you. Why don't we meet tonight if you're free and get through some preliminaries."

"OK." Rufus didn't even know why he'd agreed. "Where do you suggest?"

"Well darling, you don't mind me calling you darling, do you… well, can you get to Temporal Mansions in… better still, why don't I pick you up and we'll have dinner, say around 7.30. I know where the hospital is. What do you say?"

"Fine, 7.30 it is"

And so it came about, with the preliminaries taking all evening and well into the night. Mercy Cryer, was a mover and shaker. She had plans for Rufus far beyond his wildest imagination. She was not only an agent, she told him, but a producer and she already had a very well-known writer at work on a drama series based on microsurgery but featuring Rufus in a different relationship with infatuated women intent on seducing him in each episode.

At first, Rufus's almost puritanical sense of moral rectitude resisted such a notion. He was a doctor first and foremost, but he believed in the sanctity of pure love and respect for what he called the God-given privilege to indulge in sexual congress in order only to procreate. But Mercy was determined and plausible. She was also a very beautiful woman. Expensively and seductively dressed, she made Rufus feel like a gauche youth, in his tee shirt and jeans, pliant and gullible in her experienced hands. He found her perfume intoxicating and after featuring in the television reality program, he couldn't deny the satisfaction his ego felt by her proposal. He was vulnerable.

"Your private life is sacrosanct," she told him, her eyes glinting with desire. "No one can ever touch that or even influence the morals and ethics that guide you. But as an actor you stand outside of all that and represent nothing more than an image, an object perhaps, of the desires and yearnings of the people. The ordinary little people who want to believe that their lives can change. The folk that need to be taken to that special place outside of the mundane existence that daily swamps them. Trust me darling, you have a huge role to play in this world. Oh, I know that you are already a brilliant microsurgeon, but believe me, you could become another Dr Kildare".

Rufus didn't know who Dr Kildare was, but he was already being seduced by the soft purring voice that was so convincing. She ran a beautifully manicured finger down his cheek. And this was just the preliminaries. Before he knew it, he was committed to 'negotiating' with her. Firstly on the couch in her lounge and then in her bedroom. She really did know how to 'negotiate' and Rufus found no problem at all in agreeing to continue 'negotiating' every evening for the next week or so. 'Henry' was forgotten and old ideas soon became... old ideas.

However, the 'negotiations' came to an abrupt end ten days or rather nights, after Mercy had managed to get Rufus to sign up for a "guaranteed successful career as an actor" as she put it. In practical terms it was as the star of a series of seven dramatic episodes, with an option for a second series. She also made sure that in her presence, the brilliant microsurgeon contacted the producer of the reality television program and officially turned down any further episodes. It was a coup for Mercy, who had previously promised the head of a rival television channel that she would ensure that the highly rated ***Through the Microscope*** would not be spawning another series. Certainly not with Rufus Pild MD, anyway. He could, she assured him, rest easy in the knowledge that the non-commercial station that had carried it would no longer provide any threat at prime time for the commercial channel's main reality show: ***Big Momma meets***

Big Daddy – which examined why so many obese people meet up and marry.

That TV attraction had started off with much audience interest and good ratings that brought in wonderful advertisers like McAndrews, maker of the two pounder, Alabama Chicken, Hungry Fred's, Fat Pete's Pork Pies and – Guts Galore, a new self-service fast food chain where the customers paid a standard fee of ten dollars – five dollars for under three year olds – picked up a big plate and then stepped onto a moving walkway. Alongside it, a smorgasbord of pies, pasties, hamburgers, hunks of pork crackling, cream cakes and pastries of all shapes and sizes were all travelling slowly in the opposite direction. The idea was to grab and stack as much onto your plate before your moving path took you to the end and out of reach of the flab-making goodies, which were heading, inexorably, beyond the longest arms.

Initially, before it was properly policed, this exciting innovation in gross consumption had some teething problems. Until customers really understood the process and limitations, there was trouble when some tried to backtrack even on the moving path. Inevitably, greed even led to fistfights and food throwing. However, by speeding up the electric belt controlling the movement of the food so that it whizzed past the stretched out hands of the battling customers, a pause and some decorum was created and once again, controlled plate-filling was established. Of course, the management soon realised how easily they could manipulate the amount of food that was being taken for the ten bucks even by the most honest and docile of customers. After some trials they discovered just when to "speed up" the process ever so slightly to ensure that plates were rarely filled and they made an enormous profit.

Anyway, in return for her good work in subverting the competition's future plans for Rufus, Mercy was guaranteed a slot for a drama series with the commercial channel, which would feature the subject of her most recent attentions. For the young doctor, it was fortuitous that decisions had been made.

The 'negotiations' had begun to affect his work at the hospital. Inevitably, the normally scrupulously efficient surgeon, made a serious mistake. Luckily for him, though, he was protected by a love greater than any negotiation with or without Mercy could ever bring. A love he never really appreciated.

He was actually with Mercy. It was the day that he'd fulfilled all the agent's requests. He'd phoned the television station and turned down a second series of **Through the Microscope**. He'd signed the contract for exclusive representation by the Cryer agency and was just enjoying a post-negotiation cup of tea when his bleeper called him in to the hospital for emergency surgery.

The operation was routine, any one of a number of microsurgeons on the hospital list could have attended, but, he was told there was something special about this situation and the hospital registrar had insisted on calling him in. Apparently, a man had somehow chopped off the middle finger of his right hand. Fortunately, the man's wife had picked up the finger and wrapped a packet of frozen peas around it before calling the ambulance. The victim had been distraught. Both the man and the finger were waiting for the genius that was Rufus Pild.

When the surgeon arrived, the patient was already sedated and waiting to be taken into theatre. While he was scrubbing up, Marlon Mandrake, the anaesthetist opened the washroom door and called to Rufus.

"How d'ya feel about cricket?"

"Cricket? Can't stand it, why?"

"Oh, never mind. Just that you might have been interested in the guy on the table."

"Yeh, who's that then?"

"Only one of the best spin bowlers in the world. Something funny up, too. The police want to speak to him as soon as he recovers. Good luck."

The theatre staff all seemed expectant as they went about their duties when he joined them, masked and fully covered. They obviously had something on their minds in the presence of the comatose cricketer at their mercy. So did Rufus, but it wasn't the same thing. Something about the lights perhaps, but his full attention was never there that evening. Within seconds, he was back in Temporal Mansions, 'negotiating', mentally anyway, with Mercy. He just went through the motions of the operation and as usual, the nursing staff and his female assistant were more interested in looking at those deep blue eyes above the mask and admiring him rather than watching what he was actually doing. It was only when he'd finished and his brow had been lovingly patted dry for the last time, that someone, Veronica, the head nurse, noticed something, but her tongue just wouldn't move and she was unable to speak, to warn…

When Rufus and the others had left the theatre, expecting the junior nurse Ann Tizer to clean up and arrange for the attendants to take the patient through to the recovery side ward, suddenly Ms Tizer also saw what Veronica had seen.

"Oh, my God!" she exclaimed.

The severed finger had been sewn on backwards, with the nail facing inwards rather than outwards. As always, the actual surgery was immaculate, but this blunder of judgement was one of awful proportions. Veronica calmed the other nurse and considered her next action. Had he done it on purpose? Was this his comment on sport and particularly cricket? She knew this maestro of the micro was not interested in organised games, but no, he wouldn't, he couldn't… she acted quickly. She decided she could repair the situation and save both his embarrassment and his reputation. But, no one must ever know. Veronica "became" the microsurgeon, reliving everything she had ever learned from her work with the man she secretly loved; the man she first met when she too was a medical student.

At that time, she had been sure he was as attracted to her as she was to him. She was petite, confident and very intelligent and several other male students had been drawn to her big brown eyes, but she could only ever focus them on the tall, slightly awkward boy who seemed to exist in a space of his own. Because of her persistence, they dated a few times, a few innocent times and she even managed to invite him to her parents' home for dinner. When he accepted, he seemed oblivious to the generally understood significance of that arrangement, but it turned out to be quite an occasion.

The Milstein family were very well off and they lived in a large apartment with a view of the ocean on three sides of their dining room. When the couple arrived, the father Cec, a stockbroker, was affable enough, on the surface, anyway, and mother Milstein managed to combine a sweet, almost seductive, charm with the concentrated intent of an assassin.

After the formal pleasantries and the obligatory viewing through the lens of a huge telescope set up by the window of an upstairs bedroom, sadly, things didn't go quite as Veronica had hoped. On reflection, the seating arrangement had probably been a mistake. Poppa Milstein sat at one end of the table and Momma at the other end. Veronica and her date sat on opposite sides. However in a slightly cheeky, flirty way, Mrs Goldie Milstein had set Rufus's place fairly close to her own. It proved to be a fatal error.

Actually everything was going quite well, initially, although Veronica was constantly wincing at her parents' pointed remarks about the guest's non-Jewishness. They were an orthodox pair but their daughter proudly proclaimed that she was an *unorthodox* Jew, so the meal, or any gathering that gave her the opportunity, quickly provided Goldie with a chance to lecture not only the outsider but also their own maverick daughter on the injustices perpetrated against the Jews throughout history. With a look that cut like a laser beam from mother to daughter, she would proclaim that anyone born Jewish should be proud of their heritage and eager to perpetuate both the race and the religion.

"You're not Jewish Mr Pild are you." It was a statement rather than a question and Mrs Milstein managed to make it with one smiling, kindly eye on Rufus and at the same time with her other eye still aimed at her daughter.

"No, I'm not, I'm afraid, but I belong to a spiritual movement that has Jewish members, and Christians, Hindus, Buddhists, Muslims…"

Suddenly the condescending half smile died on Goldie's heavily painted lips.

"Muslims? Terrorists? You have terrorists alongside Jewish people in your organisation? What kind of people are they to allow terrorists in?"

"Don't be ridiculous Mom, Muslims are people just like you and I, in fact, some of my best friends are Muslims".

"Well they wouldn't be welcome in this house." Mrs Milstein brought her clenched fist down with a bang on the table, rattling the several bracelets that adorned her wrist.

Veronica shook her head, looking at her date and hoping he hadn't taken too much notice of her mother's comments. Cec Milstein leaned forward and helped himself to some water.

"Are you a Muslim, Mr Pild?" Goldie was still on the attack.

"No, I'm not and I don't know any terrorists at the moment."

Rufus seemed unaware of any visual reaction to that last comment, like the cold flick of the eyeballs from mother to daughter. Indeed he just continued to smile awkwardly through the melon *hors d'oeuvres*, and the sugar-coated barbs that were flying about, until, just after a large plateful of roast was put in front of him, his bladder gave him a reason to excuse himself from the table for a momentary respite.

That's when it happened. His plate must have been slightly, oh, ever so slightly, over the edge of the table. He was a big man, and as he got up from his seat, at the same time turning to his hostess intent on apologising for his lack of forethought, the buckle on his belt caught the edge of the fairly full plate and over it went.

Unfortunately, Mrs Milstein was dressed in a very expensive-looking light cream dinner gown, and as she reacted to the first assault of food that hit her lap, two slices of brisket, a hunk of noodle pudding and a fair dollop of sauerkraut, she in turn, in a spontaneous act of protection, accidentally pulled at the once crisp white cloth and brought over a glass of water and a jug of rather fatty gravy… again much of it finding her evening dress.

The air was suddenly filled with wails of anger and disappointment. Mrs Milstein's hands were held to her eyes and then high above her head, offering up her grief and beseeching her maker to hear her as she uttered dramatic claims that it would be impossible to ever get the gown clean, it was ruined and it cost, well never mind the cost, it was an original, "oy, oy" and tears. Then came the clear instruction to her daughter to "get him out of my house" given in a low, chilling voice meant for Veronica only, but said at a pitch that seemed to make all the glassware on the table rattle and caused Cec to stand and adjust his *yarmulke* that had slipped in the excitement.

Rufus tried to apologise, but ears were closed and heads turned away, so, he excused himself rapidly and hurtled from the scene, never to return. Once outside, in the dusk of a beautiful evening, the air filled with the heady perfume of the jasmine flower, he could bear his urinary discomfort no longer and was forced to relieve himself over the very shrubs that produced that fragrant blossom. Cultivated around the side of the apartment building entrance, they were planted specifically to lift the spirits of all who entered. However, on this occasion they had served to lift the spirits of one who was leaving.

After that things seemed to cool between the couple and although Veronica tried everything she could to get him to forget the incident and to prove that she was quite different from her parents – she even went out of her way to order bacon sandwiches when she sat near him in the university refectory – he made it clear that he just wanted to be friends and nothing more.

However, Miss Milstein's ardour never faded and she knew that one day he would come to her and all would be well again. Well that was her hope. She even dropped out of the medical school and turned to nursing with the clear intention that somehow she would contrive to be near to him in his future work. She would transfer to wherever he was working and be right by his side. That way she could share some of him and perhaps, as time passed, she could share more and more. And so it came about. Never envious, she always felt the glow of admiration for Rufus as he progressed through his medical studies, his specialisation and emergence as a brilliant microsurgeon. Although throughout all that time, she ached to tell him how much she loved him, she was content to just witness his genius at close range. It had always been a wondrous experience… until that fatal day.

★ ★ ★

Veronica checked the theatre window to make sure that everyone had cleared the area. Then she swore the other nurse to secrecy and with a sureness that surprised the junior, added a small measure of anaesthetic to the patient, checked pulse and heart and then, after applying a tourniquet to the wrist, she severed the offending digit precisely across the recent suturing of the surgeon's. With a deftness that even further amazed Ann Tizer, the senior nurse, seemingly inspired, was now rejoining the finger to the hand with the nail and knuckle on the outside as they should be. When finished the work was almost as perfect as Rufus's except that the member was slightly off kilter. Too late now for any further correction though, as the anaesthetic was beginning to lose its effect and the blood was now released to flow into the cell tissue to start the healing process.

The finger was bandaged and then double bandaged to the next one in the hope that it would act as a splint and perhaps help to straighten up the wounded digit. Then the table was cleaned up and the attendants called.

Outside, an anxious wife, the manager of the national cricket team and two men from Police Special Investigations branch all waited for the patient to recover.

When Veronica finished changing from her hospital uniform, she checked through the window of Rufus' office, although she had no idea what she would have said had he been in there. Fortunately he'd already left.

Still totally captivated by the woman who seemed to be the key to a new direction in his life, the surgeon had driven straight back to Temporal Mansions in the hope that he could continue 'negotiations'. When he got there though, he was to be disappointed. Either she chose not to answer his persistent buzzing on her intercom or she was out. Whatever the reason, there just was no Mercy and Rufus felt a sinking feeling. It was very late and there had been no indication when he left her charms to rush off earlier, that she would be going out. He rang her phone. A voice invited him to leave a message. He phoned her mobile. It was switched off. Realisation finally came and further tainted his pure soul. The 'negotiations' were over. She had got what she wanted. He was set on a completely different path in life, a path he was determined to explore with the promise to himself that he would be as successful as an actor as he was as a surgeon. Even without any formal training, he knew innately that he was a performer and resolved to show everyone that he could make it with or without Mercy.

Now, though he had to cut all his other ties. He would retain his membership of all the professional associations that he had been accepted into, but he would no longer practice medicine in any form. Rufus's situation was beginning to crystallize. As he made his way back to the hospital, he realised that he had been in a kind of fog. It was almost as if his will had been taken over and he was just going through the motions of his life, like a plane on automatic pilot. He could hardly even remember the last operation he'd performed, even though he'd been told how important the patient was. He did recall that. But how did the operation go? He'd been in such a hurry to return to his romantic reverie in Temporal Mansions, he hadn't given either his work in the theatre or the patient a second thought. His main intention now, though, was to clear his office of all his personal effects and in the morning to make his resignation official and known to all. He'd worked at this famous hospital almost since it was built and endowed by a grateful Saudi Arabian family before the wave of paranoia towards people from the Middle East swept like a tsunami across so-called Western societies. Located in Sydney's western suburbs, the hospital was established as a symbol of goodwill to the people of Australia and welcomed patients of all creeds and religions. Originally it was established to serve the needy, who couldn't find a bed in the general hospital system, but as so many specialists chose to be associated with it, a private wing was opened for the wealthy like the maimed cricketer. The money from the private section helped to subsidize the rest of this huge hospital, but the money wasn't really needed. The Saudis were committed to totally fund their gift in perpetuity. Just who the benefactors were was a mystery. All business transactions were conducted through a Swiss bank and overseen by anonymous lawyers. Of course there were rumours as to its *raison d'être*, this apparent incongruity in a land that still paid homage to the English Royal family. One wild theory was that the hospital was a gift to Australia in gratitude for its support of America's determination to destroy Iraq's ability to compete with the Saudis in the world oil market. Another was a really far-fetched story that suggested that an Australian mercenary had rescued a Saudi princess from a gang of marsh Arabs who had daringly abducted her and demanded a huge ransom. The hero, it was claimed had been raised in the western suburbs of Sydney, where now the name of King Abdullah was both famous and respected.

★ ★ ★

When Rufus arrived in the hospital precincts that evening, he noticed that although most of the building was dowsed in the usual subdued night light, the hospital boardroom fluorescents were blazing and as he walked through the reception area, a head bobbed up from behind a computer.

"Oh, Mr Pild, Doctor, I'm so relieved to see you. You're wanted… look here's your bleeper, you must have left it behind when you rushed off this evening… been trying to get you on your phone…"

"Why, what's up, is my patient alright, the cricketer guy, eight o'clock, finger off."

"Yes, well I don't know… but you are wanted in the boardroom, by the hospital Super and the police… please go up straightaway, I'll ring them and tell them you're on your way."

Rufus was met with mixed reactions when he entered the boardroom. The men were all sitting at the solid oak table, which was littered with empty coffee cups.

"Oh Rufus, good, glad you're here." The hospital superintendent looked relieved.

"These gentlemen are from the police and they want to ask … well we have a bit of a situation with your last patient… nothing to do with you of course, but they want to ask you a couple of questions that may help them. This is Inspector Blitzen – Don - and this is Sergeant Mann – Constantine Mann… er Con for short, isn't it? Con Mann, oh dear that doesn't sound too good for a policeman does it, ha, ha," the man blundered out, laughing to cover for his embarrassment.

The two men stood up to greet Rufus, the sergeant warm and enthusiastic, the inspector leaning slightly back as he offered his hand seemed to be examining Rufus from top to foot.

"Hey, it really is you." The sergeant was like a little boy meeting his idol.

"I watch every program, you know, my wife too. She thinks you are just wonderful".

Rufus smiled modestly and suggested they sit and get started on whatever they wanted to know.

"What's the problem, then?"

"I'll come to that in a minute". The inspector took over.

"First if I may, I'd like to ask you a couple of questions about the chopped finger. Now, you must have seen a lot of chopped off fingers in your time, doctor…"

"Oh, boy, I'll say" burst in Sergeant Mann, "remember that episode in your series when the man was distracted whilst he was using a circular saw… what was it, two or three… still had the thumb, though, I remember…"

"Thanks Con, can we let the doctor answer the questions, how about a cup of coffee all round… can you Con? … Now, doctor as I was saying, you must have seen a lot of chopped off fingers and you must have been able – just through sheer experience – you must be able, just by looking, you know, to sort of say how they came to be chopped off, or separated, so to speak from the main part of the hand. Would I be right in assuming that, sir?"

"Well, I don't know… I suppose you can make certain assumptions from say the type of cut or injury to the member. Whether it appears to be the result of a clean slice or blow, made by a sharp implement or a jagged cut, made by a saw or a blunt instrument or something without a, you know, sharp edge."

"What about the type of implement?" The inspector leaned closer.

"Well that would be difficult, particularly by the time I get to see the wound and the detached finger. You see if there was rust or any tell-tale sign like that, it would be cleaned off and waiting in antiseptic fluid for the operation. I can tell you one thing about this particular op that one of the nurses mentioned just before we started." A smile teetered on Rufus's mouth.

"Yes, what was that?" Inspector Blitzen's eyes widened.

"Well, apparently the member, the finger, came into the theatre wrapped in a bag of frozen peas and the anaesthetist, Marlon, who's a bit of a wag called out "Ah, McCain, you've done it again! You know, the TV ad for McCain's frozen peas?" Rufus couldn't restrain himself now and his boss, hospital Superintendent Rizal Humphries joined in the laughter. Inspector Blitzen, however, was not amused and he turned and snatched a cup of coffee from the sergeant's proffered hand, spilling it down the front of his trousers and onto his shoes in the process.

"Oh, Jesus, you stupid"... He was not a happy man, but he quickly recovered.

"So, to summarise: can you please confirm whether the finger was removed by a single blow, by a sharp instrument?"

"Yes, I could say that." Rufus was serious again.

"And was there any bruising on any other part of the hand, arm or any other part of the patient's body?"

"Well, I really was only aware of the hand and that seemed free of bruises before the operation anyway. I'm sure you've inspected the other parts of the patient since you arrived?"

The two detectives looked at each other, the senior man's eyes, just slits. "Yes, well... now," he turned back to Rufus, "finally, we know your time is valuable, but any help you can give...so, in your opinion could the injury have been self-inflicted, or is it possible that it was caused by a third party? In your opinion."

"A third party?"

"Another, or some other, person or persons unknown."

"I'm sorry, Inspector, by the time I saw the patient and his severed finger, there was no way I could form a judgement of that type. All I was aware of was finger and a vacant space. Sorry."

The policemen were on their feet, offering their hands to Rufus and the hospital head.

"Thanks anyway, we'll be on our way and please keep this whole thing to yourselves, if you would. We are still following up our enquiries and it would be a disaster for all parties if a sniff of anything suspicious were to get into the media. We'll let ourselves out, goodnight."

"Keep what to ourselves? What's all that about?" Rufus frowned at the Super.

"Oh, well, you'd better know, but please keep it all to yourself. Don't tell a bloody soul. Want another coffee?"

"No thanks."

The hospital boss placed one large buttock on the table top and then crushed it with the rest of his ample body. "It seems the police are sceptical about the story that the wife told the triage nurse when she brought her husband and the finger in to emergency. She said he had hacked his own digit off as he was chopping up some ribs for a barbecue. They said, that's the police, said, they thought it was a bit odd that the index finger was the one that was maimed, for one thing, but they had far more serious doubts about the accident. In fact they feel it may not have been an accident at all, but rather a deliberate assault on that finger, his main spinning finger, by, as they said 'a person or persons unknown'."

Rufus was tired, but now he was really puzzled. "What! What... who on earth would want to do that to him? I hear he's played around a bit but I can't imagine how even a furious cuckolded husband would, could do that... could he?"

"I don't know." Rizal Humphries shifted his weight off the now numb buttock and slid down onto a chair. "But Inspector Blitzen has hinted, well more than hinted, that they think he has been paid back in this cruel fashion for passing false information to some Indian bookmaker. They claim, they had a tip off that our friend had been offered a generous sum of money for a pitch report and detailed local weather forecast for a test match he was playing in a few days ago. There might even have been more to the arrangement than that, it seems. However nothing much could be proved, apparently, except that the weather forecast that the bowler had phoned over to them – which he got in good faith from the meteorological office – was, as usual, completely wrong. Instead of the expected baking sunshine which would have favoured the other side, the match was completely distorted by humidity and rain... and the home side won hands down – against all the odds. Particularly the ones being offered by the Indian bookmaker. He lost a lot of money, they claim, and threats were made. That's why our friends Blitzen and Mann suspect foul play and they don't mean on the cricket field. So now you know, but try to forget it all and just concentrate on your work and your patient. We must do all we can to restore him to his former very talented self, if that's possible. The country needs him. But, I don't need to tell you that of course. How are you anyway?"

"Me? Oh, I'm fine." Rufus hesitated for a second. "But, look, I really should tell you, I guess."

"Tell me? What? Sounds serious."

"No, not really... look, the fact is that I came to the hospital tonight to write out my resignation. You see, I don't intend to practise in any capacity in future, either privately or publicly... I'm sort of changing course."

The hospital Super was standing now. "Changing course? That's ridiculous, my boy, you are the best in the business, you know that. You have a talent... an incredible talent, as a surgeon, you can't just walk away, you're still so young."

"Well, that's really why. I want to try something else while I am still young and I've had an offer that excites me... what can I say?"

Rizal could see that a decision had been made, but he continued nevertheless: "Look Rufus, I don't know what it is that you want to pursue, but have you really talked it over with anyone else? Your colleagues, or your father... I know he's a great influence... what is it anyway?"

Rufus was getting ready to leave:

"No, I haven't talked about it ... I don't need to. It's all set, I'm going to be an actor... I have to go now but I'll keep an eye on that patient of course... cheers."

2

Back, or perhaps forward, to Master Control. Parapip, an assistant to Calisthene was monitoring calls and making notes in a computer of the various comments being offered in response to the earlier broadcast call from the intergalactic helper. A small, studious looking being, Parapip was from a planet other than earth. Happy now that he had left his outer form behind, he was totally dedicated to his work and the beings he served. Following instructions, he had created two data pages: one for complimentary comments and the other for uncomplimentary ones. Also whenever there was a pause, "Pip" as he had come to be known, was viewing visual footage. He had access to pictures taken over many years, of the actions and whereabouts of one Henry Pild - recorded by unseen surveillance vehicles that circled the earth, recording the activities of every single person born on the planet and archived for uses such as the present one. This was an extra and valuable source of information on the subject, to be used in any needed arbitration before a decision was taken on whether Henry was worthy to receive advice and if so the kind of advice to be given.

"Hey, take a look at this guy…" Pip, made the comment in perfect English, in fact, he could have made it in any one of a thousand languages or methods of communication that he was qualified to use. On this occasion he was addressing another assistant working nearby. She was an attractive earthling, or rather she had been before she was called, prematurely, her husband and family thought. Now, like Pip she worked in the Master Control of the intergalactic research centre.

"Wow, what a dish!" Danilda was impressed at what she saw over the shoulder of her colleague. "Who is he and where is he?"

"Relax, my friend, he's still down there. He's my subject, in fact. He is Henry Pild, but this was taken several years ago when he was still Rufus and had completed the first four years of his degree course in medicine. He was twenty and a near perfect earth specimen by all accounts at this stage."

"Who's the girl he's talking to? Seems pretty friendly." Danilda returned to her own place of work.

"She's really interesting, I believe. I spooled fast forward just now and they were together in a cinema. Heat seeking infra-red cameras captured that. Amazing isn't it. She would certainly be one I'd like to get a report from or some comment on his character and behaviour towards her. Her name is … Veronica Milstein… she's a couple of years older than him… just a minute while I see what I can get from her"…Pip was clicking on various keys in front of him.

"Oh, that's a shame. She's still down there, too, still on earth for a while yet and won't be able to give any kind of comment unless Henry himself requests it from her to substantiate his case for consideration." The researcher double checked the name: "Milstein, Milstein… I've seen that name here somewhere…"

"The violinist? Nathan Milstein, lovely man, he's in the celestial orchestra now, you know".

Danilda still seemed half interested in the work being done on Henry – "the dish".

Pip was scrolling through the images again. "No, no relation..." He pressed a button marked *Time Transference* and when a graph appeared on his screen, he put in a date, months ahead in earth time. "Here it is, Goldie Milstein and she has something to say about our subject, listen to this."

"My name is Goldie Milstein, well it was Goldie Weinstein before I married Mr Milstein. You ask me if I would like to say anything about Henry Pild. Well I certainly do and so would Cec, my husband, my first husband, if you asked him. This man is no good... this Pild person. His name was Rufus when my daughter brought him to our home. A terrorist. Belonged to some strange spiritual group, that's right and he brought terror to my home, completely ruined a beautiful Versace dress I was wearing. Versace designed dress, that is, from Hong Kong. I'd hardly worn it. I'm telling you, it was some dress. I bought it when I went to Florida one year. White with gold trim and... anyway, he ruined it. Couldn't wear it again. Couldn't get the stain out. The man was *mishiga*, hopeless and clumsy. How he became a surgeon is hard to imagine and worrying. Knocked a lovely dinner I'd prepared all over me, gravy, everything. Never got the stain out. Tried everything. Had to give it to a charity shop in the end. The man's no good. Behaved terribly towards my dear Veronica too. Ruined her life. She would have done anything for that man, even though he was a terrorist, but he just discarded her... that's my opinion anyway. You were lucky to get me today. Cec and I – I went back to him before we both... well before we both.... Yes, Cec and I had been to a reunion of former earthlings from our part of the world, you know, where we lived when we were... well anyway, there were several hundred I would say, yes a hundred at least, and Cec said he didn't recognise a soul. Recognise a soul, get it? He's a funny man sometimes. Is that all? Is that ok? Right."
And the words and image stopped.

"Poor Veronica" Danilda called over. "Where is she, that woman, what level?"

"Earth time or our time?"

"Well, I know you went forward quite a few months, so, when that was recorded."

"Still on the material. Still circling the stratosphere. Still attached to all her former worldly goods and desires. Keeping an eye on them so to speak. What she doesn't know is that Henry, or Rufus to her, will be her salvation, but that's in the future, her future. Meanwhile, she remains her old bitter, selfish self. Actually, I think Mrs Milstein heads up the uncomplimentary comments, but he's got some good ones in the other data file". Pip called up the other file to his screen. "Like this one, from a grateful patient he once tended, or so the man thought. Wanna hear?" Once again, Pip entered the time transference zone and applied a date to come, in the future.

"Oh, ok... I've got a wee window. Just pretty well finished a complete file on a very unpleasant piece of work who is finally seeking redemption... anyway, what's this about then?"

"Well, it's a bit of a joke, really. You see our, subject, Mr Pild – 'the dishy one' - was just about to go into free fall in his spiritual life, when he was called in to perform an emergency operation on a famous, very famous cricketer. I didn't know what cricket was until I got this case. Anyway, the guy had had a finger chopped off under mysterious circumstances and Henry (Rufus) had to sew it on again. I should tell you that he was a brilliant microsurgeon at the time – the best. However, because of a lack of concentration, he sewed the finger on backwards and was completely unaware of his action. However, his head nurse, who just happened to be the Veronica you were sympathising with, saved his arse so to speak, by re-severing the digit and then sewing it back on. Without him knowing a thing, would you believe. Now everything would have been hunky dory if it hadn't been for the fact that when the second operation was over, it was discovered that the finger was re-attached slightly off-kilter. By now of course it was too late to do anything about it and even though it was Henry's responsibility to do post-operative checks, he never got a chance".

"What d'you mean?" Danilda had moved over closer to her colleague.

"Well, as I mentioned there were mysterious circumstances surrounding this incident. The police were even investigating the cause of the so-called mishap – that's what his wife had called it when she brought him in. The police, though, were following up leads that pointed to some rather nefarious goings on and apparently an Indian bookmaker had fingered, oops sorry, had named this cricketer as being involved in a scam. We have all the facts, along with some vivid vision of course, and I'm not going into all that right now. The main thing is that the patient, apparently a genius at spinning the ball, didn't wait for any post-operative checks (or more police interviews) and instead persuaded a nurse to give him a plentiful supply of the necessary medication to prevent any cell degeneration and skipped out of the hospital and away. His wife was waiting outside with the car.

Later he assured the hospital that his personal medical adviser would look after any further treatment for his finger and along with a letter of thanks to the staff – 'particularly the microsurgeon who had performed the crucial operation' - he sent a very generous donation to the hospital. Actually there's lots more I could tell you. But I must get to the kernel of the story. Is that the right term, kernel?"

"It'll do, and...?"

Pip couldn't resist a smile. "Well the fact is that rather than being furious when he discovered that his index finger – his spinning finger – was not straight and in line with the rest, he was thrilled. Apparently, ever since he had learned to spin a ball, he had tried to curl that finger in the process, to achieve great and novel variation. However, for any extended period, this method was painful, even if it was effective. But, now that he had a permanently twisted finger, it would be painless and even more effective, to bowl what he called his 'wrong 'un'. And so it proved. When he was able to play again, he was like a demon bowler, completely unplayable by most oppositions. The problem was, though, that although he was almost exalted in the cricketing arena, he had a weakness, what you might call a social weakness, that inevitably proved to be his downfall and the reason for his early demise."

Pip paused and gave Danilda a strange look.

"This is beginning to sound interesting". She still hadn't completely eradicated all earthly feelings and knowledge. "So, need I ask, what was his social weakness?"

"Look, my dear colleague. It means nothing at all to me, personally. To my knowledge, it relates only to sensations peculiar to earthlings. Once it was more commonly associated with the male of the species, but now it apparently is experienced by both male and female sexes. I refer to extra-marital sexual gratification, whatever that is. I understand that what was originally a sacred act of procreation, has, over the centuries, descended to the level of base acts, all perpetrated simply for sensual pleasure or the transitory enjoyment of sexual satisfaction. It seems to take many forms, at least in this cricketer person's case: from sending dirty text messages to women, talking dirty talk over the phone whilst masturbating, as well as the more normal adulterous relationships."

Danilda was inwardly blushing a little as the scenario was described in completely unemotional terms by her fellow researcher. "I get the picture, Pip. So what happened to him?"

"Well, the inevitable I suppose. You see, after several warnings from his wife, she realised that he was so addicted to extra-marital sexual activity – beyond all hope she felt – she took things into her own hands. Er, I hope you don't misunderstand that last phrase... sometimes my English tends to favour double *entendres*, I really must do a refresher course. Anyway, she decided to act decisively. One night, after sedating his cocoa, that he always insisted on before he went to bed, she cut his sexual member off and worse still, this time instead of wrapping it in a bag of frozen peas to preserve it for another brilliant operation by a microsurgeon, she threw it to the dog. It was a callous act, I suppose, but considered a desperate one by the wife… and it nearly went all wrong for her. Apparently the dog sniffed at the article and decided he didn't want to touch it, so the woman, now frantic at the screaming and bleeding of the man in the bed and disappointed at the rejection of what she thought would be a treat for Buddy the wolfhound, turned to the only alternative means of disposing of the troublesome phallus. She flushed it down that place where earth beings evacuate their bodily waste, you know, the bog."

"Toilet."

"Ok, toilet."

"Oh, no, how could she!" exclaimed Danilda.

"Well with some difficulty, apparently. It took three flushes to send the offending piece on its way. Meanwhile the still groggy cricketer, now aware of the situation, managed to staunch the blood and phone his medical adviser. He also furiously questioned his wife why she had done what she'd done, but she just laughed hysterically and called back 'Guess?' He demanded to know where his missing part was and when she told him, he called his legal adviser, instructing him to send for the police. Then he phoned back beseeching the man to instigate a search in the sewer pipes that led from his house and joined with all the others that sent the neighbourhood effluent surging on its way to the treatment plant."

Pip could tell a good story, even if he didn't really understand the significance of much of the detail. Where he came from the inhabitants knew nothing of genitals or the problems they could cause when motivated by lust. Procreation was an intellectual exercise between male and female. Coupling was simply an exchange of electronic impulses, activated from the natural respect one creature had for another. Love was pure and selfless.

Suddenly, Pip received a time signal from his computer. He turned to Danilda: "Look, I'd better get on, this is all taking much longer than I expected, but to cut to the chase – oh dear there I go again – to get to the point – that's not much better is it? Well the simple truth is that no trace of the missing part was ever discovered and so the poor man was left with a severe shortage in the genitalia area. But he was determined and faced with the prospect of a rubber bladder slung between his legs and enforced celibacy for the rest of his life, he sought a transplant of the desired organ from any donor that could quickly be found. Once again, microsurgery was called upon, but not this time in the King Abdullah Free. No, he was whisked off discreetly to a small private clinic where all the staff were masked both above and below the eyes, and sworn to secrecy over what they might witness.

"When the recipient was shown the donated member that he would be inheriting, at first he was very pleased. It seemed to more than match his own original body part. The operation was a success, in appearance at least. However after a short period of rehabilitation, when he tried to stimulate himself, he found nothing but a flaccid handful. Watching some pornographic images did nothing more for him and soon it became apparent that the donated organ had in fact belonged to someone with severe erection problems. Again, though, the cricketer was not going to take things lying down (ouch!) so he tried a drug that boasted all kinds of properties that would ensure, what it described as the ability to make a piece as hard as a rock. It didn't work and so after trying any and every other product on the market and after consulting every pudenda specialist in the country, the spinner had to give up and accept both his loss and what he had gained in its place. He was a changed and depressed man from then on and could hardly raise a smile when he visited his wife, who had been imprisoned for her cruel act of retribution.

"He played a bit more cricket, but by now, the crowd seemed to know something was missing and he was no longer regarded as the wizard of spin. In fact his fans that once idolised him, starting calling him "wicketless" or old "middle stump". His total misfortune had obviously been leaked by someone with a vengeance. The unfortunate man died of a broken heart, after a massive build up of sperm in his testes, burst their sacs for lack of use!

"Nevertheless, despite all, he'd always remembered the good days; the wonder period when he terrified and completely bamboozled batsmen, thanks to his finger being sewn on off-kilter. His words of compliment for our subject – remember? Henry? Are effusive – if completely mistaken - and more than compensate for the rather negative view expressed by Mrs Milstein. But there are others for me to check out, so if you'll excuse me, I really must get on."

"Of course" said his colleague, "but just out of interest, save me looking it up for myself, where is he now, in future time, I mean. What level is he, this cricketer person?"

Pip was patience itself. After pressing two buttons, he turned to Danilda and said: "He's actually been put on the vegetable level. That's it really, until or if he gets released to progress. He wasn't a person who was dominated in any way by all the material success he enjoyed, so he skipped the material level. He might well at one time have been a perfect candidate for the animal level, because of his anger and his lustful ways, but after he lost his ability to fornicate and then of course when his bollocks exploded… that is right isn't it bollocks, you know, his testes?"

Danilda nodded.

"Well after that, he was just a prime candidate for the vegetable level. Ok?"

She nodded again and they both resumed their work.

★ ★ ★

A few days after Rufus, (Henry) had officially cut his ties with the hospital and his private practice, he finally received a phone call from Mercy Cryer, his agent and prime negotiator. He'd been trying without success to make contact with her ever since the night he was called to the hospital to operate on the cricketer. In fact he felt slightly in limbo. Not only could he not understand her sudden disappearance from his life at a time when they seemed to be really in harmony, but he needed to know more about his new career prospects as an actor.

"Hello, Mercy, what happened?"

"Rufus? Look, I will explain everything when I see you… not at my apartment, though. Can you, can you meet me tomorrow in Manly, say around noon? Outside the ferry terminal. We can have lunch and have a chat. How does that suit?"

"Fine, I'll meet you there, sure… but Mercy, but, are you, are we…?" Rufus was struggling.

"I've got to go, see you tomorrow, 'bye." The voice on the phone was cold and abrupt.

Rufus was beginning to have serious doubts about his decision to follow the blandishments of Mercy, and the very lucrative financial carrot that had been dangled before him. He was not naturally attracted to material affluence. His God was not mammon, but the creator or great life force that had hitherto guided his way and given him confidence in everything he did. Now, he felt vulnerable. He wanted to confide in his spiritual colleagues. Wanted to ask his group helpers to test with him whether the course he had chosen to follow was the right one. That it was, as they always used to say: "in accordance with the Will of the Almighty." He knew, though, or suspected, that if he did try to get their advice, he'd have to tell them the whole story and that would mean describing the sometimes torrid 'negotiations' that he and his agent had been involved in. Negotiations that took him away from that inner guiding light and into a realm of sheer physical pleasure that he'd never before suspected could exist. Certainly not in a shared way with another person. Oh, he had experienced bliss of a different kind when he stood and felt the inner movement of the spiritual exercise that he had practised. Not always, but at certain times when his heart and mind were quiet enough for him to totally surrender to its influence.

He couldn't discuss his predicament with his parents. He respected them too much to reveal that he wasn't exactly the son they thought he was any more. They had been shocked at first when he told them that he was taking a break from medicine and planning to become an actor. Although, perhaps it shouldn't have been so much of a surprise, since his father had been an actor in an earlier stage of his life. Neither parent had ever tried to influence him in that or any other direction and they were both relieved and very proud when he chose to study medicine and developed into a talented and celebrated microsurgeon. How they would react to the more personal elements of his relationship with his new agent/producer, is another thing. They always assumed that he was determined to stay virginal until his true life partner was identified. They hoped it would be someone who was a member of the same spiritual movement that they, and later their son, had been such strong adherents to. But he always seemed less than interested in the young women that he came into contact with in that society, however attractive they might be. To Rufus, those women, young or old were his sisters, just as the men of whatever age were his brothers. Now, though, his innocence was lost and he didn't know who he could confide in or even whether he should do so anyway.

★ ★ ★

An Eagle Eye UAV flew low overhead on its monotonous circling of the harbour surrounds, the sun glinting on its sombre shape. These Unmanned Aerial Vehicles were now a regular feature of the famous skyline and if you didn't want a visit from the federal agents later, you didn't carry anything that would look the least bit suspicious to those surveillance drones. Now that tourism was the economic mainstay of the city of Sydney, security was kept at a very high level. Armed marshals always rode the buses and trains and anyone carrying suspicious packages was forced to reveal all contents before being allowed to board all public transport. The opera house, now considered one of the wonders of the world, was not only heavily guarded, but like every place of public performance, its program selection or repertoire was now subject to government censorship. The opera Otello (the Moor) for instance, could never be staged there or anywhere else in Australia, although a maverick company did do just that in the gymnasium of a high school in Kalgoorlie, in the far north west. Unfortunately for them, though, a deposed and embittered former federal MP for the area heard about the production and dobbed them in to the anti-sedition forces. The whole company was seized in the middle of a performance, arrested, charged and sentenced to a year on the island of Nauru. The thirty or so members of the audience were also detained and taken for de-briefing and brain cleansing in the fully equipped facilities of the local branch of the Australian Patriotic Task Force.

Rufus felt a slight sense of excitement as he purchased his ticket for the next ferry, aware that several pairs of eyes were on him and everyone else intending to make that journey. The signs clearly pointed out that after being scanned for any hidden weaponry, dark haired passengers should pass through one set of turnstiles, whilst fair haired travellers enjoyed much easier access to their platform. However, even these privileged folk were subjected to unseen scrutiny, above their eye level. Its effectiveness was made evident to Rufus as he ran the security gauntlet. Suddenly two guards appeared from nowhere and apprehended an apparently very blond man in his forties. There was a slight scuffle before he was led away from the concourse.

"What was that all about?" Rufus asked one of the men scanning for metal.

"Hey you're that doctor on TV aren't you?"

The man had been completely distracted from his duty for a moment and Rufus cursed the fact that he'd taken his dark glasses off and had been so easily recognised.

"Yes, that's right, but do you know what happened over there just now, with that man who's been taken off?"

The scanner man smiled. "Mate, it happens all the time. Crafty bugger had dyed his hair to try to pull a fast one. The camera up there picked it up. Black hair roots, you see and that swarthy skin gave him away. Can't take any chances can we... have a nice day" and he returned to his work, checking for metal and anything middle-eastern.

Rufus made sure he had his sunglasses back on and his white fedora pulled well down when he boarded the ferry. Nevertheless, he was an imposing sight even if he wasn't recognised and plenty of female eyes noticed his presence amongst them. But his interest was elsewhere. As he watched the harbour police boats buzzing around with binoculars observing every passing craft on the water and every bit of movement on the surrounding land, he was thinking of Mercy and wondering what she really wanted in asking him to meet her in this mysterious way.

A seagull almost collided with the Eagle Eye drone as it came low over the water. Surely it wasn't expecting a submarine to infiltrate, he thought. But in the minds of the government, all possibilities for any would-be terrorist strikes were being considered and every potential route, however unlikely, was constantly under scrutiny. As Rufus made his way forward to be amongst the first to disembark when the ferry docked, he brushed against a large sinister-looking man leaning with his back on the rail surveying everyone along one side of the boat.

"Pardon me" he said.

The man had frowned at the accidental collision, perhaps annoyed that Rufus had bumped against the firearm concealed inside the other's jacket - identifying him as a marshal. A low profile security agent.

"I hope you've got a licence for that." Rufus turned to say, but in a flash the man had disappeared. Once off the ferry and another row of turnstiles had to be negotiated before passengers were finally free of cameras and scrutiny. Outside the terminal building, under the clock, Mercy was waiting, but he almost walked past her as he looked around.

"Rufus…"

The soft tones were unmistakeable, even if they came from a woman with very large sunglasses and a headscarf that almost completely hid all sign of her naturally radiant blonde hair.

"Mercy? Is that you? I didn't…"

The lady was already on the move. No embrace or even peck on the cheek this day.

"I thought we might just walk along the front for a while… before we eat… is that ok with you?"

Rufus would have walked into the sea with her if she had suggested it. At last he was with her again and the smell of her nearness was as enthralling as ever.

"You look great, I've been trying to…" Rufus attempted to put his arm around the lady's waist, but she pulled away and kept walking.

"Listen Rufus, I'll come straight to the point and it will be better for all… both of us. The fact is that things can't be the same any more".

"What do you mean?"

"I'm married."

"What!" Rufus was stunned. "I don't believe that. What just like that. What about all those meetings at your flat, what was that all about? Were you married then or is it something that you've just drummed up?" Rufus had stopped walking and turned her round to face him.

Mercy's voice was low and cool. "I've been married all the time. For four years if you must know and, well, my husband was away and I was … Look Rufus, I really don't want to hurt you, but my relationship with you was one of convenience. It was for one thing and one thing only, to get you to leave your television program and sign a contract with me and the chance to be a real performer in television. There you are, it may not be nice but it's the truth and I'm not particularly proud of it. But you haven't seen me for a while and nothing really has changed. Nothing important has changed. The program series is pretty well scheduled now and you will go into production next week. Everyone is still excited about it and ... but look, there is one other thing."

Mercy took Rufus by the arm, like a father might take a child when he was about to dispense some really meaningful advice. She led him to a vacant seat away from ears or eyes.

The doctor felt drained. A sense of shock had been replaced by first the impact of betrayal and then disillusionment and finally an awareness that he was very much alone. Even his own inner had let him down. No guidance available it seemed because he had chosen to enter a world outside the world that had sustained him since he was a teenager. Now, he knew he really had to choose. He could turn back and reinstate himself in his former life. Throw away the dreams and enticements that had managed to find his ego and feed it, or else he could accept where he was and what he had committed himself to and follow and experience whatever presented itself.

"You see, oh Rufus don't think too badly of me. Really, I do have great affection for you and I did enjoy all our 'negotiations', you must believe that. Can you forgive me?"

Rufus sat and looked at something a thousand miles away. He had nothing to say.

"It's so important that whatever has happened, whatever ... however I behaved, it's important now to forget it and move on. We have to work together. Well, I have to work for you and I just know that you have a wonderful, brilliant future ahead... So, can you forgive and forget, can you?"

Rufus nodded.

"Oh, great", Mercy opened a small brief case she had been balancing on her lap. "Ok, now there is one other thing that we must get sorted." And she pulled out what looked like a contract. "You see, the television company has discovered that your father is a Mohammedan, or Moslem or you know. Is that right? They say his name is Ridwan Pild, not Sam as you told me."

"So what?" Rufus showed the first sign of anger that he had ever displayed.

"My mother is too or at least she has a Muslim name: Renita. That's right, when they wish to use their Muslim names they are Ridwan and Renita Pild. When they choose otherwise, they are Sam and Kerrin. So what?"

"Do you also have a Moslem name then Rufus? Are you a Moslem?"

"No, I'm not and I don't, but if I did want to embrace Islam and if I did want to use a Muslim name I would, even in the atmosphere that exists nowadays."

"Oh, well, that's just the point, you see. Because of the way things are, you know, with so much suspicion of these middle eastern religions and terrorism and so on, the company want to make a few suggestions… to get rid of any possible suspicions and so on… what with your future as a very high profile person."

"Middle eastern religions? You mean Judaism or Christianity?"

"No, no, you know what I mean. Mohammed… er Moslems you know. Anyway, they want you to change your name for one thing, just in case there is any association with, well Ridwan Pild really. Anyway it's no big deal, most actors adopt theatrical names that will be more suitable for their career and their, you know, image. I got together with their publicity people yesterday and we came up with a name that we all feel is good for you. Look at me, Paisley."

"What?"

"Paisley!"

"Paisley? Me, Paisley?"

"Yes" Mercy was beaming. "Yes, oh, looking at you now, I see it is just right. Paisley Rathbone is the full name and it suits you down to the ground. So there it is, you will …no, from today, you *are* Paisley Rathbone and there's just one other little thing…"

"Just hold on a minute. What if I don't like the name and won't use it from today or any other day?" Rufus started to get up from the seat.

"Please sit down Rufus, I mean Paisley. Look the fact is that the lawyers have drawn up addenda to the contract. You may have noticed when you signed, that down at the bottom of your contract, in the small print, you agreed to any new cultural points that the company may introduce at any stage to enhance both the artist and/or the company. The name is one such cultural point. Another is that you must never be seen near a mosque or with known Mohammedans – including your father – that is, not to be seen with them and... that you will be publicised attending Christian ceremonies in churches or the cathedral or even socialising at church bazaars or sausage sizzles". Mercy was now cold and businesslike.

"So here's the official document with all the details or addenda and you just sign ... here... and here, where I've put those little crosses." She laid two copies of the document down on the seat, put a pen on top and eased along from it for Rufus to sign.

"Oh, no lady, you've gone too far. This is ridiculous. Unethical ... it's against everything... and what if I say screw you and them, I refuse to sign this piece of ..."

Mercy looked around and took her sunglasses off for the first time. Her eyes were cold and her lips tight, until she opened them to say: "What will happen? I'll tell you what will happen. They will sue the arse off you and destroy you in public. Sign the bloody thing."

Rufus also took his sunglasses off to read the document, then after a withering look at his companion, he shuddered and reluctantly signed...*Paisley Rathbone* and handed the top copy to the agent.

"Goodo, that should be just fine" Mercy checked his signature, folded her copy of the document up and put it neatly back in her briefcase. Then slipping her sunglasses back on she said: "Great, now let's go and get some fish and chips... make sure you put your sunnies back on though… Paisley! We don't want you to be mobbed just yet."

3

Samuel Langhorne Pild had a couple of secrets he hadn't revealed to his son, and coincidentally they both contributed to his feeling of unease at the change of direction Rufus had decided on.

Born in London, during the Second World War, Sam had been a bit of a rebel in his youth. His father, who he doted on, served with distinction in the British army and survived the Normandy landing which paved the way to victory in Europe. He came home a hero from that conflict, but sadly, he was killed six years later, after volunteering to fight in the Korean war.

An act of God, had taken his daddy, Sam was told. That was something he found difficult to understand. God doesn't kill people, he thought. People kill people. God doesn't make guns. People make guns. Maybe, even his own father had killed people. He knew he had a gun, he'd seen a photo of him as a soldier, in a kilt, proud and smiling, with a rifle in his hands. But even if his dad had killed people, he still loved him and missed him. So, along with his older brother, he was raised by his mother, with a little help from a small army pension, his grandparents and the money the boys could earn delivering papers, assisting on milk rounds, bread rounds, anything.

His parents must have been a fascinating twosome. The elder Pild, an engineer, was originally from Scotland and, apparently, he was a voracious reader. In fact, he was such a fan of the writings of Mark Twain that he gave his first son the name of Mark Sean and his second son, Samuel Langhorne, the author's actual first names. His mother Caitlin, was as Irish as the shamrock and her hobby was cage birds. She had a room full of them and she used to speak to each and every one of them by name in the strongest brogue you could imagine. But if she wasn't in the bird sanctuary, which had been the living room, she was offering tea to anyone who called by.

"Would you like a nice cup o' tay" was her mantra for making a soul welcome and to assuage any concerns or anxieties that she may have detected that needed her special healing powers, contained, she claimed, in the strong brew she served up. She was originally from County Cork and she'd migrated to England to find a husband, so she said. How she and "Jock" Pild had met and got together, Sam never did find out. Whenever he tried to broach the subject, she would laugh girlishly and say:

"I'll just make us a nice cup o' tay, that I will."

Sam was a bright lad and had done exceptionally well at school and then, initially, at university. But he became bored and decided that he wasn't interested in an academic career after all and dropped out. He once claimed that his greatest accomplishment, during his brief spell as an undergraduate, was to drink six pints of lager and eat a chicken Vindaloo in one hour and then to vomit it all up in 45 seconds on someone's neat lawn on his way home to his digs. A friend had timed the second part of the achievement with a stopwatch.

After that and after firmly refusing his mother's suggestion that he enter the church, he spent a short period in art school and then managed to win a place to an acting academy. However the only real success he had there was in bed with one of the teachers, a Laverne France, who was several years his senior.

Actually almost like his son Rufus and his sudden and passionate liaison with Mercy Cryer, Sam didn't seem to know how this improbable relationship came about. It was on him before he knew it. Later he was to discover that the woman had a bit of a reputation in this regard, but as a new and willing pupil, he had been completely trusting. However when he found himself, under her personal instruction, participating in a completely abandoned love scene in her flat, he was lost, snared like an innocent rabbit.

Through the teacher's advice, Sam seemed always to be involved in scenes in class that required him to make love to an actress and Laverne used to take notes then invite him back to her place to discuss the work, criticize it and, under her expert guidance, discover how to improve on his performance. It didn't last for too long though. As handsome and physically attractive as Sam was, Laverne seemed to tire of his *naïveté* and she soon moved on to the next and latest pupil to come under her tutelage, discarding her last young lover completely.

At first the young ex-virgin was puzzled. He seemed to be learning so much in these sessions and the acting was so real, he was convinced he was ready to take the plunge, leave the academy and try to get some commercial work for himself. And he did just that.

He rarely saw or heard anything from his brother Mark Sean. The last time they met, he had told Sam that he was a "lazy git" and he should get himself a trade or some training in something. Sean, as he preferred to be called, was considered the success of the family. At first, to please his mother he had enrolled in the priesthood and become abstemious and to Sam, annoyingly pious. Just about everyone was impressed by his devoutness. Well nearly everyone. Not Sam, though. By the sheerest of coincidences, he'd just happened to see his big brother emerge from a seedy strip joint in London's Soho one afternoon, clothed, Sam noted, in not one single item of the trappings of the priesthood.

Sean was striding off, head down, fairly quickly at the time, but his delighted brother caught up alongside, put his arm on the other man's shoulder and said: "What are you up to then, you dirty old dog."

Sean went white. "What do you mean? I'm meeting someone near here."

Sam was enjoying this immensely. "Come on man, I just saw you come out of a sex show... look right there, the one with all the flashing light bulbs and big boobs in the window. You sanctimonious old sod, you. Was it any good?"

Sean had been shaken to his shoes. "Look, shut up will you. I was doing some research... and..." eyes narrowed and lips just thin threads... "don't you say a thing to anyone, or I'll bloody kill you." And he strode off away from his younger sibling.

"OK, Onward, Christian soldier" he called out after the disappearing Sean.

The next time the brothers met, the priesthood was just a memory. Although he was still a devout Catholic and regularly accompanied his mother to Mass, Sean had changed his vocation to studying mechanical engineering. Sam had moved on too, but without a great deal of success. He was sharing a small flat in Hampstead with a young oboe student, named Saul. They got on extremely well, both living on the dole, but with a little support from Saul's parents and whatever he could get from busking whenever he had no study periods. He did extremely well at Christmas, he said. "You could pull in five quid for certain with each rendition of *"The First Noel"*.

Sam tried to make some money on the streets, too, by reciting various monologues he had learned at the acting academy, like Cassius's speech to incite Brutus to action in Shakespeare's Julius Caesar: *"I do not know what you and other men think of this life, but for my single self, I would as lief not be as live to be in awe as such a thing as I myself"* and so on... Unfortunately, Sam was really not a great crowd puller and his acting of the classics amongst the shoppers of Watford for instance, was so histrionic as to be absurd. For some reason, he had developed a very questionable hand movement as he orated. The result was that if he was lucky, after a curious initial glance, people would just walk on by smiling. If he was unlucky, he would get hurtful comments on his performance like "Where's yer skirt, poofter?"

He wasn't much more successful in his attempts to get acting work, in the profession either. After writing to every agent in the business and every casting director in theatre, television and film, he finally made contact with someone who said she could help him, for a modest fee of 33⅓% of anything he earned. So, he had an agent and whenever he got himself an appointment with a casting director or for an audition, he proudly put his agent's name at the top of his totally spurious resumé.

Finally, he got his break. Well he thought he had. There it was on the mat, a letter with the embossed emblem of the Royal Shakespeare Company. Wow! This was it. The reply he had been waiting for.

"Could you prepare two pieces for audition, one Shakespearean and the other modern, no longer than ten minutes and present yourself at the Aldwych theatre on Friday next at 2pm. Please confirm".

For the next week or so, poor Saul had to endure endless recitations of monologues from Julius Caesar and Luther, John Osborne's dramatic play about the protestant rebel, Martin Luther. Whenever Sam looked up for comment, he praised him. Whenever Sam looked down, he shut his eyes again. After a while, Saul couldn't face it any more and rather than come home to the constant demand on his time and interest, he slept rough in a London underground station. Inevitably, he was picked up and arrested by the Metropolitan police as a vagrant. Fortunately, his parents bailed him and insisted that he return to the flat with Sam, no matter how painful life had become. Subsequently, in deference to his flatmate's sensitivity, Julius Caesar and Martin Luther were taken up to Hampstead Heath for regular airings, with the space between two huge trees serving as a make-believe proscenium. Here, after every bird in the vicinity had taken flight, the odd stray dog would watch and listen for a short while, before running off barking loudly.

Eventually, the budding actor decided his audition pieces were near perfect and in his mind he was planning a wonderful future with the Royal Shakespeare Company. But sadly it was not to be. In fact his debut at the Aldwych Theatre was little short of disastrous.

Auditions were well underway when he arrived and checked in. From the Green Room where he was asked to wait along with several others scheduled to show their talents, he could hear the vague echoes of the voices of earnest triers orating on an unfamiliar stage. He felt confident. One by one, his waiting companions were called. Each one's name was intoned over the intercom by a bored production assistant, to move, in advance, to a waiting station adjacent to the stage, so that they could follow on after the last actor's efforts with the minimum of delay. Finally, his turn came. At least he took it to be his turn although the loud booming voice he heard said: "Samantha Pild, please!" He got up, smiled sheepishly to the hopefuls still there and left the room, a little angry at the mistake of his name and presumably his gender. Anyway, in this slightly agitated state, after he left the green room, he took a wrong turn and then a wrong door, which led him down into a dark space that eventually revealed itself as a large area underneath the stage. Above him the last actor was just finishing off his audition pieces which seemed to be received with a positive comment or two. Then came the name again: "Samantha Pild. Please!" … it was repeated with a touch of impatience.

At this point, Sam was beginning to panic as he searched in the darkness for a way out. Then he suddenly realized there was a set of stairs that led from his murky surrounds up to somewhere where there was light. He decided to mount them and luckily his hunch was right and while the people conducting the auditions were staring with anticipation towards the wings to greet this Samantha person, Sam suddenly popped up through the floor like a jack in the box and appeared centre stage.

Looking out, he searched for faces in the stalls and in the most macho voice he could muster declared. "I am Sam, not Samantha, but Samuel and I am a man. Thank you." He then went on to perform his two pieces to a stunned silence and when he finished, the voice that thanked him for coming was disturbingly light. So light in fact that he realized that he had destroyed his chances with one person at least, after his testosterone-charged announcement on arrival. He never got a call back.

In fact, apart from some bit parts in television, his career as an actor didn't seem to be going anywhere. Faithfully offering a third of the small payments he did get from his efforts to his agent, to encourage her to look out for him, he still relied mainly on the dole for his sustenance. In return for his "largesse", his agent called him once and asked if he was willing to play a bit part in "Charley's Aunt" in a show at the end of the pier at some south coast seaside resort. She said it was worth ten pounds a week and would be running for six weeks. At first he was excited at the prospect of a job, but, then he considered: a third of the salary would be taken by her for starters. He would still have to pay his share of the rent on the flat in London, plus he would have the added cost of paying for accommodation and food by the seaside. He was no accountant, but he figured he would actually be out of pocket if he took up the offer. So he declined it, and told her he would no longer be requiring her services as he was going overseas. Well, that was what he intended to politely inform her. However, in the event, he just said: "Get Stuffed!"

At this point, it hadn't occurred to him that perhaps acting wasn't his thing, the bug had got him and he convinced himself he had a future in it. But not in England where he had failed every audition he had managed to get. No, after seeing Marlon Brando on the screen, he realized that like that actor, he was more a realistic type of performer rather than the superficial one-dimensional characters that English acting schools produced. He would try his luck in America. Even though everyone and his dog from all over the Commonwealth was beating a path to London to "swing" and be photographed in Carnaby Street, Sam was sure his future lay elsewhere. New York was the obvious place for him.

Unfortunately, however, when he applied for a visa to settle in that country, he was told he would have to go on a long waiting list. Meantime, all that the US embassy could offer was a visa allowing him to land in the Home of the Brave and Free and pass through. Actually it was suggested that once landed, he'd have to move on, as rapidly as possible, to somewhere else…Canada for instance. All he needed to do then, was to emigrate to that country and, perhaps from there, launch his talent onto the North American theatre scene through the side door so to speak.

★ ★ ★

Goodbyes had been short and not too painful. His mother was confident he could look after himself and anyway, she had her birds to care for and tea to make. His brother Mark Sean had met a girl at a dance and was soon engaged to be married. He apparently couldn't wait to expunge his past interests as a celibate trainee priest and on the very few occasions when he and Sam had met up, the meetings were always cool and polite rather than brotherly. Indeed, when Sam was invited home to the house of birds for Sean's official engagement party, the older brother's eyes were challenging slits as he introduced Sam to his betrothed, a rather buxom, giggly young hairdresser named Greta from Streatham, a south London suburb.

"Interested in mechanical engineering, then?" The younger brother was going away soon so he thought he would have a bit of fun before he left.

Greta looked bemused.

"No, she isn't, why?" Sean had turned away to go, but he spun round to quickly intervene.

"She's a beautician and hairdresser as it happens and she could do wonders with that mess on your head."

Sam's hair was long and tangled. It always looked as if he hadn't even tried to comb it. In fact, his appearance, usually in clothing he'd purchased at the army surplus stores, probably didn't help him much in his quest to convince casting directors that he was a disciplined and easy to work with actor.

"Oh, a beautician and hairdresser, oh… so you'll be up with the latest fashions and everything. Do you know anything about the salons in the West End… say…Soho? You know up in…"

That was as far as he got with that. His brother steered his lovely Greta away saying, "Come along darling… must mingle, look who's over there" and with the subtlest of pushes he sent her off in the direction of another buxom blonde by the buffet. Once he had got his girlfriend clear of the danger, he turned back to his brother and coming very close indeed, so that no one else could hear, he hissed "I told you before, I'll bloody kill you one day. Now do us all a favour and piss off to Canada."

That in fact was the last time he saw his brother or Greta and he never got to see the six children they subsequently had.

★ ★ ★

Sam arrived in Toronto on April 1st, with $50 in his pocket and a letter of introduction to a man who ran a small art gallery in the city. His flatmate had given him the name and details of "a friend of the family", who, he said, "owed them one".

En route, he had endured a rocking, rollicking sea journey from Liverpool to New York, sharing a cabin with an alcoholic Irishman who boarded the ship when it made a short stop at Cobh in southern Ireland.

Tommy, as he introduced himself, was short and slight and seemed to be held together by a strong tweed suit. He'd been on holiday in the place of his birth and he explained how he worked as a locker attendant at a golf club in Yonkers in New York City and made enough money from tips to holiday each year either back home in Ireland or in Florida.

Whatever he did on his holiday, the Irishman seemed to have plenty of money left over and he tried his hardest to spend it all in the ship's bar, which had two results. The first was that he attracted a lot of friends on the voyage and the second was that he was regularly brought down to the cabin, almost unable to stand up, and lowered down onto his bunk by a steward. Once there, he would manage to light up the strongest of cigarettes and blow the smoke from, these, mingled with the fumes from his alcohol soaked breath, up to the bunk above, where Sam was almost permanently lying, groaning from sea sickness.

"I've to lie low for a while, y'know." Tommy confided to the young man above him, on the first occasion. "Made a bit of fool of meself in the dinin' room d'yasee.. Geez I could use a dhrink, couldn't you?"

Sam answered by climbing down from his bunk and dry retching into the sink. At least nothing more was coming up. After the first meal of the voyage, the young would–be actor had vomited everything up that had gone down. Now he was existing on a diet of dry crackers and ginger ale. He would just have to be patient and hope that his new Irish friend would soon recover and return to his favourite part of the ship. However, his torment was invariably exacerbated by the tap tap tap on the door and, "Are you dere Tommy? Can we come in?"

The simple enquiry was enough to bring the man from Cork to his unsteady feet and swaying across the room to open the door. Then after the warmest of greetings, four or more of his bar cronies would pour in with a table and chairs and set up a card game in the middle of the cabin. Very soon after this, the steward would mysteriously arrive with a bottle and glasses and the room was quickly converted to a bar, complete with smoke, fumes and loud voices. On these occasions, Sam would summon up the strength to get out of the cabin and find somewhere to lean. Preferably close to the toilets. Nobody was more pleased to see the Statue of Liberty when they finally made it into New York's harbour, not even the European migrants earlier in the century.

Tommy had sobered up for the disembarkation and before he swept off into the city he loved, he had a few words of advice for his cabin mate. "You're too smart for that place up dere y'know. Too intelligent. Place is controlled by the bloddy church. Dey've everything tied down, tied down, sewn up and restricted, d'yasee. Dey call it Toronto the Good, but dere's nuttin' good about a place ya can't get a dhrink on a Sunday or buy a bottle widout fillin' in a government form is dere? No, you should stay in New York, dere's nuttin up dere for ya. Good luck". And after a couple of whiskey induced twitches of his mouth, he placed his fedora over his brushed down, greased hair and was off.

Sam couldn't wait to get his feet on dry land either. He also needed to put something down into the cleaned out cavern that had once been his stomach. He tested it out with a quick hot dog from Woolworths and a fast trip up and down in the lift of the Empire State Building. Then he was off to Grand Central station and on a train for Toronto. He had no choice. The visa in his passport effectively said "don't hang about". So, suffering another long and sleepless night, the budding Marlon Brando arrived in Toronto to start the first leg of a new life.

The cab driver he chose to ride with had never heard of the "Downstairs Gallery" which Sam had assumed from what his friend Saul had told him, everyone would know. Then, when Canada's latest migrant read out the address to the man, he answered in a heavy Ukrainian accent, "Dislonkway. Dis'll ride yer costume fewdollars, ok."

Sam said "OK" and spent most of the journey trying to work out what the driver had said. Actually his concentration on that problem was made even more difficult when the man uttered a few other phrases on the way, which Sam either nodded to, in answer, or said "Yes".

After leaving Union station, the driver headed up the main street of the city: "Disyung – main street", the passenger was later to recognize as "this is Yonge Street", which he came to know as the spine of the city leading from south to north. However, after a couple of blocks, they headed west and past a modern piece of architecture that stood out dramatically from the heavy stone colonial buildings: "Seetyall" the driver prodded the air to his right with a huge fat finger. Fortunately, Sam had read a bit about his new home-to-be before he started out and knew of the new City Hall that everyone was so proud of. Then they were in Chinatown and before the driver could say anything, the newcomer did it for him.

"Chinatown?"

But rather than being appreciated for his obvious desire to join in the discovery route being taken, it drew a scowl from the tour operator and a grudging nod. And so it went on. And now Sam's pocket would suffer, as the trip continued the long way to its destination. North, then east, the Englishman was sure they had been around the university with its old buildings flanked by lawns at least twice, but he just smiled and scanned the scenery for himself, all the time trying to work out what the man had said when he first got in the cab and showed him the address. The riddle was solved when the cab drew to a standstill alongside a building boasting a sign proclaiming "Downstairs Gallery", several kilometers outside the city.

"Towdja", the Ukrainian said, pointing to the meter. "Few dollars costume and return back also, costume. You got?"

The gallery turned out to be a part of a two story apartment, which also served as home for the owner and his partner and an office for the man's several business affairs.

Lenny Berger and his current girl friend Jilly were both painters themselves, but they felt there was more money to be made from selling other people's paintings than sitting dabbing and daubing themselves. So they had bought the apartment and converted a sub-basement into a large gallery. Whatever his artistic talents, Lenny was a very shrewd businessman and whilst he was establishing the business, he continued with his lucrative side enterprise of supplying prizes for radio and television quiz programs. It took up a fair amount of time, but, as Sam was to learn, boy was it a winner.

The young man from England and the two painters eyed each other up at that first meeting. After Lenny enquired about Saul's family and their health, he opened up a bit and told how he had spent a year or so in England at one time and Saul's father had not only given him a job in his art studio, but had given him the money for the fare back to Toronto. Now he was doing well, he said and prepared to help Saul's friend all he could.

There was a spare room in the flat and Sam was offered that for a bit of work in return. The work was connected with the radio and television programs he was told. All he had to do was go down the list of manufacturers and wholesalers in the yellow pages and phone each one with an offer they couldn't refuse. For a quantity of their products, so the spiel went, "the firm, *Showtime Winners* would guarantee X amount of free advertising coverage – vocally descriptive on radio programs and visually on television programs that reach millions. You couldn't afford to buy the kind of marketing of your products that we can guarantee for just your wholesale costs. You are interested? We'll send a contract by next mail and we'll give you the address of our warehouse to send your goods. Thank you".

Sam had little choice but to accept the kind offer. He had given the Ukrainian cab driver most of his money and he needed to eat and sleep. He was also intent on furthering his acting career, and when he told Lenny about that, the man was generosity itself again.

"Look my friend, I have a few contacts in the business myself and I'll help you. But if I may say so, you will need to do something about your appearance. Have you got a comb? Also the clothes are not completely right for Toronto. I can help you with that, too. In the garage, you'll find shirts, jackets and pants in boxes all labeled. They're all prizes that are waiting to be offered to those programs I told you about. Go and get yourself fitted out and take a watch too, there's a case full of them, then we'll have a chat about something else you can help me with."

Lenny was married to a lady living in Montreal, where he had originally come from. Now they both wanted a divorce and because of Ontario's strict laws in this area, the only sure way was for one party to be sued for adultery.

Already the "arrangement" had been agreed to by both parties and their lawyers, but it required Lenny to be discovered in a compromising situation with Jilly, his live-in business associate. However, because of commitments, neither could spare the time to go off to a hotel somewhere to be discovered by a private detective, a witness, who would be handsomely paid for his observations at the time and for his recollection of those observations, as evidence, later in court. Now Sam had come into their lives and as a tenant sharing the accommodation, he'd do very nicely thank you, to observe right there, the "naughty goings on" between Lenny and Jilly. Or, rather, he would be briefed to testify that he *had* observed them to the divorce trial judge. He would be a totally reliable witness, coming from the old country and all, particularly if he combed his hair and wore the clothes he'd been given. And, better still he'd pick up a few dollars in the process, not as much as the private eye would have demanded, but enough to make everyone happy.

Meanwhile, as he settled down to this job of soliciting for prizes, he did also make a few forays into the television and theatre world. But again, success didn't come easily. A tight little clique seemed to control the work in that profession so, while he waited, with the little money he had acquired so far, he signed on for evening acting lessons with Elias Brook, a teacher of the Stanislavsky Method who was from New York and who, it turned out, knew just about every naturalistic actor you could mention. Marlon Brando? Knew him well. James Dean, knew him even better. And so on, and so on. He was a charismatic character who sat at the front of the class of hopefuls with a large fob watch on the table in front of him. Students were invited to the stage area in turn to perform various exercises or later, to work with each other on scenes from various plays. These they subsequently had to perform in front of the class, where they were subjected to "observation" or criticism from both the other students and the teacher.

This seemed to be what Sam had really been looking for. With its emphasis on seeking an inner truth in creating a character, the way of working taught in these classes seemed to open up his true creative ability. He loved every bit of it. The exercises to strip away inhibition, heighten the sensory awareness and instill great concentration, soon made him conscious of just how bad an actor he really was. But, as he worked with others on scenes suggested by the teacher, Sam not only improved over the months, but he also attracted the attentions of several of the female students. Here we go again, he thought, when one of the more mature women taking the course not only asked him if he would do a scene from Streetcar Named Desire with her, but she insisted that they should rehearse at her house.

Marie-Ann Dryden, was already an experienced actress who worked fairly regularly in both television and on the stage of one of the few professional theatres in Toronto. She also had an agent in New York and occasionally got calls to appear in that city. Or so she told everyone in the class. Anyway, she had been trained in the old school of acting where so much was indicated to an audience rather than felt by the actor, so she was now trying out this new method. Marie-Ann's house, in one of the wealthiest areas of Toronto, was like a mansion to Sam and his eyes nearly popped when he saw not one but two Cadillacs parked in the drive.

Her husband was apparently overseas on business at the time and so the cars weren't actually being used. She explained that he owned the two luxury cars because if anything went wrong with one, he was so impatient that he couldn't wait for it to be repaired or rectified, so the other one replaced it. Marie-Ann had a smaller car herself. Just the one.

Rehearsals were slow and awkward at first, but when she suggested that they should do some improvisation to really explore the relationship between her and him, things became so steamy, that they had to stop the improvisation in the large lounge and continue rehearsals in the bedroom.

So, while he was soliciting prizes for Lenny and helping in the gallery during the mornings, most afternoons and evenings during this period were spent improvising with Marie-Ann in any one of several rooms in her very large home. When they finally felt they had done enough on the scene, which was around the time that the actress's husband was due home from Europe, they performed it in the acting studio for the rest of the students and for the appraisal of the teacher. It was considered to be extremely good work on both actors' parts. Elias said it demonstrated the kind of realistic acting that everyone should be aiming for. It was obvious, he said, that both parties had been working on something very strong to motivate them so passionately.

After that, the invitations from female students to work with him on scenes increased to such an extent that after six more months of night classes and daytime rehearsals - with their concentration on "improvisation", Sam had to take a rest and pause to reconsider his situation. Did he want to be a great actor or an overworked stud? When he had measured the pros and cons of both roles, he decided that he would concentrate on trying again for acting parts for now and also look for a more permanent situation in his working and domestic life.

He had managed quite successfully to acquire a good supply of watches, bicycles, prams, ballpoint pens, fridges and washing machines for the programs, but as he was running out of people to phone, he was also running out of interest in the job and less than happy living in his little room adjacent to the bedroom of randy Lenny and Jilly. He had also fulfilled his part in the other bargain by fronting up as witness for the Bergers' divorce.

"Yes your honour, I did see Mr Berger and Miss Curzon come from the bedroom scantily dressed. Yes, I did hear the sounds of love-making regularly."

Now it was time to move on. He'd met a Scottish guy in the acting class who was looking for someone to share his flat, so he moved out of Lenny's and into Simon's. However, he desperately needed an income from somewhere to pay the rent and support his acting quest. Preferably a job which allowed him time off for all the parts he planned to get. Lenny had written a flattering reference on *Showtime Winners* letterhead paper and as Samuel Langhorne Pild, esquire, he wrote all his job applications on photocopies of some spare paper he'd carried around with him for years that proudly boasted the name of his old, distinguished university. He never really purposely set out to deceive, but the spurious BA Hons after his name, might, he thought, be a helpful touch. He assured himself that had he not dropped out when he did, he would obviously have been awarded one.

The only real talent he had, though, was revealed during his brief period at art school in his teens, so, he compiled a relevant C.V. and applied to design studios and advertising agencies in the city. Unfortunately, he told them, he'd left his portfolio at home in England and just heard that his mother had thrown it out with a lot of other stuff she had found in the loft. Most of the people he managed to get interviews with were unimpressed, even with the BA Hons, but the head of one old-established firm decided to give him a chance... starting at the bottom, but with the opportunity to both learn and to prove himself. However, as he had let slip his acting interests, he was warned, he had to choose between the offer he was being given and dedication to the agency and forget any thought of taking off for acting parts. In fact no choice. The firm wouldn't entertain the latter. So, once again, his acting career came to a halt.

Sam settled into his new job and surprised himself by very quickly adapting to the regular hours and expectations of his position. He was a quick learner too and made his way up the ladder in the agency with remarkable ease, impressing the head, Cyril K. Grover (C.K. to his intimates) so much that within two years he had moved from being the office *gofor*, through art design for print advertising and then television commercials to the trial position of producer of commercials for radio and television. So successful had this period of his life been, that he'd pretty well given up the idea of becoming an actor.

His private life had also changed. Living with Simon didn't quite work out the way he had hoped. The problem was that Simon, a hairdresser by trade, seemed to take a great deal of interest in his flatmate's hair, constantly touching the crown of his head and wanting to comb his generous locks. At first Sam assumed that the other man was just taking a professional interest, but when the hair caressing hand continued down his neck, Sam decided that the two were not really compatible after all. He moved out fairly rapidly and found himself firstly some temporary accommodation in a boarding house and soon after a studio flat of his own.

For the first three years of his new life, Sam had stayed celibate. He figured he'd more than done his duty to the opposite sex during his period as a student. Now, work and a desire to live in a completely disciplined fashion were his driving force. That is until Angela came into his life.

As he progressed in the advertising agency, Sam had been almost adopted by Cyril K, his boss. Cyril was not only impressed by the young man's talent and diligence, but he was also aware that he had no father of his own. Cyril K. felt he could fill in a bit in that respect, so he introduced Sam to his golf club. He also invited him to his home for dinner with wife Janey and his son, Cyril Junior, who was visiting. The younger Grover was a mining engineer working in northern Ontario who hardly said a word either to Sam or his own family members.

The dinner date became a regular occurrence and it was when Sam was visiting the Grover household on one of these occasions, that he first met Angela and her two sons, six year old Lyall and four year old Kevin. Apparently the one daughter that the Grovers had been blessed with had been living for several years in California with her husband Rick, a chiropractor. He didn't immediately discover why Rick was still in California while his family was settling in permanently in Toronto, but after a couple of weeks, Cyril K. decided to tell Sam all about it, whilst they were playing a round of golf one morning.

"What do you think of our Angela then young man?" Cyril K. took the oblique way to introduce a subject.

"Oh, she's beautiful, yes, lovely... and the boys are just great, you must be very proud."

"You're darn right there Sam." Cyril K. emphasized the point by sinking a very tricky putt. "Had some rough luck though, my little girl. Husband's no good. The bastard's left her. Left her stranded with the boys. Yep."

Sam missed a much easier putt, but with a sick smile said: "That's terrible C.K.... left his own sons? That really is miserable."

Cyril K. was swinging for a drive to the next hole, and he seemed to be putting everything he'd got into the shot. "Well, they're not exactly his sons, you see... it's a bit complicated..." Cyril K. shot his club back into his bag as if he were spearing an enemy through the heart. "Go ahead son and as we walk down I'll tell you."

Sam drove his ball a fair distance, but unfortunately he found a bunker.

"Good shot, you'll soon get out of that. How much we got on this game by the way?"

"Just fifty bucks" the younger man groaned as he swung his bag of clubs onto his back. "But you were saying, about the boys, Angela's..."

Cyril K. had a set of wheels to carry his clubs, so as Sam struggled along under the weight of a full set of steel and wood in its heavy leather bag, his boss strode out puffing on his cigar and shooting a spit here and there as they walked.

"No, you see Angela has been an unlucky soul in the matrimonial stakes, you might say and it was another guy, her first partner – she never actually married him – who gave her the two boys and then upped stakes, the bastard, and went off. Ange was devastated, as you can imagine and when she found out that he was in Los Angeles, she moved down there with the children and tried to track him down. Needed a bit of maintenance y'see. Bit of financial support. Oh, she had money of her own, money she'd earned as a model – you've seen what an attractive woman she is – but she felt cheated and tried her damnedest to locate him and remind him of his responsibilities. She couldn't of course. Not in a city that size and who knows what name he was using. Anyway, in the end she tried to make a life for herself down there – modeling and such like – and then she met this guy Rick Meltzer, the chiropractor. Now he's legged it, too and Ange has given up California and come home. Problem is still there though, d'ya see. Those boys need a father. Someone solid and reliable. Anyway, we'd better get on, you've been bunkered remember... don't forget to come over for dinner tomorrow."

Care for the two young sons of Angela, was now playing on Sam's mind. When he'd learned they were fatherless, it struck a chord of pain in him that wouldn't go away. He knew the ache of losing his own father as a young child and the big gap in his feelings this had caused as he grew up. As he reflected on his situation, he realized how much it had contributed to his restlessness and lack of discipline for so long. Now, he was more settled and had the support of Cyril K., his fortunes had changed and he felt more fulfilled than he had ever done. Perhaps, he thought, I can help these children avoid what I went through. Perhaps I can be the father figure that they need.

In this frame of mind, Sam presented himself at the door of Janey and Cyril K. Grover for his weekly visit and dinner.

When he rang the bell, the door was opened not by Janey, as usual, but by Angela, who looked stunning.

"Hi, come on in. Mom and Dad had to go out to a special function tonight, but that's ok, isn't it. I've ordered in some food and the boys can join us for a cosy dinner. Is that alright? Give us a chance to get to know each other much better. Come on through." And so it came about that Sam got his wish to become a father figure to the boys.

The wedding took place, under the proud and relieved eye of Cyril K. and the slightly tipsy smile of Janey, with Angela in a beautiful white gown and her sons in matching white suits. Neither of her two previous liaisons had been legitimized by any formal marriage, Sam was told, and now as she stood amongst her old school friends and her family, Angela even managed a tiny blush for the camera. Only her brother was absent, deep in a nickel mine up north. But there were one or two youngish men around the groom had never seen before but who seemed very friendly with the bride, judging by the way they embraced her after the ceremony. Cousins, he supposed.

Mother Pild had been invited with all expenses paid, but she declined, saying she couldn't leave her birds. Brother Mark Sean and his family had migrated to South Africa and he also wired that it was impossible for him to leave either the project he was involved in, or his wife who was on the verge of giving birth.

The honeymoon was in Florida, and when they returned to Toronto, Cyril K. surprised the couple with the keys to a three bedroom apartment just north of the city. A little gift for his baby, he said. And there was a partnership in the business for Samuel Langhorne Pild.

Initially, the marriage seemed to be working out just fine, although Sam was a tad surprised to discover how much he had to contribute to the domestic side of the partnership when he returned from work each day. Angela had told him that she had low blood pressure and needed to rest a lot, so it would help so much if he could pick the boys up from their after-school activities some days and perhaps do some of the housework and cooking. Of course, any questioning of his role was quickly assuaged by the satisfaction he got from making love to his beautiful wife occasionally and by helping the boys with their homework or joining in their leisure activities on the ice or at the little league baseball games, depending on the season. Then there was the cottage. The family cottage on the shores of Georgian Bay, where they could go any weekend or summer holiday time. The elder Grovers had told them it was theirs to enjoy any time and for the boys to appreciate country living along with the delights of swimming and boating in the unspoilt water.

Time passed and Angela decided to renew her modeling career in a modest way. However this apparently proved to be so tiring that she felt she couldn't always also cope with the demands of her young sons. Of course Sam had taken quite a bit of that responsibility away already, feeding and looking after them whilst she spent at least one evening a week with her girl friends. But he only wanted the best for everyone, so when Angela later suggested that she really did need a break and that occasionally she should just get away and drive up to the cottage to spend a couple of days on her own, her husband found no reason to object. Just as long as it refreshed her and made her happy. And it did.

After a few more months of family bliss and great success in his work at the agency, Sam had a strong feeling he should visit his mother back in England. Naturally, he wanted to take his wife and the boys along to show off to her, but it wasn't to be. Angela had no interest in visiting England, she said. "I was there once before and it is just cold and damp. No darling!" She also explained that she had quite a lot of modeling jobs lined up that would be taking her to Montreal and New York. She suggested that of course he should go… and perhaps take Lyall and Kevin with him, if he liked. Or else if he wasn't away too long, her brother could take them up to stay with his family in Sudbury.

Sam felt it would be decidedly weird to turn up in England with two young boys he hadn't fathered and no wife, so he decided on the latter plan and traveled back to London on his own.

4

It had been quite a few years since the young aspirant actor had thrown a kit bag over his shoulder and left England for Canada. He'd been back a couple of times to be at the funerals of his grandparents and to visit his mother, but he hadn't seen her for almost four years when he returned this time and he wasn't at all prepared for what he saw.

The outside of the family home desperately needed painting, but that was nothing. When his mother's face appeared at a side window evaluating him from the edge of a pulled-back curtain, she seemed a bit vague and very slow in recognizing her own son. Then when she finally let him in, he had to cover his ears to quell the sound of who knows how many birds as they serenaded each other or fought for attention. Looking around the house, he discovered that two of the main downstairs rooms were now completely occupied by cages of all shapes and sizes containing birds of all colours and breeds. A third room that had been a study was stacked from floor to ceiling with newspapers, magazines and books about exotic birds. There were even two grey parrots in the kitchen. Not surprisingly, when he entered that room, one of them called out: "Would ya like a cup o'tay, then? Would ya like a cup o'tay, then?" Until his mother spoke to it and told it to hold its tongue.

"Hold yer tongue!" it repeated. Then, when his mother said to Sam that he could wait in the garden whilst she fed her babies, he realized that something serious was wrong with her. His worst fears were confirmed when he ventured upstairs to the bedrooms. Empty tea cups and dishes were everywhere and one room was virtually a store room for bird seed and all the other needs of a well run aviary.

Sam decided he had to act decisively and quickly. Downstairs again, he searched for any of her private documents or any information he could find that would help him first to get her to her doctor and also to discover how she managed her finances.

Meanwhile, Caitlin Pild, *née* O'Meara, was busily humming and chatting away to her birds as she filled their little seed boxes up and replenished their water. She was rewarded by sounds that varied from squawks to the most beautiful trills. By the time she'd reached the last cage, the house resounded again with bird song and sounds. Sam wondered what the next door neighbours thought. So he decided to find out.

Apparently even the long time neighbour and friend on one side of the Pild home had tried to persuade his mother to find other interests away from the birds. She'd suggested that they go together to a senior citizens club nearby, but Caitlin had always insisted that she couldn't leave her birds. The only time she went out was to do a bit of shopping – essentials for the birds and a few food items for herself. Friends who used to drop by for "a cup o'tay" no longer called and yes, another nearby resident had complained to the council about the birds. However, whenever anyone of any authority called, they were never allowed in and had to retreat after being assaulted by a mixture of Irish curses and a high pitched chorus from the birds.

Sam managed to find out the name of her doctor, then he went back into the house and tried to talk to his mother. He told her that he wanted to take her back to Canada with him to meet his family and enjoy the life there. He even talked glowingly of the Canada geese she would find. But she was immovable. Her life was here with her birds and that was that. However, her son was as stubborn as his mother.

"What is your favourite, mum, which bird do you like the most?" Caitlin smiled at his interest in her charges.

"Well, I can't say really. To be sure I love dem all, to be sure, but maybe the budgie dere and the lovely, lovely canary over dere and then dere's ..." Her son cut her off, telling her he was off for a short while to visit some friends. He assured her he'd be back and gave her a kiss on her cheek and a hug. The hug he'd wanted to give her when she first opened the door to him but never got the chance. The action seemed to distract her from her feathered friends for a moment.

Sam moved fast. First he visited his mother's doctor and after questioning how often he'd seen her, insisted that he come with him later that day to the house to examine her. Next he contacted the hospital to get the name of any specialist psychiatrist or neurologist that he could bring his mother to. When he got a name, he made an appointment for the next day. Finally he went in person to the health department and explained the situation that his mother was living in. He said if and when he got his mother out of the house, he would get her into some temporary accommodation where she would need a live-in welfare or social worker to look after her for a short period whilst he sorted things out back in Canada. He would pay generously for the help. Finally, he made contact with an aviary and arranged for someone to come to the house once his mother was out of it and to take all the birds away. When he had satisfied himself that he'd covered all his needs, Sam picked up the doctor and went back to his mother's house. Caitlin peeped through the curtain suspiciously when he knocked, but smiled when she recognized her son. The other man she didn't acknowledge, but she assumed that it would be one of her boy's friends come round for a 'cup o'tay' no doubt.

Once inside, the doctor was diplomatic and very interested in all the birds and even more so in the cup of tea he was offered. Then when everyone seemed relaxed, he asked her if she ever had any illnesses or any problems she would like to discuss. The answers he got were rambling and so irrelevant that he was quite convinced that the lady needed help. As he was leaving, he told Sam he would pass on his report to the specialist and help in any way he could to get somewhere else for his mother to stay.

Now the man from Canada, who was very used to all the comforts of a quality life in Toronto, would have to get himself something to eat and then bed down in one of the less than fashionably furnished rooms upstairs. Probably the one currently in service as a seed store.

Next day, by convincing her that he wanted to take her out for lunch as a treat, he managed to get his mother dressed and after assuring her birds that she would soon be back to feed them all, she came out of the house and into a waiting taxi which took them to the consulting rooms of the specialist that Sam had contacted. By now, Caitlin seemed to be in a different state of mind altogether. Out of her environment she became docile and a little bewildered holding tightly onto her son's hand. It looked as if things weren't going to be as difficult as everyone had anticipated. When his mother sat down opposite the specialist, she looked like a small lost child and when her son pulled away, at first she started to get up, but when he smiled at her, she relaxed and sat back in the chair.

Seeing her sitting there smiling at nothing, the full realization of the state of the woman who had raised him, given him courage and all the encouragement he ever needed for everything he ever attempted, really hit him and he had to swallow hard and leave the room. Now she was in the right hands, he felt, and whatever was subsequently needed he would ensure it was provided. Whatever it was.

After examining and testing his mother, the specialist confirmed his suspicions. She was, he said, in the early stages of dementia. The man wanted to do more tests and observe her over a short period and he suggested that she could be comfortably housed in a small annex to the private hospital where he was a consultant. He agreed that some companionship was essential, to replace the woman's total dedication to the cage birds. The health department had referred Sam to a private company that employed highly qualified care workers, so he contacted them right then and made the arrangements for someone to care for his mother whilst she was at the hospital.

Before he introduced Caitlin to her temporary accommodation, Sam took his mother to the best restaurant he could find in the area and bought her the promised lunch. He told her he wanted her to stay awhile in a place where the doctor could carry out some more tests and despite her protestations, he insisted that she had to be out of her house for a while anyway. It needed painting inside and out, he told her, and for her future comfort he would have it all done whilst she was in her new place. The birds would all be fine and looked after, he assured her, and all the better for a change themselves. Then he took her to the hospital and together they met her new companion, a young Australian woman named Kerrin Stewart.

Like Sam, Kerrin originally had had ambitions to be an actor. She'd had some success in her home town of Melbourne, and so she had traveled to London to try her luck. But none came her way. So, again like Sam, she turned to the one thing she had some qualification for and, as it turned out, considerable aptitude. In Melbourne, she had graduated from university with a social science degree and once she had made the decision to quit trying to be an actor, she took practical courses that equipped her for what really became her calling.

Once Kerrin introduced herself, both mother and son were immediately attracted to her and Sam left the hospital confident that dear Caitlin would be well looked after. All he had to do now, was to organize the removal of the birds from the house, get it fumigated from top to bottom and painted inside and out.

Then, he thought, when he had taken his mother to live with him in Toronto, he would arrange to put the house on the market. First though, Sam phoned his wife to let her know what he had planned; that he'd be home earlier than he had initially intended, but would be going back again to fetch the lady who would no doubt keep everyone happy with her 'cups o'tay'. He felt the boys would love her. However, although he tried the line several times during the day and evening, he failed to get a response. Sam assumed that she was working somewhere, so he made all his other arrangements for the birds and the house and booked into a hotel for a couple of nights before his flight back to Toronto. He wanted to leave it a day or so before he visited his mother in her new environment.

Once again he was assured that all was well. She and Kerrin obviously got along but even so, Caitlin's eyes lit up when Sam showed her a gift he'd brought for her. It was the bright canary that she had said was her favourite. Well one of them. "Oh, Sammy, come here will you now. You brought Jenny, so you did" and she started cooing and chatting away to the little creature. Then she said: "Have you met Kerrin, then, my daughter Kerrin, dere. She's a lovely girl is she not. Let's all have a nice cup o'tay. Will you have one Sammy?"

★ ★ ★

Next day, tired and a little apprehensive, the one time rebel turned brilliant organizer flew back to Toronto to an empty apartment. He had no idea where Angela might be or what she might be doing. Her modeling generally only took up a day or so of her time, he recalled. He rang Cyril K. but neither he nor Janey knew just where she was at this time. Then he rang Cyril K. Junior who presumably was in touch as he was caring for Lyall and Kevin her sons. That's when he got confirmation of the feelings of foreboding he had experienced when he boarded the plane to return home.

Although Cyril K. junior was not exactly known for his loquacity, he seemed to want to get something off his chest right away. "She's at the cottage. She came up to get the boys yesterday. She and Barry that is. They came and got the boys and they're all at the cottage....look..."

"Barry! Who the hell is Barry?" After a flight with no sleep and an empty home to greet his return, Sam was not a happy hubby.

"He's her ex... her first husband, the father of the boys, you know. Oh, boy, listen, perhaps I shouldn't be telling you this, but she was, she is, married to their father. The marriage was never annulled and in fact she left him rather than the way she tells it, but she has been back with him several times since the so-called parting. She loves the guy. Oh, I'm so sorry Sam. She obviously didn't waste any time after you left for England. Now she's in deep shit, eh? Bigamy's a crime isn't it? I don't know what to..."

Cyril K. Junior never got to finish his sentence. The phone in Toronto was dropped down onto its cradle and the deceived 'adopted' son of Cyril K. Grover and partner in the most successful advertising agency in the city, stood stunned, looking out of the window at the gathering clouds – heralding a summer storm.

When all the thoughts and possible courses of action fought for space and acknowledgement in his mind, he tried desperately to quieten them, so that he could make the right decision. He had been living with a lie, born, it seems from the connivance of Cyril K. and his own naïve belief that he could and should give a scarcely known woman's sons his paternal care. He even thought that his "bride" had wanted him for himself, for what he was as a man. He was under no illusion that the pair had married because they were in love in the conventional way, but there did seem to be an attraction from the time they first met and over the years that they had shared, they had had a good life. As a family, they had had great holidays in Hawaii and Mexico. They had skied and had snow fights in the Laurentian Mountains in Quebec and rode every possible ride in Disneyland in Los Angeles. He had watched the two boys grow up and develop. His plan had been to move from the apartment and to buy a house that would be home to his wife, the boys and his mother. Now the dream had been smashed. What should he do? The storm was gathering momentum outside, but he decided that he must face his wife, tonight, whatever the consequences.

The drive to Georgian Bay would normally take about an hour and half, but the further north he went, the worse the storm became. It was obviously over the whole of southern Ontario, coming across the lakes. Then, when a blinding flash of lightning struck close by, Sam was sure he had seen his wife's face looking at him through the windscreen. He almost skidded off the road. The image was in agony. Was it real or had he imagined the experience? Or was it a sub-conscious wish from his tormented mind. Sam decided to pull over to the side and then turn the car round to return to the city. He had been driving for half an hour and the stress of his situation, his lack of sleep and the intensity of the storm was taking its toll. He desperately needed a rest and once he'd made the decision, he felt a quiet calm develop in him. Either the pain and shock had anaesthetized him or he was experiencing some sensory phenomenon, some inner balm from somewhere…

When he arrived at his apartment block, Sam got out of the car like someone walking in his sleep. The calm feeling had stayed with him for the half hour return journey. He even stayed within himself when he sat amongst the chatter and clatter of a sandwich bar where he'd stopped along the way. He couldn't really describe it to himself, but he seemed to be in thrall to something he couldn't comprehend.

Inside the apartment, the phone was ringing. Sam was in no hurry to answer it, but when it persisted he finally lifted up the receiver: "Yes? Who is it?"

An agitated Cyril K. senior was on the other end. "Oh, thank goodness I've... Sam, I've got some bad news, some very bad news..."

"If anyone here," the younger man interrupted, "has any objections to this couple being married," he continued... "let them speak now or forever hold their peace..." and he put the phone down.

Immediately, it was ringing again and once again he let it ring for a while before picking it up. "Yes, father-in-law?"

The man was now obviously emotionally distraught. "Sam, oh, my God, Sam, she's dead. Angela's dead, and so is Kevin. The storm... lightning hit the boat... it's just horrible. We've just had a call from the police at the bay. Will you come over, please."

★ ★ ★

Janey Grover was very drunk when she opened the door to her "son-in-law", her latest son-in-law, and she collapsed sobbing into his arms. Cyril K. then ushered him into the study and offered him a glass of whisky before attempting any words. When they did come, they were punctuated by shaking shoulders and sobs.

It appears that Angela, her boys, Lyall and Kevin and their real father, Barry, had all been out on the lake in an open boat when the storm hit. Angela was actually struck by lightning and the boat capsized in the turmoil. The older boy was a strong swimmer and after a struggle searching for his mother and his young brother, he gave up and made it to the shore dazed and in shock. Their father had recognized the inevitable with Angela but desperately tried to recover his younger son, without success. A poor swimmer himself, he had hung on to the upturned boat and screamed and screamed for help. After a while, a boat came out from a nearby cottage and he was dragged from the water. When the accident was reported to the local police, they searched the area and eventually recovered the dead bodies of the woman and her son.

Sam received all this information without any outward show of emotion. It was as if he knew what was coming and was prepared. The stillness that had descended on him after the graphic premonition in the car, remained with him. He no longer wanted to punish his so-called father-in-law for his role in the subterfuge that led to the bigamous marriage. He didn't care how much or how little the man really knew about his daughter and her devious behaviour. He knew that he himself had been scarred, but also that he would get over it. The dreadful end of a precious life for the boy Kevin was now the only hurt he felt. When Cyril K. said he would be driving up in the morning to speak to the police and visit the survivors who were recovering in the local hospital, Sam automatically offered to accompany him. He wanted closure of this episode in his life.

The journey next day was a sombre affair. The elder man mumbled an apology and hoped that his business partner would forgive him and the unfortunate Angela… his princess. Sam just touched the other's arm gently and the two remained silent for the rest of the journey.

At the police station, an inspector specially called in from the nearest large sized town confirmed the details of the accident and his finding that there had been no foul play. He knew that the woman victim had bigamously married and that her first husband was still being treated for shock and hypothermia. He was recovering and had been able to supply the police with all the information they needed. The bodies were in a mortuary and the two men were asked to identify them. The experience brought shudders of pain to Cyril K. but surprisingly, Sam was unemotional, as the stillness seemed to enshroud him. He felt somehow protected. The feeling stayed with him too, when he met his rival husband Barry and his former "son" Lyall. The latter was surprised to see the man he'd lived with for the last four years. "I thought you were in England", the boy said, his voice shaking. "I know what's happened, dad. I know what's happened, I know they're dead, they're drowned, it was terrible. I tried..." and he crumpled in his former stepfather's arms.

On their return journey, the silence between the two men was even more pronounced. Everything had been pretty well settled. The bodies of the victims would be brought back to Toronto for burial. After the funeral, the legitimate husband, Barry, would be taking his son Lyall with him, to live in Montreal. Sam had realized there was nothing left in Canada to keep him. He decided he wouldn't attend the funeral. However, he couldn't get away until he had clarified his situation legally. Cyril K. and Barry Shand had to sign affidavits establishing their innocence or otherwise in the bigamous mix up. Then both marriage certificates and Lyall's birth certificate had to be traced, and a considerable fee for the lawyer had to be found to ensure that any reference to any marriage between Samuel Langhorne Pild and Angela Grover had been expunged from the official records. Sam also formally resigned from his partnership in the Grover agency, receiving a very generous settlement from a devastated Cyril K., who now planned to sell the company and retire. His wife Janey was admitted to a special treatment centre for alcohol and drug abusers and he felt that when she came home she would need his support full time.

5

On the flight back to England, Sam felt almost excited. Behind him a life he had almost stumbled into and worked so hard to make a success of, was now just a bad memory. It was a life lived on the outside of his being, bending this way and that to please or impress. A life almost without a real purpose. Now, he felt quite different in himself. It was absurd he knew, but somehow it was as if he was being guided to a new destiny. He didn't understand it, but destiny was the word that kept reverberating in his mind. He had been away a little over two weeks and in that time the psychiatrist had completed all the tests necessary to confirm Caitlin's condition, which, he said, would inevitably become progressively worse. She really did need constant care.

Fortunately, his mother had accepted the presence of Kerrin as her carer, or rather as her "daughter" and when Sam called in to visit them, they both seemed happy to see him, although Kerrin had to gently remind Caitlin, who he was. First stop after leaving the hospital was to a lawyer's office in order to officially and legally invest in Sam the power of attorney over his mother's affairs. Just happy to be in the company of her son and "daughter", Caitlin signed the necessary form without demur. In fact she nodded wisely and smiled as she put her name to the paper.

The family home was a good sized semi-detached house in Mitcham, close to the common, where every year a convoy of colourful caravans and lorries brought groups of exotic looking people to set up a giant funfair. Now, redecorated and refurbished, the Pild household could provide room enough for a guest or two to stay at any time, along with Sam and his mother.

Arrangements had been made for Caitlin to leave the hospital permanently and return to the place she'd lived in for nearly forty years. She and husband Jock had bought it with a legacy he'd inherited from a wealthy aunt, not long before the Second World War started. The beautiful Mrs Pild, as she was known, long before she became "the bird lady of Talbot Avenue", had sheltered, shielded and soothed her two boys there throughout the war years. Together, they weathered bombing during the London blitz which spread to all suburbs, terror from the unmanned flying bombs they called doodlebugs and finally the cowardly V2s or rocket propelled warheads that arrived without warning and devastated whole streets along with their innocent occupants.

After the cleaning and repainting, Sam had arranged for the place to be completely and tastefully re-furnished. Everything he could think of was done so that when his mother did return, he hoped she would be impressed enough to forget that the place once housed about thirty of her little feathered friends. Fortunately, his plan worked and with the gentle Kerrin as companion, Caitlin seemed to find a really happy place in her mind and that allowed her to enjoy her 'new' home. She especially liked the large back garden and before long, shrubs and flowers seemed to completely replace the caged birds that she had been obsessed with.

Once everything seemed settled, Sam set about exploring business opportunities. He had quite a few contacts in London that knew of his reputation and not his recent history. But whatever advice they offered, it was obvious that it wasn't intended to advance his cause in this city. He was on his own, he realized and if he had ever considered most folk who worked in the advertising field in Canada shallow, then the stiff white collars and striped shirts in the business in London, he found transparent. He very soon got the impression he was intended to get that "there really wasn't any room for anyone else in the game old chap, perhaps you should have stayed in Canada!"

After eight years or so living in a relatively egalitarian culture, Sam had forgotten about the stuffiness and snobbishness that permeated the middle and upper echelons of England's class structured society. He realized that if he was going to stay in the country of his birth for any length of time and survive, he would have to find a way of insulating himself from it. When he was young, his natural rebellious character allowed him to remain relatively unscathed. He had managed, even without a plummy accent and the right old school tie, to find his way and make his mistakes as an independent soul. Of course he was aware that he was looked down on as some kind of coarse alien, when he had tried to make his way in the acting profession. He was considered not only untutored but uncultured by the 'luvvies'. He never forgot the occasion when he was invited to a director's flat in Central London to do a reading for a Shakespearean play the man was staging. When he had finished, the smiling response had been: "Awfully sorry old chap, but your voice has quite the wrong *timbre*, d'you see. Lovely meeting you though."

Those words and his experience auditioning for the Royal Shakespeare Company always came back to him like flashing red warning lights whenever he had entertained any further notions of trying to be an actor. Meanwhile, even though he had been going through the motions of feeling out the advertising situation in London and his possible involvement in it, he realized that he had felt no great enthusiasm from the start. His first priority now was to ensure that the remaining years his mother had left were spent with some contentment. He had no urgent need to rush into anything. He had a very healthy bank balance and a regular modest income from his Toronto apartment and if he ever needed to, he would sell it. There was one thing though that he had to deal with as soon as possible and it was a task he wasn't keen to undertake: the phone call to his brother to bring him up to date with everything that had happened to the lives of both himself and their mother.

Having re-established a study in the room that formerly had served his mother as an overfull library of newspapers and magazines, Sam checked that he was alone in the house and decided the conditions were right and the time difference was correct for the dreaded phone call to South Africa. He needn't have worried. Sean was reasonableness itself after his first reaction of surprise at the news of his mother's state and incredulity at what had transpired in Canada. In fact, he first thanked his brother for all the care and attention he had paid to Caitlin and then sympathized with him over the tragedy he had suffered.

Sam didn't even intimate that in fact, he felt somehow relieved that his situation had changed. That a massive distraction had come and gone and that now he felt he was on his right path for the future. It had never been easy making conversation with his older brother and he still recalled that on a couple of occasions when they actually talked face to face, Mark Sean had threatened to kill him. However, even now when he would have liked to open up a bit and perhaps even confide in his own kin, he felt that the voice at the other end of the phone would not really be interested, let alone receptive, to anything more profound than the basic facts. In fact he sensed that his brother's real focus was elsewhere. That he was anxious to get away from the phone. When Sam asked how work was going and how the family was, his suspicion was confirmed.

"Well that's just it, really, look I'm up to my ears just now and, did I tell you, well Greta is about to give birth… I was just going up to the hospital with the other kids… this one will be number four. OK, anyway thanks for calling, tell mum about the baby will you, I'll try to send some photos, cheerio." And the connection between London and Johannesburg ended.

Mrs Pild and Kerrin came into the house from the garden and the social worker called out, "would ya like a nice cup o'tay, would ya?" impersonating Caitlin perfectly and bringing a smile to her face.

"Indeed I would, to be sure." Answered Sam in the same brogue and they continued the banter as two old hams improvising a whole scene that would surely have fitted into a Sean O'Casey play.

When the tea was made and being drunk and everyone was now talking in their normal accents, the young woman from Melbourne told Sam that she wouldn't be able to continue living in the house. She explained that she had a life of her own and interests that she wanted to share with others and that although she would be happy to be a day visitor, she suggested that if he felt it was necessary, that he might employ someone else's services for the evenings and nights. What she didn't divulge, was that she was concerned that her feelings towards the son of her charge were beginning to disturb her. Kerrin had a boy friend and yet this man who employed her and who was several years older was beginning to have much more meaning in her life. She started to feel embarrassed at the situation she was in, since she had no idea that he was no longer married to the beautiful model he'd told them about when she was first hired to care for his mother. At that time, he talked of preparing a place in Toronto for his family that would include Caitlin. She was aware that things had changed of course, but she had no idea of the full implications of that change.

Sam said he completely understood her need to have a life of her own, of course. He said that he'd try to manage by himself. Initially, he had no plans to go anywhere in the evenings, and everything seemed to be working out with Kerrin just coming in during the daytime. He was happy to take care of his mother's needs after she left. However, when one evening, after dark, he discovered his mother in the garden with a flashlight, counting all the flowers, and talking to them, he decided that both he and Caitlin needed help, so a night nurse was employed.

The woman sent by the agency was middle-aged, efficient and seemed not too interested in the person she had to tend to, or Sam. In fact the contrast was so marked, that when he next saw Kerrin and his mother together and noted the real affection they had for each other, he decided he really should be more open with his mother's "daughter" and tell her his story. He found the opportunity when Caitlin was in the garden, talking gently to the flowers or some unseen object in their midst.

When she was asked to come into the study for a chat, Kerrin's first thought was that she was about to be told that her services would no longer be required as he was taking his mother back to Canada with him. At first, he was finding it difficult to put into words what he wanted to tell her, indeed, he could hardly believe what he was telling her himself. It sounded like some sort of soap opera he had seen on television. He was talking in a strangely detached way, still feeling emotionally separated from the tragedy that had turned his life upside down. In fact he couldn't help smiling when he recounted his former wife's penchant for collecting husbands. He said he couldn't be at all certain that even the chiropractor she lived with in Los Angeles wasn't married to her before he skipped off. However, the recollection of the death of the younger boy, Kevin, seemed to sober him up and after listening to the whole story in silent amazement, Kerrin detected in his eyes and voice the grief he must have felt but tried not to show.

"So that's how it is", he concluded "and that's why I really hope you can stay on ... for a while anyway... Caitlin...we really need you. Ok?" his words seemed to catch in the back of his throat and he jumped up to cover his embarrassment.

"Well, now…ahem… look", the man had a quick glance at his watch, "I have to go out now, but I hope to see you later or if not, in the morning." And the *tête à tête* was abruptly over.

★ ★ ★

Sam had finally managed to catch up with his old flatmate Saul. When he phoned and discovered that he was "resting", after a stint playing with a large orchestra in the Midlands, they arranged to get together for lunch.

They both had plenty to tell each other. First Sam quickly recounted his sorry story, pushing away any overtures of sympathy.

"Look, I'm ok. I'm fine, just fine and I'm more interested in hearing what you've been up to, you look great by the way. Something about you that's different, what is it?"

Saul found the quick change in the mood a little disconcerting at first but he was relieved. He was bursting to tell his old friend what had happened in his life since they last met. For one thing, he was married and had a son. No, Sam hadn't missed a Jewish wedding. To the everlasting chagrin of his parents, it was a mixed marriage and as far as he knew or really cared, they might still be sitting *shiva*. His home was now in Hertfordshire, but he kept the flat, the same flat that the two young men had shared, in London. It was so handy for much of the freelance work he managed to get.

Sam congratulated him on his marriage and his freedom, but said he also detected something else. "I don't know what it is, but there's something different in you. What is it? I just get a feeling that there's been a change in you too. A change that I have had a sense of in myself, something I can't explain. What is it, man?"

"Well, I'm married and a father. I am doing well as a freelance musician and…"

"No, something else. Something that I can feel from you. It's like, oh, I don't know..."

"OK, look, it's not easy to explain, without it sounding a bit odd coming from me. You know. Well, you remember that I always fought against formal religion, yeh? Well a couple of years ago, I was introduced to this sort of spiritual brotherhood. Well it's not anything to do with spiritualism, but it's a kind of receiving of a force, that, well, it's called an exercise. They use an Indonesian word for it, and, anyway, men and women do it separately in groups. It's an experience where your inner self is touched by the power of God, or the Great Life Force and Sam, it's like being re-born and by doing the exercise regularly, your inner is nourished and gradually cleared of all the baggage it's normally lumbered with and so on..."

Sam's eyes were gleaming as he listened and inside he felt first that calm that had descended on him during his time of trial in Toronto, then a slight, almost imperceptible, but real, inner vibration as he indicated that Saul should continue.

"Oh that's just a flavour, there's much more to it all, and there are people called helpers, who've been doing this thing for some time, who can explain it much better and books of course and printed talks from the founder of the movement ....explanations, you know. But for me and my lovely wife Mary, it's just wonderful and the movement is multi-religious, multi-racial and multi, multi disturbing to my dear parents. Does that all sound weird to you?"

"I knew it was important to meet up with you, you old bastard." Sam was smiling and he had tears in his eyes. "Now I know why I've come home. I don't know if it's weird, or what you call it, but I want it. I want it to confirm the feelings I've had and not been able to understand, that I have been open to a force or power that guides... that can guide us. It may sound spooky, but listening to you, I recognise the truth, you know. I can easily accept the *reality* of your experience and I want to share it. How, do I..."

"Get the contact? Get opened?" Saul took a diary from his inside pocket. "Well, I'll give you a couple of names of helpers and you can give them a call if you are really interested."

Sam couldn't figure that out. Here he was with a friend who had apparently received something special that he also wanted and yet he couldn't just pass it on himself to him. What was all the mystery for? "Why can't you and I get together and you show me all about it?"

"For a lot of reasons. Here, write these names down and the phone numbers. Got a pen? Right, now the main reason that I can't just open you to this thing, this receiving, is that I am fairly new to the whole thing myself. All enquirers are called applicants and they literally are applying to become a part of the brotherhood. There is a process, you see... and the first stage is to meet up with helpers. Anyway, after the initial meeting, where they tell you about it all, you can ask anything you want to know, there is a kind of cooling off stage, which is called... you'll like this, it's called a probation period. Three months. Well a minimum of three months that is and you are referred to during that time as a probationer."

Sam couldn't help smiling. "So, for just asking a few questions, I'm put on probation. No trial, no judgement, no chance to defend myself, one friendly enquiry and I am on probation. And these guys are what did you call them, probation officers?"

"Helpers, smart arse. People who have been in the business for a while, quite a while in fact and who have the experience to answer all your questions and to tell you all about it. They are also... the helpers that is, they're the only ones who can do the opening or, induction, the actual introduction to the experience. They will be your witnesses. Listen Sam, I really think it's best if you talk to them before I blather on any further. I'm a very inexperienced member and I'm just learning what it's all about myself. Give one of them a ring and please don't take the piss when you do. This probation thing is good really. It's a chance for you and them to get to know each other and for all parties to test each other's sincerity about the whole thing without anyone committing to anything. You're living in Mitcham, did you say? Yes? Well there are groups all around you. You're spoilt for choice. But one thing at a time. And if you decide that you are not interested after all, then don't call me, I'll call you. Just joking. Let me know what happens, won't you?"

Sam promised he would and travelled home to think about it and his life in general. He'd give it a little while to filter into his being before he made any calls to either of the names Saul gave him.

Meanwhile, there was something else for him to think about. He had been attracted to the idea of writing and illustrating a children's book. The idea had come to him whilst he had watched his mother enjoying her garden, marvelling at the various creatures that visited it to gather up their needs from the flowers. She would "ooh" and "aah" at the dazzling dragonflies as they hovered and then zipped off as if suddenly propelled by a rubber sling and then she'd reach out with the gentlest of intentions to try to touch a multi-coloured butterfly as it swerved and fluttered around her head. He knew she loved the colourful creatures and, remembering his own childhood, so did most children he supposed. But what about the not so beautiful ones? The moth for instance. Moths had always fascinated Sam, from the time his mother started to put moth balls into his clothes drawers and make everything stink like a public lavatory. He had also had a friend in his pre-teen years who had a collection of moths – all of them big and ugly – and all of them stuck to a board with pins. To Sam, the poor moth was an unfortunate creature. Despite the fact that he could fly and perform all the gyroscopic manoeuvres of his beautiful cousin, the butterfly, the moth generally was not liked. In fact most of the time, if a poor creature was spotted in a house, it was swatted like a fly. People didn't like moths and children learned this illogical attitude towards them from their parents. So, that's it, decided Sam, I'll write a book about a butterfly and a moth and I'll illustrate it in such a way that children will be able to discern beauty not only in the stunning butterfly, but also in the plain old moth, once he had given them characters. Perhaps, if he could get the message across, some young readers might even recognise the fact that discrimination, any form of discrimination, is usually based on ignorance and passed down from parents.

The project excited him and he didn't give a second thought as to whether or not he could get it published. He was an excellent illustrator and now he had to learn on the job how to write for a particular market. He needed to do some research. His mother had managed to throw away all his books from his own childhood, along with all his meccano sets and lead soldiers, so he bought a wide range of books for young people and brought them in to his study.

Every afternoon while his mother was resting, her aide, Kerrin, used to take her afternoon tea with Sam. It was the only time these days that they could have a chat about Caitlin's condition, whatever new problems had presented themselves and what, if anything, was needed. After he had opened up and told her about the tragic circumstances that led to his returning to England and moving in with his mother in the family home, the young woman from Australia found herself becoming more inwardly attracted to Sam. Nothing overt could be detected, she made sure of that, but she really did want their exchanges to become a little more reflective and less businesslike. She would be patient, but when she saw all the children's books, on the desk and on the floor, she wondered if he was experiencing some kind of post tragedy stress – as far as the death of his young step-son Kevin was concerned.

The man noticed her puzzled look as she glanced at all the children's covers and before she could say anything, question anything at all about them, he said: "Don't worry Kerrin, you don't have two patients to care for. I haven't regressed to my earlier years, no, I'm doing some research. Trying to see what kids like or rather what parents and others buy kids to read or just to look at. I am going to join the market myself. Yep, I am going to write and illustrate a book for nippers. Don't ask me about it now, but really when I've got going on it, I'd love you to have a look and tell me what you think. Will you?"

Kerrin readily agreed. At last a breakthrough, she thought. Now, perhaps they would be a little closer and their relationship could become a little deeper. She had no outward reason to suppose it, but her instinct told her that there was something between them, something they were really both denying. She knew that it would take time for Sam to recover from the events he'd experienced and that he was protecting himself by keeping everyone at arm's length emotionally. Finally though he had taken her into his confidence and that, she felt was a big step. However, nothing further developed in the short term and life in the Pild household continued with everyone respecting everyone else's space and role.

Apart from the shared meals, all three occupants pretty well lived separate lives. Sam trusted Kerrin implicitly to be carer and companion to his mother and for his part, he applied himself to a daily program that started with a brisk walk across the common, breakfast and then as much of the remainder of the day in his study, spent writing and sketching. He had no social life. Never went out in the evenings and made no attempt to seek company of any sort. Even rapport with Caitlin was becoming more and more difficult. They were now very much on different wavelengths and although he hated himself for it, he found he had little patience with some of her demands and eccentricities. More and more he would avoid having to be alone with her and more and more he relied on others to supply the care and the companionship she needed.

After a couple of weeks of work on the book and a lot of self-examination whilst he was alone in his study, Sam decided he would phone one of the names his friend Saul had given him. The phone call was easy and the man at the other end of the phone, a Stephen Madson, invited him to come to the group centre to meet some of the other helpers and have a chat. A time was arranged and with just a touch of apprehension, Sam turned up and was ushered into a small room where three other men were sitting, with their eyes closed. As soon as he joined them, though, eyes were opened and smiles were presented as they introduced themselves to the newcomer.

The atmosphere was quiet and the conversation slow. Did he have any knowledge of the brotherhood? Only what he'd been told by his friend. Then each one, sometimes in turn, sometimes overlapping each other, gave him information about the exercise that was the core or *raison d'être* of the whole business. Someone said it is called a *latihan*, actually *latihan kedjiwaan* which roughly translates to *spiritual exercise* and it had come originally from Indonesia.

"Well", someone else went on, "of course it is our belief that it came from the Almighty and was passed on through the first person to receive it, a man respected by everyone and known as Bapak. A sincere Muslim, when he was a young man, he'd had a miraculous experience which took him out of his body to witness incredible happenings and then when he returned, he had to undergo a year or so of purification of his soul. This was the speeded up process. It might take a lifetime and more for the rest of us. Once purified, Bapak was given a mission to serve his creator by passing on the *latihan*, the very experience he had himself received, to whoever asked for it".

"So, once a person asks, there's a period – we call it the probation period – usually about three months…"

Sam nodded in acknowledgement.

"… after that if the enquirer still wants it, an arrangement is made for that person to be opened".

"Opened?" Sam queried.

"Yes", it was explained, "your inner, your soul, that has remained dormant from birth, lumbered or handicapped, affected or influenced or whatever, by everything you inherited and everything that you have acquired during your life, is officially opened to the power of Almighty God or the Great

Life Force and once opened, it's nourished by the *latihan* so that it can be purified and so that it can grow and guide your life.

"Right now, folk are guided by their heart, or their mind, their emotions or their intellect," he was told, "both of which, most often, were influenced, if not dominated, by the 'lower forces'".

"The lower forces?" Sam was on to that one immediately.

"Yes," two of them chorused: "the lower forces, or as we call them the *nafsu*, another Indonesian word. They are the material, animal and vegetable forces that are below the human level and that should be man's servants, to work for him, but which so often become his master".

Everything was related in a quiet, almost reverential tone and Sam found himself taking some of it in and losing some of it. They had tried to make it sound as simple as possible but although it was probably all true and according to their credo, it was, after all, he thought, coming from their minds and who knows how "purified" they were.

The actual "opening" it was explained, was a short, simple sort of ceremony, introducing the *latihan,* or the contact so to speak, to the individual, and this is witnessed by the helpers. Following that, the exercise or *latihan* is done initially twice a week, for about half an hour each time. Men with men and women with women.

"You will stand with others and having quietened your mind, you will experience your own individual receiving. What is right for your purification and development. You do nothing, just follow whatever you experience… it might be a physical movement, it might be a vocal sound. You just go with it."

Then Stephen, the man who had invited Sam along, stood up and said: "Don't worry if you didn't understand everything you've been told tonight. It's not easy to take it all in straight away and you will have concerns and questions you want answered as the time ticks away during the next three months. Try not to think too hard about it all. We can give you some literature that also explains the fundamentals of the process etc.

and the structure of the organisation in case you're interested. Ok. We'll be here every week at the same time and available for you and any other applicants that may turn up... ok? And of course if you have any real worries in between these meetings, then you have my phone number... and I'll give you the other helpers' details, and you can just call any of us any time." And there was handshakes all round.

As he left the building, Sam caught a glimpse of a few women arriving, presumably for their bi-weekly exercise. He found it fascinating to see how they all seemed to be wearing long dresses and carrying little pairs of slippers.

It had been quite an experience. Whether or not he believed or even understood what they had told him, applicant/probationer Samuel Langhorne Pild, felt very comfortable in their company. In fact, once again there was that little flutter of excitement deep inside him and he knew that he had taken the right step and was determined to reach complete fulfilment by being "opened", as they said. And if it were so, he couldn't wait to purify some if not all of the garbage that he had managed to collect in his life so far.

He arrived home that evening feeling positive and happy. Even the awkward situation in the house with his mother and her carers fell away from him for the moment. That is until the message waiting by the phone hit him like a bombshell. The note told him that Kerrin had phoned to say she wouldn't be coming in tomorrow. She'd had a telephone call from Australia to say that her father was dying and she decided she must return to Melbourne as soon as possible. The agency would be told first thing and a replacement would be there as soon as possible. The young carer said she hoped Sam and Caitlin would understand. She'd miss them both.

The news was not only unexpected, but unwanted and disturbing. Suddenly he was shaken out of his self-preoccupation. He hadn't realized how much her quiet strength had supported him. He had taken her for granted and now her companionship would be sorely missed by him if not his mother.

Next morning, he tried to phone her, but the line was constantly busy, so he gave up and told Caitlin that Kerrin wouldn't be coming in to see her, as she had to fly back to Australia for an emergency. Surprisingly, the woman who was living more and more in her own world, didn't seem at all troubled by the news. "Ah, well, you can't keep these youngsters in a cage can you? If they want to fly, they will, to be sure."

Sam was beginning to envy the selflessness behind many of his mother's comments, however questionable the logic might have seemed.

★ ★ ★

The new care worker was quite different from her predecessor. A married woman in her late thirties, Magda Wilson was a no-nonsense, efficient Scot, who had, she said, lots of experience in assisting dementia patients.

She fitted in quite easily, but seemed to create a much cooler atmosphere in the house than had previously existed. Tea with Magda was not the same as tea with Kerrin and whereas the younger woman hadn't minded a bit about clearing and doing a bit of washing up of the breakfast dishes if Sam hadn't got around to doing those chores, under her regime, Magda simply pointed out that the sink area was cluttered and she couldn't use it unless it was cleared. So, the pattern of life was changing at number 6 Talbot Avenue and the man of the house had to adapt and do a bit more domestic work himself than he really favoured.

His work on the book was progressing well, though. Something was really motivating him. His attitude was changing both towards his mother and importantly, towards himself. He went again to a meeting with the helpers in the spiritual brotherhood and again he felt calm and good inside whilst there and for some time after. He learned of the real pillars that will assist in the success of the exercise he would receive, the three key attributes, *surrender, submission* and *patience,* all three traits that were really strangers to his character. He had much to learn, it seemed. The essence of this brotherhood, the real and personal experience that his new friends had described, he felt an instant empathy with, and he had no problem with the notion of the *latihan* being an act of worship. But he had been a restless soul for most of his life and wondered just how much of his personality would be changed. Could he learn to surrender his will and have the courage to submit to the guidance of the *latihan,* whatever it suggested, wherever it pointed to? And would he have the patience to persist with a regular twice-weekly arrangement to benefit from a process that would really be a commitment for the rest of his life?

Big questions that only he could answer and whilst he was also focussing a lot on his writing and art work, he felt he needed something to take his mind off all these undertakings - a distraction. He decided he'd get himself a dog. Great for walks on the common, morning and evening and he was sure Caitlin would love to have one to play with in the garden. There would probably be a negative reaction from Magda about fleas, falling hairs and the occasional dog turd on her shoes, but she'd have to get over it. He never even gave a thought about how the almost anonymous night carers might react. They were obviously on some kind of roster and they came and went without leaving a trace of their personality behind.

So, a dog it would be. But not a puppy, Sam had no time or patience to train it. No, he needed a trained, content and mature creature that perhaps had been abandoned or just left by someone who had moved on. He didn't have to look far. The nearest RSPCA dog compound had a brown and white cocker spaniel that had been discovered, lost and ownerless, just a month previously. The dog was about seven, the assistant said, and was well trained and lively and in need of a good home. The people at the pound had no real idea what its name was, so they had been calling it "fella". They didn't want to pre-empt any preference a future owner might have for names. Sam was sold on it, "fella" was bought and the two of them hit it off right away. Even in the car on the journey home, once it had been introduced to a big blanket on the back seat and told to lie there, the cocker spaniel obeyed without a murmur.

When he got it home, he put a collar and leash on "fella" and proudly introduced him to Magda and his mother. Although she had been forewarned, Magda was predictably unimpressed. Caitlin was all smiles.

"Oh, he's a great one for sure, let me take him round the garden." And off she went talking away and telling the dog all about the bushes and flowers and the old tree which a very young Sam had often climbed and fallen from.

"What shall we call him mum?" The man had watched the joy this newcomer had already given her, and he was sure that even in her progressively worsening state, she might well find just the right label for this lively bundle. He wasn't wrong. Every now and again, Caitlin seemed to have a space in her mind, a few moments of clarity and when she heard her son's question, she just looked straight at him and said "Rufus. He's Rufus", and went off with him again for another tour. Sam hadn't expected that, but it came so positively that he felt it would be ok. Rufus was the first name of his own dead father. What it now meant to Caitlin he couldn't even imagine, but for the moment "Rufus" lived again in the form of a very happy dog. Once ensconced, the animal proved to be a real boon to his owner, except when he had to go out on business. Then it was a plea and a wink to Magda and a smile to Caitlin and with fingers crossed, Sam could leave the house. In the evenings, there was no problem. After a good run on the common, Rufus seemed to just want to sleep.

The book was finished and he took it to the most prestigious publisher of children's books in London. Somehow, his background in the advertising business in Canada had equipped him with the necessary *élan* to get past the usual barriers to any would-be author and he managed to get it into the hands of the managing editor. The result was both good and bad. The bad part was that the publishing house weren't happy with the writing of his story. The idea he was trying to convey was good, they told him, but not written well enough for the target audience. However they were impressed with the illustrations, very impressed and they wanted to have a meeting with Sam that they felt could result in something positive for both parties.

The meeting did indeed prove worthwhile for the illustrator and erstwhile wordsmith. It convinced him that he was not a writer but it also established him as a freelance illustrator. His first book, about the moth and the butterfly was re-written by a well known children's author, inspired, he generously said, by Sam's illustrations. The publisher offered him a two year non-exclusive contract. So once again, the aspiring young actor, whose personal rebellion had taken him to Canada and into the world of advertising and marketing, was now entering a completely new chapter in his life. He set up the study in his home as a studio and embraced his first love, drawing, enthusiastically. He had also embarked on a new inner quest – for spiritual fulfilment - and his days of navel gazing seemed to be over.

6

The 'opening', when it came, was pretty well as the helpers had informed him. His introduction to the actual experience was witnessed by them, standing with him in the centre of the hall, some smiling benignly, before they again all closed their eyes. The real action started, though, with Stephen, his first contact, reading a statement, which was pretty obvious in much of its content - reminding him to just stand, relax and follow whatever happened. Then he was off. With the word "Begin" came the unexpected, the unimaginable by the rational mind. With his eyes closed, and aware but not distracted in any way by the movements and sounds of his comrades, Sam's being seemed to be vibrating from top to bottom and the action taking place was completely involuntary. He felt to do nothing about it. Just witness it. When he did start to think about it, the action stopped, so he quietened his mind again and off he went. The vibration changed to clear movements of parts of his body. His arms shot up and down and his legs took him for a walk somewhere, anywhere and amazingly, even with his eyes closed he managed to avoid either bumping into anyone else, or into a wall. The others were now singing sounds almost in harmony, but certainly not in the acknowledged meaning of that word. Undisciplined by musical etiquette terms, their melody came, unforced and untutored. Even Sam started to make vocal noises that were strangers to his consciousness. Some even sounded like the guttural resonances of Arabic. And so it went on.

After about thirty minutes, the one who had said "Begin" then said "Finish" and slowly, as he walked back to his chair and sat, the probationer who had now become a member, realised he was surely 'opened' to a different world, a higher one, he hoped, as he was aware that his whole person had embraced it unhesitatingly. He hoped too that this new reality that he had a taste of, would either permeate into the material world that he, like everyone else had accepted as the true reality, or replace it. But perhaps the last wish was a wish too far.

The next time and all subsequent times that he would do the exercise, he would be in the company of a lot more voices and swinging arms and legs. On these occasions, even with his eyes closed most of the time, he realised that both the sounds and the movements were so varied, that the concept of this process being a very individual experience was easy to accept. For some it appeared to be smooth and effortless, others emitted noises that could well have been born of pain – inner pain and struggle. One or two didn't seem to express anything. They either stood silent or walked around the hall. Oh, well, he thought, it's a process and who knows where it leads. Sam had telephoned his friend Saul to tell him that he was now opened and become his spiritual brother as well as his friend. He wanted to get together to tell him about his experiences, but that would have to be delayed, as his old flatmate was off with an orchestra on a three months' tour of the Americas – north and south. The two agreed that they both hadn't done too badly in their professions. Not for two guys who spent their earlier years sharing their weekly dole and busking earnings.

Like Saul, Sam's life was becoming increasingly full. He was illustrating for several authors and having to keep up with their deadlines. Now too, a couple of his evenings a week were spent at the group's premises doing the *latihan*, meeting the brothers and sisters and in a very minor way socialising and getting to know some of his new "family". He noted that some of the women who came there were quite nice looking, but that basic acknowledgement was as far as his interest went, or was likely to go at that time. Whether the spiritual process was already guiding him in his judgement, or whether some reflection on his past personal relationships was influencing him, Sam had decided to stay celibate for the present. Maybe for all time. Or at least until he felt he had met his soul mate.

Despite his mother's carer's protestations, there was now a new member of the household. Morag really didn't welcome her presence at first, but the impact she had was soon noted and appreciated by all. Mrs Alvira Grinnage, was a large, cheerful, West Indian who came to the house every day to clean, cook, wash, iron and shop for Sam and his mother and anyone else around. She was married to a bus conductor and she kept everyone laughing at the stories that he told her about the passengers he encountered on the 152 route. However, her ebullient and happy presence was in contrast more and more with Caitlin's mental state. Sometimes, the childlike lightness she could express, would quickly change to heavy depression. When she cried, it took more than Morag's skill to change the mood and even she was grudgingly pleased when the constantly smiling Alvira lent a hand.

Sam had a feeling that his mother didn't have a lot of time left in this world and that feeling made him more attentive and much softer in his attitude to her. But death was certainly in the air and when he suddenly received a letter from Australia, he knew before he opened it, that the portents weren't going to be good.

Kerrin had been back in Melbourne for about six months witnessing the disintegration of her father as he battled against the cancer that finally took his life. She knew that it was inevitable that he would succumb, but even as positive as she always was, it had affected her considerably. It had also taken its toll on her mother who had suffered a stroke and who now needed Kerrin's skill in caring and her love as a daughter. Apparently there was another daughter, who lived in Queensland with a husband and a young family, who had offered to share her home with her, but the mother had decided that she wanted to stay put in Melbourne, in her own home.

Kerrin wrote that she had thought that perhaps she would be able to return to England sometime, but that thought was looking a tad optimistic now. She asked how progress on the book had been and how Caitlin was faring these days and really hoped that he would be able to write and keep in touch.

Sam didn't waste any time at all in answering. Immediately, he sent a telegram offering his condolences on her loss and telling her a letter would be following. In it, he told her of his mother's continuing decline, about the austere Morag and the jolly Alvira and of course about Rufus, his dog. Was it only six months since she had left? So much had happened in his life. He knew she would be happy at the book's fate, because it had defined for him his future work and then he told her a little about the spiritual movement that he was now a member of. He didn't go into details, for one thing he had been told that in this brotherhood, proselytising was discouraged and anyway, men talked to men about the content and only women should talk to women. Nevertheless he gave her a tiny flavour of its effect on him and he also told her that it was a worldwide organisation and there was probably a group in Melbourne somewhere. Then he sent it off and felt an invisible flame was being kindled. Or perhaps, re-kindled.

It was another four months before he heard from her again. Her mother had made such a good recovery, that she had insisted on taking a world cruise - with plenty of side trips - paid for by money from her late husband's insurance. Creating enough doubt about her possible vulnerability by travelling alone on such a mission so shortly after her recuperation, she had prevailed upon Kerrin to accompany her. They were away more than a month and witnessing her mother's wilful strength return, the caring daughter realised she had been used.

In fact Kerrin had never really got along well with her mother. The older woman was an academic and accomplished musician and had little time for anyone, even members of her own family, if they too weren't either very successful or accomplished in some way. Her husband hadn't really measured up to those high standards and his shortcomings were always blamed for any friction or major *contretemps* that developed in the household. After the early years of marriage and the birth of her daughters – some years apart - any love that had been there at the beginning seemed to wither and the relationship fell apart. They had stayed together as husband and wife in name only really. The mother indulged her interests and relationships elsewhere amongst the gifted and ambitious.

As the family had disintegrated as a unit, Kerrin found herself becoming closer to her father. In fact she dearly loved and admired him. He was a General Practitioner, a term his wife used to throw at him in a pejorative fashion with the emphasis on the *general*. Just an ordinary GP. No ambition from the start, she claimed. He could have specialised, he could have become a surgeon, anything other than a five or six day a week doctor to all. But local doctor he was and local doctor he remained until he succumbed to a disease in his own body that he couldn't cure. All his patients were shocked and saddened by his illness and many turned up for the funeral. He was liked and respected by everyone and even if his wife treated him with disdain, his daughters were both proud of him and his dedication. Now, his worst critic and bearer of his daughters was happily sharing the financial fruits of her husband's years of commitment to others.

Kerrin wrote that once they were back home from the world trip, she had decided that her dear mother was fit enough and well able to look after herself. She had so many interests and plenty of friends still interested in her, that her life would continue just as if nothing had happened. She realised in fact that she, devoted daughter though she'd been, would probably just be a nuisance or hindrance as the merry widow re-engaged in her old lifestyle. Then came the words he wanted to see written. She had decided to return to England in a month or so and was really looking forward to seeing him and Caitlin again. There was also a postscript.

"Oh, by the way", she wrote, "I have not only made contact with that group you mentioned, but I have met several ladies and I'm a probationer or whatever they call it. Had no intention of joining really. But I found the place in the telephone book and just went down to have a nose around and see what you were on about. Then it all seemed to happen and now I'm waiting to be 'opened' before I fly back... seeyer later!!"

How to get Morag out and Kerrin back in, was the first thought that crossed his mind after reading the letter. He would say nothing to his mother at this stage, but he knew that if he could hit one of those really clear moments she had from time to time, she would be very pleased at the news and it would be 'cup o'tay' all round. That was about all she was taking into her system lately. She claimed she had no appetite and wasn't interested in any of the food put in front of her. The doctor had said there was no physical reason why she wasn't eating, just disinterest.

Three weeks later, on the last day of the week before the Easter weekend holidays, the long convoy of caravans and lorries arrived on the common to set up for the traditional annual fair. It was a sight the Pild brothers had thrilled at when they were young. Before their father died, the family always went together, to join in the screaming on the most frightening rides and gamble their pennies and sixpences, determined to win something from the many tempting stalls. Usually it was just coconuts that they carried home, as Jock was a great shot. But the memory was one of fun, and the great enjoyment that his mother always seemed to get from those occasions.

Sam had been out early morning with Rufus jogging across the grassland nearby. It was chilly still, but a clear blue sky suggested that this year there'd be some sun for a change. May even get warm. Twelve hours later, when he drove out past the fairground to go to his *latihan,* he marvelled at the fact that everything had been constructed and prepared for the grand opening next day.

That evening, during his exercise, he suddenly had a really light flowing feeling and then an image of his mother's face. He knew it presaged something inevitable and it didn't really disturb him from the blissful state he was in. When his thirty minutes were up and everyone was preparing to leave the hall, Sam suddenly remembered the last time he had had a premonition with an image of the woman he thought was his wife looking in his windscreen. How different that was. The agony and the ecstasy, he thought.

When he got home, the night nurse was about to retire. She said his mother still wouldn't eat anything and seemed very frail when she put her to bed. His mother's room was next to his own, so before he went to bed, he looked in to see if she was awake or not. As he got closer to the bed, he looked down on the very face he'd seen in his *latihan.* She lay gently sleeping with the hint of a smile on her lips. She looked beautiful. He kissed her forehead and left.

She passed away that night. The nurse found her, still smiling, when she took a cup of tea to her early next morning, before finishing her shift.

When the doctor left this time, he handed Sam the death certificate which cruelly sent her off to the records office as a victim of senile dementia. She wasn't all that old, just turned seventy and he always thought of senility as an affliction of the very old and ga-ga.

"Do you have to put that there? That senility bit?"

"Afraid so old chap", said the doctor

"Why not natural causes or something like that?" Sam tried.

"Daren't. Fact is that anything vague like that at her age and there'd be… there'd have to be an autopsy. Now, you wouldn't want that would you? I'm very sorry."

The night nurse had really proved her worth on that last day. Before she went off duty, she had phoned the doctor and washed the body.

When Morag arrived, for once her austere presence was at least appropriate for the occasion. Her goodbye was a little warmer though. She actually kissed Sam's cheek and said how sorry she was. Only Alvira the housekeeper would come and stay and she was as comforting as a mother to Sam, making him a cup of coffee you could stand a spoon upright in.

The piece of paper in his hand suddenly reminded him that he had to inform his brother. First though, he arranged for his mother's body to be taken to an undertaker's parlour and also pencilled in a day for the actual funeral. Now to give the news to Mark Sean in South Africa.

"Hello, is that you Sean? Hope I didn't get you out of bed or anything."

He obviously had, as the voice at the other end of the phone was anything but welcoming. "It's late, what do you want?"

Sam thought for a fraction of a second just how to phrase what he had to say, then, "Mum's dead!" came out.

"What? What d'ya mean, she's dead, what happened." Sean was waking up.

"What happened?" The other repeated. "What happened is she died. That's it. She died last night in her sleep. It was a peaceful passing over. You know just how you would have told us all if you had become that priest person. She's dead, Sean and I'm calling to tell you and also to tell you that the funeral is in four days' time, so get your arse over here."

Sean had suddenly been reminded of his past: "Did you call the priest? Did the priest come and give the last rites? Did he?"

Sam was losing patience: "No Father Sean, I didn't call the priest, because I didn't know, couldn't be sure if she was dying or when she might succumb. I wasn't standing over her with a bloody stop watch and for all I know the priest could have been out on the piss in one of the pubs round here. She died Sean.

She lived and then she died. And we won't be having a wake either. Get it!"

"Take it easy Sammy, don't get too excited now. Look things are very difficult right now. Greta's having a pretty stressful pregnancy and the birth could be premature. Jesus, this is not easy. Y'see I just can't leave here right now for another reason too. It's my work, a special project that's at a crucial point and…"

The younger brother had suddenly lost his inner quiet completely. "Crucial point eh? You're rutting away like rabbits and your work has reached a crucial point. What the fuck are you making Sean, some nice new torture equipment to use on the blacks, eh? What are you doing over there in that bloody racist whorehouse anyway? Don't bother to answer that. Listen, the funeral of your mother, of our mother, the woman who raised you, arsehole, is on Thursday at the church of St Anselm's at 11 am. Cheers!" and he put the phone down in time to see Alvira turn her head away as she hid the broad grin on her face. Five minutes later, he caught her in the kitchen sobbing. And he envied her. He felt no grief, just a deep feeling of relief for his mother. Now she was free of the torment that had not only affected her mind, but more and more was were taking a toll on her physical body.

★ ★ ★

Just as Sam had expected, his brother didn't turn up for the funeral. Instead, a large wreath of expensive flowers played surrogate son. Alvira was there and so was her husband. There were no relatives, as they had all either moved country, died or just long since lost interest in the bird lady of Talbot Avenue, let alone the independent Sam. One or two neighbours who remembered her in her better days had made it along and his friend Saul was standing alongside him in the front pew. He was also there with his arm on his shoulder, when they lowered the coffin into the ground.

Finding the right plot had been easy. It already had a stone bearing the name of Rufus (Jock) Pild, killed in action in Korea, but the grave had not previously been dug. There had been no body returned to Caitlin, just the news from the defence department that her husband had been reported missing in action. When she discovered that there was no way of verifying just how he had died, she decided to pay homage to his soul by marking his passing with the stone and a place for his body to lie, if it were ever recovered. The plot had been waiting there for more than a quarter of a century. Now it would be the final resting place for Caitlin Pild and a new stone would remember them both.

After the final prayers had been said and the handfuls of dirt thrown, the priest in charge and the undertaker approached Sam and asked if they could have a word.

Here we go, he thought, the body's hardly cold and they want their money. But he was wrong. They wanted him to know that his brother in South Africa had telephoned both parties to ascertain the costs of the funeral, all the costs. Then he had wired a cheque to each of the main parties in the operation.

When Sam told Saul of the conversation, his friend said "My God, I know what Jewish guilt can do, but if that's Catholic guilt that's just amazing."

With the few mourners beginning to drift away, Sam thanked those he could for coming, refused Saul's offer to accompany him, and returned to an empty house in Talbot Avenue. Once there, he sat quietly in his study, looking at the wall, until without seeking it, his *latihan* started up spontaneously and made him stand. It was all completely involuntary and unplanned, but before he could do anything, the force went through him and he started shaking and sobbing uncontrollably.

After fifteen minutes or so of this action which also took him down onto his knees, it suddenly stopped and changed altogether. It was as if his heart had been cleared of grief. The grief he had denied. Now he was experiencing a clear light shining inside him and an uplifting feeling of joy. Finally he was sobbing in a completely different way. When it all finished, he checked his watch and it had been exactly thirty minutes. If there had been any tiny doubts about the efficacy of this *latihan* thing, they were now washed away, along with his sorrow for his dear mother.

"Now for a cup o'tay Caitlin", he said out loud.

Then he phoned his brother. He now felt he had to make his peace with him and be a little gentler and less challenging in his attitude. It was a good time to phone.

"Not busy?" Sam started a little tentatively.

"No, I'm fine for bit. Just finishing breakfast. How did it go?"

"Well, it went ok, I suppose. Yes, it was fine. Simple and fine. Your bouquet was there and we put it on the coffin in the church. By the way, thanks for sending over the… for paying for it all. I haven't really checked on mum's assets yet, but I doubt that they would have covered it. So thanks, and I hope it hasn't stretched you too much."

"It was the least I could do". They were both obviously making an effort. "You know, I really and genuinely couldn't come there myself right now. I can't leave the home for anything other than my work and the company has even allowed me to do much of that from the house. Greta's not well at all just now and… well you don't want to hear about it. The fact is Sam, that yes it is a racist regime here, but not everyone is racist and right now, I have, or rather we have a very good life without hurting anyone. I am now quite well off and, you may not like this, I'm also buying a farm in the country outside of Jo'burg. As you say, we are "rutting like rabbits" although I would prefer to call our sexual habits, natural procreating, and I want to make sure that this large family we're building will have a good material future, and that's not unchristian, is it?"

Sam was still glowing from his *latihan* experience: "Whatever grabs you brother. Look, I want to apologise for my attack, for my unchristian attack on you when we last spoke, I guess I was a bit distraught. I'm ok now and I had no right to be so vile, so forgive and forget please. Like to see you and your family sometime, though, who knows when. Please give Greta my best wishes and prayers for a safe birth for number, what five is it?"

Down the phone line came the unmistakeable sound of dishes crashing into a sink and children's voices before Sean came back on. "Sorry about that, one of the boys clearing the breakfast things with a bit too much exuberance. Yes, you're right it is number five and it could come any time we're told. As for your vile attitude, well of course I forgive and forget. I'm quite used to it by now - that's a joke. What will you do now, yourself. Are you planning on selling the house and moving out of Mitcham?"

Sam hadn't given anything much thought, but he answered as if he had. "Well, I haven't been able to do a lot right at this time. I have a fair amount of work to get through in the near future and a dog that needs exercising. But seriously, the will has to go to probate. As you know, everything that mum left is to be split equally between the two of us. Oh, I believe there is a small legacy for the RSPCA - bird division. So, yes, once it's sorted I can make all the decisions necessary. If there's any valuables that can be converted to cash, I think it would be an idea to set up a trust fund for your kids and put it in there. Up to you. Just now, I don't really want to put the house on the market. For one thing I like living here and my studio is here, but more importantly, the housing market is pretty dead just now and if we do decide to sell, we might as well make the best deal we can. So, if it's ok with you and you're in no hurry, I'll leave it like that and keep in touch. This phone call's probably going to cost me a week's earnings. I'll say goodbye for now, right?"

Sean sounded relieved that the conversation was finished. He seemed to have a fair amount of action going on around him as he tried to listen. "Yes, that all sounds fine. I agree about not trying to sell the house of course, and that's a really nice thought you had about setting up some kind of trust fund. I'm sorry Sammy if you have been left with all the work again, but you seem to cope so well nowadays. Good luck with your work. Cheerio."

Alvira was letting herself through the front door. She had Rufus with her and he was pleased to be home. The housekeeper had taken the dog earlier and left it with a friend of hers while she and Sam were at the funeral. She told him she wouldn't disturb him if he wanted to work or anything, but she would just clear up a bit, do some washing, and make him a meal before she left.

Work, however, was not on the agenda today. He really wanted to try to stay in that wonderful place he had visited during his *latihan* experience. He wanted to let his mind take a bit of time off, so he put the leash on the dog and went off for a long walk across the common. While he walked, though, his mind demanded some attention. Where was he at? A house, a career, a spiritual life and the comradeship that that could bring and a dog. Still something missing, and he knew just what that was. But even as he considered his situation and what or who could possibly change it, he was reminded of those three tenets: *surrender, submission* and *patience*. He had enough faith and nous to know that he couldn't hasten anything. He just had to continue developing in everything he did. Then he suddenly realised he hadn't told Kerrin in Melbourne that her charge, his mother, had passed away. A selfish thought earlier had prevented him from doing so in case the news would stop any plans she had for returning to England. Now, he would write and tell her, but just the bare facts.

By the time he sent the letter and it was delivered to her in Australia, Kerrin had been become a member of the spiritual brotherhood Sam had told her about. She'd bought her ticket, phoned her old girl friends to make sure of a bed when she arrived and was preparing to send a telegram to the residents of 6 Talbot Avenue, Mitcham.

The news in this envelope she'd been so anxious to open, however, seemed to stun her for a moment. It can't be. How could it be that dear Caitlin was no more. Why didn't he let her know. Let her share his grief. Perhaps he had someone else that he could lean on now. She was unsettled. But she still went ahead and sent the telegram. "Terrible news. So sorry. Leaving here in a day or so. Will phone you when I arrive. Kerrin". She decided to keep the message vague. She could have given flight details, but she didn't want to put any pressure on him. She would play it cool and see how things turned out.

★ ★ ★

The next time Sam visited his local group, he learned that the founder of the brotherhood, which had spread from Indonesia to countries all over the world, was to travel to Europe in a month or so to give talks with explanations about the *latihan* and conduct testing sessions with the members in Germany, France and Holland. There would be no visit to England this time, so any members interested in travelling to those countries, should register their intention.

More explanations? thought the new member from Mitcham who had little regard for the significance of this future happening. What's to explain? And what's this *testing* business? His friend Saul had hinted at it at one time, but nothing was really made clear. Sam thought perhaps that it was the next official stage in the process. First, probation, then the opening and receiving and next, each person had to be tested to see if they were doing it right and still qualified. Could that be it? A kind of first year exam? He wondered what he would have to do when his turn came, so he decided to phone and ask one of the helpers about it. The best way to explain what testing is, he was told, would be for him to go along to the next helpers' meeting and they'd give him some practical experience.

It all sounded mysterious and he couldn't wait. In the meantime, he booked a flight to Cologne and a train ticket to a town in North West Germany where he was told Bapak, the father of the brotherhood, would be staying for a week or so. It would be a fairly long train journey, but he wanted to get a glimpse at least of some of the places his father had mentioned when he talked to his sons about the war and his experiences. Then he phoned Saul, who was "resting" and asked him if he had planned to go to Europe to see the man. His friend said he had been toying with the idea and now that Sam was going, he'd like to go with him and they could share a hotel room over there. After explaining why he wanted to take a train ride through the country of bad memories, Sam also mentioned that their destination, the venue for the gathering, was not a great distance from Celle, where the notorious Belsen concentration camp was sited.

"Can you handle that?" He queried.

"I knew about that and I can now. Handle it, I mean. But if you'd suggested a visit there when we shared a flat together, all those years ago, I would have floored you with my oboe. But don't tell my father."

So it was all fixed.

"By the way", Sam added, "I'm going to be tested at the end of this week. I have to go along to the helpers' meeting."

Saul smiled at the other's phrasing. "Great! That's great! Let me know how you get on, I'm sure you'll pass".

★ ★ ★

It had been two weeks since the telegram arrived from Australia announcing Kerrin's decision to return to England. Had she arrived? He had heard nothing further and although part of him was anxious to see her again, he also had a feeling of trepidation. What would she expect of him? Perhaps nothing.

Maybe she wasn't really interested in seeing him at all. It could be that she had just taken up with her old friends, including a boy friend and he was now fairly low on her list of priorities. He had plenty to think about anyway. The work was still coming in regularly and his reputation as an illustrator was growing fast. Next week he was due to fly to New York for a meeting with a publisher there who was anxious to use his talent. He'd have to find a dog sitter for a couple of days then and for a week or so when he travelled to Germany.

Two days later, the phone rang in his studio and it was her. Apparently things hadn't gone all that well since she'd landed. First a girl friend who had promised her a bed temporarily had reneged on the undertaking, because her man friend and his flatmate had been kicked out of their rooms in Earls Court for not paying their rent and had moved into her place. At short notice, Kerrin had managed to get a room at the YWCA and soon after she moved in, she'd either lost her handbag or had it stolen by some itinerant thief posing as a young Christian. The police couldn't help her, so she'd had to go to the Australian High Commission for some immediate assistance, while she phoned home and asked her mother to wire her some money.

She explained that she felt too embarrassed to get in touch with him earlier, but she had contacted the woman whose name she had been given for the London centre of the brotherhood and she'd given her a room whilst she sorted herself out. Sam hadn't really been able to get a word in. Kerrin seemed to want to get it all out as quickly as possible.

"Work's another thing, I've got to arrange… I've got to get in touch with my old agency and…"

"Good to hear your voice." He decided he would step in there. "Like to meet up with you sometime, can you, would you like to have a coffee… I don't know where you are exactly… look, you know where I am, if you have the time, why not pop over here?"

She arrived two hours later and was greeted at the front door by Alvira, Rufus with his tail wagging madly, and, in the background, Sam.

After slightly awkward greetings all round, the saga of Kerrin's re-entry to England continued to be related for a while. Finally though, she apologised for her total preoccupation with her own problems and asked about Caitlin's last days and her passing. She wanted to know everything and what Sam couldn't supply, Alvira soon filled in. The mood all round had certainly changed, and the young woman from Melbourne who felt much closer to Mitcham, Surrey, asked if she could look around the house. When she came back down from Caitlin's room, she couldn't talk to anyone but just wanted to walk on her own in the garden, closely followed by Rufus.

Sam had noticed how quickly both Alvira and the cocker spaniel had taken to this stranger and he knew instinctively, that his own future was inextricably tied up with hers, so when she returned to the house, he invited her into the lounge for what he said was some tea and some chat. If she was to be working from her old agency in this area and she no longer had a flat in London, why not move into 6 Talbot Avenue, he suggested. "Share the house, have your own room, any one, there are lots of them up and downstairs. No strings attached. You can padlock the door if you like and come and go as you please. Alvira is staying on and she's a great cook and Rufus will take you for a walk any time he feels like it. You can even pay me rent if it makes you feel better, what do you say?"

"Can I think about it ? Of course I'd pay for my rent and keep. Always have… let me think about it for a bit, ok?"

"Of course, of course. Now for the selfish part… Kerrin, I have to go to New York in a week for a couple of days and then in about a month, I'm going to Germany for a week or so. Get it? I need someone to dog sit for those times. Just in the evenings and nights. Alvira is here every day, all day and she loves having Rufus around. So there's the catch. You've got to get to know and like my dog in a week, or no deal. Just joking. But if you can let me know soon that'd be great."

A short while after, the switch from Melbourne via London to Mitcham was on. After re-registering as a freelance carer with her previous employer, Kerrin had called to say she'd like to take up the offer of renting a room in Sam's house. She told him that she was hoping to get a permanent appointment with the social services department of the County Council and living in Mitcham would be very convenient. All very formal and not a hint of how she really wanted to be near the person who was the real reason she had returned to England.

That evening, Sam went along to meet the men helpers and to learn about testing. No words, no big discussion, but an invitation to join them in the spiritual exercise. When it had finished, everyone stood in a circle and Stephen, the man who he had first made contact with said:

"Staying with the *latihan*, may we each receive how do we worship Almighty God? Receive".

Then for just a few moments, every one reacted from their inner selves and did their own thing which Sam was barely aware of. For his part, as soon as the question had been asked, he experienced all the sensations that he normally felt when he stood and received his *latihan*.

Stephen then said "finish" and again it all came to a halt.

"So there you go, said one of the other men, that is an example of what testing is. You are asking a question and seeking the answer from the source that allowed you to be opened. Get it? OK?"

Sam nodded and smiled.

"Yeh, I think I get it, pretty amazing really. So can you ask any questions then?"

Another man took over.

"Of course you can, but depending on the nature of the question will come the clarity of the answer. If you are not ready to follow the result you get, then you could become confused, so at this stage, we keep the questions simple and, hopefully, spiritually relevant and we do the testing as a group, so that there is a consensus of answers. We are all at an early stage in our own development and can quite easily be influenced by our minds or hearts – still unpurified, you see – so we have to have a safeguard. We need it to stop us from going off half-cocked with some answer that may well fit in with our wishes or desires, but also to remind us to respect the wonder of the testing. It's like a prayer really, a prayer for guidance with something that might be troubling a person and which he or she cannot come to grips with from their own reasonings. The true purpose is for spiritual questions, but unfortunately some use it for all kinds of needs and if it is abused, then you can easily be given a bum steer so to speak, a misleading answer or an answer that misleads".

"That's right," said another voice. "Keep it simple and you won't have to use your mind to try to interpret the answer. Let's just try this one" and they all stood quietly with eyes closed.

"Let's each receive, how do I receive a "no" to a question, an indication that an action considered is wrong? Receive."

Then after a minute or so, he said:

"Now, how do I receive a "yes" or indication that something is right"?

Then after a pause, he said "finish" and asked Sam if he had felt the difference. The newcomer to this business certainly had. There was no doubting for him what he received for each of those tests. After the first question, he felt heavy and down. Whereas his response to the second question was light and positive. He even felt his arms involuntarily shoot up above his head

"Fantastic!" he exclaimed and then told them all just what he had experienced.

Then as Sam was taking all this in, Stephen said: "Principal rule is not to do testing on your own. Make sure, if you need to, to get two or three helpers to do it with you. Anyway, if you are going to Germany, you'll get the real low-down from the top man. The one who brought us the *latihan*. Bapak may even talk about testing, but he surely will do some with us all. His testing will be quite different though. When he tests a group of people, he asks questions that seem to be relevant to each individual standing in front of him. He is able to see through us all and to understand what we each need to either show him where we are at, or to unlock any little blockage we may be experiencing in our *latihan*. Anyway, main thing is not to rush anything. That's enough eh," he looked around at the others for agreement or for any further comment they might want to make. Everyone nodded so he continued:

"Alright, let's have a coffee." And it was all over.

★ ★ ★

The next morning, Kerrin arrived in a taxi with two cases and a backpack.

She surprised Sam by asking if she could have Caitlin's old bedroom and would he mind if she bought some extra furniture and turned it into a bed-sitting room. They were standing talking at the foot of the staircase when her new landlord joked that if she was to have that room, she must be aware that it was next to his, so unless she had other intentions, either she or he had better put an extra lock on the door.

"Anyway, I thought you had lost your wallet and everything or had it pinched, what are you going to use for money, after you've paid me an exorbitant rent?"

"Oh, don't you worry a thing about either of those little problems", the girl from Oz came back with. "As far as the closeness of the rooms is concerned, I should have told you earlier I suppose, but I do have a brown belt for Karate and I sleep with a white mask of cream on and that's not the most attractive sight for anyone at night. Money, no problem. My mother has transferred the money my dear dad left me to a bank here, so I'm fine, just fine for a while and anyway, I'll be earning a salary very soon. That is apart from the charge I'll be making for looking after the dog while you are away. Where's my rent book by the way? How much would you like and do you want it weekly, monthly or when you get it."

Sam was enjoying her feisty attitude. She was revealing more and more of her personality and he liked what he saw. "Oh, let's say the first year's rent's free and we'll talk about the next year's when we get there. Meantime, I also reserve the right to drive you to the local *latihan* group twice a week, whether you want to go or not."

Kerrin was about to haul her cases up the stairs.

"Sounds good to me cobber, but I reserve the right to buy some of the food we all eat, including Rufus's and some new wallpaper I want to put up in Caitlin's old room. Shake?"

He shook her hand as strongly and firmly as he could.

"Fair dinkum, old mate, that's a fair dinkum offer from a fair dinkum Aussie," Sam teased, in a poor imitation of the Australian accent.

The business trip to New York proved to be very successful and after staying a couple of days to show some rough sketches, a publisher signed a very lucrative contract with Sam for a series of children's books based around the adventures of one character, a young boy who always forgot crucial things, called *Tippletop*. There was also an option on a second series if the illustrator met a very tight deadline. As he also had other commitments in London, he knew he was going to have to keep his head down with no distractions at all before he set off for his trip to Germany.

When he got back home, he told everyone, including Rufus, not to expect too much from him for about three weeks. However, he still managed to attend his two *latihan* sessions at his local group and introduce Kerrin to everyone he knew there. They travelled back and forth like brother and sister, neither daring to express what they really felt about each other and during the first trip, he told her all about the visit of the brotherhood founder Bapak and how members were encouraged to attend if they could. She said that any other time she would have loved to go, but not while she was re-settling in England and looking after a dog.

These drives were the only occasions when they could have any kind of conversation and as she had brought the subject up, Sam told her she was welcome to use his car any time he wasn't using it, but to be watchful for where the dog was when she drove out of the property. He had apparently developed a habit of lying under the car.

7

Working every hour he could, Sam completed everything he'd promised his clients and with hardly a breather, he was off to Germany with his old friend Saul.

The flight was uneventful, although his former flatmate did get a bit boring when he insisted on talking about his lovely family down in the country. By now, his wife Mary had given him another child. The midwife had held up a daughter this time and he couldn't stop telling, the man strapped into the seat next to him, all about the birth and just what a beautiful creature she was and how clever they both, his son and his daughter, were. Sam suggested that they must take after the mother which set him off again. Saul didn't bite but instead raved on about what a fantastic wife he had and how understanding she was about his peripatetic existence with his work as a musician and even agreeing without question that he should go off to Germany with his bachelor friend. Thank goodness for the *latihan,* he said and recounted how Mary had actually been opened before him. That's how they met, at a gathering in London. Oh, there was so much he had to recount but in the nicest way, his companion reminded him that they had plenty of time ahead of them, including a long train journey from Cologne.

The tearoom at that city railway station was their next stop and the highlight of the next leg of the journey, for Sam anyway. He had travelled about quite a bit on British railways and accepted that the ticket you purchased for a trip, was also invariably payment for dirt and discomfort. If you dared to order refreshments you got tasteless tea or coffee and dry sandwiches, all served with wonderful English indifference from the crashing trolley that seemed just too wide for the carriage aisles. This travelling snack bar was a vehicle ingeniously designed specifically to clip everyone's elbow on its clattering way. Alternatively, if you decided to seek a little light snack in the station concourse of your destination for instance, it was invariably to be taken standing, or if sitting, on food-stained chairs with someone else's crumbs still waiting for you at tables that hadn't been cleared for a day or so.

But in the tearoom or rather the grand restaurant adjacent to the tracks at Cologne Central, it was quite different. The interior was elegance itself, both in design and decoration. The tables and chairs were arranged with plenty of space in between and your order was taken by a waitress in pristine white apron and delivered efficiently and gracefully. What a contrast Sam felt. However, things went a little downhill from then on.

The train seats in each compartment seemed to have been designed for thin people but patronised by fat people and a lot of the latter variety were travelling on the particular train the two Englishmen had booked on. It left much later than they had expected and their tickets entitled them to the trip only and no seat reservations, so for the first part of the journey, they were standing or leaning in the corridor. And that was when Sam first smelt it. He mentioned the sensation to his companion and asked him if he too could smell it and, better still, identify it.

Saul said he could smell it alright, a sickly sweet smell that seemed to be emanating from their fellow travellers. A bit later, after a couple of stops, when the two men had found seats, a vendor came around the carriages with a big basket over his arm and that's when Sam figured out just what it was he was finding less than attractive. The man was selling chunks of meat, pork meat for which there were plenty of customers. The mystery odour was created by a diet of pork mixed with the sweat that inevitably came from fat people wedged into thin spaces on a long warm journey. That was the theory anyway and the two men discussed it in whispers in this German-speaking travelling abattoir. Saul was no help at all of course. He'd been raised in an orthodox Jewish culture and pig meat was never discussed, let alone eaten. Sam owned up to having eaten and liked bacon and ham, but thought that perhaps the smoking treatment those two examples got managed to extract and eliminate that sweet sickly aroma. Then in case the two of them needed further convincing, at the next station, someone got out and the space was quickly taken by a new arrival, a very attractive young woman. Both men, despite their current commitments – in the case of Saul, or the hoped-for future commitments of Sam - couldn't but be attracted to this nubile creature. That is until she lifted her case up to put it on the rack above her. With her armpit exposed, they got the full force of an effluvium that must have been created from pig meat eating, sweat and a not too expensive perfume. Neither man had any further interest and so they both left their seats and recovered their places leaning in the corridor. When they looked at each other with relief, Sam said, "Is this really happening? Are we going to be dogged by this unpleasant whiff all the while we are over here?"

★ ★ ★

The venue for this gathering of kindred spirits, was a refurbished farmhouse on the outskirts of a small city. Its renovation had been accomplished by the local members of the brotherhood and apart from the main house, across a cobbled courtyard, a large barn had been transformed into both a comfortable place for the group to do their regular *latihan* and also a cosy coffee bar.

On this occasion, the man from Indonesia and his small party would be staying in the house and because there were so many visitors who'd travelled from all over the world for this visit, a school hall nearby had been hired for *latihans*, talks and testing sessions.

Sam and Saul had been booked into a hotel a few kilometres away, but after a night there, they moved out convinced that the odour they'd found so offensive on the train was following them. Their fears were confirmed, it seemed, when they experienced the same unpleasant flavour to the environment in the room of another hotel. Were they being paranoid? Or what? The joke that they'd enjoyed earlier no longer seemed so funny. Sam was now convinced they were being shown something and swore that he would never eat another piece of pig meat again.

But they still needed a safe house so to speak to spend the rest of their time at this gathering. Fortunately, they got talking to an American member in the coffee bar who was actually living in the town and who said they could crash on the floor of his bijou flat. He also assured them that he was Jewish and didn't eat pork, so they should be able to breathe easy.

As things turned out, they had missed very little by these distractions. Someone must have had the dates wrong, because Bapak arrived a day later than expected and nothing really got going with him until the two Englishmen had settled their accommodation needs.

Now, happily breathing in pig-free air, Sam and Saul were there, to see the man step out of the car dressed not in some eastern robes and garlands like the mystic gurus that had had much influence in the West in recent years, but in a smart business suit and fedora.

All the local German members of the host group had been sitting inside the house that would accommodate this holy man and his party, being quiet. On cue, they came out, locked the heavy wooden door behind them and joined the rest of the hundreds of visitors who were waiting in dignified silence. Then one of them introduced himself to the man from Indonesia and with a flourish, presented him with a key to the closed door at the end of the pathway. Smiling broadly, the distinguished guest just pointed past the key bearer to the waiting door and as we all witnessed, it was opening by itself. Still smiling, Bapak then made his way through the waiting members, into the house. Even after a long car ride, he held himself in a dignified posture as he walked and there seemed to be an aura around him that both attracted and distracted the watching eyes. It was like he was there, but he wasn't.

That evening, the *latihan* was a revelation. About a hundred men of several nationalities and different religions stood quietly together to hear the person who had brought this miraculous experience to mankind, say "Begin". Sam felt as if he had been opened once again. The sensations he had felt before were magnified and like everyone else around him, he was expressing sounds and movements all peculiar to him yet in a kind of harmony with all the others.

And so it went on. The days were free for the visitors to meet and mix with brothers and sisters from many countries around the globe. Young and old had been drawn to Europe at this time like iron filings to a magnet. The evenings were devoted in rotation to *latihan*, talks and testing sessions and each morning the daily chat amongst the clusters of folk who gathered in the courtyard was full of wonder at what had been witnessed or experienced the night before.

When Bapak sat up on a simple stage, sipping occasionally from a cup of tea or a glass of orange, whilst his words were being translated, he could almost be ignored. But when he spoke, always starting with his eyes closed momentarily, he seemed to hold everyone spellbound. No histrionics, no flamboyance, just the softly enunciated *Bahasa Indonesian*. His voice carrying information and explanations of the *latihan* that seem to come from somewhere deep inside or from some other source just passing through him. It was as if he was receiving what he was saying and hearing it himself for the first time. Whilst he talked, his eyes lit up and his smile, when he talked of Almighty God, was like sunshine pouring from his lips.

Whether it was the original Indonesian being spoken or the interspersed translation from a man sitting at Bapak's side, Sam found that his mind was not able to take it all in. He sat quietly listening and when it was all over, he felt full and satisfied. Then when he checked some of the points that he had managed to remember, with Saul and others, he discovered that they had all, without exception, heard something quite different. So, he realised that the lesson was not to try to understand with the mind what was being related, but to just absorb it all and hope that comprehension would come to the listener in its own time.

The testing was something else again. It consisted of groups of women or men separately standing before this amazing man, being asked questions that seemed innocent and almost irrelevant to a spiritual gathering, but which proved to be keys to open up some blockage or release some stunted feeling in the individual. At the end of some tests, Bapak would single out someone on their way back to their seat with a puzzled look on their face and say "Don't think about it" and the face would relax.

★ ★ ★

When they were on their way home, the two friends started to compare notes on what they felt were the highlights of the trip and they came to a fascinating decision. Sam reminded Saul that Bapak had said that of course this movement had come at a time of great materialism in the world. That it embraced all religions and in fact that through the *latihan,* by doing the exercise regularly and sincerely, a person would get to really understand the true significance of one's own religion, whether it be Christianity, Judaism, Islam or whatever. Anyway, they both realised that neither of them had a religion that they followed. Saul had abandoned any interest in Judaism and Sam had long since rejected Catholicism. However, during the first and subsequent *latihans,* he had started to involuntarily intone the phrase Allahu Akbar… "I think that means…"

"It's Arabic for 'God is great'". Saul broke in.

"But I don't know any Arabic." Returned the other. "So where d'you suppose that came from… I made other noises like it too."

"Don't know", his companion said. "Your inner must know Arabic, I suppose."

Sam then recalled how, in the last session, he found himself on his knees with his head on the ground in the prayer position of a Muslim. He had no idea how he got down there or really what it meant. He remembered that he had seen pictures of people praying in a mosque, but that was ages ago. This was yet another dawning for the rebel from Mitcham. He said he felt he was closer to Islam and its belief in the One God, than any other religion and he intended to test with the helpers back in the UK to see if he should do something about it formally.

"I might do the same." Saul was smiling. "I know I can't talk about what I receive and feel as well or as fluently as you, but I've had some strange feelings this week too and they may well coincide with yours."

Now, Sam was beaming.

"A Jewish Muslim? You must be joking. What will your family do if you become one?"

"Probably disown me, but that's their problem really. We each have one life and we must each proceed on our own spiritual journey and follow our feelings in the process. So to you and to me: *Mazeltov!*"

* * *

When he got home, he was glad to see that both Alvira and Kerrin were in the house. He had something to say to the two of them and the sooner he said it the better, so he ushered them into the lounge.

"It's good to be home and great to see the two of you, I must say. I had a fascinating time over there, you know, in Germany and I learned a few things. One of them was that I will no longer be eating pork meat. Yeh, that's right don't look shocked. Gone off pork, permanently. So, Alvira, no more of those delicious spare ribs, what is it that you call them Jerky ribs?"

"Jerk ribs, Mr Pild, Jerk is the sauce we make – it's a favourite of Jamaicans." Alvira looked a little hurt.

"Well, I'm sorry, but from now on the spare ribs are out and the bacon and ham things, too. So, Kerrin, if you fancy a bacon and tomato sandwich in future you'll have to have it in your room. I don't want to even see the stuff. I'll put a cooker in for you."

"Don't bother, I can live without it, if it's a banned substance, I'm a social worker don't forget. By the way, I got the job with the council I was after. Permanent, full time and all. Didn't tell them I hadn't got British citizenship yet."

"Oh, that should be alright. Once you're a regular civil servant, you're in the club. It's probably like Freemasonry. Anyway, congratulations that's great." Sam got up to leave the room signalling that the chat was over, but Kerrin had a question for him.

"What's this pork thing about anyway? Did you get orders from someone about what to eat? I thought you were going for spiritual nourishment, not to satisfy your belly, which is a bit smaller than when you left by the way. In fact you look fitter all over doesn't he Alvira? Probably starved himself though, and got a lot of exercise dodging pork pies and bacon sandwiches.

Eh, take it easy, Mr Pild," the young woman objected, pretending to be offended as Sam took her arm and led her from the room and pointed out the stairs leading to her bed sitter.

"I'll tell you all about it later, 'bye for now, oh, yes, I want to see that wallpaper you put up too" and he disappeared into his studio.

The next time they travelled together to the local *latihan* group, he told her of his sickly smelling train journey and its lingering impact firstly on his ordinary sensory equipment and then, he claimed, on his psyche. He also hinted at what he felt was a profound receiving that could have quite an impact on his future and how he wanted to do some testing with the helpers to check it out. He asked if she'd mind waiting while he did so. Before they got out of the car, he also handed her a gift from his visit overseas. A bottle of Chanel No 5 perfume. Taken aback at first, she queried, "Is this because you think I smell like your beautiful girlfriend on the train?"

Then the first real contact: he was given a kiss on the cheek and thanked profusely.

The helpers were happy to do the testing with Sam. It was simple and straightforward, he assured them. However, once he had shared with them his feelings about his possibly becoming a Muslim, the normally quiescent attitude of the four men he had come to know a little, changed to a slightly animated one, even challenging the questioner's reasoning and asking what, if anything, Sam knew of the Islamic religion. For instance: Didn't he feel he should find out what he wanted to get into before he made any move in that direction? What about his own background? Catholic wasn't it? What was wrong with that then? Why not pursue that and try to understand the basis of the culture he was baptised into and confirmed in? And so on.

Well, this was a new and unexpected reaction and all he could do was to maintain his own 'quiet' and strength of conviction. He told the ones that were most vociferous that he hadn't really come there to discuss or debate anything. He merely wanted to confirm or deny a conviction that was growing in him. Perhaps, he suggested, they should leave the testing for another time, so that their concerns didn't cloud the testing of the simple issue he wanted to pursue.

He knew that one of the four helpers present was a Muslim and ironically, he was the one with the most questions designed to make Sam doubt or at least re-examine his wish. However, like all the others, this man, Rahman, was smiling at Sam's quiet defence of his request and his gentle reproach that they were there to test something of great spiritual significance. Here he was a comparative newcomer to this business, reminding the helpers of their roles. There was a moment or two of sheepish silence before Stephen who always seemed to be on hand, suggested that they all do a few minutes *latihan* to quieten their minds and then test what had been asked.

It turned out to be a good and worthwhile experience for all of them. The testing proved conclusively that Sam's feelings were right and coming from the right place. No desire, but a genuine indication from his inner, that his true religion was Islam.

When it was over, the helpers thanked him for his patience and for the opportunity to witness the very powerful receiving they had all experienced in the testing.

Then Rahman, a South African Cape Malay, embraced Sam and told him he would be happy to give him any information or advice about Islam and also that he would be happy to take him to the Mosque when he felt he wanted to formally embrace his new religion. Sitting him down away from the others, Rahman said he would bring him a book which outlined the basic tenets and a list of the taboos for Muslims, such as the dietary requirements: no shellfish or pork meats and no alcohol. It's all explained in the early pages he said.

"No alcohol?" Sam gave a wry smile. "I just bought a bottle of the best whiskey duty free on the flight back from Germany. Wasn't receiving too well there was I."

"Now that you're on the path that you have chosen, you won't miss it, I promise. In its place you will be able to know the joy of fasting and abstinence. Oh, by the way, I hope you don't mind me asking, but are you circumcised?"

"Not that I know of, laughed the new Muslim, you mean do I still have a foreskin? Well yes, last time I looked, I do. So, has that got to go? Along with the pork and the whiskey. Why?"

Rahman sat for a moment before he answered. He wanted to get this as right as he could.

"Look, there are various reasons postulated by scholars and so on, the most common being the simple fact that it is cleaner and healthier to keep the penis head free. However, Bapak, who as you know is a Muslim, says it doesn't need to be confined to just Muslims, because he says that by removing that extra flesh, you are ridding yourself of ancestral bad blood. I also personally feel that for a mature man to be circumcised, it also purifies spiritually, the effect of ... perhaps, past sexual misuse of that organ...by the individual. Please don't take that personally, I am speaking generally of course. Anyway, don't hesitate to ask me about anything else you want to know."

Sam, quite involuntarily scratched his crutch as the two men stood up, preparing to leave. "Hey, thanks for all that Rahman, I do want to know as much as possible, and if you have the time, perhaps you could come over to my place for dinner one day this week and we could talk a bit further."

On the way home in the car, Kerrin learned why she had had to wait. He had confirmed his feelings about Islam and his life was about to experience quite a change... again. He kept it all a bit mysterious, though, by first asking her if she would like a bottle of whiskey and when she said she didn't really like liquor, he decided to give it to Alvira as a Christmas present.

★ ★ ★

After Rahman's visit to Talbot Avenue, Sam decided that he should get his foreskin removed even before he went to the mosque for the official induction ceremony. He rang Saul and told him the result of his testing and asked him if he knew how he should go about getting the chop. Saul explained that he didn't know much about it as he had been circumcised as a baby, but he'd get back to him with a name of a foreskin specialist in London after making some enquiries. He also congratulated Sam on the result of the testing and his determination to follow it through. He said he hadn't yet tested for himself, but he would as soon as possible, because if it was right for him too, he would love to embrace Islam, in any formal procedure at the same time.

Next day, Sam got the name of a doctor who carried out minor surgery at a small private hospital run by the Catholic church in Notting Hill gate. The nurses, Saul informed him, were all nuns, so he shouldn't get any ideas whilst he was in there. "They know all about minor operations on minor parts," he quipped and gave the would-be patient the phone numbers of the doctor and the hospital. As it turned out, Sam didn't have to stay in overnight even though he was to be fully anaesthetized. It all started early in the morning and shortly after he came round and had a quick inspection of the stitched up pathetic piece between his legs, the doctor was at his bedside, along with a nursing nun.

"Everything ok, let's take a look", and he pulled the sheet back quickly and roughly to expose his work to the nun and anyone else passing through the ward at the time.

Still recovering from the effects of whatever had been pumped into him to put him out, Sam looked again at his member, now wreathed in a crown of nylon stitches, looking like a miniature Roman ruler, and said: "Doesn't there seem... look isn't there still some of the foreskin there... I mean I can only see the top of the actual penis head, d'you see?"

He was sure the nun/nurse was smiling as she turned away.

"Ya, Ya, that's fine… for when it grows, you know, when it gets big." To illustrate his point, Dr Galewski put a crooked finger out and then straightened it up abruptly. Wasting no further time on his post-operative check, he threw the sheet back over the patient's private parts as if he was bored and wanted to get away. "Do you have a cheque book?"

Sam pointed to a pile of his personal belongings on the side cabinet. The doctor made a grab in that direction and within seconds had the book open, had written his own name in the appropriate place and also filled in the amount he was to be paid.

"Here, sign here please." This man was definitely in a hurry as he passed the pen over and helped Sam up into a sitting position.

"I don't have my glasses, I need reading glasses… I wasn't expecting…"

Before he could finish the sentence, the good doctor had snatched his own spectacles off his nose and thrust them at the other man. "Here, use these."

And so, squinting through totally unsuitable lenses, and sore from the handiwork of this man, Sam managed to sign his name. He didn't have a clue what he had put his name to and really didn't care.

About an hour or so later, after tea and biscuits in the ward and a painful pee in the toilet, the man with a skin trim he would not be able to talk about at home, made his way slowly and carefully from the hospital and back to Mitcham.

Now he had to face Alvira and later Kerrin, who would surely notice the strange, tentative way he was walking and worse still, Rufus, who was certain to jump in one bound onto his lap.

All that and more happened. First Alvira asked if he was going to take the dog out for a run as Kerrin hadn't been able to earlier. The dog got the message at the same time and leapt up to hit Sam with both paws in the danger area. Then, gasping with pain that he was trying to disguise from the housekeeper, he made a big mistake in moving too fast to get to the phone which was ringing in his studio. Lunging across the desk to make sure he didn't miss the call, he managed to catch his vital part on the corner of his drawing board. He then gave up the attempt to get to the phone and collapsed into his armchair nearby. That's when Rufus struck again, predictably jumping up onto his lap in an attempt to persuade his master to go for a run.

Somehow Sam survived the rest of the day without too much suspicion from Alvira, but when Kerrin came home and invited him up to her room to see the decorating she'd done, he said he was too busy. He was actually reclining on a couch in the lounge.

"What's the matter? Are you sick? If that's busy, then my busiest hours are spent in bed and don't you dare say anything smart. You know I live like a nun."

"And I spend my days and nights like a monk, and it's got to stop, but not right now. Oh, ok, I'll come and see the room, just help me up, will you." Sam sat up and swung his legs round ready to stand.

Kerrin took his hands and pulled him up. "Eh, there really is something wrong with you. Can you walk?" Then when she saw how uncomfortable he was doing that, she continued. "What have you been up to, getting the chop?" she laughed.

"How on earth... what do you know?" Sam was both surprised and embarrassed.

"Not a lot, just putting two and two together, really. I have done a bit of research on Muslims and when you said you were definitely going to become one I got to wondering if you had ever had, you know what. Anyway, seeing the way you are walking, there is obviously something giving you discomfort down there so... No, your friend Saul didn't say a word."

Sam saw the twinkle in her eye and so he thought it was time to lay his cards on the table.

Yes, he had had a circumcision operation and yes it was a requirement of all Muslims and Jews. And yes, as soon as things settled down below his pelvis, he intended to go to a Mosque with Rahman to formally embrace Islam. Would she like to come to be a witness too? Then he explained what he really meant about his living like a monk:

"The fact is that after what happened in Canada and, well even before all that, as a young man, I really couldn't handle the whole sex thing. So, anyway, after that mess in Canada I just felt I wanted to stay celibate… I certainly didn't want another relationship for a while, maybe for ever. I know it sounds funny, but I didn't feel worthy or something and I didn't want to make another mistake, I suppose. Then you came into my life and whether it's destiny or whatever, you have become very important to me. Look, we have lived in the same house for a while now, we both have the same spiritual interests and you now know all about my private parts. Don't run, although this seems really bizarre now, me like this and all, but I think… well I think I love you".

Kerrin had waited a long time for this and when it came, she just burst out,

"And I love you, and have done for a long while." And she grabbed him in such a powerful embrace, he fell back onto the couch.

" Eh, hold on, take it easy, jeez that is painful. Look, plenty of time for that when we're married. Will you?" Sam pulled her down beside him.

"Too bloody right I will, oh, are Muslims allowed to swear?"

"Right up until the ring is on the finger and that's going to be pretty soon as far as I'm concerned. Hey Alvira", he shouted out for his surrogate mother in the kitchen "Alvira!" Then when she burst through the doorway, thinking there was an emergency, he said. "We're going to get married. Kerrin and me, married, Alvira, to each other. What do you think about that?"

The buxom West Indian who had shared his life and house for quite a while now; the woman who had helped to care for his mother and who had witnessed his loss and who would do anything for him that he ever asked of her, just simply beamed and said: "About time. Now I've got a pie to make." And off she went.

Having established a code of behaviour in the house, the couple agreed to maintain it until they were wed. They continued to occupy their own bedrooms and share the house just as before. Outside the house, they now socialised a bit, with visits to the London galleries, the cinema and theatre, learning for the first time their individual tastes and behaving like a regular courting couple. Soon, life for both would be taking on the simple disciplines of becoming Muslim.

★ ★ ★

A month after his circumcision, Rahman called to say he'd made an arrangement for Sam and Saul to officially embrace Islam at the Woking Mosque in Surrey. They could all meet at Talbot Avenue and travel together.

To both men, the Mosque sited on a most appropriately named Oriental Road, was an amazing sight: a beautiful Indian designed place of worship with its pillars and tastefully shaped archways surrounding the dome, and there it was in the most English of counties. Rahman had told them a little of its history on the way there, so they knew that it was oldest purpose-built mosque in the UK and probably in Europe, built in 1889.

They were all met at the doorway by a smiling Indian or Pakistani man who introduced himself as the one who would be conducting the ceremony. He indicated that they should take their shoes off and then he ushered them into the building.

Beautifully carpeted and cloaked in a feeling of peaceful stillness, when Sam later tried to describe the place to Kerrin, he found that apart from a shining gold chandelier and an impressive stained glass window, he could only really remember the quiet atmosphere and the gentle manner of the Imam.

The ceremony was very simple. All that was required, was for the two to make the declaration, or what the Imam referred to as the *Shahada* which they repeated after him in Arabic: *La ilaha il-Allahu, Muhammad-ur-Rasullah*. Then, still smiling, he embraced them both and said, "What you have just said is: There is no God except Allah; Muhammad is the messenger of Allah". And it was all over.

When they had their shoes back on and were making their way down the pathway from the mosque, this gentle, holy man, who was strolling between them put his arms around Saul and Sam's shoulders and said.

"Main thing. In Islam, we worship the one God. We recognise and praise all the messengers or prophets - from Abraham to Moses, to Jesus Christ and finally to Muhammad. The rest you will learn as you go on." Spontaneously, before they left him, the two new Muslims embraced the man, who half an hour earlier had been a stranger to them.

On the way back home, Rahman reminded them of some of the practical requirements of the religion they had just joined. The five prayers a day, the fast of Ramadan, the giving of *Zakat* or a charitable donation, at the end of the fast and one day, perhaps, the *Hajj* or holy journey to the shrine of Muhammad that all Muslims are expected to make.

As the man talked enthusiastically about the pillars of Islam, Sam drove and nodded, but inside himself, he knew that although he'd make an attempt to learn the prayers and do the fast and so on, his first priority was to continue with diligence his *latihans* and to follow what he received from that amazing source. He couldn't deny that he had been impressed by the whole experience he'd shared with Saul and Rahman, but he also knew that he couldn't wait to get to his house and see his bride-to-be. Now that all other formalities seemed to have been completed he didn't want to wait any longer to get married and he hoped, have children. His own children.

★ ★ ★

The marriage took place in the County registry office. Alvira and her husband agreed to be witnesses. Then a few days later, the newly weds stood in front of the same Imam in the Woking Mosque and were joined together in a religious ceremony which was almost as simple as the declaration that Sam had made when becoming a Muslim.

This time, Saul and his family were on hand and a number of Sam's brothers and sisters from the local group where he practised his spiritual exercises. Later, there was a small party at the mosque, with fruit juice for champagne. After which, Sam confided in Kerrin that "boy do I need a drink".

With Alvira successfully bought off by the gift of the special bottle of double malt whiskey that Sam had been eyeing again and again, she agreed to be housekeeper and dog minder for two weeks whilst the couple flew over to Spain for their honeymoon.

Two months later, while they were settling down to married life in Mitcham – Kerrin announced that she was pregnant.

Sam was now 36, more than six years older than his new wife and this was the news he wanted to hear more than anything else. The words he had thought he would never hear and the idea that he had almost dismissed from his mind: he was going to be a father. They shared the excitement and joy together and early as it was, started to make plans for when the newcomer arrived. Which room would be his or hers? When should they buy the pram and the cot and so on and so on. But amidst all this planning and expectation, Sam suddenly felt a wave of sadness go through his consciousness. He didn't understand it and he quickly dismissed it. It must have been some deep doubt in him of his ability to be a father. Perhaps some inner guilt at how he had lived his early life, from which he had made himself believe for years that he didn't deserve real happiness. Whatever it was, he wouldn't allow it any significance and as a defence mechanism, he tried to be unusually buoyant and positive about everything to do with Kerrin and the creature growing in her body.

However, try as he might, he knew that the feeling he'd had was meaningful. A kind of foreboding. That was the reality. All the excuses he'd made for himself were unreal and that was confirmed when he felt the same sadness descend on him whilst he was alone, working on illustrations for a new children's book intended for the very young.

Three months later, Kerrin miscarried and they were both shattered. Two weeks before the child was lost, the young woman had felt some uncomfortable pains and dismissed them as being just natural happenings during pregnancy. Now she felt guilt. What had she done. Work, that was it. She shouldn't have continued with her job as a social worker. She obviously wasn't as strong as she thought she was. She was taking on other people's problems and must have been too vulnerable. And so she tormented herself with everything negative she could come up with to blame herself for losing the most precious gift she had wanted to present to Sam.

For his part, the recognition that the premonition, that he had desperately tried to deny, had once again been a harbinger of death, haunted him. It made him also turn his confusion into guilt and blame. He tried to console Kerrin with his conclusion, that in fact the child had not been allowed to be born because of his past. He told her that he really did believe that every person carries in their soul something of previous sexual behaviour. It was a concept he knew that was understood by some indigenous peoples of North America and Australia. Something he didn't want to understand or recognise, but he now realised that however well-intentioned his conduct towards her had been, he carried baggage from his past that had to be purified before a sexual bonding between them was clear and uniquely theirs.

Despite the emotional state she was in, Kerrin's mind cleared enough to recognise something of the truth he was expressing. However, she didn't want him to think that it was all his fault. If his theory was correct, and it really felt right, she told him that she too had not been an innocent when they finally got together. She too had experiences in her past that she now regretted.

Then after crying and hugging together, they both felt they had already cleared something. Now their relationship seemed to be on a new, higher plateau. They could talk to each other in a new, spiritual, way and know that they each could understand and *feel* the significance of what they were saying or trying to say.

★ ★ ★

For another year or so, the two reverted to being the nun and the monk in their attempt to cleanse anything from their beings that would affect their ultimate hope that they could really consummate their partnership with a child. An infant, they hoped, born of love and conceived by two people who entered into their union in a state of quiet surrender and not from physical passion.

Throughout this period, their love never wavered and even though Sam's workload seemed to increase and intensify the demand for his talent, his dedication to the *latihan* also seemed to strengthen. He became a keen student of the ways of Islam and with the help of Rahman had learned not only the necessary prayer movements, but also many of the actual prayers, if only in phonetic form. Arabic could come - might come - later.

Now, he thought, if I really am to be a Muslim, I should have a Muslim name. Sam had learned from the helpers that most members of the brotherhood - both men and women had at one time or another felt the need to ask the founder, Bapak about the significance of names. Whether they were in harmony with a person's soul. Sam wondered if perhaps his moniker was wrong and whether that too had been a contributing factor in the miscarriage. He decided to check it out by writing to Bapak for advice and at the same time to ask for a Muslim name. He also talked to Kerrin about this name business and asked her if she felt comfortable with hers. She said she felt fine with the name but if he was writing, then he could perhaps get a Muslim name for her too.

It took little more than two weeks to get an answer and Sam's Christian name had pretty well been ignored, so his parents' choice couldn't be too far out, he felt. However, he had a new name as a Muslim. Bapak had written that his correct name was Ridwan and that his wife should be known as Renita.

The airmail letter that carried the information seemed like a personal blessing on the two of them and when they saw that they had both been given the initial R, they felt that they really were destined to be together and that their lives would surely one day be blessed by the birth of a healthy child.

And of course, there was another R in the family, the faithful old cocker spaniel Rufus.

8

Another year went by and both Sam and Kerrin (or Ridwan and Renita) felt that the pain from the miscarriage had been healed. They also felt that they would only have sexual intercourse after first being aware of the spiritual nature of what they were doing. They were really offering up a prayer that they should be blessed with a child as a result of their act. Because of this their lovemaking became an act of worship. Not a performance of physical gratification and sexual relief, but something that seemed to take them away from their bodies into an idyllic place, where they truly became one.

Neither had ever experienced anything like it before and they both agreed that they had really discovered the real purpose of the sexual union.

Within two months, Kerrin announced that she was again pregnant and this time, she insisted that she would stop working and resign from her post as a social worker. She didn't want to take any chances at all, particularly as her workload had increased and she was having to minister to a wider range of problems, including drunks and drug addicts.

Sam was as thrilled as before and he knew that soon Kerrin's biological clock would be running down a bit for a first child. He felt light and happy and they both made their plans again for the arrival of this newcomer. Nine months later, almost to the day, Kerrin's water broke and she started to time the contractions. Although Sam was at home it was Alvira who was in closest attendance and offering all the advice she could draw on from her own experiences with the three childbirths she had had.

"You know you mustn't leave it too long my dear, the hospital warned you didn't they? They want to keep an eye on you because of what happened before. This time, it's going to be wonderful my sweet, but don't leave it too long. It don't matter if it's a false alarm you know, you can always come back home."

Kerrin feared that this running commentary would carry on until she left, so she decided to go sooner rather than later. Everything was packed in her suitcase and Sam whisked her off to the local maternity hospital where she was booked in for a preliminary examination.

The anxious husband sat outside the ward for over half an hour, finally wondering if the birth had occurred and they'd forgotten to tell him. He had mooched off to get a coffee at one time, perhaps he had missed the whole thing. Then the door to the ward opened and Kerrin was standing there, still as big as she was when he brought her in.

"That Alvira is a witch I swear. False Alarm. Just as she intimated". Kerrin was obviously fed up. "Can't come home though. They want to keep me here now that they've got me. Doctor's examined me, midwives have examined me, I think the orderly had a look in too. Anyway, they said it could take a while yet but who knows. The main midwife said you might as well go home and they'd call you if anything starts to happen. There'd be plenty of time and they won't start without you. Give us a hug."

Sam went back to the house and sat about a foot away from the phone. Alvira made him something to eat and then asked if he wanted her to stay for a while.

"Please do, yes, that would be great. Just in case I have to dash off to the hospital any time soon. Yes, thanks. Would you like to ring home and tell them… go ahead now, here", and he thrust the phone into her hands urging her with his eyes to make it quick.

After her call which wasn't quite as short as he would have liked, he thought, oh, what if they were trying to get me then. So he phoned the hospital and enquired if anything had happened to his wife, yet. Was she in labour or whatever, or contracting at all? They told him that nothing had changed since he had left her just twenty five minutes earlier and that Kerrin was sitting in an armchair with a cup of tea, reading magazines. Better for him, they suggested, if he relaxed too. Perhaps get some sleep in case he was called late in the night.

There was no way that Sam was going to get some sleep. He had no intention of moving more than a foot from that telephone, however relaxed he became. In fact, he was just on the point of dropping off for a doze, with his latest illustrations under his flopped down arm, when the call came. He had been waiting three hours. The voice from the hospital said: Mr Pild? Is that Mr Samuel Pild there?"

"Yes, Yes!"

"Wilson Hospital here, maternity. Yes, things seem to be happening and the contractions are getting more and more frequent, so if you'd like to come along now it would be a good idea". He wasn't aware of it in his rush from the house and into the car, but that dash signalled the end of his dog's life. Unable to consider what might have happened when he drove over Rufus in his haste to get to the hospital, he could only think of his wife and the birth they both wanted so much.

When he arrived, he was given a mask and a gown and allowed to stand at the side of his panting wife. She managed to smile up at him as she followed the orders of the doctor and midwife in attendance.

"Bear down now dear, come along, everything's going just fine."

"Bear up" Sam quipped and received a less than appreciative look from the doctor.

And so it went on, until a calm and smiling Irish midwife brought out a big, healthy baby boy and held it up for his mother to see, before shoving it under the nose of Sam who quite involuntarily, just mouthed the words "*Allahu Akbar*". The doctor and the midwife looked confused at the expression and so the proud father said to them: "I'll explain later". He then kissed his wife and told her: "thankyou, thankyou so much, darling Kerrin. I have to wait outside now, while you're cleaned up, but I'll be back." And he left the ward with a smile from ear to ear and with eyes full of tears that were welling up and would soon spill over.

Once he'd recovered, he phoned home and told Alvira the news. She congratulated him and asked him to give Kerrin her love, then she told him about the crushed dog. She had found him in the driveway when she had gone looking for him after he'd failed to turn up for his supper. She was very sad, she said. And she had arranged for him to be taken away.

"Can't have Mrs Pild seeing that poor old Rufus like that, when she comes home, can we."

★ ★ ★

The joy of the arrival of Pild junior and the sadness at the misfortune that had befallen their much-loved dog, was still with the couple when Kerrin received a telegram from Australia that managed to affect both emotions.

It had been only a matter of a few weeks since the new mother had phoned both her sister in Brisbane and her mother in Melbourne to give them the news: the exciting tidings of the birth of their new son. The first call, to her sister Ann, had been greeted with enthusiastic congratulations and an offer to send over any baby clothes that might be needed. The second call to Rosemary, her mother, received a grudging recognition that she had been presented with a new grandchild. Actually the fact that there was another addition to the family in itself was no problem, but it was its progeny that seemed to give grandmother some scarcely hidden difficulty.

When her daughter had previously phoned to tell her of her marriage to Sam, dear mother's response was: "Who is this man?" followed by "What does he do?" then, "Oh, an illustrator. *Just* an illustrator, a book illustrator, you say. Not an author or an artist. He just does the drawings". The last comment was delivered in the same derisory tone that one might use to describe the work of a lavatory cleaner.

Anyway, the latest news from Australia was not good. Rosemary had suffered another stroke and this time it was very serious. Apparently she had been berating some music critic over the phone when she was struck down. Much to his credit, the critic had called the police. Actually his initial intention was to try to prevent or at least stem the constant abuse he had been getting from the woman, but when he had a second thought about her strangled cry, he sensed that something had happened that needed some official attention. Much of this information had come later, when Kerrin phoned and spoke to her sister. The telegram had just indicated the bare facts, but the full story was even more depressing than was first thought. Their mother was in a coma and the doctor expected her to be quite incapacitated if and when she recovered consciousness. Worse still, there would be no relatives left in Australia to give the much needed care that would be required. Ironically, Ann's husband had been offered a diplomatic post in Japan and the family were moving there in three months. So, unless they decided to put Rosemary in a home, it was assumed that, if it were at all possible, Kerrin would take over from her sister at the appropriate time, at least to be on hand to give some comfort and care to their mother.

Suddenly, the Pilds of Mitcham were faced with a major upheaval in their lives. They both agreed that even if they had planned to go to Australia some time, these were not the circumstances they would have envisaged that would have persuaded them. However, it seemed that they had no choice, assuming that Kerrin's mother survived. Faced with the prospect of caring and probably providing for this woman who had made no secret of the fact that she had no time for him at all, Sam surprised his wife by insisting that they make all the necessary arrangements for the family living in Talbot Avenue to transfer to Melbourne permanently.

It took very little effort to get the necessary confirmation from the Australian High Commission that the British/Canadian and his Australian wife, along with a healthy bank balance, would be welcome to re-settle in the Antipodes.

A call to Johannesburg to consult with his brother Sean about the disposal or otherwise of the house in Mitcham brought the inevitable news, that yes, wife Greta was pregnant with number six. Sam had said nothing before about either his marriage or his new son, so he took the opportunity of doing so then, saying that the five, soon to be six young South African nephews and nieces, now have a cousin who would soon be travelling to Australia.

Sean was a little unkind in his first reaction, suggesting that perhaps Sam had been using factory seconds condoms, but when his brother informed him that he had also become a Muslim and if he didn't raise the level of his comments on this subject, he would organise for a *fatwa* to be put on his head. This brought profuse apologies down the line and a little latin incantation that was meant to be a blessing on the child.

When the property was discussed, it was agreed that it could be leased out until the housing market made selling it a more attractive proposition than it was at the time. A good agent would be appointed and Alvira, his trusted Alvira, would keep an eye on things and send reports on the future use and condition of the house. So, everything was set and the news came that Kerrin's mother was sufficiently recovered to return soon to her own home.

Sam informed all his clients about his departure and in the beginning at least, they were happy to continue their association. After crating all his studio equipment and anything and everything that Kerrin wanted, sad farewells were made to Alvira and his dear friend and spiritual brother Saul. Actually, by this time, Saul had adopted the name of Suleiman, a fact that this son of a strictly orthodox Jewish family decided not to share with his parents. They would never understand that, for him, Abraham had become Ibrohim. Then the three Pilds of Mitcham flew out of Heathrow airport to face who knew what on the other side of the world. They only knew that more than ever, they would have to be faithful to their mantra: *Surrender, Submission* and *Patience*.

★ ★ ★

Kerrin's sister, Ann, had flown down from Brisbane earlier and when they met up with her at Melbourne airport, they were informed that mother was in worse shape than expected. She was going to need a good deal of care and attention and Ann was all apologies for landing them with the problem. However, she convinced them that she had no choice since the transfer to Japan for the family had been confirmed.

Rosemary was due to leave the hospital in a few days, which would give them time to settle in and sort themselves out before they brought her home.

The family house was in the lower middle class suburb of Carnegie and although it was a big house that stood out from the rest in the street, its location was a key factor in the mother's snobbish dissatisfaction with her husband throughout their married life. He wanted to practise his medicine in just the environment that existed in that area, and he always went out of his way to help new migrants and the less advantaged. His wife on the other hand wanted to live in the smart and expensive district of Toorak, close to her musician friends and the social life she craved. Now, though, all that would be memories to share only with her daughter. Her so-called friends seemed to have all disappeared.

Sam was concerned at just how much demand his mother-in-law would make on Kerrin's time and strength. She already had the unfamiliar role of being a new mother to cope with and he was anxious that this other responsibility should not be a burden. As he feared, though, once she was re-established in her own home, the badly disabled stroke victim needed almost as much attention as his baby son. Initially, Sam helped out wherever he could. He would be the first to admit, though, that he was a bit out of practice in the domestic arena. For the past few years, he'd been spoilt by a housekeeper who did everything for him. Nevertheless, he tried his best, either with the cooking and cleaning and sometimes, even with the feeding of the patient. However, he felt that he also had to get on with other aspects of his life. He started to make contact with whatever publishers he could get to show his work to and more importantly, he went along to the Melbourne group of the brotherhood that both he and Kerrin belonged to. He was very conscious of his recent neglect of his spiritual life and when he made contact with members down under, it proved to be very propitious.

At a small gathering of his Aussie brothers and sisters to welcome him to their group, he discovered that a woman member in her late fifties had recently retired from her occupation as a nurse – one, as luck would have it, experienced in the nursing and caring of stroke victims. When they talked and Sam described the situation that he and his wife were in, the lady, whose name was Miriam, offered straight away to lend a hand and at least give some relief for Kerrin, with her mother.

Miriam proved to be just the right person for the job. Her attitude was a mixture of love and strength and she made light of what to Sam seemed a very heavy task. The stroke had really taken a toll on Rosemary. Her left side was paralysed and her face and speech badly disfigured and when they arranged for a specialist to examine her and assess what could possibly be done therapeutically to perhaps reverse the damage and improve her condition, the news was not good. In fact they were told there was little hope. Apparently, considerable brain damage had been caused and this examination also revealed that the woman had an enlarged heart and could suffer heart failure any time. Some tender loving care and some mild medication was about all that could be prescribed. So they all waited for the inevitable.

It came four months later, after sister Ann and her family had settled in Japan. Mother suffered a third and fatal stroke. Rufus was just nine months old when his grandmother died. There had been virtually no rapport between the two, so he wouldn't miss her. He now had no grandparents left alive, just an uncle and aunt and cousins in South Africa and an aunt and uncle and cousins living in Japan. He really would be raised as an only child now unless his mother and father could come up with a sibling in the near future. For their part, they never stopped trying, but it wasn't to be.

After the funeral, the house in Carnegie was put on the market and, as the will had stipulated, all proceeds were to be shared equally between the two sisters. The onus of selling the property was left on Kerrin's shoulders. Meanwhile, Sam had experienced an inner receiving indicating clearly to him that their future was not in Melbourne. It tallied with his general impression of the city that he had acquired during his investigation of the market for his work. He told Kerrin that he was surprised that there was such an élitist attitude in many aspects of life there and when he had to meet a potential client in the Melbourne club, he said he found it pretentious and that he might as well have been in some exclusive English establishment. The reminder confirmed his feelings also that the family wouldn't be returning to England, so, whilst the house was waiting to be sold, he flew to Sydney to scout around to assess the potential work situation there and look for a place to live.

He found positive signs on both counts. One big publisher of children's books told Sam that his work was well known to them and they would very much like to employ his talents from time to time.

Sydney felt good to the man with Irish and Scottish blood in his veins. Indeed he phoned Kerrin to tell her that he felt his soul had found its true home and that probably at least one of his ancestors must have been amongst the convicts shipped out from England to Botany Bay to settle the new colony and give it its rebellious nature. He said it must have been an Irishman who designed the opera house, for sure and Irish labourers must have built that magnificent bridge over the harbour. He convinced her that in all ways, he expected the capital of New South Wales to be an exciting place to be.

The area to live in came just as easily. After driving around various suburbs, Sam felt most comfortable in Lane Cove. It had almost a village feeling about it, with a pedestrian precinct, a little band rotunda, plenty of shops, a neat little police station, a good library, a huge public swimming pool and access to the Paramatta river. It was also very handy for travelling into downtown Sydney where the local *latihan* group premises were.

Happy at the environment, he checked out the real estate agents, and came up with three properties that all had what he was looking for: plenty of space, a garden, good views over that river. It would be a quantum leap from his home in England, but what the hell, he thought. If it's there and you can afford it why not have it.

He had been away from Melbourne for just four days, but for Sam the trip had been most successful. Next step was for Kerrin to share his enthusiasm for both Lane Cove and one of the three houses he had seen. Two months later, they were moved and resettled and had all taken a dip in the pool that sat glimmering in their own back yard. This then was where the future Dr Rufus (Henry) Pild, was to be raised.

9

A buzzer sounded from the speaker on Parapip's computer and almost immediately, the image of Calisthene appeared.
"How's it going, then? The research on Henry Pild?"
"Good, yes it's going good". Pip hit the pause button on his machine. As a matter of fact, I've just been talking to his former headmaster in his junior high school. He seems to have had quite a close interest in our subject from his very early years. Do you want to know anything now? I was going to have a chat with Danilda about what he said as she's quite interested in this project, but she seems to have disappeared from Master Control."
"She's on a special project. Back to earth. But what's with the headmaster business. Don't we really want to know what he was like to others once he had matured. How he used his persona, in the treatment of others he came into personal contact with?" Calisthene's voice was gentle, yet it seemed to carry a slight edge to it this time.
Pip was as diplomatic as ever. "Indeed, Calisthene, that was the implicit remit, I know, but if you will allow me a wee leeway, I wanted to explore the development of this unusual being from his earliest days. I truly believe that those early years played a significant part in the final nature that we are trying to assess. And with the greatest respect, what I have uncovered so far indicates that the Almighty created a very, very special person."

The image on Pip's computer had obviously been distracted by something as this last statement was uttered.

"What, what's that... ok, well what have you discovered then?"

"Well, apparently, the boy was brilliant at just about everything he tried, whether it was academic, mechanical, artistic or musical. And from a very early age. The man I was talking to, Simon Wallis, got to know the family first through the spiritual brotherhood that they both belonged to. That was a coincidence wasn't it?"

"No. But carry on."

"Well, almost from the time that Sam and Kerrin - or Ridwan and Renita, to use their Muslim names - moved to Sydney with their baby, the teacher became a close acquaintance and witness to the development of the child. He says, he was constantly surprised at its precociousness. Of course both the parents were quite talented, but only in certain things. Ridwan was a very good illustrator, still is I think, and Renita is able to empathise with most folk. Indeed after the boy, Rufus, reached puberty, she returned to her work as a social worker and counsellor. She has also developed her love of painting and has shown considerable talent at that too."

Suddenly Calisthene interrupted the flow and with an even sweeter smile, said: "Pip, I actually know all about Ridwan and Renita. They are both scheduled for a meeting with me in a few earth years, so I have already had research done on them. By the way, you didn't mention that Ridwan - Sam, seemed to have a special gift of intuitiveness, a clarity of receiving. In fact it is because of his and his wife's devotion to their *latihan* and their understanding of the guidance that comes through it that the son, is able to use a direct portal to us. They are amongst the few who fully realised that their guide was and always will be their conduit to the Almighty."

Parapip sat back in his chair. He knew he was in for a lecture and all that was required of him was the occasional nod. He knew also that the voice and image that was addressing him required total attention, as it continued:

"I'm sure you know already, but I'll just remind you, that after the founder of their spiritual movement on earth - which was not really any different from the one you followed on your planet, incidentally – after he departed from his followers in the earthly sense, it seems that his mission hadn't been fully understood by all those people all over that planet who had been passed the contact. Despite all the explanations and talks he gave on tour after tour of the countries where the brotherhood existed - well into his old age - including the dynamic message that his inner was such that his head was at the North Pole of planet earth, his feet touched the South Pole and his arms outstretched embraced the globe east to west, the majority of the members failed to recognise his true significance – that he was *our man* on planet earth. Worse still, even though they seem to be progressing in some ways, many don't realise fully that this *latihan* that he brought them was their true key to receiving their individuality, for themselves. In fact the advice for each one of them to stand on their own feet was implicit, if not explicit in whatever he said.

"However, he also knew that the earthlings had embraced organisation and structures throughout their history. They love to be told by someone else what to do and how to do it and because that world is a material world and has become dominated by materialism, the need to be guided to rise above it, can easily be abused by the wrong people if they are put into any position of power. Then of course the guidance can subtly become manipulation. Look at the actions of the fundamentalists in all religions and particularly, the rise of the politico-Christian movement: a powerful and spreading influence which may satisfy the heart and mind, but certainly doesn't touch the soul.

"Oh, dear, I think I am being judgemental and that's not right is it? Only the Almighty can and will make judgement. But back to what I was saying. Aware of mankind's weaknesses, even in the movement that was based on submission to the will of God and true guidance through the *latihan*, the founder, they called him Bapak, set up a structure, initially to assist him in his mission. It was wryly called a horizontal hierarchy. Anyway the idea was that when he was called home, this set up was intended to replace his role amongst them as a guide. It was a kind of insurance, and it consisted of local helpers, then, regional or national helpers and finally international helpers. But for all of them the main and most important aspect of their role was to help or assist the members. They were expected to do this objectively and unselfishly. Are you following this ok?"

Parapip nodded.

"He also knew that because of man's inherent desire to exercise his ego and dominate, some used their roles to implant their own opinions that came from their minds, instead of receiving guidance from the *latihan*. In fact, this is really the main reason why members like Henry seek direct help from us in Master Control."

Pip moved forward again to be closer to his computer, thinking the lecture was over. But he was wrong. Now Calisthene was back to where he first started his explanation or slight chastisement of the researcher. "Oh, by the way, you didn't mention Sam's mother who loved to talk to birds? Did you know she has had many conversations with St Francis since she arrived here. He tells me he couldn't understand a word she was saying unfortunately and she kept repeating something about a cupatay, whatever that is. Meanwhile, please keep to our subject if you can and I do really appreciate what you are doing." The smile broadened and then died.

Pip decided to ignore the irony and apologised for the digression: "Sorry, just wanted to indicate the good pedigree, I suppose. Anyway, the boy, our subject, could read and write by the age of three. He could also paint abstract paintings full of feeling and when he was four, he was not only able to play the piano without any teaching whatsoever, but he amazed his family and their friends by composing and performing his own minuets. Anyway, although obviously aware of his brilliance and huge potential, the parents resisted the temptation of sending their son to a special school. They wanted him to learn to live and share with other children who perhaps were not so talented. So, throughout his school years, the boy attended state school and despite the fact that he stood out as one who had absolutely no interest in sports, he was always popular and well liked. In fact Simon, the head teacher I mentioned, says that his very presence seemed to have an impact on all kinds of situations. If two boys were fighting for instance, he just had to stand nearby and within a couple of innocent blows, the protagonists would stop and end up walking off together as friends.

"As you know, he is a big chap and he would also use his strength and size to help others. For instance, on one occasion, he had been with some mates at one of the beaches on the North Shore of Sydney in Australia. That's apparently over a bridge across a harbour."

"Please, Parapip, spare me the geography lesson – anyway I know it well – we've got melanoma victims coming in from there all the time."

"Ok, right, well whilst they were there, one boy got swept up in the sea and carried rapidly along by a rip. Rufus apparently raced along the beach to try to head off the unfortunate victim who ended up slammed against some rocks. Although he was a poor swimmer, our subject plunged into the water, reached his injured mate and managed to get him to the shore. Then, when he saw the cuts and abrasions on the other's arms and legs, our man lifted him up and carried him like a baby off the beach and for about half a mile to a first aid post. He was the most unselfish child that the teachers had known and completely unspoilt, despite his brilliance. In fact he seemed to emanate a kind of love towards everyone and he would help any other child with whatever they needed. In class, if a teacher's explanations to complex problems in mathematics for instance were not easily comprehended by all the pupils, the boy Rufus, would re-state the explanations in a simpler form that everyone seemed to be able to understand. Even the teacher. It seems that as he progressed, he passed all exams with the very highest marks and he was always about two years ahead of his age group. He was ready for University and a course in medicine at 16." Pip paused and the intergalactic helper who'd been listening jumped in.

"Ok, fine, sounds good and that's all recorded isn't it, I mean you have both the oral and visual records. Yes? By the way is that Simon Wallis, the same man that came in last year and is now working in the languages laboratory? He's a lovely being."

"He is indeed. Oh, by the way, please give my regards to Danilda. That is if you have any contact…" but the image was gone and the channel closed before Pip could say any more.

10

Rufus had decided that he wouldn't tell his parents or anyone else for that matter, what had transpired in Manly when he'd met up with his former lover.

He had turned down Mercy's offer of a fish and chip lunch and instead caught the next JetCat back to Circular Quay and a taxi to his apartment, wrestling with his conscience all the way. Once home he wanted to re-consider his situation and how he should respond. If he backed out now, a lawsuit would bring publicity and ignominy not only on him but also on his family. He felt he couldn't ask for any spiritual assistance at this time. It was all too embarrassing. So, he went over once again some of the thoughts that had come to him earlier. On his own and facing only himself, he felt he was in no man's land, between two worlds. The one he had grown up in where he had been secure both in his spiritual life and in his work. Perhaps, he thought, he had been too secure, too protected from the vicissitudes of the other world. The world he now found himself about to enter. Perhaps, though, with his relationship with the devious Mercy he had already entered that world and indulged in its temptations. When he thought about it, he felt both sheepish and at the same time strangely fascinated at what had happened to him over the last few weeks. Would it be possible to combine the two worlds? To live in and enjoy both? The only way he would ever be able to answer that question would be for him to explore the possibility. As his father always told him, whatever else, we are individuals and we must stand on our own feet and follow our inner guidance. We may well make mistakes along the way, but the most important thing always to remember is reflected in the last phrase of the advice from Polonius to his son Laertes, in Shakespeare's *Hamlet*.

"This above all, to thine own self be true, and it must follow as the night the day, thou canst not then be false to any man."

Recalling his father's words comforted Rufus and he convinced himself that the dramatic change to his life that he had committed himself to, had been inevitable, whatever difficulties it had already thrown up. Now, he felt strongly and without any doubts or feelings of guilt, that he had to continue on this path and prove that he could be as successful in his new role as he was as a specialist doctor.

Next morning a package arrived by special courier. Addressed to Paisley Rathbone, it contained a script and a production schedule, along with a welcome aboard letter from the television series producer. This confirmed that the series was to be called, **The Specialist** and that a car would be picking him up at 8 am on Monday for him to meet the director and cast and have a read through of episode one. Then there was a press conference called to promote the new series and to introduce the doctor's reincarnation as Paisley Rathbone, lead actor. It also told him that for the few days before and during rehearsals, he would have the services of an acting coach, one Sandy Tebbit.

Rufus read the script and prayed inwardly that it would end up better on videotape that it did on paper. There were elements in it that he didn't like at all. All references to microsurgery had obviously been researched for accuracy, but in the depiction of their practice, the writer or director would be getting some further advice from him.

With this on his mind, he made contact with the medical association and requested that he be kept up to date with all the latest developments in that discipline everywhere in the world. Then after wincing again at that name on the outside of the envelope and mindful of the fact that he had been given the name Henry as his true name – the name that was most in harmony with his inner self, he rang his father to warn him of the change that was going to be announced to the public in a few days. He also ignored the contractual stricture of not being seen with his father, Sam, simply because he was also known as Ridwan a "dreaded" Muslim. They arranged to go to the *latihan* together that evening. He swore then that he would never neglect his spiritual exercise and the opportunity to be with people who would only know him and refer to him as Henry. The conviction was gathering strength. That was reassuring. However, although he didn't mention it to his father, as they got out of the car to enter the brotherhood premises, the younger man noticed someone on the other side of the road, suddenly move out from the shadows to take a closer look. When Henry paused for a moment to try to identify the figure, it moved back into the shadows, so he just registered it in his mind and then ignored the incident. Perhaps he was imagining something, but if not he was now alerted.

★ ★ ★

On the way to the television studio, on his first day as an "actor", the driver identified himself as Bert and referring to Rufus as Mr Rathbone, told his passenger that he would be picking him up and dropping him home every day during rehearsals and production.

"For security reasons, you see." And the broad-shouldered driver ran a finger down the uneven contours of a large broken nose.

"Ok, well, in that case, as we will be seeing a bit of each other, let's drop the Mr Rathbone bit and just call me Henry, how about that." Rufus, who was sitting in the front alongside Bert, held out his hand. The driver awkwardly took it and shook it briefly, before resuming his concentration on the road.

"Henry? That'd be a nickname would it?"

"Yes, that's right. It's what I prefer. Is this the place?"

Bert stuck his head out of the window and flashed an ID card at the security guard manning the double set of gates. The first one had opened automatically after the driver had punched a code into what looked like a bank ATM.

"Ok Bert" said the man who had now stepped out of his booth and was checking the car interior, the boot and the underparts of the car with a special bomb detector.

"Sorry sir, Dr Pild isn't it, can't be too careful these days can we" he said and then returned to his booth, hit a button and raised the second gate for the limousine to drive into the studio precincts. This procedure was repeated every time Henry was brought to the studio.

The room he was directed to was large and spare. High windows and plain cream walls. The only furniture seemed to be the stacking chairs that an assortment of people were occupying.

"Hi, er... Good morning Doctor ... er come on in." A balding man in a black leather jacket turned from the circle of men and women he'd been amongst, stood up and waved a plastic mug in Henry's direction. "Come and meet everyone, he gushed...Trish get Mr, er ... Rathbone, er Paisley, a coffee, black with?"

"Without" answered Henry.

"Great. How's it going, honoured to meet you, I mean it's just lovely. I'm Mason, I'm the director for the first three episodes of the series. Better tell you now, my full name is

- 157 -

Mason Dixon and we've pretty well exhausted the Mason-Dixon line joke, so. So now meet the others" and he went round the circle introducing everyone as they stood up, almost glazed eyed looking at the man they all knew from his former television reality series. He could have been a Hollywood star that had just stepped in the door and he found it intensely uncomfortable. In fact when he sat down on a proffered chair, he decided to change the atmosphere.

"Look guys, I think it's going to be easier for all of us if you realise that I know next to nothing about acting in a drama. You are the ones who will be carrying me and teaching me as we go along how to react and relate, so forget whatever misconceptions you may have about me. Don't forget I am just a doctor now trying to be an actor. Mind you if anyone loses a part of themselves during rehearsal, I will gladly return it surgically to its rightful place." They all laughed and relaxed.

"That was just great Pais..." Mason wanted a vicarious share of that sort of camaraderie. "Now, if you've got your script with you, yes? Right we'll have a bit of a read through and I'll explain things as we go along. No pressures everyone, and do ask me any questions you like when we've finished. Paisley, I'll cue you in each time for you just to get used to things. Oh, whilst I think of it, the press conference is going to be at the Hilton Hotel. Got to be there to make sure there's plenty of food and booze around for the greedy bloody media people. The whole cast will be around and your leading lady in this first program, Norma here" and he indicated a dark-haired actress that Henry (Paisley) recognised from somewhere. "She'll be up at the table with you and me and Rupert the producer, who'll be along in a little while to meet you. Righteeho, then, let's have a little read, shall we."

But before they could get started, a small thin man with ginger hair, a worried look, a red striped shirt, and arms that to Henry looked too long for his body, came in the door and looked around.

"Oh, sorry folks", Mason stood up to get full attention, "one more thing Pais, this is your acting coach Sandy," the new arrival flashed Henry a shining eyed look. "He'll sit in and have a chat with you after the reading about how you're going to work together. How are you Sandy? Sit down luv." And the reading finally got underway.

Henry's reading of his part was stolid and, by comparison with the others, expressionless. Throughout, the "star" of the show, was aware of his new mentor Sandy folding and unfolding either his arms or his legs, demonstrating to everyone his anguish at what he was hearing. To be fair, it was all a pretty stilted experience for everyone, with the director interrupting throughout, setting the different scenes and filling in the background. However, they got through it and at the end, when they were all asked if they had any questions, Henry told them all that there were several inaccuracies in the procedure and practice of an operation requiring microsurgery and he'd be happy to correct them.

"That's great Pais... I think Walter, Walter Jansen – he's the writer – yes, he thought you might like to check out anything that was wrongly represented. So, hey that's just great man. We'll get together first thing tomorrow if that's ok and I'll get Walter in to join us. Great! Now I just know that Sandy is dying to have a chat with you so, you stay here, want another coffee? And we'll all piss off and meet up again at the Hilton. I'll be in the bar lubricating my favourite journos. Seeyer later."

Sandy moved over to sit next to Henry and introduced himself officially. "Well now, we've got some work to do haven't we. Yes, we have. It's pretty obvious I know nothing about microsurgery, and you know nothing about acting. So, we've got to bring you up to scratch. OK. First things first, and that's your speech. Now often I have a problem with the theatre people, you know, they have developed great big voices to project to everyone, but we don't want that in television or film acting, no, not at all. Anyway, that's not your problem. No, you have the opposite difficulty in a way, you are just not expressing yourself, you just don't have any personality there at all. Could be a bloody computerised voice, do you know what I mean? Sorry to be cruel Paisley – that's a lovely name by the way – but I've got to be cruel to be kind, you know. Don't get disheartened, I think we can get over the problem by doing some improvisations – I'll create some situations that will help you to react naturally and hopefully with some emotion or feeling," the last phrase came in a tone or two deeper than the rest of his remarks. "Just a minute, I'll get one or two of the actors back in, won't be a peep ..." And he was off through the doors like a ballet dancer about to make an entrance onto the stage of the Opera House.

When he returned he was accompanied by two other actors – and for the following hour, the three were set various character roles within situations that Sandy contrived on the spot, with a view, a hopeful view, of loosening Henry up and bringing some drama to his voice. When the hour was up, Sandy was smiling just a little. "Ok everyone, thanks for that, that was lovely. We'll do some more tomorrow – I'll arrange it with Mason. Now off you all go and have a lovely lunch. I wasn't invited but I don't mind, I don't want to spoil my figure anyway... terraa!" And he was off, acting his way to and through the door.

★ ★ ★

Henry had no idea how the others got to the hotel, but for him it was a limousine trip again and Bert at the wheel. When they arrived, the 'star' invited Bert in to join the others for lunch, but the burly driver had to refuse, he said, as he had to stay with the car - not leave it out of his sight - until his charge was ready to be taken home.

At lunch Henry met the producer, Rupert Goodyer, a suave, confident man in his thirties who managed to talk so much throughout the meal that it saved Henry divulging anything personal about himself. In fact the man's loquacity was a blessing for the 'star' of the series as he pretty well dominated the press conference, leaving Henry little more to do than smile and say how he was looking forward to the changeover from reality television to drama. Just how much of anything would be reported and gain publicity for the Channel and the new series, let alone this new leading actor called Paisley Rathbone, everyone would have to wait to see. To Paisley (or Henry or Rufus) watching from the table, most of the assembled questioners and listeners had been so well wined and dined, he didn't expect much more than what had been provided to all of them as official press handouts at the start of the proceedings.

The press headlines the next day were both dramatic and predictable, with the story taking precedence over the latest death count following an earthquake in the Philippines.

"Microsurgery loses its most distinguished surgeon" was one banner. Followed by the words, "Former Australian of the Year, Rufus Pild, considered to be the most brilliant microsurgeon in the country, abandons the operating table to become an actor. The man who made microsurgery a household word via the reality television program **Through the Microscope,** *has changed his vocation and his name. Starring in a new drama series called* **The Specialist,** *this time for commercial television, the twenty eight year old has now adopted the name Paisley Rathbone. Speaking in Sydney yesterday at a press conference, Mr Rathbone said he was looking forward to the new challenge. Dr Rizal Humphries, head of the King Abdullah Free Hospital, where the surgeon had carried out many of his most complex operations, said, 'We will never be able to replace his genius, but there are other highly-skilled people in this discipline who will ensure that the high standard of microsurgery at this hospital will continue'."*

★ ★ ★

Former head nurse Veronica Milstein, was now re-established in her medical degree course. After leaving her nursing post, she had been able to rejoin her studies where she'd left off in the fourth year. The unsung heroine of the operating theatre, who had saved Rufus from humiliation, reflected only sadness when she read the news. Despite everything though, she still retained her love, her unrequited love, for the man she had known as Rufus from the time they were both students together.

The name Paisley Rathbone brought a weak smile to her face and she wondered what his parents thought about it all. She knew what her own parents thought. It wouldn't matter one little bit what his name had been changed to, even if it had been Asa Goodman, Goldie Milstein would still despise the man who managed to knock a meal over her beautiful *neo* Versace dress years earlier.

At this point in time, visiting her parents had become a bit of a chore, using up precious time she wanted to apply to her studies. The main problem was that the Milsteins had separated. It was a "surprise" that had been coming for some time. The father, Cec, seemed to be spending more and more time away from their luxurious apartment finding more and more contentment in his business, or someone who worked in that business. When challenged by Goldie, he was always sweet innocence itself and so discreet were his actions, with whoever he was more and more content with, that even the private detective that his wife hired, could find absolutely no evidence of the 'vile perfidy' that Goldie suspected.

Anyway, so dissatisfied was she with the neglected existence she was forced to bear with Mr Milstein, that she decided to go on a world cruise. Alone. It proved to be the catalyst that resolved the domestic situation by splitting the couple up.

It all really came about because, after having a wild affair on board the cruise liner, with a steward half her age, she then met a man in Venice who was also travelling alone and who, amazingly enough, came from Sydney. They were both about the same age and after no more than two days of sharing time together as tourists, they decided that they should share beds together as lovers. The man, a widower named Jacob Reisner, had a much better hotel room than Goldie, so she packed her bags and upgraded.

When the holiday was over and they both returned to Sydney, they continued the liaison quite openly. Goldie's hope was that her husband Cec, would be so angry at the turn of events that he would demand a divorce and move out of the apartment until it was achieved. In fact, he did no such thing, so once again Goldie had to be the one to move. This time, she transferred herself and her ample personal belongings into Mr Reisner's large house in the exclusive suburb of Double Bay. The irony was that Cec knew Jacob Reisner and when he next bumped into him at a shareholders' meeting of a company they both had interests in, Cec shook Jacob's hand warmly and wished him well in his new relationship. Then with so many spare rooms in the apartment that Goldie had vacated, he offered one to a certain Sarah Wiseman, a widowed lady and employee of his who he had managed to find some comfort with from time to time.

Consequently, for Veronica, visiting her parents became a double chore, potentially taking up the best part of two afternoons or evenings whenever it was arranged. As time passed, she managed to neglect that little task and although Goldie made a big fuss on the phone about never seeing her, Veronica got the distinct impression that all parties were relieved when her visits became less and less regular.

Away from any influence of her mother, the younger Milstein was still determined that one day Rufus, the man she loved would return that love. That it was fate that they should be together. She knew it was going to take time. He would have to go through whatever it was that turned him away from his great medical talent and into the acting profession. The name Mercy Cryer meant nothing to her, so she knew nothing of that person's blandishments and "negotiations" with the brilliant doctor that resulted in his metamorphosis. Veronica just knew that whatever the future brought to the relationship she so desperately wanted, she would never ever tell him just what had happened on that bizarre evening when she had covered for him.

So far there had been no reaction to the work she had done, despite it being far from perfect. She had initially waited in anticipation of an outcry when it was discovered that the key digit had been sewn back, slightly off kilter. She'd been aware that the cricketer had signed himself out of the hospital the next day and she feared there could well have been dreadful repercussions once the bandages were removed. But no, the only reaction reported to her was that the man was so grateful and impressed that he had made a very generous donation to the hospital. After learning of that, a surprised and relieved Veronica determined that she would concentrate on her medical studies and hope to become qualified in the very specialty that Rufus had excelled at.

★ ★ ★

The next day, when he arrived at the studio to meet up with the director and writer, Henry discovered that Mercy was also there in deep conversation with them both. When she realised that he had arrived, she looked up and waved to him saying "Won't be a jiff darling… then a quick word and I'm off."

Henry sat down and started reading the script before his agent slipped into the chair next to him and confidingly told him why she was there. Apparently she had been unable to attend the press conference, but had later met up with the series producer Rupert. He'd briefed her on what he knew of Henry's first day, including the fact that "Paisley had pointed out some inaccuracies – procedural and practical inaccuracies - in the writing, you know, from his knowledge as a real microsurgeon," she repeated.

"He told me that you had volunteered to correct things with the writer and that's why you're meeting with him, with Walter, there and Mason, yes? Well I wanted to check it out and now I'm off to see Rupert, you know, the producer. Oh, my dear I hope it's not all too confusing all these new names… anyway, I want to meet up with Rupert and get a credit and payment for you as consultant on the series, because that is what you really will be, as well as being the star. Just want to protect you Paisley" and her smile lit up the room as she strode off. "Be in touch."

Mason, the director, introduced Walter, the writer, to Paisley the star, saying, "We may have to delay any specific discussions until dear Mercy has sorted things out with Rupert. She's a stickler you know" then under his breath, "*the bitch* and as she's also one of the executive producers on this project, she will probably get what she wants. Anyway, you've now met Walter and we can get together again later. Meanwhile, if you don't mind, perhaps you could just pencil in any alterations to the script that you feel are necessary for accuracy from a medical point of view. Walter doesn't mind, do you Walt?"

Walter obviously did mind, judging from the struggle he had to produce a nod and a weak smile to the director's comment. Lean and looking stressed out, the poor man had obviously done some research, but for the man who as a surgeon had always insisted only on perfection – apart from that one glitch – that research was not completely adequate. Henry (Paisley) nodded and stood up to stretch. He hadn't said a word yet, just listened and taken in the characters and temperaments of the two men who he would be putting so much faith in.

"Right, then that's fixed, great. Give you a buzz later and we'll fix something up Walt ok? Is that all ok?" The director seemed always to want to quickly wrap things up.

Walt had picked up his bulging briefcase and was about to give that sickly smile again, when he paused and said: "Actually Mason, Dr Pild, I mean Rathbone, I'd prefer to be called

Walter if you don't mind." Then looking down at the ground he strode off out of the studio.

"Well. Get him. Thinks he's Arthur bloody Miller, cheeky bugger. Now, must get on... where's Trish, we'll have some coffee when she turns up and Norma Gleeson. I'm expecting Norma early, to go through a couple of scenes you have with her. Sandy will be here too to give you any coaching he feels you need. Oh, here she is. Hello Trish, what kept you dear, didn't I say 8 o'clock, yes? Well come along, come along... look, we've got the star here, Paisley, here, absolutely parched for coffee..." The performance was for Henry, "off you go and get one for me and one for Norma, she lives on it, oh and see if you can get a fruit juice for Sandy he'll be here soon".

"Now, Pais, if you turn to page..."

"Hang on a second, Mason" Henry interrupted. Look, while we're discussing names... as you were with Walter a moment ago... I would like you and everyone to call me Henry, my nickname, if you like. The other name may be fine for all the publicity and nonsense that goes on to attract attention, but amongst us, Henry, ok?"

"Fine, fine, Pais, sorry Henry. What about Harry?"

"No."

"H?"

"No."

"Right, fine, Henry it is then. Great, yeh, I'll tell everyone. By the way what happened to Rufus, you know, your real name?"

"He's resting." Mason liked that and repeated it:

"Resting... that's good, Henry, that's good."

One by one as each of the cast and later the crew were involved in anything with Henry, they were told how to address him. In future, everyone had to use his "nickname" and to forget that Paisley business. Most of the people were completely unfazed by the sudden change, with the exception of Sandy that is.

When Mason introduced the subject to the acting coach, his response was mock shock and hurt.

"Oh, no, you're not a Henry are you. No you aren't. Well, don't take any notice of me, will you, but Paisley is such a gorgeous name and just right for a big handsome hulk like you... but *Henry*, oh dear."

The subject of this reaction greeted the whole act with a smile and then said: "What about my acting, any quick tips before I have a go at these scenes with Norma?"

"Yes, well, I was going to have a look first and then make some notes, but as your dear leading lady hasn't graced us with her presence yet, there are a couple of things to fill in with. Stand up dear, that's it, now just loosen your body, relax and loosen up, yes, that's it. Now, remember when you are relating to another actor, unless the director wants something different, always remember to look at their eyes. If it's a woman, don't look at her tits, or her hair, as they used to in those early Hollywood films, and when you have a conversation, listen to what is being said to you and try to pretend you are hearing it for the first time. Don't need to use Stanislavsky method or anything, or worse still, don't attempt to indicate anything, just be yourself. And don't mumble. You've got a good voice and clear diction, so let's hear it. Get my drift? Ok, that's a couple of quick tips. Here's another one. Right, now, let's see... look, in the second scene, you will come into a room where Norma is actually sitting in a seductive pose, waiting for you. The room happens to be your private dressing room in the hospital and although you are familiar with it and its normal contents, on this occasion, before you enter, you don't know anyone is in there, not anyone, let alone someone who wants to seduce you if she can. Sooo, ok, let's just try it. Henry, Oh, my God, *Henry* yet, right here we go. The door to the room, your dressing room, is there and you are going to come through it, after performing an amazing piece of microsurgery. You've been in the operating theatre for six hours and this is your first break. So, how do you feel?"

"It depends on how the operation went, I could be tired, I could be exhilarated, in which case…" Henry was getting into it.

"You are shagged! Ok, you are shagged out and you are coming into your room to change and whatever, but that's not the point at this stage. Look, you are not expecting anyone to be in your room when you come in, but the woman, Norma is sitting there, waiting. Right, so there's the door, open it and enter, let me see you do that."

Henry badly mimed opening a door and entering, then he darted a look straight at where the woman would be seated.

"OK, that was not good." Sandy was frowning. "I said you don't know there's anyone there and you bloody looked straight at her, or where she'd be. Now, this time just come into an empty room. There's no one there, right?"

Henry repeated the action of pretending to open a door and walked into the space without looking at anything in particular.

"Great, my boy, great. That's how you come into a room. Then when you are in there, you happen to notice you have a visitor, and you react to that then and only then. Got it. Fine. Now, remember this, the director can cover for most of your deficiencies, by keeping his lens tight, keeping you in close up, but if he does that, your reactions have to be absolutely truthful or you'll look like a silent movie comedian indicating everything. And it restricts his freedom and selection of shots. Now here comes Norma. Hello darling, you look as if you've seen a ghost, so pale. Yes, you can look at your watch, you are late, bloody late and I just hope that Paisley no, Henry, will excuse you. Yes, Paisley is not Paisley any more, he wants us to use his nickname Henry. OK and you better have a good excuse for Mason, he can go ballistic if his schedule is bollocksed up. Here he is now."

Mason came into the room along with another woman who was dressed completely in khaki: a top with pockets everywhere and shoulder epaulets, trousers with even more pockets, visible as appendages, and desert boots. She was carrying a big roll of white tape, scissors and under her arm, a clipboard full of paper.

The director's first comments were for Norma and his accompanying look was withering.

"Oh, darling, how nice of you to pop in. Just twenty five minutes late, that's all, and please put that bloody cigarette out when you come in here, my dear, lovely Norma. You won't keep us all waiting every day will you sweetie, do you have a rehearsal schedule? If not Jackie here will give you one. Oh, everyone, this is Jackie Fallow our floor manager. Jackie, you know Norma I know, but this is our new leading man and star of the show, Paisley, sorry Henry. Yes, you can change the schedules if you will, he wants to be called Henry. Right, great." And he rubbed his hands together in anticipation while Jackie got busy laying tape on the floor to mark out bits of the set appropriate for the rehearsal.

All this time, Norma had stood still trying to control her temper at the spiteful remarks that had been thrown at her and the humiliation that she felt. Now she was ready to counter.

"Mason! And you Sandy, before you throw your insults and bile around in future, perhaps it would be better if you attempted to find out why for instance I am late this morning? What about that, you know, that old-fashioned courtesy of actually being concerned or interested in another person's welfare."

Everyone seemed to stop doing whatever they had started and just stood looking and listening at this injured woman. And the injury wasn't just to her feelings. She had a bandage on one hand and the blood was beginning to seep through a part of it.

"In case any one of you wants to know, I bloody near cut a part of my finger off this morning, when a brand new knife that I've got, slipped whilst I was cutting a melon for breakfast. Ok, I managed to make a good gash and sorry, oh, so sorry, this slight misadventure held me up for a while and hence, bloody hence, I was twenty five was it Mason? Twenty five minutes late. I haven't been to the hospital or even a doctor, because I didn't want to hold things up here, but perhaps, if and when we get a break this morning, I can get some help. Perhaps you, Doctor Pild, can take a look."

Mason was all contrition. "Oh, darling, you know I didn't mean it. I just get anxious and I'm a bit constipated this morning, please forgive me. Silly old thing, all you had to do was call in. What do you think Henry?"

The former surgeon took the actress's hand in his and asked her specifically what part under the bandages was cut and how deep. When she told him, he first joked: "Well I am really only qualified to sew something back on that has been severed completely, but listen, from what you say, and from the leakage of blood coming through, I suggest that you get to the hospital for some stitches right away. Take a couple of Panadols in the meantime. Can someone drive her there?"

"Well, we can't do the scene without her, so I'll take her down if you like." The floor manager put the tape down and led Norma along with her. "I'll call you and let you know how things are and when we might be back, Mason." And that was that for the moment.

The director was not a happy man. "That's just great, that is", he said to the air above his head. Then he turned to Sandy and Henry. "Well, I suppose she'll be alright to rehearse, but when we come to production, we're going to need a bloody good bit of make up on that hand in the intimate seduction scene."

"Perhaps you don't need that scene. At least in the way it is written now. Does seduction have to be so sexually overt?" Henry looked at both Mason and Sandy for a response. "I bet it could be played just as effectively in a subtle and suggestive way, rather than flesh all over the place. When I meet up with Walter and you for that other stuff, perhaps we can discuss that too. I mean, why do we feel we have to attract voyeurs to get an audience. Most people are seduced or make love in privacy don't they? They tend to close the blinds rather than open them up for everyone to have an eyeful of their intimate moments.

"If I may say so, with respect, I would have thought that the point of this series is to combine the extraordinary with the ordinary. That is the amazing accomplishments and potential of microsurgery and the dedication of the people who are involved in this work and then illustrating how they are all, no matter how brilliant they may be in their specialist environment, they're just like anyone else in their private lives. If anyone is tempted and even seduced, it's totally unnecessary to show every aspect of their intimacy. To my biologically attuned senses, the sexiest parts of a woman or a man are not the genitals but the eyes and you don't have to take each other's clothes off to appreciate those. Right Sandy?"

"Don't ask me love, most of my associates wear dark glasses."

Both Sandy and Mason had sat politely listening to Henry's lecture, but what they thought of what he'd said, wasn't at all clear, judging by their expressions. Mason gave Henry a deferential look: "We'll talk. We must. The producer has also got to have some input, though, don't forget. Anyway why don't we go up to the canteen and get a bite of something. Can't do much else here just now. They'll page us if anyone calls. Is that alright guys? Or did you want to do any more work with Henry, Sandy? Look if you want to run over one of the scenes, without the marks down yet, I could play Norma's part, if you promise not to ravish me, Henry. Or you could Sandy, just joking. But what do you say Sands, anything you can do with Henry on his own? I mean, acting wise of course."

Sandy pushed a quiff of red hair back in a mock seductive pose: "Well of course I can always think of something that I could do with Henry on his own, but no, not in the coaching field, no. We did a couple of things earlier this morning and I would prefer to see how they are put into practice in a real rehearsal situation with a few props and another actor. Then I can see how best to proceed from there. So, let's go."

But before they could get to the door, Mason's mobile rang. It was the producer Rupert calling to say he had been talking to Mercy and he now wanted a meeting with the writer, the director and the star to sort out a few things about technical consultancy. Mason as he always did, said "Great!" and suggested also that Henry had some other points to make about the script and the way it should be played.

When Rupert asked who the hell Henry was, Mason informed yet another member of the production that Paisley Rathbone or the distinguished Dr Pild wanted to be called by his nickname and that's the way it was. The director wanted to get this meeting underway as soon as possible to get things sorted. He suggested they have it in an hour and that if he hurried now, he might catch the writer in the canteen. The producer agreed.

As Mason had predicted, Walter was still sitting at his table, with two coffee cups in front of him, surrounded by pages of script. When the others entered, he was the only one in the place that didn't stop whatever they were doing to turn and look at Henry. Everyone seemed to recognise this man, a real celebrity wherever he went, who right then wished that he'd kept his sunnies on and worn a beard or something. The idea of having a meeting whilst he was still in the studios seemed positive to the writer, but when the subject of changing some of the script other than for medical accuracy came up, the frown he'd demonstrated earlier came back with a vengeance and insisted on a prime place on his very lined face.

"We won't go into it now, though... wait until Rupert gets here, so that Pais... sorry Henry, doesn't have to go over it twice, OK? Great! More coffee, Walt, er... Walter? And who's for bacon and eggs?" He had no takers for the last offer, but Sandy said he'd get himself some fruit. Mason persisted though with his star.

"Are you sure there's nothing I can get you, Henry?"

"No, I'm fine I'll just get myself a glass of water, no problems."

When Henry sat down again, although he was sitting opposite him, Walter didn't seem to dare to look up from his papers, let alone engage in some kind of conversation. So trying to ignore the stares from the other tables, the former medico tried to contemplate his situation. As a microsurgeon, his life was disciplined and his time was occupied with essentials - decisions and actions. A recognised authority, he hardly needed to be even conscious of the personalities of the people he had to work with. Everyone had a well-defined role and rarely did an individual's temperament or character intrude on his awareness. He was always focussed on his role and self-contained. Now, he found himself witness to the behaviour and conduct of a completely different set of people, different from him in every respect. The only way he could deal with this transition period of his life, was to observe, stay objective and accept that it was a great learning curve. One thing he had already decided was that however things turned out, he would not allow himself to get completely sucked in and become too active a player in this strange charade that everyone he had met so far considered so significant. It all felt like a parody of real values. Nevertheless, he had signed a contract and he would have to pretend to play their game it seemed. For a while at least.

He wondered how long it would be before they stopped looking at him, or in Walter's case avoided looking at him, as some kind of super being, because of his reputation. He had tried to break down that strange barrier that is often erected unconsciously by those who regard with awe someone who has achieved fame in some way or other. It was important for him now to be seen and acknowledged only as another cast member, even if it were to be one who had the *chutzpah* to make his feelings and opinions known. Soon enough, he felt, that reverence would turn to disillusionment when everyone really became aware of his acting ability.

More personality traits were to be displayed and sorted out when, well within the hour, suave Rupert bustled in, just stopping at the doorway to dump the butt of his cigar in a bin and the meeting got underway. The business of giving credit to Henry (as Paisley Rathbone or Rufus Pild – a point to be settled later) as medical consultant was resolved quite easily. The writer, was more than ready to accept that Henry's expertise, his unique knowledge of microsurgery would obviously be of great value in correcting any mistakes that had occurred from the research. Then came the real point of contention. Mason asked Henry if he would mind spelling out his problem with the current script suggestions for the seduction and sex scenes. Walter's frown was almost out of control as their leading actor started to reiterate the points made earlier to Mason and Sandy, but he didn't get very far before the producer interrupted.

"Look, just a minute, Henry," he smoothly slid in, "look, if I may. I am aware that this business is all new to you and of course I understand that you might be a bit doubtful about your ability to handle it all with the same superb skill that you demonstrated in your previous occupation. We all know of that, Henry, of your, er... fame, and we are so happy that you are aboard on this venture, but I have to tell you, that this is commercial television we are talking about now, not public hospital surgery. This little baby, seven episodes in the first series, is going to be produced to make money. Big bucks, Henry, not just for you and everyone else here, but more importantly for the owner of the channel. Big bucks from advertisers, my friend, and that means we give them what sells. You understand sir? Look, apart from all the money that the channel is more than willing to invest in it, in *you,* that is, and believe me that is the sort of gamble that the owner of this little lot rarely takes, we also have to get big sponsorship funding. I have a man now, a bagman, working the rounds on that very source. He is as crooked as a bent nail, but he can raise funds, and we'll all breathe easier when he gets his part of the deal sewn up. Do you see where I am going Henry? We've all got to make sure that we produce something that sells and attracts a big audience and believe me two people rolling around with nothing on does that very well. Sells and attracts, ok?"

Everyone sat back and looked at Henry for his capitulation. But it wasn't to be. With all eyes still on him, the microsurgeon-turned actor, smiled from an inner confidence, even though he was now operating in an alien environment.

"Well, I'm not sure that Walter here wants his characters to roll around with nothing on exactly, but I must say I am amazed to hear what you have just said. I was told that you were a creative producer, one of the most creative in the business and yet you have just treated us to the most eloquent defence of the *status quo* in television programs. Correct me if I'm wrong, but I am sitting here because you and your colleagues convinced the owner of this outfit to try something very different. You wanted to build a drama around someone who is already very well known in this country if not overseas. I was told that by making me an actor in a program, a drama program dealing with the subject that I have a bit of a reputation for, you would destroy the opposition ratings that had been achieved by my old reality show."

Rupert had never listened that long to anyone else before and he was impatient to get back with his own views. "Yes that's right, but look ..." was as far as he got.

"I haven't finished yet, *my friend*," parodied Henry. "If you had allowed me to expand a little on what I felt about how relationships can be portrayed on television for viewers rather than voyeurs, you might have re-considered some of the more brash parts of your argument."

The director and the writer were looking at the producer to see what his reaction might be to this articulate response, but he showed nothing yet except an indulgent smile, which disappeared slowly as Henry continued: "Why can't you really express your creativeness by doing something different. You suggest that simulated sexual acts or visually titivating interpretations of personal and private moments in relationships are needed in dramas to sell them. Well, with the greatest respect, I say that's rubbish. Is the intention of the series merely to attract people who need to have a regular serving of gratuitous sex displayed for them? Or is it a series that looks at the most advanced form of surgery and technology but in a way that humanises the information by relating, in parallel, the private life or lives of the main practitioner and his associations, partnerships or whatever."

The producer was starting to look very uncomfortable and shifted in his chair as if he wanted either to leave or to say something more himself. Control of the situation seemed to be slipping away from him and the high ground was being held by this person, this person from outside who was lecturing him on his own subject. Something he didn't like one bit. Mercy had assured him that this Paisley Rathbone or whatever his name is was a big handsome pussy cat, but he was now acting more like a tiger. However Henry wasn't finished yet.

"Please just hear me out, and I'd also like to know what Walter feels about this, right. Forget the current premise that the main character is successfully seduced each episode by a woman and that seduction is displayed graphically, or that he beds a different woman every week as some oversexed Lothario who just happens to also practise a bit of micro-surgery on the side, but instead, consider this: the audience never really knows whether he gets seduced or not, does it taper out unsuccessfully? Does he bed a woman a week or not? Will she or he achieve their desires next week? The cliff hanger concept raises more interest, I'll bet, than a display each week that is a fleeting and poor imitation of any porno video you can get over the internet or from your friendly video store. So why not be bold and try something different?"

Sandy had long since left the table, but the other three now looked at each other as if silently asking what each felt about the proposal. Then Rupert spoke, trying to appear chummy, despite the fury he felt at being chastised in front of the others:

"Well, Henry, I've gotta hand it to you. I think we all are more than impressed with what you say. I'm not saying you're right by the way, no sir, but you certainly have made some points that could possibly be given a bit of consideration, what d'ya say Walter?" The writer nodded enthusiastically and Henry noticed that the frown had all but disappeared. One down and two to go, he thought.

"The fact is," Rupert continued, "that whatever we decide, we have to convince the boss, the channel head. Now, if you agree, Walter and you Mason, perhaps we can re-arrange things a little, not too much of course, but enough to cater for Henry's disquiet and alternative ideas, and we'll make a pilot to show to the money boys and see how we go from there, what do you say? Yes? But you have to realise that I am not really promising anything more than that. If the powers that be insist on more graphic scenes being depicted, why then we'll have to live with it and do our very best to make it work and come up with the great success they are, we all are, expecting. Ok, guys... ok Henry. I'll certainly talk up your views. You can rely on me, but in the final analysis we are at their mercy and convenience... ok?"

"No, I'm afraid it's not ok" Henry didn't believe that the producer was really a hundred percent behind the idea. Not at all. He was just trying to slither away from a difficult contretemps that he really had no answer for.

"No, Rupert, I know of course that you will do all you can to promote the concept I have expressed, but I have to add the bottom line from my point of view. That is, the bottom line, Rupert, is, that I will not, as a principle, even as an actor, engage in any gratuitous acts of a sexual nature for this or any other series. I'm sorry if this comes as a shock to you and that you have only just been confronted with it, but the fact is that there's nothing in my contract that forces me to do anything against my will, so I won't. Thanks for listening."

Henry stood up, offered his hand to be shaken by everyone, and strode towards the door then, before he opened it, he turned and called to Walter, "If you and Mason want to spend some time adjusting things in the script and you need me, give me a call and we can either do it at my place or down here somewhere... cheers".

11

When Henry got back to his apartment, before he did anything else, he went into his study and found the two contracts he'd signed for Mercy Cryer. The first one that had been produced after all those nights of serious "negotiations" with his seducer, committing him to star in seven episodes of the drama series, he had signed *Rufus Pild*. The second one, was the one that the devious Mercy had confronted him with after telling him that there'd be no more intimate relations between them as her husband was back in town. This was the one that imposed all kinds of restrictions on his social life and activities. The one that dared to prevent him from being seen with his father in public because the elder Pild had a Muslim name; that endeavoured to commit him to be identified only as a Christian and as such to be seen attending church services and even sausage sizzles. The one, the very one that had been produced under the dubious addenda clause, which had changed his name from Rufus Pild to Paisley Rathbone and yes, "thank God", Henry exclaimed out loud, he had signed this one *Paisley Rathbone*, so it wasn't worth the paper it was printed on as a legal document. That's all he wanted to know.

So far he had managed, without any great difficulty, to ensure that everyone he had had anything to do with on this new drama project, called him by his true name. Now, with the spurious contract out on his desk where he wouldn't forget or lose it, Henry was ready to play his next card. He had placed the document immediately below a small plaque on the wall which had the words his dad had passed on to him: "*To thine own self be true.*" He sat down in one of the big leather armchairs and for a moment allowed himself to enjoy in anticipation what he intended to do. The professional certificates and degrees in their frames around the wall, reminded him of the dignity of his life as a surgeon. It was in marked contrast, he felt, with the superficial world he had put his foot into. And although he knew he had no one else to blame for the commitment he'd made, the blunder he'd made, he was determined to see it through, but on his terms and with his values. No more compromises. Then just as he was about to get up and make himself a cup of tea, the phone rang and, as he'd expected, Mercy was on the line. He'd been home about fifteen minutes.

"Hello darling, how are you?" The opener was spoken in her warmest tones.

Then when he said he had never felt better, she changed tack completely.

"What the hell's going on mister? I've just had an earful from Rupert about the changes you are trying to have made to the scripts. What's all this rubbish about not portraying sex, you bloody fool, have you flipped or something? Do you ever watch television? I saw that script when it was completed and I personally passed it. It's good, just what's required for this type of program. What's the matter Paisley, have you become bitter just because you can't have me any more? Smarten up, you're supposed to be a mature adult, not a poor hurt child. Do you... are you listening?" Henry let a couple of seconds pass before he answered.

"Oh, hello Mercy, how nice to hear your voice. Are you well?"

"Don't give me that shit". Now the beautiful seductive blonde was ablaze with anger. He was taunting her and she didn't like it one bit. Her hold on him had completely gone it seemed and she was struggling to retrieve it by verbally bullying him.

"Your career is over pal. After this series, don't expect anything more from me or from the channel and, well, in the meantime you get in touch with the producer and you tell him that it's all been a mistake and you are happy with the script as it is. Do you hear? Then perhaps we can think again about our future working relationship, maybe."

Henry became the microsurgeon in charge of a large team engaged in the most delicate and dangerous of operations. He had to inspire confidence in everyone and show that he was in total command of what he was doing:

"Mercy, I'm so glad you rang, because apart from the business of changing the script, I have something else to tell you. First though, here's what I say about the script. I have made my opinion known and hopefully after you hang up, I'll get a call from Walter and Mason to get together to make the changes. Yes, my dear, the changes will be made, or else I won't be in the series. Do you understand? As I pointed out to them, there is nothing in the contract to require me to do anything against my will. It's as simple as that. Ok? Now, as far as any suggestion that I am reacting to the fact that you decided to break with me, I have to tell you that after the initial surprise to find that you had been deceiving your husband all that time, I was, I am, relieved. Relieved that I'm not any longer involved in a deception that came so easily to you. Still there honey?"

Mercy was almost shaking with rage at this stage. Not only because she had been embarrassed at the studio, but because he was now talking down to her, almost like her father used to. "You, you are going to regret this, Rufus..." she managed, "why are you doing this? Why? Everything was fine... you wait..."

However, Henry was not in the mood for any more bile from this woman. "Right, now I don't want to waste too much more of our valuable time. I'm sure you have lots to get on with, I know I have. But before you go. I no longer will be known as Paisley Rathbone, ok? My name for all purposes in future is Henry Rufus Pild. That's my name and that's how I wish to be known."

"Don't be absurd, please, it's not possible now." Mercy suddenly thought she had him back in her court. "You signed a contract, Paisley, remember the addenda contract you signed at Manly? Well that's when you agreed to a change of name and also to avoid any connection with those Mohammedans or whatever they are that your father belongs to. It's all in the contract signed by you and you can't get out of that or we'll sue the arse off you, as I told you before, so let's get real, shall we."

Henry was smiling as he answered the agent. He had sensed her sudden little flood of self-confidence and now he was about to demolish it.

"Ok, how's this for *real*. The contract isn't worth a cent. It's not a legal document, because it was signed by a non-existent person, this Paisley Rathbone. Sorry Mercy, but getting me to sign with that name was a *real*, get it, *real* blunder. Now, not only will I no longer use that ludicrous name, but I want you to make sure that the publicity boys make it known that the star of **The Specialist** wants to use his name, his *real*, get that, his *real* name in both his new professional life as well as his private life. I've just added Henry to the name Rufus Pild. That should get some more publicity for you. And it makes good sense for the program. Also I want it known that I am the son of Sam Ridwan Pild, one of this country's best-known book illustrators and I'll be seen with him any time I like. Even if he wants me to accompany him to a mosque. Ok? And while we're on the subject, have you or anyone at that television channel been spying on my movements?"

Mercy was completely thrown. "What? When... where? What, have you seen someone? I don't know anything about it, I didn't..."

Henry wanted to finish this conversation. "Listen Mercy, if I discover that I am being watched, for whatever reason, I will take legal action against whoever I find has initiated such a vile intrusion into my private life. Ok? So, you now know where I stand and what I intend to do and now I think I'd better get the line free in case I'm wanted for something. Bye for now." He put the phone down. Then he made himself a cup of tea.

★ ★ ★

Henry didn't see or hear anything from Mercy for a few days after that. She had had to accept defeat in her struggle with the man she had hoped would make her famous and respected in all television circles. The woman who had been so dominating in the past in one to one relationships realised that in order to reap any benefit at all from being associated with Dr Pild in the future, she had better endeavour to go along with his wishes. She was going to have to call a meeting with the producer and the owner of the television channel. She would say as little as possible about the ineffective contract she had tried to saddle him with and hope that the big boss didn't make a point of wanting to see a copy. The ditching of the name Paisley Rathbone *per se* and its replacement by Henry Rufus Pild wouldn't have been too much of a problem if it weren't for the fact that this maverick star now wanted it to be acknowledged publicly that he is the son of Samuel Ridwan Pild.

Most interested viewers of the reality television program that featured Dr Rufus Pild, would have been well aware that he was the distinguished son of Sam Pild. However, the addition of Ridwan now added a different dimension to any discussions she would have with the channel head, Becker Clayton. It would be a big hurdle to overcome, because it was out of deference to that man's total dedication to the Christian religion that prompted the show's producers to insist on all the anti-Muslim restrictions. Fervent Christianity was almost as important to the man as making money and the fact that he was part of a mass congregation church that seemed to direct all its prayers towards that same aim, reinforced his belief. He and perhaps his fellow worshippers, would be among the most enthusiastic backers of Australia for Australians, if possible of Celtic or Anglo Saxon backgrounds. They were in total support of any government measures or actions that suitably fitted them for the "Crusader nation" label. They didn't like Jews a great amount and they hated Muslims and they saw nothing wrong at all with all the fear and anti-Islamic hype that now permeated society and caused distrust and division. No measure to regulate the lifestyle of the people was too draconian for them. Checkpoints, phone tapping, email monitoring, ID cards were all regarded by the good people of the church as absolutely necessary. "If you've got nothing to hide, then you've got nothing to worry about" was their often espoused belief. So for Mercy, the task of revealing the Pild connection, was something she was not looking forward to at all.

As things turned out though, her worries were all for nought. When she and the producer informed the channel head of their star's desire to avoid any participation in any visually explicit or even simulated sex scenes in the series, the man beamed his approval.

"Of course, of course", he exclaimed. Our star is Rufus Pild, a very distinguished man. Of course he doesn't want to be demeaned and I am frankly getting a bit bored with the incessant flow of sex and nudity in the programs myself. Don't forget I have to see them all and sometimes more than once and now some of my fellow worshippers at the church are asking for free copies. So no, great, good on him. Yes, what else?"

The producer and the agent seemed almost like pygmies in contrast to the physically huge man who sat opposite them behind an enormous desk. Like the man and the desk, Becker Clayton's office, was large and luxuriously furnished. All around him, if the walls didn't have windows for him to gaze out at his empire, they were adorned with expensive paintings or crucifixes and framed quotations from the bible. Side rooms leading from the main one contained a bathroom, a kitchen and a bar. This was second home, office and church to the man whose media empire was just one string to his wealth-making bow.

Mercy stepped in with the most naïve of smiles. "He wants to use his own name, his full name of Henry Rufus Pild instead of…"

"Paisley… what was it, Paisley Rathbone." The big man interrupted.. "I should think so too. Stupid bloody name if you ask me. Did you ask me?" The boss took a swig from a glass of some coloured liquid that had been waiting by his elbow.

This time Rupert quietly affirmed that yes indeed they had all been asked about the name dreamed up by Mercy.

"There is another thing, sir, Henry Rufus wants publicity to make sure that he is known by everyone, that everyone is reminded really, that he is the son of Samuel Ridwan Pild the well-known book illustrator."

The man behind the desk, who personally controlled just about everything at the television channel apart from the main gate, paused for a second, looking straight at Rupert and then at Mercy before he said: "So? Where's the problem there?"

The two supplicants were both taken aback. They expected the mention of a Muslim name to throw the boss into a tantrum of terrifying proportions. However, fortunately for them, the big man was not the worldliest of men. He could recite all the books in the New Testament and many of the psalms, he could tell you most of the day's movements on the stock exchange, and where every colour of a roulette wheel was placed, but Muslim names, apart from Muhammad, were not his strong point. The information about Henry's dad's name meant absolutely nothing to him.

"Makes good sense to me. Adds a bit more charisma to the man, too. Great for publicity and tells everyone, particularly the bastards at that other commercial channels, that we've got the big one. Ok, good to talk to you. Just produce a damn good series and I'll be happy and please do give my best wishes to Dr Pild and his dad when you see them." And with that he took another swig, drained the glass and left the room.

Mercy and Rupert sat for a moment looking at each other in disbelief before Rupert said, "Well we had better tell publicity to get on to this, perhaps we can get a good press release out ASAP... just find a reason for the name change ... and yes, then get onto some of the magazines and get some interviews lined up for Henry Rufus Pild, MD FRACS, OA, who is trying his hand at acting and who has some very definite views on what today's television should or should not contain. Leave it with you Mercy." And he leant across the table, picked up the boss's glass and smelt it. "That's not holy water, I can tell you. Wonder if there's a bottle around somewhere."

Before they left, the producer and the agent found the bar and the bottle of whiskey that had only recently been opened. They both took a slug to relax their stressed out states and then went on their way happy and relieved.

12

"Hey, so, you're back, good to see you." Parapip jumped up from his bank of computers and went closer to his colleague Danilda who was sitting in her old workplace again. "Special mission, eh? Earth I heard. You must be happy to be back, from what I've learned about that place."

Danilda just smiled and moved her body round to indicate that she was anxious to get on with her work. However Pip had been totally focussed on his assignment for so long that he wanted a break. He needed to communicate with someone on his level for a change.

"So what was it about, this special mission for the Intergalactic Helpers?"

Danilda put her hand up with a finger against her mouth, "Can't say anything until I am de-briefed, sorry," Then as she brought the hand back down to her lap, Pip spotted something.

"What is that? Let me see. What is that phosphorescent glow? Did you have an accident?"

Danilda pulled her hand away from his view:

"Nothing, it's nothing. Please. Anyway, how are you and how is your project going? Interviewed any good witnesses lately?"

Pip returned to his work area. "No, not really, so I've been reviewing an interesting period in Henry Pild's life. The phase when he ceased his work as a microsurgeon and was lured into the world of television acting. It's been very interesting and when a certain woman agent called Mercy Cryer passes through, she will be quite a resource. Mind you, she's still quite young and unless she has a sudden fatal illness or accident, or if someone takes her out, you know, eliminates her for some reason, chances are we won't be able to make contact for some time. Only Calisthene knows when she's due. Anyway during the changeover of occupations, Henry went through quite a quick and drastic series of changes of personality."

Pip looked over to his colleague to see if there was any reaction… "From strong, disciplined man of ethics and morals, to a limp, infatuated fool who allowed himself to be manipulated by the aforesaid Mercy, who endeavoured to show him none. Mercy, I mean. But then suddenly, this gauche, innocent, turned again and returned to the strong-minded man he'd been before he let his guard down and indulged in an indiscretion. Yes, Danilda, and the funny thing is that the change back, the re-emergence of the real person that is Henry Pild, came after a woman named Norma James, an actress in the television series that Henry starred in, cut her hand. She said she had cut it by accident whilst preparing her breakfast and although I can't swear to the exact part that got the blade, because I could only see some blood seeping through a bandage, when Dr Pild held her hand, it looked remarkably similar to the area of your finger there that you are hiding. I can double check if I spool on and take a look at where the stitches were put in if you like…"

"Don't bother Pip." Danilda was on her feet. "I've just received a message that I am to be de-briefed by Calisthene. I'll have to go into the booth for this as he knows that you understand just about every language and code that exists and for now at least things have to be kept … er, confidential.

Excuse me." And she was off to a space without walls within the main space.

Once inside, she became invisible.

The de-briefing was a formality really. Calisthene had seen the same video as Parapip.

"Just tell me about the entry and exit, please, any problems?" a voice and image was visible only to Danilda.

"It was a very easy mission all round. Bit disappointing in the short time there to notice so many changes in the environment since I originally left to come here, but entering the woman at night whilst she slept was completely without incident. She was actually dreaming about Henry the new star, at the time. Then I exited after she had been treated for the cut I made and returned to work. I know it was not in my remit, but I wanted to witness any changes in Dr Pild."

"You weren't supposed to know that we were intervening, that your mission was to be a catalyst for a change, you know. But you are a very clever person, we all know that and I can understand you're wanting to discover the true reason behind the exercise and by staying on you now know that it worked as we wished. Well done. Be careful though about what you tell anyone, particularly Parapip, he's as bright as a button too. Let him do the talking if necessary. He'll probably work it out for himself. That's it. Thanks again and you're right about the planet's environment. Socially and climatically, it's got much worse since your time. The people there don't deserve such a beautiful place. But I shouldn't be judgemental, not my place. Goodbye."

When Danilda reappeared at her work area, Parapip turned to her immediately: "Can I see your hand please? Your left hand."

Danilda was half expecting Pip to renew his interest.

"Why, why do you want to see it?"

Pip turned back to an image on a computer in front of him. It was an image of a hand with stitches where a cut had been made.

"Oh, you know, I'm just a wee bit curious about that scar. I've got Norma's stitched up hand right here look. Coincidence if your scar matched that wouldn't it be. Especially as you've been on a secret mission. Let me see?"

Danilda got up and moved closer to Pip. She held out both hands for his inspection. Since leaving the booth and her debriefing, there was no sign at all of anything unusual. "There you are sport, satisfied?"

Pip was no fool though. "Oh of course you have been debriefed, what was I thinking. I am impressed. But aren't you just a teeny bit fascinated by the fact that you were the instrument to make a change in the good doctor. That you were privileged to be dropped back in time to enable Calisthene to re-write history. This man, this doctor must be some soul, I reckon. What do you say my dear colleague."

"Oh, I say nothing. I am just amazed at your wonderful imagination. Must get on now..." And she left Pip to reflect on the picture in front of him.

★ ★ ★

The next time Henry went to the studios, the atmosphere was quite different. Everyone there had the revised scripts that had resulted from the rewrite session with the director and writer in the star's apartment an hour or so after he had made his feelings known to them and the producer.

Only Norma had been called in for the first period, because director Mason wanted to rehearse the newly written scenes between Henry and the woman who was supposed to seduce him or attempt to. No longer was the woman character first encountered in a sexually provocative situation, but instead, the writing provided all the suggestiveness and *frisson* between the two simply and naturally and without the removal of one item of clothing or any physical contact. Other scenes between them were written in the same manner and yet the totality of their relationship, as it unfolded, developed into a fascinating mystery. It was exactly as Henry had suggested and wanted. Will he or won't he? That's what will be left in the air for the viewers to work out for themselves and to satisfy their own feelings.

After the inevitable coffee all round was ordered, Mason checked that the rehearsal area had been taped to show the limitations of movement and that Sandy was in place sitting and watching. Then he got the two actors to walk through the scenes reading from their scripts.

When there was a break, Henry asked Norma how her hand was and she showed him where it had been stitched. "That should heal in no time, he said and when the stitches are out, you can help the healing by gently rubbing Vitamin E in."

"Ok, thanks for that, I just feel such a fool about the whole thing. How that knife slipped I'll never know I'm usually so careful. Must have been trying to hurry for our dear director I suppose. By the way, I have to tell you I really like the revised scripting of our scenes, I heard how it came about. Boy, it's so refreshing to find something written about a relationship between two people of the opposite sex – or even the same sex these days – that doesn't involve actors tearing each other's clothes off and revealing everything they've got. So often young actors who are desperately keen to get work will agree to practically anything, however demeaning it is. Half the time it isn't necessary, you know, what they're required to do. Just to titivate. So, seriously, this is going to be a real pleasure and who knows, it may start a trend. Hope so."

Henry was almost purring inside himself. So it had all been worthwhile, well so far. The big test would be the reaction from the viewers when the show was aired.

Meanwhile, he had notes from Sandy, and some more advice about emotions. The coach told him that if he had to show an emotion that he couldn't naturally feel or identify with, then it would be a good idea to give himself an image in his mind of something or someone who would provoke the required reaction from him.

Henry was feeling much more comfortable with both his work colleagues and the work they were involved in, and he was beginning to think he might even enjoy this strange world of acting, after all. However there were some aspects that he wasn't too excited about. One was the measuring and fitting he had to have from the costume department. Henry didn't mind having his chest and waist measured, or even the length of his arms, but when George "you can call me Georgie" started on the inside leg, he felt distinctly uncomfortable.

"Ooh, you are a big boy aren't you" said the slender man in the colourful shirt, "long legs I mean and a big chest. Wouldn't like to meet you in a dark alley luvvy, although I don't know, perhaps… just joking Dr Pild. No, it's going to be a pleasure dressing you sir, a real pleasure. Can you come in for a fitting tomorrow, same time, yes? Lovely, see you then, toodle toot!"

Henry agreed, but he knew that next day he had a busy time ahead of him. In the morning he was rehearsing or walking through two or more scenes in taped areas that would become various wards in a hospital. This he was really looking forward to, if only to see how the other actors fulfilled their roles in that environment. Then he had a luncheon appointment with a feature writer for a women's magazine. This was the first chance he would have to make known publicly his attitude to the requirements of television.

The rehearsal went well and Henry marvelled at the other actors' ability to pretend that they were actually existing in a real hospital situation even though they had only tape guidelines on the floor to indicate hallways and rooms. Some still appeared overawed by his presence and the awareness that he was the real thing and would be in his own world, even if it was a simulated one. However, with a few modifications that the star suggested, everyone soon adjusted to their roles - participating or assisting in major surgery in the unfamiliar world of the operating theatre. Henry was satisfied that once the scripts were put aside and the sets were in place, they would all feel much more natural and his own faith in this make-believe world would be even greater.

Simulating an actual operation would be a challenge. An absence of genuine subjects, he felt, might require a quality of acting beyond him and as his director, Mason kept telling everyone that the camera never lies, they went for a safer option.

Every operation that Henry had performed at the King Abdullah Free Hospital, had been videotaped for ethical and teaching purposes, except one. Fortunately for the former microsurgeon, on the night he had to rush in to operate on the cricketer and his severed finger, because of the notoriety of the man, his wife had requested that no record of either the patient or his treatment be made on videotape. The hospital head, who happened to be an enthusiastic cricket fan, had agreed and made sure that everything was kept discreet. Apart from the non-existence of any tape of his last operation, however, there was a wealth of material recorded and the administrators were more than happy to make any of it available to the director and producer of Henry's new drama series. Especially as they could make good use of the money that would come to the hospital.

With everyone gowned and masked, it would be a simple matter to drop in shots from reality into the simulated operations that were to be featured in *The Specialist*. Without being asked, Henry said he would make himself available for the editing of those sequences to make sure that they were a hundred percent accurate. He didn't mention it to the director, but he was determined to also learn as much as he could about the various aspects of production. In fact, he was such a perfectionist that he couldn't help himself. Already he had acquired every book he could find about both television and film making and he was anxious to discover the practical application of what he was reading.

As far as the acting demands, he felt quietly confident. From the time that he had first agreed to make the change from reality to pretence, he had also read various books on the "art of acting" or "acting techniques" but already he had great faith in his studio-appointed coach, Sandy. His advice generally seemed to make good sense, particularly, his instruction: "be, don't show". Henry realised that all he really needed to do was to take on board that man's tips about relationships and emotions and to just be himself. And that was not an acting task.

With his lunchtime appointment due, Bert was called and the star whisked off to a smart restaurant overlooking the harbour. Here we go again, he thought, as many of the already seated customers turned to look at him when he entered. Although he kept his sunglasses on, his appearance was impressive enough for people to take notice, even if they didn't actually recognise him.

A waiter was soon at his elbow and ushering "Dr Pild" to a table set by the window and one of the two women who stood up to greet him was none other than Mercy Cryer.

"Darling" she purred, "don't worry, not staying, just wanted to introduce you to Marjorie here, she's the features editor of the most influential women's magazine in town, dear. Marjorie, Henry, there, now I have to go, don't say anything that I wouldn't say, will you..." Mercy whirled round in a theatrical gesture for the obvious attention of the other lunchers, and exited stage left. Having shaken hands with the journalist, and just as he sat down, Mercy was back. She leaned confidentially over his shoulder and said.

"Oh, I meant to tell you, darling, *Teleguide* wants to do an indepth article on you. And I'm certain there'll be others. I'll check on your schedule at the studio and make any arrangements, if that's ok is it? Or do you have any other commitments?"

This openly stated intimation of media interest in Henry, was as much for the woman sitting opposite him as it was for the former doctor. It was all code for "You'd better appreciate that I got you the first bite of the cherry and get your stuff out in print sooner rather than later, lady."

Henry pulled out a small diary from his shirt pocket. "Yes, I have a long standing arrangement for next Friday. I have to lecture at the medical school. Something that was set up a long time ago. Bit rusty but I must keep to it."

"Friday" Mercy was writing herself a note. "Good, thanks for that darling" and the performance was over and she retreated from the restaurant.

He was left with a thin woman in her forties, with grey highlighted hair, cut short and styled to enhance her looks. She wore an overlarge pair of glasses that to Henry's annoyance tended to slip down her more than adequate nose when she looked down and made her notes. She was sitting behind a large glass of white wine and as soon as Mercy had gone, a waiter was called over for her interviewee to order a drink and his lunch. As usual, the former surgeon's drink was mineral water and his lunch a light one.

Marjorie explained that she would be getting some basic facts down today and her pen and pad were really just an insurance. Then, as she spoke, she flicked the record switch on a mini tape-recorder aimed at Henry.

"Fingers crossed I hope to pick up everything we say despite the noise in here, but I may still have to follow up with a telephone call later if that's convenient. I would also like to borrow you for a photo shoot if you can spare a half day or so. Really need to get a few shots in different situations, you know the kind of thing. Perhaps we can sort that out later."

She didn't wait for a reply, but Henry nodded as she continued: "So, Henry Rufus Pild, can I ask firstly why you have dropped Paisley Rathbone, after it was spread all over the media?"

"I realised it was a ridiculous name for me even as an actor and particularly in the series we are shooting. Maybe all right for a Hollywood idol, but not me."

"Right, so everyone agreed to the change?" Mercy had obviously been talking.

"Yes, everyone agreed. No problems."

"Ok," Marjorie shot the glasses back up to the bridge of her nose. "What about ... how do you feel about sex?" Oh, yes Henry thought, Mercy had briefed the woman on much of what had taken place over the last few days.

"What, now? Bit public don't you think?"

Marjorie smiled, she had heard that one before, many times. "I think you know what I mean doctor."

Henry knew he was no comedian and so he started on a different tack whilst still trying to discover just how much she knew about him.

"Well, I think sex is fine, just fine, between consenting parties, that is. In fact, I'm really glad that my mother and father indulged in the act, for my sake."

Marjorie had started to make a note, but as her glasses slid down again, she stopped and gave Henry a mirthless smile.

"What about sex in television programs?" At last she cut to the chase and gave the man sitting opposite the chance to make his views known publicly. And as he talked, the editor's head was down and the pen was working away frantically. When he finished, she smiled again and suggested that he was certainly taking a big risk by insisting on his "very old fashioned notions" in such a modern medium as television. He realised that there might be an element of cynicism reflected in her article so he countered her comment by talking about standards. He told her that he strongly believed that in life we get a choice to either lower or raise our standards as human beings. If she was intending to ridicule his views in any way when she publishes, he wanted her to also consider this viewpoint. He said he was ready to take any risk that might help to promote decency instead of encouraging the prurient. He repeated once again, that in his opinion, as there were so many avenues available for people who wished to be voyeurs of soft or hard porn, that he found it completely unnecessary and irrelevant for television programs, or films for that matter, that had a serious central theme, to compete and try to satisfy that same market, just because human relationships might also be depicted in those programs. Why should they be an excuse for titillation?

"If that's an old-fashioned notion" Henry concluded, "then fine, but it's one that I respect and one that I suspect a lot of other people do. And by the way I really would appreciate it if I can get to read the draft of the article before the photos are taken."

Marjorie was not used to that kind of demand, but then she wasn't used to anyone like this man. Not only did he have very strong convictions, but he had a certain charm and authority that seemed to undermine her normally tough approach to her journalism. She found herself agreeing to his request and then she went on with her interview by enquiring all about his decision to change professions and how he felt about both his past one and his new one at this stage. She also wanted to know about his family and any future plans.

Then it was religion. What was his personal belief? Was he a practising Christian? She wondered if the Christian ethic had shaped his views. Or any other religious philosophy. Henry explained that he belonged to a spiritual brotherhood that embraced all religions and all creeds. That he felt privileged that, because of the wide spectrum of its membership, he had a much wider appreciation of the various ways that people can worship Almighty God. All in all it was a fairly thorough chat and when it was over and Henry had once again been assured that he would see the article before it was published.

★ ★ ★

A few days later, Henry was back in his former guise and being introduced to year four and year five students of medicine in his old med. school. Knowing that many of the young people facing him were already committed to specialising in surgery, perhaps even microsurgery, allowed him to concentrate on encouraging them in their chosen disciplines. At first he felt he was just addressing a sea of anonymous faces, but as his eyes went along each line as he talked, he suddenly stopped abruptly on the visage of Veronica Milstein. His flow was completely interrupted and he had to smile his acknowledgement of her presence, informing the others that he had just spotted an old friend and associate.

He knew she would approach him at the end of his lecture and for once he didn't mind one bit. Meanwhile, after a few jokes about possible mistakes that can occur in the operating theatre, which he noticed Veronica didn't seem to enjoy as much as the others, he then went on to tell them of his recent experiences as an actor. Throughout all aspects of his talk, he had the complete attention of his audience, many of the students just fascinated by being in the presence of such a pre-eminent surgeon who was so young and who obviously didn't take himself too seriously. When he'd finished, they applauded him and seemed reluctant to leave, almost expecting an encore or something. But he turned off all the lights on the desk and rear board to signal that as far as he was concerned he was ready to go. Before he did leave, though, Veronica came forward to speak to him. They were both a bit embarrassed at seeing each other in this place and Henry immediately suggested that they go somewhere for a cup of coffee. Unfortunately, the student doctor had another lecture that was due to start almost immediately. She suggested that perhaps they could meet for a chat somewhere at another time and she gave her 'unaware love', her phone number. Henry said he would have to check his schedule and sort something out, but in the meantime, he wanted to apologise for leaving the hospital so abruptly without saying goodbye or anything when they last worked together and he also wanted to congratulate her on renewing her studies. He said she was so dedicated she would make an excellent surgeon. They both smiled sheepishly at each other and Veronica asked him how he liked being an actor, but instead of telling her anything, he reminded her that she had another lecture and that he had to get back to the studio.

When they parted, they were both left experiencing mixed emotions at this unplanned meeting. She turned away with the same feeling of infatuation that she had been carrying around with her for years, tinged though with the growing doubt that it would ever be fulfilled. Henry found himself wondering why he actually felt drawn to this woman who he had always just taken for granted. She had been a key member of his theatre team of course and before that, little more than an old acquaintance. Apart from the calamitous time that he met her family, their friendship knew nothing more dramatic or intimate than a few totally innocent outings together as students. But after this short absence and perhaps because of what had changed in both their lives, there was something different. To his own surprise, he felt really disappointed that their reunion was so abbreviated. For the first time perhaps, he found himself actually wanting to see her.

13

By the time the first feature on Henry was published, the first episode of **The Specialist** was in the can and a new urgency had been imposed on everyone. A pilot group had viewed the program and almost to a man or in this case, woman, declared it a great success all round. The one exception, a very plain female in her late thirties felt that it lacked something that would have added to the viewers' enjoyment. She said her personal view was that there should have been more sex and less microsurgery. After the screening, the producer, Rupert, noticed that one of the male members of the viewer group, had caught up with the woman outside the building and was offering her a lift in his car.

The pressure was really building now, because the publicity for the series was increasing with every article that was published about the star. Even Mercy had been surprised at the amount of interest this surgeon turned actor was creating. When the magazine which was dominated by the feature written by Marjorie hit the stands, it was virtually snatched up by regular readers and by any customers who managed to catch a glimpse of the cover. Very cleverly, Henry was featured in various poses, looking at the camera each time with eyes that had been retouched to make them appear almost hypnotic. So enticingly presented was the publication, that even some women browsing the racks in newsagents who had intended to surreptitiously pick up a copy of Playgirl, quickly changed their mind and grabbed up this possible revelation of their favourite microsurgeon. It was a total sell out and its effect had quite an impact. When the popular press hacks got to read it and extrapolate Henry's views on sex in television programs, from the interview, they had a field day.

No sex in the city! Screamed one daily rag.

Former doctor now turned actor, has changed his name from Paisley, the one announced at his first press conference, remember, to Henry and says another change he wants, is to transform everyone's attitude to sex on the screen.

Who is this born-again do-gooder? In this reporter's opinion, Dr Henry Rufus Pild may know all there is to know about human anatomy and physiology, but he seems to know very little about human nature. And so on...

Another paper carried the headline: **The King Canute of Television has arrived!**

In a recent interview, the former microsurgeon Rufus Pild, now to be known as Henry, intimates that he wants to turn the clock back and stem the tide of what he calls "sexual indulgence" that, he claims, has come to dominate our television screens. Where has this man been during the last ten years? Thanks to the anti-censorship lobby and common sense by the regulators, the naïve, suggestive innuendo in physical relationships once depicted in television has been replaced by the portrayal of full frontal nudity and sexual acts that almost explicitly demonstrate what love or even lust between two people is really like. And we're all the more healthy for it... If his perverse views are to be found in his new television drama series then this observer prophesies a dire future for it. I say it will be set to disappoint even viewers of children's programs.

That theme or something very similar was echoed by many of the less than distinguished journalists who base their scribbling always on the negative. However, despite them, as each magazine with Henry on the cover came out they were snapped up by eager hands. No amount of bad publicity about his views could dampen the enthusiasm that was building in a community now deprived of seeing the Doctor in his reality program. The hacks had got it wrong if they thought they were going to attack someone who to many was the kind of person they all really wanted to emulate. His coolness under pressure, his obvious talent and intelligence were just some of the attractive attributes of this very handsome young man. Whatever he had to say on just about anything would be welcomed by so many folk, that the petty criticisms of the cheap media merely served to denigrate the perpetrators themselves and just helped to elevate still further the respect that Henry naturally attracted.

Meanwhile, his producer and agent were gleeful in anticipation. The channel owner had seen the pilot and was thrilled by what he saw. And from his reaction, they realised that they were both destined for even greater things if they played their cards right. The publicity the show was getting was already beyond their wildest dreams.

Rupert couldn't restrain himself from sharing his enthusiasm with Henry. Apart from anything else, he realised that by hitching his star to this man's wagon, would be a move that could help play a very big role in his own future success. However when he gushed down the phone of how the bagman had had no problem at all in getting sponsors and that the company had been forced to turn would-be advertisers away, Henry very soberly told him to hold his fervour for a moment and explain who the sponsors lined up for the program were. Oh, dear, here we go again, thought the producer. First the script had to be changed to meet the Doctor's standards and now he wanted a say about who would be sponsoring or associated with the series. Who would be paying for it in fact.

"It's not really anything for you to worry yourself about Henry. You have got enough to do in the actual production, haven't you. And then there's the publicity. Wow, have you been busy with those interviews, the publicity is fabulous my friend. Now we have to get the rest of the programs completed and scheduled. They are out there waiting you know, thousands, possibly millions… so don't…"

"Who are the sponsors you've got lined up?" Henry persisted. "Oh, and Rupert, *my friend* it really is something for me to be interested in. Ok. Who are they?"

The poor man realised that his position was being questioned if not actually undermined, yet again, but reluctantly he told Henry of the main sponsors: One was a big insurance company, who would no doubt be promoting their services for any possible surgery that the viewer may contemplate at some time. The other was a big hardware company who were often seen on television advertising their wonderful drills and their saws: from hand cutters to circular and chainsaws. It was well known that they were famous for these products.

They were the main names and hardly disguising his feelings about what he had just heard, Henry pointed out very firmly, that he felt it was less than appropriate for the latter company to be associated with something that dealt seriously with surgery. When Rupert tried to remonstrate by saying it would all be done very sensitively and discreetly, Henry just said no way, if you want me, then get someone else to replace that advertiser. He pointed out that the publicity gained so far had ensured that he or his shady bagman should have no trouble in finding a substitute. He also added salt to the wound by asking the producer to send him a list of possible advertisers already lined up, so that he could check out any further anomalies. Despite himself, the man promised that he would have them in his hands the next day.

★ ★ ★

With two episodes completed and the third well underway, acting out the role of *The Specialist* was becoming easier and easier for Henry. In fact although he wouldn't admit it to his old colleagues in medicine, he was quite enjoying the whole experience – including his script editing and the video editing. So much so, that just like everything he had ever tried in his life, if he didn't have a natural aptitude to begin with, he always set out to learn and master every facet of the particular subject or craft. By making a point of spending time with the editing and camera staff, whilst they worked, Henry was discovering and accumulating a whole world of knowledge that he felt might come in handy some time. He also used as much spare time as he could with any company camera crew that he discovered was shooting on outside locations. As meticulous as he was whilst studying medicine, the star of a television program that everyone was waiting to see, learned everything he could about all the individual roles of everyone associated with videotaping and filming. Indeed, on many occasions, he was invited by the various technical operators to take over and try his hand at their job.

Once again, just as he was as a dedicated surgeon, Henry was single minded in his determination to understand everything he could about this new craft he had become part of. And once again, he managed to neglect all personal relationships, including his parents, his spiritual brothers and sisters in the *latihan* group and Veronica, the woman he had promised to call. His total focus was on his work and he seemed to need nothing else whilst he pursued his journey.

★ ★ ★

When it came time for rehearsals to get underway for the seventh and last part in the series, the channel schedulers had decided to launch the much publicised project to air to coincide with the ratings period. Apparently the company had been concerned that its competitors were not only gaining but beginning to overtake in popularity, judging by some spot polling of viewers. That had to stop and ***The Specialist*** they hoped was the product that would turn things around. Some of the management team still had some doubts about the philosophy of cutting out the overt sex content from the programs, but they were boosted by the feedback they had obtained from the pilot viewing and the hundreds and hundreds of letters that had been received at the television station asking when they were going to be able to see the new show with Dr Pild.

On the day that episode one was to make its debut, the producers organised a luncheon for the media where they were introduced to the star of the show and all of his leading ladies. The camera bulbs flashed and an awkward Henry stood on a stage surrounded by beautiful women looking like a reluctant James Bond. It hadn't been easy to get him to participate in the display and when one of the organisers tried to slip a stethoscope around his neck, he came the nearest he had ever been to punching a man out. After the introductions and an oily, but thankfully short, speech from the producer, the food and wine was served and each person present found a DVD of the program by their plate, to make doubly sure that it was seen and reviewed.

That evening, after the show had aired, it became obvious that whatever any reviewers might say, the television station had a hit on its hands. Emails, text messages, faxes and telephone calls flooded in, all praising the quality of the production and the content. Indeed many of the responses mentioned that it was a breath of fresh air and so good to be able to see something of substance and taste without having to accept the predictable sexy titillation that cheapened so much current television fare. So, Henry's stand had been justified and even applauded, judging by the reaction from viewers. Two weeks later, when the ratings were published, ***The Specialist*** scored the highest ratings right across the board. In its particular timeslot, it out-rated its competitors two to one and several of the media hacks who had previously condemned its future to the trash bin, had to eat their words publicly.

The success of the venture meant very little to Henry though. He was happy for the writer, the director and the cast, but although it had been reasonably satisfying to participate, already, his mind was taken up with the question of what to do next. Not that there was going to be a vacuum to be filled. Even while he was rehearsing the last show, he had been called by Mercy to discuss a further series, for which she claimed she had managed to negotiate a substantially higher fee in a contract that she promised contained no addenda in small print. Henry told her to send it to him and he'd give it a bit of consideration. He also told her that he wanted a break and intended taking a trip to Europe for a couple of weeks whilst the current series was playing out. He'd be in touch later, he promised.

When the last show was taped and he'd excused himself from the cast party, the 'star' called Bert to take him home. He wanted to get some sleep and then go to a *latihan*. He also hoped to do some testing to get some direction in his life if he could. As things turned out, his rest was interrupted by a series of phone calls from old colleagues congratulating him on his success in television drama.

The *latihan* was, as usual, calming and then inspiring and he felt that he had received something of significance about his future direction. He had a strong feeling that he was to do something with poor or deprived people. He had an experience of seeing images of poverty and misery. It was so strong, that after the spiritual exercise had finished, he approached a few of the helpers who were present to ask if they would test with him to confirm or reject whatever it was he had received. The men, all of whom knew of his fame as a surgeon and now his huge success as an actor, tried, but their testing results were so confused that they were of little or no help. Some felt what he described was a "real" experience. Others thought it might have been his imagination, perhaps caused by his guilt at being so successful. That one definitely came from the mind, Henry thought, but before he gave up completely, he asked for all present to see if they could receive any indication that could guide him in his future work. Again, there was no unanimous receiving and after hearing some of the answers, he thanked them all and excused himself.

He decided to visit his father to see if he could offer some advice or even test with him. It seemed to Henry that despite the fact that although many members of this brotherhood had been doing the *latihan* for quite a few years, they still had difficulty emptying their minds and trusting in their 'inner', their *jiwa* as it was known in Indonesian. It was obvious to him that his presence tonight amongst sincere and dedicated helpers had thrown them in some way. They had been influenced by all the things they knew about him and that was interfering with their receiving.

His parents pretended they didn't know who he was. "It's been so long since you visited, I wonder you could find the place" chided his mother. "Yes, we see the programs and although I certainly didn't agree with your decision to leave your work in microsurgery, I must admit you're not bad. Not a bad actor after all. Better than your father was from what I hear. You were a Shakespearean actor weren't you dear, tell Henry about your *timbre*," she laughed.

"He doesn't want to hear about my amazing successes. Give him an inferiority complex. How about something to eat, have you eaten?" Sam had decided to change the subject although he knew that his son was well aware of his failure as an actor and some of the ludicrous situations he had found himself in. "What do you say to a hamburger and chips? Or if your mother is making it, a bowl of lentil soup and a celery sandwich?"

Kerrin threw the book she had been reading across the room at her husband in mock anger saying, "Have you read this darling?" and went off to make a snack.

"Wanted to talk about some testing really."

Henry sat opposite his father and explained his feelings and the receiving he'd had. He also told him that he didn't really get much assistance from the helpers and he needed a bit of advice or a suggestion as to how he could get some guidance.

Sam Pild was now in his mid sixties and although he had a wealth of life experiences to call on, his wisdom came principally from his inner receiving, much of it in the form of practical advice, not esoteric flashes of insight. Although he did still have the odd premonition. Like his wife Kerrin's, his workload had been wound down. It had taken some time and the removal of his natural obstinacy for him to adapt to creating his illustrations on a computer rather than a drawing board, but that's how his craft had developed and what his clients required. Nowadays, though, he was enjoying more leisure than work and Kerrin's spare time was being more and more taken up with her painting. Work and leisure apart, they were both devoted members of the spiritual brotherhood that had been a big part of their life almost since they met. Now, because of the modern trend to avoid all charges of sexism, the movement had become an "Association" not a "Brotherhood" and the Pilds believe that the change had been for the worse, even though it may have satisfied those women who felt offended by the fraternal title. Now, they felt, the essence, the *latihan* or spiritual exercise that the founder had brought to people all over the world, was in danger of being overwhelmed by the structure or organisation that was originally meant to support it. Henry knew that both his parents were long time helpers and very experienced in the *latihan* and might be able to throw some light on his little dilemma. He remembered how as a younger man still living at home, he used to just sit quietly with his father and without a word spoken between them, he could feel any burden he might be carrying, any doubt or concern, just lifted away from him as if by magic.

"So, what do you think Samuel Ridwan Langhorne?" The son had often used his father's first name when addressing him, but never the long version of all the names he had acquired.

"What do you think about this testing business? Getting worse as far as I can see, not better or clearer, is it?"

"Well, Henry, Rufus, Paisley, sorry, Henry Rufus, when was the last time you did testing? And can you remember what it was about? No. Well if you don't mind me saying so, when you went to the helpers tonight, you went with so many questions inside you, that it's no wonder that there was no clarity in the receiving. As you know, the idea of having a few folk testing with you is to try to get a consensus, a harmony of feeling. But it sounds to me as if your sudden appearance and needs were too much. Don't think I'm criticising you, because I am aware of the pressures you have had on your life recently, but if you just go to the *latihan* when you need some personal problem resolved, you really don't deserve those helpers to give up their time for you. Think about it son. How many times have we discussed the individuality of the spiritual exercise and how we get back in proportion to what we put in. Henry, don't neglect your *latihan*. Do it regularly, not just when it suits you to find time from your other life. Make your life fit in with the reality of the *latihan* and not the other way around. All knowledge and judgements are ours, if we know where to look and we are shown where to look from the moment we are opened. Oh, look, here come the celery sandwiches, or are they cucumber?"

"Cheese, cheese and tomato, to be exact, made specifically because of your cholesterol problem." Kerrin brought everything into the lounge for her men. "Actually they're made for my son here, but if you want to risk it, go for it, I've got a very good insurance policy on you, I'll do just fine. That's if I survive your snoring."

"I'll take you with me madam. Actually your sandwiches are safer than your cooking."

Sam was dodging a cushion this time, as the banter and improvisational performance came to an end. Henry was used to the way they behaved with one another but tonight, if it was for his benefit, it was wasted as he seemed too preoccupied to take much notice. He was still absorbing his father's words. "I'm going to London for a conference in a week or so, I meant to tell you earlier – been invited by the Royal College to attend a series of seminars on the latest developments in microsurgery. Whoever sent the invitation obviously hadn't heard of my change of profession. But I want to keep up with everything, so it's great. By the way, do you still have that house in England you used to talk about?"

Kerrin looked at Sam as if to say: I knew we shouldn't have sold it. "Sold it years ago when we went back over after your graduation," Sam informed him. "Sorry, did you want to stay there? Look if you need a bed, I have a very old friend in London, he's probably still got his flat... actually it's the flat I used to share with him about forty odd years ago. I'll send him a message if you like." Sam had kept in touch about once a year with his mate Saul, who became Suleiman.

"No, it's fine, they're putting me up in a smart hotel in Kensington, apparently. All expenses paid. No, I just wondered if the house was still yours I might pop over and take a look and sniff around the area to conjure up some imagery of you two when you were both young, well reasonably young. Ouch!" They both gave him mock looks that could kill.

"You can still go there, but who knows what it's like now. May have been converted into flats. We'll give you the address anyway. Got rid of it because the whole business of worrying about tenants and all the maintenance that had to be supervised became too much. Your uncle Sean agreed to sell it and we're all much better off for the fact. Also, the lovely Alvira who had been keeping an eye on it for us, got sick and said she couldn't oblige any more. Hey, you've got to look her up. She was there with us when you were born, she'd be thrilled to see you. Getting on a bit now though. I'll give you her address and you can see how you feel when you're over there."

"How's your love life, Henry?" Kerrin asked with feigned coyness. "Any lucky young lady waiting outside? Or waiting anywhere?"

Henry was suddenly reminded of his promise to contact Veronica. "Oh, plenty of time for that, mum. Still got things to do and places to go. In fact I had better get going now. Thanks for the sarnies and tea and the kick up the pants dad. I'll call before I go to England. Oh, and I'll see you at the *latihan* hall, what nights do you go?"

"We'll come along whenever you want to, but we usually go on Sunday and Thursday. By the way son, you're not completely wrong about helpers. Just like everyone else, they do sometimes allow their minds to influence their receiving. Anyway if things don't resolve themselves for you, there's always the portal." And he winked at his son.

"The what?" said Henry.

"I'll tell you about it later. Cheerio."

Once outside and driving home, he promised himself that he would call Veronica and try to set something up in the next few days. However his belated consideration was to be thwarted. When he did get around to phoning, he was told by a flatmate of his former head nurse, that she was out of town for two weeks on a special course somewhere… the woman thought it was interstate. So Henry made a mental note to try again to contact her, perhaps when he returned from his trip overseas and he really meant to do it this time.

Next day a new contract for a second series of **The Specialist** arrived and a quick glance informed him that written into this contract was just about all the leeway he could ask for. Even choice of director, if he favoured anyone in particular. Along with the official document, there was a personal note from Mercy telling him how much she had enjoyed working for him and hoped that he would want their successful relationship to continue well into the future. She pointed out how she had managed to double his financial return on the last series and been given an assurance that there was yet another option available to do further series after this. She then wished him well on his upcoming trip and said she looked forward to meeting him in person when he returned. Then as a little teaser, she said that she had been sent a film script from a very influential producer and that it was just possible that Henry Pild might be asked to star in it. More when you get back. It was signed: "Love, Mercy."

14

"Hello, you've been down there again, haven't you... can't take my eyes away for a moment, can I?" Parapip was directing his comments as usual to his nearest colleague, Danilda who had just appeared and sat down at her workplace. "It's amazing, every time I'm distracted, you're off these days. I had a seminar under the leadership of our dear Calisthene and off you go on another mission. I know, don't try to deny it. No Calisthene didn't mention a word, never does, I've been looking at the video though. Surprise, surprise, another character change slipped in to test someone, I wonder who?"

Danilda sat smiling inscrutably at Pip's probing. She had no intention of confirming or denying anything.

"So, it's Veronica now is it? The totally faithful lady, 'til death or marriage with Henry, whichever comes first, suddenly has a change of heart. Heart, Danilda, remember that's the thing that you earthlings and ex-earthlings have and my kind don't. Isn't it strange?" Pip had one part of him watching her like a hawk for any giveaway signs. "Really strange, you might say, that our totally dedicated Veronica should suddenly decide that enough's enough and she ain't gonna wait any longer for that selfish sod Henry. So what do you do, I mean so what does she do, but allow herself to be courted by a senior lecturer at the university. And senior is the operative word by the look of things. Old enough to be her father if you ask me. How old is he Danilda? Oh sorry, you don't know what I'm talking about do you. Good-looking man by earthly standards, eh? Just as well, otherwise I would have to say I can't see what on earth she is attracted to. What on earth, get it? Get it, on earth…"

"Yeh, yeh" Danilda groaned.

"So, what's the point of this intervention? Make our man jealous? Or make him realise how insensitive he often is in human relationships. Not that I'd know anyway, most of the humans I have come in contact with have been insensitive, or insensitised or is it desensitised, so that they ignore me when they shouldn't."

"Don't be ridiculous Parapip," retorted Danilda, "I never ignore you when you have something relevant to say, you know that. You also know that we all love you and respect your determination to find out just about everything you can about everything. But you know as well as I do that like the prime minister of that place, what's it called, Australia, 'I know nothing'." And she focussed back onto her work.

"What's it called?" parroted Pip, but adding a tone of mock incredulity to his version. "What's that place called? You've been there at least twice recently, to my knowledge. Remember the little trip you made to effect the change from Paisley the wimp to a Henry the macho man, yes? Norma James, remember? The cut? You must have had spiritual visas from you know who. Yes? With the name of your destination stamped clearly on them. Sydney, Australia. But I see I'm wasting my time, even if that's not a valid concept of the reality up here. I sometimes forget that the past, present and future are all one. Everything is in the 'now'. And I must congratulate you. You do manage to adjust almost seamlessly."

Danilda looked over but ignored the last remark: "How's it going anyway? Any good or bad references from anyone lately?"

"No, no one's passed through that had any contact or knowledge of our subject. They seem to be living longer on that planet these days. Got one coming soon though, maybe two who can make a contribution, but Calisthene wont let me use time transference for them for some reason, so in the meantime, it's all video evidence from our surveillance cameras. Mind you, with all your missions the relevance of that seems to change more often than a chameleon changes its skins."

Before Danilda could respond in any way, a buzz on his computer alerted Pip to an incoming message from the Intergalactic Helpers' area. "Yes", he said, "am I under observation?"

The image of Calisthene appeared. "Don't be so touchy my dear soul, no of course not. Well, not in the way that your defensive attitude might suggest, but, well, yes, I suppose you are in a way, although I'd like to put it that you are such a valuable member of the team that we need to keep in touch. The fact is that you and what you are doing is available to any of the Intergalactic Helpers if and whenever they wish to tune in to the constantly flowing information through your monitors. But that applies to everyone else by the way. Anyway, you must be aware that what you are researching, or, rather, who you are researching is of some unusual significance and interest to all of us. But look that's not the reason for this contact. No. I want you to know how impressed everyone was with your contribution to the seminar, they thought you were excellent and I have a message for you that I am now going to scramble, because it is for your hearing only, ok? If you put on your earphones, you can unscramble it, as you know, with your personal pin code. All set. Good. Well the fact is that there is a vacancy for a new Intergalactic Helper coming up and the general consensus is that you would be a good candidate for the job. Your all-round awareness and your ability to understand

and speak so many languages could be very, very valuable. It's not going to happen immediately, though. As soon as your current project is at a satisfactory stage, you will be sent on a few missions to various planets in the solar system first. Don't worry, you will be programmed to change both physically and attitudinally to fit the location you visit each time. Could be fun. Meanwhile, congratulations Parapip and keep this information completely to yourself. Carry on the good work, over and out."

As soon as Parapip removed his earphones, a smiling Danilda was close by. "And what was that all about, then? What's Calisthene got to say that only you can officially hear? You look too pleased with yourself for it to have been a criticism of any kind. So?"

"Dear Danilda, I could say I don't know what you are talking about I suppose, but since you were a very interested witness, all I can comment is that if I had lips, they would be sealed. Sorry. But, God Willing, you will know in the fullness of time. Patience my friend, patience. Remember … Submission, Surrender and Patience – still applies wherever we are."

"And Hubris is always looking out for new recruits." Danilda tossed back as she returned to her work.

15

It had been less than six months since Henry had walked out of the King Abdullah Free Hospital that fateful night, after unknowingly bungling an operation for the first time. And after being interviewed by police about his patient. Now that he had some space and was trying to come to terms with the dichotomy in his life, he thought about some of the people he must have neglected.

The last little while had been a whirlwind experience and now he felt he must put some things right. Certainly he must make contact with his last patient and see how he had progressed, so he went back to the hospital to get the man's particulars. He was surprised but not displeased to hear that the cricketer had discharged himself within 24 hours of the operation. Whatever the reason for that action, it eased his conscience and cleared the guilt he felt about not checking up on his handiwork – something that previously he had always been punctilious about. When Henry phoned the man, Wayne Carroll, he was welcomed down the line by a very effusive flow of words. The cricketer had just finished a match where he had had great success – taking nine wickets in a great win for his side. He said he had wanted to thank Henry or Dr Pild, as he called him, for some time and would really like to meet up, whenever it was convenient.

"Particularly like to see you in the flesh Doc, now that you're also a celebrated actor. Hear the series is a great success. Don't get to see it myself unfortunately. The wife insists on watching *Desperate Housewives*, you know how it is. I think she's one herself, she's out right now."

Henry said he'd like to see him straight away if that was ok and half an hour later the door to his large home was opened by a beaming, healthy looking Wayne who, after a strenuous handshake, ushered the doctor in. Once again the doctor was showered with thanks for the surgery he had performed and the amazing difference that it had made to his spinning ability. In genuine humility Henry accepted the praise and thanks and was watching the hand, the right hand, as closely as he could whilst they had coffee and then when the bowler stood up and showed him the action he used. That's when the surgeon noticed something that suddenly worried him.

"Can I take a closer look at the finger we re-joined, please." The man opened his hand palm up and then turned it upside down for the doctor to examine. "Have you done anything to it yourself since the operation? The finger is out of alignment isn't it?"

"But that's the whole point isn't it, doc. That's the genius, your genius, man. Since the operation I can curl that finger like I never could before. You wouldn't believe the reaction amongst the other players. They have been saying you must be some sort of cricket nut to be able to do that for me. In fact some of them have even suggested they may get a finger off, just to get it put back on off-kilter so that they can bowl better too."

"Well I wouldn't recommend it. No, well if you're happy, then that's great. Now I'll be off and thank you so much for your hospitality and I hope you have many more years of spinning. Goodbye."

Back in his car and driving home, he tried to recall the actual operation, his last. What had happened in the theatre that evening when he was called in for an emergency. He had tried not to show too much of his surprise when he took a close look at the finger that the bowler seemed to be so proud of, but he just couldn't believe that it was his work. He would never have replaced that digit in that configuration. What on earth was he thinking of? This was something that was going to bug him until he could talk to a witness to the operation. Someone who could enlighten him about that evening. The obvious person to ask was Veronica but, according to her flat mate, she was out of town. Who else was there? Marlon Mandrake, the anaesthetist, of course. Although he was usually so busy cracking jokes during operations and watching the nurses for their reactions that he probably didn't see anything of the surgery. Who else? Henry decided that he would call in at the hospital and endeavour to get a staff list for that night. He already knew that, on the patient's wife's instructions no videorecording had been made. That would have been perfect. It would have shown exactly what had happened during what he considered a routine piece of surgery. It would show in detail the re-attachment of the finger and any fault that might have occurred in the process. No, he realised the only way he could find out now would be by questioning a witness, if he could find one.

The sun was glinting off the mass of cars as Henry drove to a familiar spot to see if his reserved place was still available. No chance. Filling every available inch of the space was a dark blue BMW. I've been replaced alright, thought the man who was lionised at this hospital so recently. He finally found a place he thought would be suitable for his six-year-old Citroen, even though the white wooden bar pinned into the wall bore the name of the hospital head, Rizal Humphries. It was 3'oclock and the former microsurgeon knew that there was little chance of his old boss returning today.

After he parked and made sure he was suitably disguised with his sunshades firmly on and a baseball cap on his head, Henry walked to the staff entrance, and inserted his ID card into the computer, hoping he hadn't been deleted from the data bank yet. He was in luck, his photo came up on the screen, so he took his shades off and, looking at a tiny spotlight, mirrored his own image until the word "confirmed" appeared. The electronic door clicked and he entered the hospital and took a lift to where he knew staff records were kept.

Once inside the office, he ignored the general reaction in the room to his presence and asked for a list of staff present on the day of the emergency operation on their special patient Wayne Carroll. The office manager took over from the woman he'd asked and she just couldn't resist making a comment about his television program before she was prepared to do anything further. "We all watch it, Dr Pild and we think you're wonderful in it and oh, please let us into a little secret, when you went into the room with the woman, you know, the one played by Norma James, and you put the light out, did you? I mean does the character, does he... you know do they? We've all been wondering."

"Been wondering myself, too. Now, if you could please let me have the names, that would be great, I am in a bit of a hurry."

The woman retreated smiling and was soon at work on her computer. A few minutes later she was printing out the result of her search and she handed it to Henry. Apart from Veronica Milstein, the only other names he recognised were the anaesthetist's and one of the assistant nurses, Ann Tizer. That name had stuck in his mind, because his father was always on about a certain drink he used to have as a boy in England called 'Tizer, the appetiser'. "Is Dr Mandrake on duty today by any chance?" Henry called over to the office manager. "Is he in the hospital?"

"Oh, no sir. Dr Mandrake is overseas just now. I believe he's in the USA for something, maybe a refresher course or something. Been gone for weeks and not expected back as far as I know."

"What about the nurse, Ann Tizer, see?" He pointed to her name listed as assisting nurse.

"I'll just check." And she was back at the computer punching the name in. "Yep. She's here and she should still be in the building. I'll give her bleeper a call, hang on."

Within minutes, arrangements had been made for Ann Tizer and Henry to meet in the staff canteen.

Once again, any conversation was prefaced by the comment that his drama series was just wonderful and so on, although the nurse did seem a trifle uncomfortable or awkward at this sudden meeting. Then when he asked if she could remember anything about the operation that night, anything unusual, she stumbled and fumbled her answer. "What do you mean, do you know? Oh dear, I am sworn to secrecy, Doctor. Oh, please don't ask me anything, Veronica swore me to secrecy and I promised her I wouldn't say a word. You'll have to talk to her. I can't ... I have to go now. Sorry." And she was off like a rabbit chased by a ferret.

Well that was it. If she was privy to a mistake, and not able to even discuss it without Veronica's permission, then Henry realised there was only one person who could help him and he was going to have to wait to talk to her.

★ ★ ★

Three days before he left for London, Henry met up with his parents and they all went to the hall for their *latihans*. Once again when they were having a cup of tea afterwards with the other members, he got the pats on the shoulders the "ooohs" and "aahs" and requests for autographs that by now were becoming tedious to him. In fact, he couldn't wait to get out and to talk again with his father alone. "Tell me about that portal thing dad."

Sam had noticed his son's discomfiture inside the hall in the company of his spiritual brothers and sisters and been surprised by their actions. Previously, they had accepted Henry as the brilliant surgeon that he was and been proud of his achievements and to be able to identify him as one of them. Now, though with this superficial glamour of being a star in television drama burdening the man, he realised that the brotherhood members were reacting in just the same way as anyone else. No longer did they see a young man of some spiritual content and talent, but they saw a television personality.

"Well, it's like this son. As you know, the very best form of guidance we can hope for is when we can receive for ourselves our true role and direction in life. If we are unclear or confused, then testing is a possible way of throwing some light on the situation and you say you've tried that without success. Now the other way that I have been blessed in discovering is for you to do your own *latihan* and then follow it with a prayer for guidance by calling on the founder's name. As I probably told you, he is the conduit for all of us to receive from the great life force, what we call Almighty God, or Allah. So, if you follow that and it is God's Will, the portal will open for you and you will be able to ask for help direct. Servant to source, so to speak. You may be lucky, or you may have to just accept and having made the plea or prayer, wait for the indication to come to you later. *Surrender, submission* and *patience*, the old three you know. Good luck."

That night when he got home, he did exactly as his father had told him. However, although he felt as if he had been transported out of his body to somewhere outside of the earth's atmosphere, he couldn't recognise anything to address, any way of either asking questions or receiving answers. It had been a wonderful experience, but no shaft of instant enlightenment had resulted. He realised that he had to just continue with his immediate plans and hope that eventually, real clarity about his future direction in life would come to him. Meanwhile, he had to pack for his trip.

With one spare day before he left Sydney, Henry thought he'd try to find out where or how he could contact his former head nurse. The puzzle of just how that finger was replaced out of alignment still played on his mind and was testing his patience. The person who held the key was away somewhere, so he was told, but he didn't want to wait another two weeks or more to find out the answer he sought. Apart from wanting to satisfy his curiosity, though, Henry had the feeling that he was also using this problem as a reason to just make contact. He felt guilty that he had neglected to call her as he had promised after their meeting at the medical school. But something else was vying with that guilt. It was a simple sensation, but one that he'd had very little experience of. It was the wish to just talk to her, to be with her and that, after all these years, was almost as much of a puzzle as the crooked finger.

When he again phoned the number she'd given him, expecting either no answer or the voice of her flatmate, he was surprised to hear a man say "Hello."

"Oh, I'm trying to locate Veronica Milstein, have I got the wrong number?" Henry must have sounded a bit hesitant. For some reason, this was the last thing he had expected.

"No," said the other's voice, "You're right, can I tell her who's calling?"

"Oh, err, it's just an old friend, yes." The confident microsurgeon turned star of television felt strangely at a disadvantage. Then when he heard the words: "Hold on then I'll get her," he wanted to just put the phone down and walk away. But he held on to hear:

"Yes, hello, this is Veronica Milstein, who's calling?"

"Hello, there, so glad to have caught you, I mean to have got you. It's Henry Pild, you know, Rufus". The pause from the other end, forced him to continue. "Just calling really to apologise for my tardiness, you know, I said I'd call and we could get together for a cup of coffee or something.... But I don't know, things just got on top at the time…"

Veronica recovered her composure: "No problems, I know you've been busy, I saw the photo of you and your lovely women co-stars in the paper publicising your show. You must have had a good time doing it. Yes, great fun."

"Well, look, I … do you want to hear about it in person. I mean, can we get together sometime… today. I called a few days ago and someone told me that you were away interstate on a course or something, but well…" The lack of an enthusiastic interruption at his belated invitation suddenly caused Henry to dry up.

"We, I was away, but I think my flatmate, Jenny, was really laying a false scent. She always does that when I have a great workload as well, and…" As she talked, Veronica's words were hardly entering his consciousness. He was just aware of the twin reasons for his call.

"Yeh, ok, so, what do you say I come round and we go for a coffee. I can be there in fifteen minutes."

"I can't. Not now."

But Henry persisted. "What about later? Unfortunately, it's got to be today, as I'm flying out to London tomorrow and… Veronica, I really want to see you. Do you understand?"

Veronica was practically in tears, her voice shaking a little. "Henry, I can't see you. I'm going, I'm going with someone. Sorry, I have to go now."

So, with one reason crushed, he still had to find out something about the other reason for wanting to contact her.

"Oh, that's great, Veronica, I'm very happy for you," he lied. "Perhaps we can all get together when I get back from the UK." He was the supervising doctor on the team again and he was talking to his nurse. "Look, nurse, I mean Veronica", he chuckled, "If you've got a minute or two. There is something else."

"Yes, Dr Pild, oh, I mean Henry Rufus, go ahead." She had recovered again and was playing his game.

Henry realised he had to be careful with his enquiry, judging by the state Ann Tizer had been in. "I went to see Wayne Carroll the other day. You know the cricketer, my last patient?" Another pause gave the caller a picture of someone at the other end who wanted to retreat or disappear, so he continued. "Well, he's a very happy man and completely convinced that I re-attached his finger out of alignment on purpose. Out of alignment, you understand, yes? Well you and I both know that I wouldn't have done such a thing unless I was drunk, and I don't drink, under the influence of drugs and I never touch the stuff or in some way mentally incapacitated, so what happened?"

Another pause and no answer.

"Veronica, you were the head nurse during that operation. You have witnessed dozens of similar operations and you know exactly the procedure and state of everyone in the theatre. What happened on that occasion? I know that you know something, because nurse Tizer, who was assisting, has told me that you swore her to secrecy. Not to divulge a thing. But now's the time to reveal all. What went on, what did I...?"

"Is that the real reason for the call?" Veronica decided that the best form of defence was attack. She had promised herself that Henry or Rufus, as he was, would never know the truth of that fateful night. "And I thought you had changed. My mistake."

Henry was thrown, but only momentarily: "I called, because I wanted to see you. Because I have been experiencing feelings about you that disturbed me. Good feelings. I called in the hope that we... look, I wanted to meet up and talk about them, these feelings. But what the hell, I now know I've left it all too late and I'm sorry. Sorry for both of us. No that sounds wrong. I'm sorry for myself." This was met by an even longer silence. "Veronica, please try to understand, though, that whatever I feel now about you can't completely erase from my mind what I discovered when I met that cricketer, can it. I have to find the answer to the puzzle of what went wrong with that operation and how the heck I did that to that patient. Surely you can appreciate that. Yes? So, put me out of my misery and tell me. What happened?"

"I can't tell you," she answered in a very low tone. "I can't tell you now, like this and I really don't want to tell you at all, to be honest. If the patient is happy, why worry about what happened? Look, I really do have to go, have a good trip, I guessed you would be going to that international gathering. At least, I hoped you would. Goodbye Henry." And she replaced the phone in its cradle.

Neither party would have been even the slightest bit aware of the reaction in Master Control to that conversation and the feelings expressed by both participants. In the great space occupied by the Intergalactic Helpers, when they weren't out on missions, the sheer joy at what had transpired, could almost be compared with the enthusiasm regularly demonstrated by the operators in the US space program mission control, after a successful probe launch. Calisthene was particularly pleased. Like the others he could see the reactions of each after the conversation was over and the phones were down. Quite independently and unknown to the other, they had either muttered or thought to themselves: "Oh, my God what have I done." The strategy was working and Calisthene made a note to congratulate Danilda on a job well done.

Whether Henry would ever discover the answer to his concern over the result of his last operation or not, was almost irrelevant to Master Control. What was relevant, in fact, absolutely imperative, was his realisation of his shortcomings in his treatment of Veronica. He was finally facing himself and acknowledging the importance of treating others with sensitivity and understanding. Of not taking anyone for granted. Particularly someone who, in the past, had shown him nothing but dedication and love. The fact that he hadn't recognised what the woman felt for him, was something that really hurt. Now that he couldn't have her, he realised that he had lost something precious. She had a selflessness and that was a quality that had been completely absent in just about everyone and everything that he had been involved with over the last few months.

The impact of the phone call from the man who for years she had pledged to herself she would always love whether that love was returned or not, was equally profound for Veronica. What had she done? Why hadn't she waited for his promised call, even if it hadn't come for weeks and weeks after their surprise meeting in the lecture hall. She'd always waited patiently with an inner sureness that one day they would be together and not just professionally, but as partners and soul mates. It had been her dream and then her commitment, until something strange seemed to enter her consciousness to make her change her attitude and to eliminate those feelings of dedication to that particular man. Suddenly, she was seeing things through different eyes. She found that if she allowed herself to indulge this new feeling of freedom, she realised that there were plenty of others that appealed to her. She was very popular at university, particularly after the great microsurgeon Henry Pild had acknowledged her as a former colleague. But it wasn't only her fellow students who were impressed with her. The faculty lecturers to a man or woman had recognised her undoubted talents and diligence in her studies. But more than that, at least one of the male staff was attracted to her simply because of her natural attributes as a young woman. More mature than the other students and therefore more approachable. At least that's what associate professor James Collick thought. In fact, after a one to one discussion with her on the intricacies of a certain type of surgery, he asked Veronica if she would like to go for a drink.

The man was about forty, some ten years older than her, and she didn't drink alcohol normally, but she found herself agreeing. He was good looking, charming and highly educated and she felt flattered by the attention from someone who obviously appreciated her. From that point, Henry Pild receded so far back in her consciousness that she rarely gave him a second thought. Instead, she started to form a regular relationship with her tutor. And it was that man, James Collick, who had been with Veronica at the time and who had answered Henry's belated phone call.

Now, though, as a result of that call, she suddenly felt like someone with two personalities. One she easily recognised as the person who had dedicated most of her last eight years or so, to idolising the man and his genius that she wanted to give her love to. Then there was this other person who she hardly knew at all if she really thought about it. It was as if something had taken her over and was guiding her in a completely different direction. Her previous resolve had been taken away and she had become someone else. She felt confused and very disturbed. Henry Pild had come back into her life and despite her current situation, she knew she really welcomed him back, even if she couldn't tell him so. Indeed she had rejected him. She, Veronica Milstein, had actually shown the person she would previously have died for, that she no longer wanted him. However, at the same time she was very much aware that one of her two *persona* did.

She needed time to sort out her feelings. Her shared flat wasn't very large, so she presumed that her man friend had heard much of her side of the conversation and probably deduced a good deal of what the voice at the other end of the line was saying. However, she didn't want to discuss it with him just then. She couldn't disguise her obvious disquiet though and quite naturally he offered his help. He'd be happy to talk things through with her if she so wished. She said quite firmly that she didn't, but in a warmer and kinder way, she asked her new friend James if he would mind leaving her on her own for a while. Just a couple of days she explained, as she embraced him and gave him a reassuring but brief kiss.

Something had happened that she couldn't explain or talk about and she just needed some space to put it all into perspective. However, after she had been left alone, Veronica was still in two minds, literally and metaphorically, and perhaps even metaphysically.

She was aware of several realities and somehow she had to put them into an order that made sense. The first was that she had a good relationship with someone who gave her love, intellectual satisfaction, support and demanded very little in return. The second was that the true love of her life had suddenly come back into it, although she still had a niggling little question mark over the sincerity of his wish to be with her. She knew of his persistence to discover something if it worried him and the result of that last operation obviously did worry him. So was he really being honest when he affirmed that that enquiry was not the real reason for his call. The third reality was just how she felt when he said he had feelings about her that disturbed him. She had practically melted. But another reality was that she had virtually told him to get lost and that couldn't be rectified, even if she – one part of her – wanted it to be. Desperately wanted that. He was off to the UK, well out of her reach and well out of her life. Then she thought, well, so what? I am in the most exciting part of my studies to qualify as a doctor. I don't need any stress or anxiety about relationships just now. I have a good relationship, she kept repeating. A stable one and one that supports me and what I am doing. And that seemed to be that. Until a last dangerous little thought came into her mind and seemed like a real cry for help as she wailed, to the walls. "But I do love him, I always will, and I'd give up everything for his love to be shown to me." Followed by: "Pull yourself together woman and be realistic. Give it a day or so," she suggested to herself, herselves "and then I will talk things over with James. Perhaps I should really find out what he sees as the agenda for our future together. Then I can take it from there. Yes, no need to make any decisions right now. Great. Oh, dear."

16

Henry was almost resigned to the fact that he may never learn the truth about the cricketer's bent finger. His focus now was on making the most of his trip to England. Scheduled to fly out early the next morning, he leafed through the yellow pages to find a taxi company and make a booking to be taken to the airport. As he found the relevant page, marked Taxicabs, he suddenly experienced a strange sensation, a presentiment of what could happen in the not too distant future. Instead of a general list of city cab companies, anonymous behind a set of letters, like ABC or some other cryptic name, they were listed according to their religious affiliations: Christian cabs, Jewish cabs and Muslim cabs being the main listings, with central phone numbers for each. Then there was an entry for *Miscellaneous* cabs, and under this heading came B'hai, Hindu, Buddhist, various cults who had developed successful commercial enterprises – and atheists. Australia was certainly a multicultural society alright and the different elements of it were clearly separated for everyone to be aware of.

Aided by this spontaneous insight, Henry reserved a "Muslim cab". He couldn't in all honesty patronise the others. Even though Veronica was Jewish, he was concerned that the proprietors could be dedicated Zionists who were funnelling money to Israel. He wasn't happy with what that country had done in its evolution from a state originally established with socialist ideals to the Middle East champion of capitalism and imperialism. Worse still, it was the super-puppet of the US, that now dominated the area as the only nuclear power and had expanded its territory at the expense of its neighbours.

Christianity in its modern form was even less appealing to the doctor, who was a man who hated hypocrisy as much as he hated fundamentalism of any kind. Two of its world renowned proponents, US President Bush and the former UK Prime Minister Blair had destroyed for Henry any credibility in Christian ethics and morality and any religious organisation that seems to spawn and often protect paedophiles, whilst preaching the gospel, made him sick at its duplicity. No, apart from anything else, he couldn't call a Christian cab and be seen to be even vaguely associated with the zeal now spearheading the great crusade against "people of middle eastern appearance" that was sweeping through the white Anglo-Saxon-Celtic world. A zeal that had cynically re-named terrorists "Islamists."

Next day, when the cab driver turned up exactly on time, Henry was not at all surprised to see that the man was Lebanese, but he was mildly disappointed that the cab carried the very un-Islamic symbols of "City Cabs". It was back to reality.

The driver apparently had no idea who he was picking up and was thrilled to discover who his fare really was. He had not only seen both of the television series that had featured microsurgery, but he had also met Henry's father Ridwan, as he referred to him. "I am a Muslim, Doctor. My name is Rashid, sir and I met Ridwan during *Eid ul Fitr*, our big celebration after Ramadan. A wonderful man is Ridwan and so is your mother, I mean she's a wonderful woman. They don't come to the mosque very often, but when they do, they are always welcomed and smothered with questions about you."

The man grinned the entire way to the airport, until they approached the outer perimeter, where the signs indicated the exact lane for him to take. That's when Henry's premonition started up again: Here at least with the routes marked out clearly, the separation of religious factions was a little more subtle, presumably in order to avoid giving offence to tourists. With his driver completely unaware and just concentrating on the road, the vision that came to Henry was stark: he could see that each cab grouping that he'd envisioned, when he'd scanned the yellow pages of the telephone book, had particular colours featured in the lettering of their number plates. Muslim taxis were distinguished by lettering in red and green. That fact was confirmed when Rashid had to make an awkward angle turn to follow the signpost marked: Red and Green plates only. However the full significance of this became apparent, when his driver turned to him apologetically to announce that he could only take him to a search station a good fifty metres from the overseas terminal. Fear of a possible act of terrorism, he explained. Doctor Pild, who even in sunshades was most obviously a perfect example of Anglo-Celtic breeding, waved away the apology, paid his fare with a very generous tip, took his bags and as he started off towards the departure lounge, he noticed that his cab had driven into the open search area and was being examined inside, outside and underneath. It was the only search station on the concourse. He noticed that, like him, the examiners were Anglo-Celtic gentlemen.

The vision faded as the taxi pulled up outside the overseas departure building. Henry got out and when his driver handed him his bags, he rewarded him with a very generous tip on top of the fare.

"God be with you, Doctor, have a good journey." The man smiled warmly and looked around to make sure other cabbies could see him. "And please say hello from me to Ridwan when you see him." Henry shook his hand and promised he would.

Without being aware of anything happening, as he entered the terminal, Henry passed through an electronic beam that encircled the entire building. No sirens wailed or bells rang, so he'd obviously not taken his stethoscope with him. Inside the airport, pairs of heavily armed policemen were patrolling every area and eyeing up people everywhere with suspicion. Henry kept his sunglasses on until he was face to face with an airline official checking his luggage through. Then when he removed them and also showed his identity card, the young woman behind the counter immediately exclaimed: "Oh, it's you. Oh fabulous, I mean I think you are fabulous in the television series, you know, **The Specialist.** We all watch it."

"That's very kind of you, I'm glad you enjoy it." Henry was squirming, very conscious of the people behind him in line. "Now, can I have the ticket, please, my ticket."

"Of course, excuse me" she said as she was punching the keys on her computer "Window seat? Oh, I have a message against your name, Dr Pild, Yes. You've been upgraded to first class sir. Pretty well any seat you want."

"Upgraded? Why? I'm happy enough to be in business class or even..." He couldn't think of the name of the main passenger area.

"It's a company courtesy instruction sir, apparently they don't want you to be bothered by any of the other passengers on the trip. There you are, have a good flight."

Next obstacle to overcome was immigration and another small baggage and body check and although he knew he had an up-to-date passport and it tallied with his civilian and hospital identity cards, someone was sure to recognise him and go through the same monotonous routine. He would have worn a false beard if he had suspected that his life was always going to be intruded on. In fact he concluded that it might have created a bit of fun if he had done so on this occasion.

Eventually, he passed all the hurdles and settled down in the luxury of the first class cabin and a chance to read some of the reams of information about the Royal College convention that he had taken off the internet. That was after the chief cabin attendant, the pilot and the co-pilot had each approached him and welcomed him aboard. And that's when he got a shock. For some reason he really had been too caught up in his own problems and concerns to give much thought to the symposium he was travelling to attend. Now, though, he was suddenly confronted with something that he was completely unprepared for. There, in the notes he was trying to scan, was an announcement that it was hoped that 'the distinguished Australian surgeon, Rufus Pild would be attending some of the seminars. It went on to remind all fellows and affiliates who would be attending, that Dr Pild had made his discipline and his skills popular with his television series **Through the Microscope** which had recently been shown in England. A video of one of the episodes in the series would be screened during the seminar'. Oh, boy, there goes my anonymity again, he thought.

It was a direct flight to London. No stopovers, no further embarrassment of being identified and gushed over and the comfort of a good sleep. In fact, when he washed and shaved half an hour before the descent into London's Heathrow, Henry felt refreshed and not unhappy in the least that he had been upgraded. Indeed, he now hoped that the same privilege applied on the return trip. However, the luxury and feeling of comfort ended once he'd cleared the first class lounge and both immigration and customs had been satisfied.

If Sydney airport was security conscious, by comparison with London it was relaxed and friendly. In the country where the so-called threat of terrorism was ever present, the concourse bristled with CCTV cameras and armed military personnel. Suspicious eyes and electronic scanners searched everyone and everything. After running the gauntlet of scrutiny which must have required a massive bank of monitors, Henry finally saw a sign saying "Welcome to England."

The irony of that welcome was emphasised when he stepped outside the airport and hailed a taxi, he then felt the climatic reality of that twelve thousand miles that separated the UK from

Australia. He had left Sydney on a warm and sunny October day, down under. Now he was attacked by the rain and wind of an early autumn day, up over. He couldn't wait to get into his cab and, shortly after, into the hotel that would be his home for the next two weeks.

Surprisingly, the whole experience in England, despite the weather and the overt security precautions everywhere, proved to be very fulfilling for the young doctor. Not only did he enjoy participating in the content of the convention and meeting colleagues from around the world, but he found his acting experience had come in handy. After his program had been viewed by a large audience, Henry had been invited to talk about his experiences in front of a camera. Starting with his involvement in the reality series, he went on to tell them how it had led to his becoming an actor. He held everyone's attention when he told them of the beautiful women he had to fight off in each episode and how it had created a real problem for him to solve. He suggested that all those assembled there might be able to give him some assistance with the question he had to resolve in the next few weeks. Should he return to the operating theatre and continue to risk his reputation, increase his stress level and pay a huge insurance premium for the pleasure of surgically reassembling a part or parts of an anonymous human being?... or cruise down to the television studios in a chauffeured car, spend the day pretending to have affairs with beautiful women and in return acquire fame and three times the salary of a surgeon. Wearing the most serious face he could affect, Henry said: "It's a difficult one as you can see. What would you do?"

"Go for the women!" they yelled back. "You lucky bastard." And the audience, which included many eminent men and women practitioners of his profession, broke up in laughter.

Once again, he had shown the aplomb of a man much older and experienced than his years and that quality was well noted.

Apart from his attendance at the convention, Henry found time to visit some of the places his parents had suggested. He made contact with his father's old flatmate Saul, now Suleiman, who knew all about the unusual Dr Pild from his childhood on, thanks to a regular flow of correspondence from his old friend. He insisted that Henry come to his home for dinner and to meet some of his family and once there, he was pumped for an hour or so about the fortunes or otherwise of Sam and Kerrin.

In the home environment of this man, Henry felt as if he was with family, particularly when Suleiman took out his oboe and invited his young guest to accompany him on the piano. The piece he chose he said was a sonata he was trying to perfect when he shared the flat with his father, so many years ago. He recalled how he had to abandon the place on one occasion because of Sam Pild's air-renting attempts at Shakespeare for his audition pieces.

On the last free day of his time in England, he found his way to Mitcham to see the old family house. The area had changed from the description his parents had given him, even from their last visit. And sure enough, the house had too. No longer a single dwelling, it now had three separate mail boxes after its conversion to three abodes.

Alvira was the very last on his list to visit and she fussed over him as if he were the baby his parents had brought home to her all those years ago. She told him of her time with them and before that as housekeeper and companion to his grandmother. And she pulled from a sideboard drawer a folder containing a series of photos and news clippings showing the remarkable progress he had made in his career. She told him that a very proud father had sent them over from time to time. Then she gave him directions and insisted that he visit the grave where the death of his grandfather was marked and the remains of his grandmother lay. Henry did as he was instructed and took along some flowers for the grave. His homage was important and moving for the young man. Thanks to Alvira, the gravestone was obviously well tended and its simple inscription brought him close to these ancestors he had never known.

Returning to the hotel, Henry was full of mixed feelings still. He felt the pressure of commitments to people in both aspects of his recent past. Some things were getting a wee bit clearer, but he felt he still needed some advice, some guidance. Should he continue with the drama series for a short while longer. Could he put up with the ego massaging that being a so-called star of television brought. Would a further period in that business provide him with the kind of money that would allow him perhaps to do something more worth while. There was the 'receiving' he'd had about working with the poor or underprivileged. How real was that? Or should he forget all these intrusions into his real calling and return to the profession he had excelled at and which really gave him satisfaction? He promised he would definitely make every effort to resolve this quandary when he got home, whatever it took to do so.

However, that evening after dinner when he relaxed with one of his new colleagues, a further alternative was tossed to him to ponder. Had he ever considered working with other surgeons and physicians in teams deployed to areas of the world where medical expertise was desperately needed? Areas either in war zones or recovering from the effect of recent conflagrations. Or places in the third world where poverty and disease were taking lives faster every year. Where local doctors were practically non-existent and hospitals or clinics under-equipped and understocked. His companion told him of an organisation that was looking for the kind of expertise that he had and he'd be happy to introduce him to the organisers.

Despite the fact that he was aware that here was yet another complication in the equation, he felt a definite interest in the notion. But, he was off back to Australia in the morning and couldn't meet anyone or even give the suggestion any real consideration at the moment. He took the particulars and contacts for the organisation and also the details of the man who had told him all about it and promised he'd keep it in mind and make a decision later.

* * *

The flight back to Sydney was just as comfortable as the outward journey. Whoever upgraded him had made sure that the courtesy applied both ways. Once again, he was untroubled and rested by the time they flew in over the city he loved and he marvelled at the view below him. The bridge and the opera house never failed to thrill.

Henry had phoned his father from London and Sam was at the airport to pick him up. The son wanted to talk as soon as possible about his trip and everything that had happened, but more than that, about his dilemma which seemed to be getting more confusing by the day. On the way to his parents' house for breakfast, Henry said he really needed to do some testing about his future direction in life. So many things were presenting themselves that he was genuinely confused. Sam told him to try to just forget about any problems for a few days and then when he was more settled and maybe even clearer in his own feelings, he'd arrange for a group of men helpers to try to test something that would assist him. Meanwhile, both he and Henry's mother were waiting and anxious to know everything about the trip and particularly about Suleiman and Alvira.

After the debriefing by his parents, a mailbox at his apartment crammed with paper demanded his next period of attention. The bulk of the letters were fan letters and even a few offers of marriage – all forwarded from the television station. Henry threw the lot onto his desk, unpacked and then went down to the swimming pool. He would take his dad's advice and lie low for a few days, although he was still interested in finding out more about that dreadful finger operation that no-one seemed to want to talk about. Perhaps the hospital head Rizal Humphries could throw some light on what happened, although of course he had to be careful in any enquiry from that source. No pressures, he thought, but it won't do any harm to give him a ring later and pop up to see him.

When he phoned, though, he discovered that things weren't going to be that simple. Rizal Humphries, Chief Registrar and head administrator of the King Abdullah Free Hospital had suffered a massive heart attack the day before. That information was only given to Henry because the head receptionist had recognised his voice and she asked him not to say anything to anyone else at this stage. She was, she said, following instructions from the hospital board chairman. Nothing had been released to the press and all official statements would be made later that day. Dr Humphries was in an intensive care ward, under sedation and only family members were being allowed in to see him. It was suggested that Henry should ring back tomorrow. The attending physician, Dr Ronald Mates, a heart specialist, was heading a team monitoring the damage to the heart and currently considering all options.

Henry immediately rang Mates and offered his services. He said he would willingly assist in any procedures that might be attempted and that he could be contacted at any time night or day. In the meantime, he decided to clean up his apartment and then have a sleep. Despite the tiredness from jet lag, that he was surprised to discover even first class passengers felt, the sleep was restless and disturbed and in the middle of the night, he sat bolt upright as he saw the smiling face of Rizal Humphries looking down at him.

He decided to go to the hospital to discover for himself what was happening. This time, he went to emergency and checked in with the reception desk before making his way to the intensive care wards. Strangely as he approached the one where lights were blazing, he felt light and almost happy. Before he could enter, though, the senior physician came through the door with a defeated look on his face. "Oh, hello Rufus, we couldn't save him, I'm afraid. Had another bang which brought him out of sedation and with obvious pain into paradise. At least I hope that's where he is. Sorry. His wife is there if you want a word."

Henry thanked him and went in to take a last look at his old boss and to comfort the widow if he could. Almost as he expected, despite the beating his heart had taken, Rizal Humphries had a smile on his face when he died. When Mrs Humphries looked up and saw Henry, she thanked the nurses and after greeting him, asked him to come outside as she had something she wanted to say to him. She looked pale and drawn, but seemed in command of her emotions. The grief would come later, but first, she had a request to make of the young man that her husband had such a high opinion of.

Relda Humphries was a much respected public figure herself, both for her charity work and involvement in local politics. She was a cultured woman and still carried herself with considerable dignity despite her loss. She told the man she knew as Rufus, that Rizal had told her before, if anything happens to him, to make sure that Dr Pild knew that in fact Rizal was a Muslim. Really a closet Muslim because of the atmosphere in the country these days. She said although he had been born a Jew, he converted to Islam many years ago, long before his appointment to the King Abdullah Free Hospital and his wish was to be buried as a Muslim. Mrs Humphries told the young surgeon that although the family had not been raised to follow any particular religion she didn't think her children would understand. They had both moved away from home many years ago and had, no doubt, subsequently formed their own opinions, so she hadn't mentioned her husband's request to either her son, Maurice or her daughter Jessica. Maurice was in the US at the moment and her daughter lived in Perth, so she was waiting for them to arrive any time. "However, the main point is that as far as the burial is concerned, he said that you would understand and you would arrange everything if you could."

Henry agreed to make enquiries in the morning. He also told her that he thought because it would be an Islamic funeral, it might have to take place within 24 hours if that is possible, but he'd confirm that and let her know. He was sure, though, that things could be delayed to allow the family to all be there. Meantime, he advised her to call another family member or friend and go home and try to get some rest.

First thing next morning, Henry rang his father, to seek his advice and help. In turn Sam, using his name Ridwan, rang the Imam's staff at the main mosque, to organise the funeral and promised his son that he would coordinate things. A plot had to be apportioned in the Muslim cemetery and a grave dug facing Mecca. The ceremony or service could be arranged at very short notice and the Imam would make himself available whenever he was required.

Henry then rang Rizal's widow to check on the arrival of the family and to ask her just how much publicity she could accept for this occasion. Relda Humphries told him that her daughter had arrived and her son was expected later that day. She said she didn't mind who knew about the burial. Already the official announcement of the hospital chief's death had been made and the papers were all carrying the story. Speculation about when and where he would be buried was also being mooted. She said she would be ready for the burial to take place the following morning if that could be arranged and she would ring the chairman of the hospital board straight away to announce the details to the staff and all those who had worked with Rizal. In fact, she said almost as an afterthought, "as the hospital is going to look after all the costs, I will ask him, old George Twent, to contact the mosque himself, oh, he'll just love that, and settle on a time convenient for them and us. Thanks for all your help Rufus, your strength last night somehow communicated itself to me. Strangely, I feel quite light about everything and I just hope that doesn't become light-headed. I'll hope to see you tomorrow, bye, bye."

Next day, Relda Humphries was accompanied by her son and daughter when she joined with the board members and many of the medical and nursing staff who were off duty to witness the prayers and burial of her husband. Several civic dignitaries were there too.

Henry asked the Humphries family if they would like to participate with him and his father in the washing of the body, which was carried out in a side room where the body laid waiting for interment. Relda and her son Maurice took their turn in the ceremonial washing and then the body was wrapped in a cloth and placed in a very simple, plain coffin before being carried to the grave.

Much to his dismay, Henry noticed that the media people were present, so somebody at the hospital had leaked the information to them and he knew that inevitably, they would be clicking their cameras and recording their videotape on the location and the VIPs attending. Of particular interest would be Henry Rufus Pild, star of **The Specialist.** There would also be in-your-face interviews to fill in as much as possible of this very newsworthy event. The Jewish head of the King Abdullah Free Hospital being buried in accordance with Islamic tradition with the former Doctor Pild playing a big part in the proceedings. Big story for small minds.

Once the burial had been accomplished, Henry looked up to see a familiar face amongst the mourners as they started to leave. Trying not to be noticed, was his former colleague and keeper of the secret he still wanted answered, Veronica Milstein. She appeared to be unaccompanied, at least not by a man, so he approached her and asked how she was and how she knew about the funeral here. She told him that one of the nurses she used to work with had called and she had come to pay her respects to the widow and family.

Henry introduced her to his father but before they could get much further with any kind of conversation, the cameras were there and the questions being thrown.

"If you could all wait just a couple of moments, I'll be happy to answer any questions I can." Henry decided he wanted to protect other people from the media, particularly the widow and he would take them on himself. First though, he turned back to Veronica and asked her whether she was in a hurry or not. When she hesitated, the young doctor told her again.

"Look, Veronica, I really would like to have a chat, and if you have the time and don't mind, perhaps you… perhaps we… could all have a spot of lunch, what do you say Dad? Just give me five minutes." And he left them and turned to the anxious press scrum.

"Now, ladies and gentlemen, what can I do for you?" Henry rubbed his hands together as if he was really keen and interested.

"Who was that you were talking to?" One overweight and short-sighted man threw at him.

"Well, the woman was, mind your own business and the man was my father Sam Ridwan Pild."

"May we know why a television star like you has been so involved in this Muslim ceremony? Are you a Muslim Mr Pild?" A woman reporter who looked as if she was fresh out of journalism school had her micro tape-recorder under his nose.

"No, I'm not."

"So, what's the big involvement, then? You seem to know what it's all about." This came from another overweight and balding reporter who seemed bored with it all and anxious to get it over and get down to the nearest watering hole.

"My presence here and whatever I have done for all to see, I would wager is of little or no interest to all your readers. However, if you must know, Dr Rizal Humphries was a good friend and a distinguished mentor to me and a lot of other people in medicine. He spent the best part of forty five years serving the public as a doctor and as a hospital administrator. He was a good man and a generous man. I am merely paying homage, and I think your talents as writers and reporters would be better utilised in explaining in your various ways what a loss to the hospital and to the people of Sydney this man's death has caused. Thankyou." He then walked away from the cameras and the questions, went back to his father and Veronica, took each by the arm and walked them briskly to the car park, saying: "Let's get out of here."

Veronica was completely thrown. She really expected the cold shoulder from the man she had been so abrupt with when he phoned two weeks earlier. But his control of things in this situation seemed to be so persuasive that she found she had no choice. When they got to their cars, Sam told his son that he had to pass on the lunch today as he had to get away. So, Henry asked Veronica again if she'd join him. She agreed and before long they were deep into conversation about each other's lives. The place chosen for lunch was a popular Italian restaurant in the inner west of the city and once again the "star" of **The Specialist** had to put on his sunshades and wear his baseball cap to disguise himself from the inevitable attention waiting at most places he visited. The manager still managed to recognise him, though and led them to a table in a corner well away from other eyes and ears. Veronica found both the disguise and the treatment his presence attracted amusing. The last time she had had a snack with this man was when they were both students and it was in the university refectory. The last formal meal they shared, was the disaster that occurred at her mother's table. This had resulted in perpetual hatred being directed from her mother towards Henry, or Rufus as he was then known, at any mention of his name and really marked the beginning of the end of any potential meaningful relationship between the two students back then.

Once they were seated and had ordered, Veronica reminded him of their past times together and hoped he would excuse her smiling as she recounted them. For his part, at this time, he would have excused her anything. As he sat opposite, he seemed to be seeing her for the very first time. She was a beautiful woman in every way, he realised, with eyes that seemed to be full of life and full of secrets. One of them he hoped to get her to reveal at some stage.

He asked whether she was still seeing someone, the same someone that answered the phone when he last called. He discovered that that relationship was now history. The associate professor at the medical school had failed to tell her that he was married with children and because he and his wife were staunch Catholics, he would probably never be free, really free.

Veronica told Henry how she was confused after his phone call. She had previously convinced herself that he was not any more interested in her than he had ever been when they had worked together. She told him that she had realised that she had been carrying a torch for someone who didn't really care and never would, so she was vulnerable and ready for a relationship with someone else. When she put the phone down on his last call, she didn't know what to do. On the one hand, her long time colleague had thrown a ribbon of hope to her with his declaration of his feelings, but how real was that or how sincere? She didn't want to be hurt any more so she felt she had to really examine her situation at the time. To try to establish whether or not there was any real future for her with the tutor. Now she knew.

Henry told her that he was relieved to hear her news, for selfish reasons. Yes, he really did mean that he had feelings for her and if she had any feelings at all for him, perhaps they could see each other again.

Veronica felt like her life had become balanced again and her hopes were once more alive. She told him of her progress in her studies and wondered if he was going to continue being an actor. He said that he really didn't know what he was going to do, and how he had a lot of things to sort out. He had several options. He told her how if he couldn't make a decision with his mind, he was hoping to do some testing with the helpers. Then he realised she didn't know what on earth he was talking about. "Right, we are definitely going to have to meet up again, so that I can explain. No, on second thoughts, I should really have a woman explain it all. Don't worry, I have not lost the plot, although I have only had about five hours sleep since I left London. I'll just tell you that I belong to a spiritual brotherhood… hey wait a minute, now I remember telling you a bit about it years ago, Yes?"

Veronica did recall. She said she remembered him telling her and later, her parents at that fatal dinner, that it was an all inclusive association of all religions and races. "I can distinctly recall my dear mother taking objection to the fact that it included Muslim "terrorists" as she called them, alongside Jews and Christians, remember? By the way, I don't know if I ever told you, but my mother actually moved out of the house and tied up with someone else for a while, but then last week she told me that she plans to move back in with dad again. Sorry, just a bit of gossip, but back to what you were talking about, that spiritual brotherhood... it's really ironic Rufus, sorry Henry, because if we had continued our friendship as students, I was really interested and intended to ask you all about it. It's true. But it wasn't to be, was it. We went our separate ways, socially. We only really communicated at the hospital."

Well, thought Henry, if that's not a cue then I don't know what is. "Veronica, I ... you must know that my total focus was on my work. I was almost obsessed by the need to be super-efficient and try for perfection in everything I did. Yes. Well I regret that now. I regret that I didn't appreciate people... you, in particular, as a person, well not properly. To my narrow visioned eyes, you were just the nurse who I knew I could always rely on. My private life was almost non-existent. For years I formed no relationships at all with the opposite sex and life for me was my work and my worship, through the spiritual brotherhood, or I should now say brother/sisterhood, that I had been virtually born into. Just stop me if I am boring or maudlin, but, look, I don't know why I have suddenly woken up and can see things so clearly at last."

Veronica was fascinated at the revelation. Could he still be a virgin? This hero, this popular idol? "What about the last few months? All those beautiful actresses you have worked with on those programs, you must have..."

"No, I mustn't have, that's a false assumption. Listen Veronica, I don't know how we got to this point, but now that we're here, I'll tell you why I didn't run amok with all those women in the series and it's going to sound odd unless you realise where I am coming from. How I was raised. Do you want me to go on now, here? And would you like another coffee, I know I would." Henry called over to the waiter and pointed to the cups on the table.

"I'd be shattered if you didn't continue now, please, please." Veronica leant forward in her chair, like a child about to be told a story. In fact the slightly serious mood that had been gathering was lightened by the storyteller when he picked up on her movement and said: "Right, if we're all sitting comfortably, I'll begin. I believe strongly that the sex act between man and woman is really for procreation. Whenever we have sexual relations with someone, we take on and carry something from that person in our soul. Call it spiritual baggage. If we're lucky and the person we have penetrated or been penetrated by is a high soul with no previous baggage, then we might even be inspired or raised up. However if that person has been gathering other people's baggage and passing it on, then we can take on what we not only don't need, but what we shouldn't want. Veronica, don't look like that. I am not judging you. I don't know what you have done in this respect. No, this is *my* belief and this is *my confessional*, Ok?" Henry leaned across the table and although his lunch companion had sunk back in her chair, he touched her cheek and brought a smile.

"What do you mean, your confessional? Maybe this is not the right time. Maybe you shouldn't go on with what you are saying." Veronica had been touched by his explanation of how one can dirty one's soul by taking on something from someone else during physical congress. She suddenly felt guilty and shabby.

"Well, I think I will go on, if you don't mind. This is the first chance I've had to tell someone about something I now feel deeply ashamed about. Veronica, I think you know that for a short time before I left the hospital and became a so-called actor, I was difficult to communicate with. Even more difficult than before. You may have noticed that I was preoccupied with something outside of the hospital world. Outside of my work as a microsurgeon. Well I sure was and looking back I can see that I was just going through the motions of that last operation for instance and the reason was, I was thinking of a woman. A very particular and as it turned out, a very devious, manipulative woman. Did I ever mention the name Mercy Cryer? No. Well it's a wonder I didn't, because this stupid and naïve person sitting opposite you was seduced by her and held under a spell for several days, whilst she convinced me that I had a great career in television as an actor. I don't really know, can't explain what happened to me, except that I was intimate with her several times. On reflection as many times as it took for her to prepare a contract and to get me to sign it. Then, surprise, surprise, she disappeared for a couple of days or so, without a word. When she did get back in touch with me it was to tell me that it was all over between us, because she was married and her husband was back in town.

"There you are, my true confession and please don't ring a magazine and tell anyone. Believe it or not, Veronica, that very clever woman, she's my agent, incidentally, was the first and the last woman I have had sex with, and the period since of enforced celibacy is maintained because of my beliefs and in the hope that abstinence and my spiritual exercise can cleanse anything that I have taken on from her and I don't mean venereal disease". Henry drained his coffee cup and looked his former nurse in the eye. She looked awkward.

"Listen, I didn't tell you all that to make you feel uneasy. As I said what you do or did and how you feel about it is your business and your business alone. I know my views are considered old-fashioned and not for everyone. But what I would like to know, if you can confirm it, Veronica... did I seem any different, not on top of the work, when I last operated at the King Abdullah, on that cricketer?"

The young woman didn't know where to look at this, so Henry continued. "Look, we both know and so does Ann Tizer, that I stuffed up that night. I've seen the result and that's not my normal work. In fact, whether I did that knowingly or even in some strange state, I can't erase it from my mind, I really can't ... and it's one reason why I have serious doubts about my future work. Help me out Veronica, what state was I in and what happened? And why did no one tell me?"

Veronica didn't know what to do. This was a moment she had dreaded and avoided for months. How can you possibly tell a genius that he made a serious botch up in that crucial operation. The irony was that the actual re-attachment was almost routine. Any one of the consultants connected with the hospital could have done it, but because of the patient involved, the superintendent had insisted on calling in Henry, or Rufus as he then was, to take charge. Now, she was trapped. By the very fact that she was sitting in a public place with the man, the changed man, who had all but declared his love for her and who was now putting the kind of mental pressure on her that she found difficult to respond to. She certainly didn't want to destroy the very strong feelings that seemed to be building between them. But, how could she evade his probing questioning and the pleading look in his eyes.

"Sorry, Henry... I can't..." was all she could get out in almost a whisper.

"Can't, can't what?" Henry tried to lighten things again. "Come along senior nurse Milstein, you can trust me, I'm a doctor... or am I?"

"Of course you are. A brilliant doctor as everyone knows. Don't ever doubt that." Attack is the best form of defence, she reminded herself. "What happened on that night, I don't know, I don't remember, now. Does it matter really? I probably applied the wrong clamp or something. Don't you think that I haven't felt terrible myself from time to time. But then the patient was delighted with the result. Rizal couldn't believe the huge donation he made to the hospital in gratitude, so why worry now... look, Henry, I have a lecture in less than an hour, so I'd better be going." Veronica started to get up from her chair. "Thanks for lunch, for everything..."

Henry smiled, he knew instinctively that she was not telling him the truth, that she was trying to protect him and he also knew that he would be troubled by the dilemma for as long as he failed to get an answer, an honest answer from someone about the mistake that he had made. It was something that haunted him and made it almost impossible for him to seriously consider continuing in medicine.

"Can we do it again? Lunch? Or meet up sometime soon?"

The interest was genuine and she knew it, but she wanted some space again between her vulnerability and this man's insistence. "Well, yes, I'd love to, but I've got exams and papers to write for the next few weeks, so… can I give you a call later. You've got things to sort out anyway, haven't you. Oh, and really, I do want to know more about that spiritual movement."

"Fine. Here's my phone number in case you haven't got it and here's my mother's. She's the best one to talk to. I'll tell her to expect a call sometime… in a few weeks, yes? But in the meantime, if you feel I could help in any way with your… no? Ok, see you later then and good luck."

★ ★ ★

When Henry returned home that afternoon, he knew that something was pretty well resolved in him. Any 'testing' might come later. For now, he could see what he had to do. He sat in his study, looking up at the certificates that illustrated his medical qualifications and reflected his professional brilliance from an incredibly early age. Then he looked down at his right hand and isolated the same finger that he had operated on for the cricketer. He moved it one way and then another. He straightened it and packed it in between others on each side. How on earth did I do it, he asked himself. Then shaking his head and frowning he picked up the contract for a second series of ***The Specialist*** that had been sitting on his desk since before he left for England about three weeks earlier.

This time the contract contained no terms that he could possibly later find unacceptable. His success in the first series had determined that. Even the fine print was larger than normal and talked only of copyright, overseas sales and repeat payments. And they were generous. Henry read through the entire document and when he finished he convinced himself that if he did do a second series and could tolerate the "phoney adulation" that his television stardom seemed to attract, the huge amount of money being offered would allow him so much more freedom in whatever future direction in life he would be taking. Along with an already fairly healthy bank balance acquired through medicine, boosted considerably by his television performances, this sum would make it possible to consider various options, including the possibility of joining the team of medicos operating in areas of the world where people were desperate for medical attention. That is, of course, if he felt he could operate again or if he could obtain some reassurance that it was the right thing for him to do.

He was convinced, and just as he was about to sign the contract in all the relevant places, the phone rang and the architect of his troubles and his success was on the line.

"Oh, good, you're there, darling. Glad I've got you. Did everything go ok over there? You know in London at that thing you went to?"

Henry smiled at the woman's gall and guile despite himself. "Yep. Everything went just fine."

"Hope you haven't made any commitments anywhere Henry? No. Because we need to discuss something that could be just massive for you. I think I might have mentioned before, when we last spoke… there is the possibility of a film. A very big film with a world class director… I wonder, do you know Steven?" Mercy let it hang there tantalisingly.

"Steven Spielberg? Why yes, of course. Well to be honest, really it's just that I know someone who saw one of his movies. Pretty good apparently."

Mercy came back quickly "No, Henry, actually I didn't know you had such a good sense of fun, you haven't shown that side of your personality before. Anyway, it's Steven Cabot and believe me he is one of the up and coming directors that people are watching. You must have heard of him. Well, things are still very much in the embryo stage and that's good for us. In fact the producers would really like you to get a bit more exposure as an actor before this project.

"They say publicity can sell a picture better than its content. So, really, that's the chief reason for the call darling. Have you signed the contract for the new series? Mr Clayton, you know, the channel boss, is most anxious that we get your signature. He was over the moon at the response of the first series, I can tell you. The ratings were fantastic and, I really shouldn't tell you this, but your insistence on changing the… you know the, what did you call it, 'gratuitous sex for voyeurs not audiences', something like that, not only met his resounding approval, as he said, 'sex is not supposed to be a spectator sport,' but it has influenced a new series of 'Love is a Four Letter Word' being prepared for one of the other channels. Big shift Henry and you are responsible for it. Sex is out and temperance is in. But I'm rambling on… so have you had a look at the contract? Any problems?"

Throughout the phone call so far, Henry had been concentrating on his hand again and pushing the fingers back and forth from side to side.

"No problems, Mercy, it's signed and if you want to send a courier over here it's all yours or theirs, ok?"

"I'll have someone there in half an hour. And we will get together sometime soon about the movie deal… oooroo!" and she was away.

The burial of Rizal Humphries had taken place in the morning. The lunch with Veronica had been complex and revealing. Now he had made a big decision and signed the contract that would tie him up in a few weeks' time for another four months or so. It had been quite a day and he flicked on the television set to relax and watch the news. He'd even accept swallowing his anger and watching the latest attempt by America to dominate a country and covet its oil reserves. In fact he half expected a story along those lines, although there couldn't be many of the oil rich countries of the world left whose governments hadn't been undermined by CIA infiltration or trading blackmail. What he didn't expect to see as the lead item was firstly a shot of him talking to a young woman and then his comments to the media.

"Who is the romantic interest in Henry Pild's life and why were they meeting at a Muslim burial ground of all places? Well the star of *The Specialist* the top-rated television drama, screened recently on this station, was reluctant to tell all to this reporter. Seen here in earnest conversation with the attractive redhead and his own father, Henry seemed embarrassed to be discovered by the media. However, in an exclusive interview, we managed to discover that as a former consultant at the King Abdullah Free Hospital, he was attending the burial ceremony of his former boss, Dr Rizal Humphries, who died just two days ago. Humphries had converted to Islam and the religious service full of prayers and ritual had been organised by the star's father Ridwan Pild another convert to Islam. When asked whether he himself was a Muslim, Dr Pild claimed it was none of my business and stormed off with his new girlfriend".

They then showed the reverse shot of Henry taking Veronica and his father by the arms and walking towards the car park.

"Nobody is invisible in this city, Doctor," the reporter's voice droned on "and we hope to bring

viewers an exclusive interview with the mysterious woman in the actor's life, tomorrow. This is Libby Mufkin for *World News Tonight.*"

The remote was immediately in action and Libby Mufkin and *World News Tonight* despatched to the ether. Henry phoned Veronica and was greeted only by the answer phone, so he left the simple message: "Good Luck." He then rang his mother.

"Hello, oh it's you, I was just about to call you," she said. "Who is that beautiful young person you and your dad were chatting to, anyway. Yes, I did see the news. You looked good and so did your father. Wish I'd been there now. I might have been on the television as well."

"Mum" interrupted her son. "I really rang to let you know that you might, just might get a call from that young lady I was talking to at the burial. I introduced her to dad, didn't he tell you? Anyway I don't think I told him much about her, but she was the student you have mentioned from time to time. Yes, she is now back studying medicine but she was my head nurse at the King Abdullah and, like me, she was just paying her respects to Rizal. Nothing else, although I did have lunch with her and ... this is what I wanted to let you know, she could be interested in learning about the brotherhood. I haven't told her much but, she did show some interest and so I gave her your number, ok? She might call. It's possible."

"Sure, that's fine, of course. What's her name then?" Kerrin got a pen.

"It's Veronica, Veronica Milstein. I won't give you her number just now, let's see if she bothers." Henry was ready to end the conversation, but his mother wasn't.

"I'm only sorry that there's not more to the relationship, you know. Could there be? 'Bout time Henry... what are your plans now, you know, your plans about what you are going to do? Back to medicine? By the way who will take over the hospital now?" Kerrin was flying kites all over the place.

"Mum, I've got to go, but the answer to your questions is no or I don't know. I will tell you, though, that for better or worse, I am buying some more time before making a long-term decision, by doing another series of that television program, ok. See you later, down at the hall probably. Love you. Bye."

★ ★ ★

Becker Clayton, head of the television channel, billionaire media magnate and born again and again Christian, was sitting at his huge desk in his huge office facing a large television screen when the news came on. He had spent the afternoon with his mistress, following lunch in the most expensive restaurant in Sydney. Wined, dined and well pleased, he had been driven back to his base or seat of power where he magnanimously told his private secretary that she could go home early. It was less than fifteen minutes to her normal finishing time of six o'clock, but she thanked him profusely and they wished each other a good weekend. Before she left, though, she put a last minute phone call through to her boss. It was from a fellow worshipper at the evangelical, all-action church that Clayton, but not his wife, attended dutifully every Sunday.

"Hallelujah, brother" said the voice at the other end of the phone, "Hallelujah! and may the good Lord be with you always. Just a call to let you know brother Becker, that after the service on Sunday, there is to be a round robin golf tourney. Would you be interested in that brother?"

Becker Clayton was not a golfing person, and he knew enough about these tournaments to know they were mainly about business and opportunities to invest, so he declined the offer graciously.

"Well perhaps another time brother and you have a wonderful weekend. If I don't catch you in the congregation on Sunday, well, Hallelujah anyway."

The television channel head was feeling slightly guilty about his afternoon of indulgence. He thought he could push it all away from him by just relaxing and watching the television news. However, when he switched on and was confronted with the vision of Henry, star of his channel's top show, at an Islamic burial ground, mixing with Muslims and then revealing how his father was a converted Muslim, the shock was too much. He wasn't normally prone to apoplectic fits, but the sight and reality of what he saw, made him suffer a paralysing stroke, which left him sitting in his chair with his hand outstretched, one finger pointing at the screen in front of him.

His secretary Averil Cumming had left for home, security had always been warned never to interrupt the boss, whatever the hour and his wife was away for the week-end with friends cruising off the north Queensland coast. So Becker, devout Christian though he was, missed the Sunday service and stayed transfixed in the same position, undiscovered, until Ms Cumming came in to work on the following Monday morning.

She had tapped on the door of the big office, entered and found her boss pointing at a commercial for weight watchers on the still transmitting television screen.

"Oh, I know about them." She said chirpily, "what is it....?" That's as far as she got when she witnessed the arm with the hand still pointing, crash down onto the desk and the head and shoulders of Becker Clayton, media colossus, fall forward to join that member.

17

"Oh, boy, things are hotting up." Parapip had been witnessing a preview of the deaths of both Rizal Humphries and Becker Clayton. He'd also viewed the interchange between Henry and Veronica at their lunch date after the burial they'd both attended. "You certainly worked wonders when you took Veronica over – a changed woman – but now she's back to her old self I see."

As inscrutable as ever, Danilda called over to her workmate, "I don't know what you are talking about."

"No, of course not. You never went down for a while, no. It must have been my vivid imagination. Tell you what, though, remember I said we're expecting a couple of witnesses to give character references for our subject, well they have passed through in earth time and I can't wait..." He got no further when the main buzzer on his computer heralded a message from the Intergalactic Helpers' area. Then the image of Calisthene filled the screen.

"Sorry to interrupt your musing Parapip, yes, sorry, I just happened to be on the line, but as you have noted, the two expected witnesses are now available for some questions. Now, normally of course we would expect you to do the interviews and record the data, but as I have something for you to do later in connection with one of the parties, I, well we, the Intergalactic Council, feel it would be better if I take over this little chore. Ok? Don't worry, I'll fill you in later, when I tell you about the other thing I mentioned. Cheery. Oh and stop teasing Danilda there's a good soul." And the image disappeared.

"Did you hear that?" Parapip turned to the woman at the next workspace.

"Teasing… as if. Hey, they must be big numbers in the story if Calisthene is doing the quizzing. Love to be 'a fly on the wall' – is that the expression? Whatever a fly is. Really like to be able to monitor the action with those two, but our communication with the big boys is sadly only one way. Well mine is. Yours may be different as a more experienced and privileged member of staff."

"Shut up Pip, you heard what Calisthene said. And a fly is a small creature on earth with wings that can contaminate, walk upside down, and generally make a nuisance of itself. You wouldn't want to be one of those would you?" Danilda returned to her work.

"If it allowed me to discover what was happening in the sacred space, yes. Meanwhile, I'll just have to use my imagination." And Pip returned to his surveillance of the life of Henry.

Down below, or above or beside where Pip and Danilda were, in a space where neither of them had ever been or ever seen, Calisthene was addressing an image of Rizal Humphries. "Hello, Dr Humphries, I see you're still smiling, I imagine you're happy to have left that body behind, am I right?"

The image seemed slightly puzzled to be hearing the details of his passing.

"Well, yes, I am, I suppose, it did take a bit of a beating in the end there. Where am I now? And who am I talking to?"

"My name is Calisthene, I am a sort of intermediary and well, a kind of witness. I don't have any real power, but between you and me, I do have a bit of influence in certain spheres, if I can put it that way. And to answer your other question, you are in transit."

Rizal didn't seem too concerned at the slightly abstruse answers that he got. After a lifetime in medicine, he was used to giving and hearing recondite explanations for simple problems.

"So, what do I do now? And how is my family?"

"Oh, they're fine. I want to ask you a few questions about a certain Henry or as you knew him, Rufus, Pild. I don't want to confuse you, but he has asked for advice up here about the future direction his life and work should take. Now, for reasons that I'll explain later, he has access to a clear portal which brings him into contact with the Intergalactic Helpers or intermediaries who, as a council, will give him the guidance he seeks, based principally on research and interviews to discover just how he has behaved towards his fellow human beings so far. That's why I am interviewing you right now. Oh, and although I said he has been in touch with us with his question, which is whether he should return to medicine instead of acting, in your time frame on earth, he hasn't yet made the call so to speak. Different concept, d'you understand. But don't let that worry you just now. Ok, let's see. How would you describe his general character, not his talent, his *persona*."

"I wish I could just answer the question that he has posed to you and the, what did you call them, Intergalactic Helpers? I'd say yes he must return to medicine. He is just brilliant". Rizal was smiling again. He was talking about someone he had immense respect for.

"Yes, of course," Calisthene quickly stepped in. "Yes, but we don't really want a reference at this point, not a professional reference. What about his attitude to other earthlings, I mean people. Was he ever hurtful in his dealings with the other members of the staff for instance?"

"On the contrary, on the contrary", Rizal repeated for emphasis. "Dr Pild was unusual, really, in that respect. Some surgeons, some heads of teams in the operating theatre, can be officious or even arrogant and treat assistants and nurses with less respect than they really are entitled to receive. But not Rufus... Henry. He treated everyone as his equal in any work situation. Well in any situation, really. Look, I'm the wrong one to ask if you are looking for faults in his character that might influence your judgement. This is the man who is almost idolised by other hospital staff. Not only because of his enormous talent, but because he is full of feeling for his fellow man or woman. He is a rarity and I feel almost blessed that he took the trouble to attend my burial and helped wash my body with such tenderness and love. It was like he was in prayer while he was doing it. He even brought my son back to me to assist. That's all I can say. Now what's the next move for me, what happens?"

Calisthene was impressed. Not surprised, but reassured by this man's testimony and the way it was given. "Thankyou very much for what you have contributed. It is all recorded and will be taken into account when we make a final decision. That is, when we come to a consensus. Meanwhile, you will have to remain 'in transit' until you are set free to continue your journey. You see, even though it is obvious that you are a good man, your soul is trapped where it has been operating, where it has been active for most of your lifetime. You need to be 'opened' and allowed to grow through the various levels that earthlings are dominated by. Don't worry, it can be done and it will be done in your case, through your son. For now, though, you will be happy enough just being. Thank you again." And it was all over.

Calisthene then buzzed Parapip's computer. "Pip, I want you to go into the booth. I have something I want you to do."

Parapip did as he was asked immediately. In a way he had been expecting something to happen. Danilda didn't even bother to look up as he passed her and entered the unseen space of the booth. Once in it, Calisthene addressed him again and told him that he was to go on a mission. A very special mission. Whilst he was away, someone else would be delegated to take over his data collecting on his subject. Someone efficient, he was assured. Then he was given the details of the time and place of departure and the name and address of Rizal Humphries' son. He was told the nature of the mission – to bring that man to the place where he could receive the *latihan* or spiritual exercise. Then he was told that in preparation, he would have to pass through the re-orientation area so that he could take on the shape and personality of a human being and be equipped with the appropriate earthly clothing and currency to exist on that planet. Finally, he was warned to shun temptation that would surely present itself whilst he was there... and to avoid the junk food outlets.

Once he'd briefed Pip, Calisthene returned to his own work and called up another image. It was the second person in Henry's life to pass through on the same day. Becker Clayton, the media baron.

"Well now, Mr Clayton isn't it?"

The recent arrival looked worried and just nodded in the direction he thought the voice had come from.

"How's the arm?" This really threw the man.

"What? The arm, oh, you know about that?"

"'Fraid so. But don't worry, we won't hold it against you." Calisthene's attempt at humour, as so often, fell flat.

"Right, did reception tell you what this is about whilst you were waiting? We want to get a cross-section of opinion about the character of Henry Pild, you know the former doctor who starred in one of your television programs".

"Oh, that sonofabitch, yes I know him, or rather about him." Becker had obviously been waiting for the opportunity to give vent to the rage he hadn't been able to express before the stroke despatched him.

"Before you go on Mr Clayton, that wasn't a very Christian thing to call him, was it. You are a good Christian aren't you?

So good in fact, that I hear the prime minister from where you left, has arranged for you to have a state funeral. Presumably for all your Christian deeds. That'll cost a fair penny for all those you've left behind won't it. Presumably Henry will be contributing, so you might want to moderate your language a tad." Calisthene was having a wonderful time with this one.

Nobody had ever spoken to Becker Clayton like that before. Not his competitors, his wife or even his mistress and he wasn't about to take it now from someone he couldn't even see.

"Listen mate, whoever and wherever you are. I'll call him anything I like and for your information, nothing I say will be a bad enough condemnation for a … a Muslim lover… a… someone who obviously consorts with terrorists and who knows who, at that Muslim place. He fooled me, with that good Christian name of Henry. He's no Henry I'll wager. Not when he's got his skull cap on and his prayer mat in front of him. Look I trusted him. I gave him good Christian charity. I never met him and I never want to, so that's him as far as I'm concerned. As to the state funeral, well I've put enough money into that political party to pay for it three times over and as a Christian, the PM should appreciate that. Anyway, where am I and who are you? Another bloody Muslim I'll wager. Load of no hopers. Cut off your hand as look at you and stone you if you so much as look at a woman".

"You like to look at women, don't you Becker." Calisthene had listened to this bile for long enough. "Not talking about your wife either, am I? What about the little lady you have set up in a lovely house not too far from work? Oh, by the way, is it part of the Christian ethic to keep a mistress or is that classified as adultery… you know, what you are commanded not to commit, remember? Surely you know, if you really do want to indulge yourself with the opposite sex, you would do better to embrace the religion that allows for a man to take five wives if he can provide for them in all ways. But then your present wife wouldn't go for that would she? Have you told her about the other little lady you are keeping, Beck? Do you always answer honestly when wifey asks where you have been and who you have been with? You must of course, otherwise, blow me, another commandment would have been ignored. You know the one about not bearing false witness. Anyway, just a thought, you know. You do seem to have such extreme views about other religions… that is other than your Christian beliefs. Perhaps you might consider a few of the pros and cons of the whole spectrum. You'll have plenty of time to do that whilst you remain where you ended up. Circling the empire you built and attached to all the material possessions you acquired. Good day to you." And another interview was over.

★ ★ ★

When Veronica returned to her flat after a tough afternoon at the university, she hit the button on her answering machine to hear Henry say "Good Luck".

What was that about? she thought. It was a nice gesture, but she had been with him just a few hours earlier and he more or less implied it then. Was he being sarcastic about her future plans? Well that wasn't like him. But what exactly did he mean by such a cryptic message? A clue to the answer came a little later when she had gone to bed. Her flatmate had come home and was watching television with her boy friend when the news came on. It was virtually the same news that Henry had seen earlier and the reason he had phoned. Surprised at seeing her friend right in front of her on screen at an Islamic burial service, she yelled to her to come and see.

"You're on television, V," she called, "with that great hunk of a guy you used to work with… look, quick."

Veronica slumped into the lounge half asleep and watched in horror as the press were pushing Henry to find out who the woman was.

"It looks like romance is in the air for the star of *The Specialist*" the reporter proclaimed, changing her script for this later version of the story. "**But just who is the beautiful mystery woman? We couldn't find out from the good doctor, but we will, rest assured and we hope to bring an exclusive report on the affair in tomorrow's** *World News Today*, **this is Libby Mufkin, Sydney.**"

Veronica sat in an armchair away from the television set and just laughed.
"What a lot of bullshit that woman has just spread across the airwaves. Oh, boy, I'm in for a ribbing at uni, just when I should be concentrating on my studies. Now I know what that message was all about... look, I have to get some sleep..." but before she could leave the room, her flatmate Deanne, said:
"Oh, no, you're not getting away with it that easy. What's it all about, this romance with him, Dr Wonderful, only the most eligible bachelor in town, that's all... so, c'mon?"
"I've got to go to bed folks, you'll have to find out all about it in Libby Mufkin's exclusive report, tomorrow, g'night."
Then the phone rang and an agitated woman's voice asked to speak to Veronica.
"For you," with hand over phone "Are you in?" Deanne called softly towards the bedroom door.
"Who is it?"
"I'm not sure where she is, who is this please?" Deanne lied.
"This is Goldie Milstein, Veronica's mother and I must speak to her as soon as possible this won't wait!"
"Your mother, and she sounds very disturbed, ok. We'll go into the other room and give you some privacy, here..." and she handed a very reluctant Veronica the phone.
"Mum? What's up, I was in bed."
Goldie was immediately on the attack. "In bed, in bed, were you... who with, may I ask... that terrorist... that man... that person you were with on the television. Romance in the air, my God, what have you done? I brought you up a good girl

and now what have you done? How do you think I am going to face my friends now? Tell me, do you enjoy hurting? Does it give you satisfaction to hurt your mother? Shame on you. Haven't I done enough for you? And your father is so upset. Do you ever think of his feelings? Why do you do these things?"

Veronica just closed her eyes and swayed with the punches until there was a pause.

"Mum, I am in bed on my own. I've had a hell of a day with exams and I don't need this. Listen, please... Mum, I don't know any terrorists and the man you saw me talking to on television was at the funeral of a man we both knew, Dr Rizal Humphries, the superintendent of the hospital where we worked. We were there out of respect. But..."

"Respect, yet. You were at a Muslim place and you talk of respect. What about respecting your mother sometimes? You never ring. You know nothing about what's going on. What we are going through. You just don't care do you. For your information I am back home and happy with your father. He is a fine man really. A bit boring at times, but a good man and I wish you would pay him some respect too. So, tell me where did you get that suit you were wearing? It's a smart suit, and another thing, that man, that man on the television, the television star doctor person, is that perhaps by any chance the man you brought to our house years ago? The man who destroyed my dress? I certainly hope not. I should have sued. Are you with him, you know, do you..."

Another pause and the daughter grabbed it.

"As I was about to say," Veronica really wanted to end this and get back to bed... "I am so tired, and I am really happy that you and daddy are back together... *mazeltov*. Now can I go, I'll call you sometime soon when I get a moment... and no I am not with him and we don't. Goodnight mum, give my love to daddy." And she crawled back into her bed.

* * *

Next morning, all the news media carried the story. And without exception, they relegated the actual funeral of the well-known and much loved Superintendent of the King Abdullah Free Hospital to a paragraph at the end of the speculative report on Henry, the television star and that red headed woman in green.

Henry had been out early in his usual disguise for a brisk walk along the promenade that skirted his local beach. On his way back home, he picked up a paper and when he saw the huge picture on the front page, he knew exactly what he had to do. He had about two months or so before he was supposed to start rehearsing for the second series of **The Specialist**, so he decided he would not just lie low, but leave the country completely for a few weeks.

It was early enough for the time difference between Australia and England to allow him to call the man he'd shared a room with at the Royal College conference. The man who just a few days ago had told him of the humanitarian work of a group of doctors in various parts of the world. Henry wanted to know if he could volunteer to work with them in some capacity for just a few weeks initially. The man at the other end of the phone said that it may not be possible to get him set up in a particular area of their operation for just a short time, but that it might be good for him, anyway, to be taken to various of the places the group were either working in or expecting to work in at any time. He could then see for himself just how they functioned in the field and he could decide later perhaps if he felt this was what he wanted to participate in and in what capacity. Henry thought that was perfect and planned to leave Sydney for London the next day.

Later he phoned his parents and told them of his decision. He asked them if they would take any calls on his behalf if he re-directed them to their phone. Then he said: "By the way, don't believe a word you read in the papers, we are just good friends... still. I'll be away for a few weeks and visiting a few places around the world to see for myself how this medical service works. Then it's back from the real world to the world of make believe and lots of money... wish me luck, love you both."

Meanwhile, the over-zealous Libby Mufkin had tried every way she could think of to track down the woman with Henry Pild at that burial. She had questioned everybody she could identify from her video report, including Henry's father. But Samuel Langhorne Ridwan Pild told her nothing. Well, he told her that he didn't have any idea who the woman was, but that he would very much like to know her. Yes, he had been introduced, but he had a very short memory span these days apparently and somehow he couldn't even remember the woman's name. However, he would be really interested in her exclusive report that she had mentioned. Or is it too late for that now? Henry's phone number or address? Again Sam couldn't help.

"Don't know his latest, he moves so often you know. You'll find that his phone number is ex-directory and we don't even know it. He's a very private person, you know," his father assured the reporter.

Undaunted, Libby rang the producer, the director and finally Mercy Cryer to try to get some contact number or address for Henry, their star. But it all proved to no avail. The producer was in the USA, the director was on a yacht in the Tasman Sea, somewhere between Australia and New Zealand and Mercy was just not giving out a thing. Libby had met her match there. And lost her deadline. Fortunately, the intrepid reporter thought, it was the weekend and she could fudge things until Monday. Meanwhile, Mercy told her that when it was convenient she would be issuing a press release herself on Henry and whoever he was having any relationship with, so "cool your heels lady!" was her advice.

Completely unaware of all the attempts by the press to trace the woman in green that seemed to be very friendly with the star of *The Specialist,* Veronica resisted her desire to call Henry and chat about it all. She was really determined not to let anything romantic or even unromantic between them interfere with the pursuit of her medical ambitions. There was something comforting about the simple "Good Luck" message that he'd left on her answer phone and that was enough for now. But she knew that she would be calling him once her current exams were finished.

★ ★ ★

Despite everything that had transpired in their relationship, Mercy still regarded Henry as her property. After all, he was under contract to her and even though her interest was now just the fifteen percent he'd agreed to, that was enough for her to want to protect and promote him. He was without doubt the star in her stable and a meal ticket she wasn't going to let go too easily. Certainly not to that red-headed bitch she had seen him with on the television news. So as soon as she had chased off Miss Libby Mufkin, she decided that on Monday, she would phone Henry and get the information for herself.

Before she could carry out her intention, though, a very blue Becker Clayton had been discovered by his secretary and the news of his demise spread like wildfire, warming the hearts of his debtors and worrying the minds of many who relied on him for their jobs. Mercy was shocked and then thankful that she had managed to get her contract with the television channel approved in time. Now, more than ever, she had to make contact with her star and make sure he was still a hundred percent behind the project. Who knows what might happen under any new administration. The network might even be sold. She also wanted to know who that woman was. However, when she did phone later that day, the re-directed call brought her no satisfaction at all. On the contrary, when Kerrin Pild answered the call and told the agent that her son was out of the country for a while and couldn't be contacted, Mercy was not a happy person. All she could splutter was that if he did contact them, could they ask him to get in touch with her. Mercy was sure, she told them, that he would want to know that the television channel boss had suddenly died.

★ ★ ★

When Henry booked in at the overseas terminal this time, the reaction to his presence there from some of the airport staff and immigration was a little different. There was certainly the same blushing enthusiasm from the young woman who took his baggage and issued his tickets, again upgraded to first class, but he met a mixed reaction from the other guardians of security and protection of the state. This time his hand baggage and his body received a far more thorough examination than the previous cursory one. The knowledge that he had been consorting with Muslims was obviously being taken into consideration and a veil of suspicion was evident, despite the superficial smiles.

This time, immigration officers wanted to inspect both his passport and his personal identity card.

"Off again Doctor? When do you plan to return sir?"

Henry knew he had to be back in two months at the latest.

"No idea, right now, mate. Depends where I go from London, is it important?"

Was it because of his fame through television that he was getting the attention of two immigration officials he wondered. Officer two now spoke: "No, not at all..." Then officer one spoke up again.

"Well, unless you do know where you will be going... it's just a formality, you know. By the way sir, did you know that you haven't filled in your religion on your ID, look in the space there."

"That's because I don't have a particular religion. Is that really your job, though?" Henry looked at both of them and officer two shook his head and smiled. Officer one though had more to say:

"Well, not really, but as we have to check folk in and out of our country, it's good to have all the facts so to speak. But if you have no religion, you have no religion, ha. And you are not sure where you are going, was it?"

Henry had had enough of this nonsense:

"Well, to be honest, I do know some of the locations. I'm pretty sure that I'm not going to Iraq, but I will go to the Sudan, I could go to Chechnya and I'll more than likely spend a fair bit of time in the Palestinian territories. Is there anything you'd like me to bring you back? A prayer mat for instance?"

Officer one wasn't going to bite on that, so he closed the passport and ID card and handed it back.

"Have a pleasant journey sir, thankyou." Then Officer two slid a piece of paper across to Henry and asked him for his autograph for his wife.

When he arrived at Heathrow airport this time, he was met by the man he'd been in contact with, Dr Patrick McEnery, a former practising paediatrician, now the main administrator and organiser of the emergency medical group. Henry would be travelling to several countries where the organisation had permanent doctors or nurses stationed for periods of six months and up, depending on the need for their services. The man from Australia hadn't known it when he had some fun with the immigration officials, but Sudan and the Palestinian territories were just two of the places he was expected to visit.

However, he wouldn't be travelling from London for a couple of days or so, as immunisation shots and visas had to be organised. The schedule had still to be finalised, but it looked as if he would be visiting doctors in the field in Colombia, where deaths and injuries were constant because of the war between the authorities and the drug barons. To Somalia, where the innocent were constantly victims of the factional rivalry. Possibly Chad but certainly Darfur in the western region of Sudan, where drought competed with tribal conflicts to provide the need for much medical assistance from the group. Uganda may be on the schedule, but the Palestinian territories certainly would be. Henry would be witness to the misery of the refugees and others in the Gaza who seem destined to suffer ongoing pain and injury, either from their Israeli "occupiers" or as a result of the factional hatred between fellow Arabs. Hamas versus Fatah.

Also, like all tours of the middle-east, it wouldn't be complete without a visit to the West Bank, where Fatah were being openly lauded and supported by Israel and the West, whilst their Hamas brothers in Gaza were branded terrorists and marginalised in all respects. But if the guns were silent there, people still suffered the mental stress of being constantly observed by Israeli guards and having to pass through checkpoints each day to get anywhere and from the anguish of being cut off from family members and needing passes to get to their land on the other side of the giant wall that their worried neighbours had erected through it. Whatever freedoms they'd be granted in the unseemly public courtship by Israel that followed the breakup of the peoples of the Palestinian territories, Peter McEnery's team knew that the psychological scars would be in need of help for years to come.

As Henry remarked to his host and organiser, the next few weeks would be fairly different from the life and work he was engaged in back home in Sydney.

★ ★ ★

When she had finished her exams and had some space, before she did anything else, Veronica phoned Henry. Despite the niggling concern that he might not have believed her explanation for the botched operation that worried him so much, she really wanted to be in touch again in the hope that the relationship could develop. The voice at the other end of the phone wasn't the one she expected though. It was his father, Sam, who told her very simply that Henry was overseas. But when she identified herself, he started to tell her about the venture his son was involved in. He stopped himself from giving away too much and instead he told her that before he went away, Henry had mentioned that she might be in touch to talk to his mother about the spiritual movement they all belonged to. Veronica hadn't really given that possibility a lot of thought since the lunch, but her interest was still there and when Kerrin got on the phone and introduced herself and invited her to come for some lunch the next day, she suddenly found it very easy to accept the offer.

Although she hadn't yet been traced and contacted for that so-called *World News Tonight* exclusive interview, when Veronica got dressed to visit with the Pilds, she avoided the green suit she had been filmed in at the burial ceremony, and completely covered her easily identifiable red hair with a scarf, just in case, she told herself, someone was watching the Pild house. She had heard many stories of how paparazzi staked out places for days and days to get pictures they could sell to newspapers and she figured that if Libby Mufkin could sound so determined, she was sure others in the media might also share her obsession, however ludicrous it really was.

When she arrived at the house in Lane Cove, without being aware of any intrusive camera lens, she was welcomed and immediately invited to have a swim in the Pild pool before lunch. Veronica declined the offer, because she was really more anxious to learn more about these people and their spiritual way and she didn't want any distractions. At lunch the small talk was pretty well focussed on Henry and that's when she learned more about his new interest overseas. They'd had one call from him following his trip to Somalia and he told them of his shock and distress at what he had witnessed there, despite the inspiring work of the medicos. He didn't say where he was off to next, but he had promised to keep in touch.

After lunch, Sam went off to his study and Kerrin took Veronica into the lounge for what she had really come to hear.

Mrs Pild was a long time helper, but after she explained the basis and aims of the actual spiritual exercise, just as she herself had been told many years earlier, she suggested that it was best if the young enquirer attended an applicants' meeting at the group's hall in Sydney. There she would meet other women helpers and hopefully other applicants or enquirers and get a better feeling from being with them all.

Already though, after a mere half hour of listening to Kerrin, Veronica felt even more attracted to this unknown, mysterious 'receiving' that she had talked about. She got the address and times that she could attend and after being assured that Kerrin herself would be there with the others, she took her leave.

How does, or how would this new reality fit in with the conventional, practical, medical attitudes to diseases and the treatment and cure of the human body that suffers from them? What about organ failures and transplants and the repair of physical injuries? As she made her way home, even though she really had no doubts about the veracity of what she had heard, the questions were coming in. Challenging questions from the other reality, the empiricism that she had embraced all her professional life. Can the two co-exist? That is what she was determined to discover. Presumably that was what Henry had discovered and what motivated him. She knew that his faith and belief in a Creator's existence influenced if not actually ruled his medical life. Now, perhaps, she had the chance of finding out for herself.

A few weeks later, she had the opportunity of actually discussing the subject with the man himself. But not before a tragedy had entered her life.

Less than a month after she had made an inner commitment to seek the contact with the *latihan* that Kerrin and later, other helpers talked of, Veronica's life was turned upside down. First had come the news that she had been awarded a first class honours degree in medicine and with it the knowledge that for once she'd have done something to really please her mother. Then the bolt out of the blue that sank all her joy.

Goldie and Cec Milstein, now back together in apparent marital harmony, had decided to really consolidate that harmony, by having a second honeymoon. They booked a flight to the most exclusive resort in Northern Queensland, where they had a reservation in the best hotel. Up to this point, although the couple were back living together under the one roof, what with Cec's business commitments and Goldie's determination to re-furnish the home, they hadn't got around to consummating the revived marriage. This was going to be the jewel in the crown for the second honeymooners. The cherry on the cake and to get the very most out of it, they thought of everything.

Goldie bought herself a very flimsy and sexy nightgown and without reference to him, she'd also bought a pair of silk pyjamas for her husband. Unfortunately, she hadn't bothered to check his waist and chest size for some time and whilst she had been out of his life, Cec had really indulged himself and put on quite a few kilos. Even before all his additional avoirdupois, Veronica's father had a weight problem which she had constantly warned him about. Because of his mainly sedentary work and lack of exercise, he had very high blood pressure and cholesterol levels.

The mistake in the size of the pyjamas wasn't discovered, unfortunately, until that first evening. The couple had wined and dined very unhealthily in the most expensive restaurant and instead of walking the short distance back to their hotel, they had taken a taxi. Back in their room, relaxing with a quick bicarbonate of soda, and a glass or two of the magnum of champagne that the hotel always provided for the "bridal suite",

Cec struggled out of his clothes and made a valiant attempt to force his huge body into the silk 'jamas. Meanwhile, Goldie wafted in from the bathroom, soaked in very expensive perfume, in her new see-through nightgown, made one mannequin-style circuit of the room and then climbed onto the king size bed. The vision was too much and the fragrance too overpowering for the "groom" who gave up the fight, tossed the recalcitrant silk bottoms onto the floor and threw himself onto his now seductively reclining wife.

It was a wonderful gesture on both their parts and as memory survives the grave, it's something they'll always remember. However, they won't get a chance to tell any of their friends or associates about this re-entry into marital bliss. Tragically before either party had experienced paradise, Cec's heart gave in and he died where he lay. Unfortunately he was lying on top and actually still inside Goldie at the time and so powerful was the grip he had around his wife's frame and so heavy was this lover, that either at a point just prior to ejaculation or simply through over exertion, his body crushed all the life out of his partner.

They were discovered next morning when a bright young waiter brought the pre-ordered breakfast to the room. It was a sad case of *flagrante delicto morte* as the local newspaper was later to describe it.

A doctor and the police were called and when two officers failed to get Cec off the crushed woman, a bath crane was brought in from a nearby nursing home.

Massaging his strained back after his effort, one of the policemen, said, out of the corner of his mouth: "Case of What God has put together, let no man pull apart eh?" The other officer glared at him and helped attach the lifting device to the deceased.

When he was raised, like some giant beached whale, Mr Milstein was still in a state of *penile erecti*, (sic) as that same newspaper informed its readers. It was also soberly reported that there had been no signs of foul play.

Death certificates were issued and when Veronica's name and phone number were found in Goldie's diary, she was contacted and informed of the sad news.

She was alone when the phone rang and she suddenly felt fragile and in need of some support. Her flatmate was at work and she really had no colleagues available to share her shattering news with. Then she felt to ring Kerrin Pild, the woman she already had a good rapport with and who was both sensitive and strong. It was a good move. With almost no time lost at all, Henry's mother was at Veronica's flat, comforting her and organising all the things that needed attention. First thing was to inform the synagogue and arrange a funeral. Kerrin knew that religious laws required that, like Muslims, Jews had to be buried within a very short time of death. Arrangements were then made for the bodies to be collected from the local mortuary and flown back to Sydney. The older woman even offered to accompany Veronica on the flight north to collect them.

Throughout the ordeal, Veronica displayed the strength she had always shown in the operating theatre and in her determination to return to her studies and earn her degree.

The funeral wasn't easy, but again, Kerrin helped in organising it. There were several relations to be informed and invited and several friends of the couple who lived close enough to attend at short notice. Out of regard for her parents, Veronica went through the motions of traditional mourning. She covered all the mirrors in the apartment that had been their home and, after the ceremony, sat *shiva* whilst the invited and several uninvited folk came to pay their respects to her as the sole survivor of the immediate family.

Two weeks later, Sam and Kerrin Pild were asked to attend the graduation ceremony that should have been a joyful and proud time for the Milsteins as they witnessed their daughter's achievement. A time which would have united the mother and her offspring in a way that hadn't ever previously seemed possible.

Veronica had moved from her shared, rented flat and was uncomfortably ensconced in the luxury of the far too large apartment she had inherited. She knew she would not be staying there permanently and had already arranged for a real estate agent to value the place. For the present though, it was a haven that gave her the privacy she needed whilst she prepared herself for the future. Did she after all want to specialise in surgery and particularly microsurgery? Did she want to specialise in anything? She had an excellent degree and she knew that whatever course she chose, she would next have to serve a couple of years of internship. And after that, what? She assumed that she would still be unmarried and wondered if she would also be unwanted. Meanwhile, she also now knew that she was clear in her mind about wanting to be opened in the *latihan* or spiritual exercise that she'd been introduced to. Perhaps that would bring the guidance she needed. Would need. But there was no hurry. No pressure at all. Certainly not in any material way. She was now a wealthy woman and the guidance she really wanted was to do with her personal life and future relationships and perhaps her spiritual path.

18

When Henry Pild returned to Sydney, instead of coming back with answers for his future in medicine, he carried with him even more questions. His tour of the various areas throughout the world where the medical team had bases, had been both an eye-opener and a cause for deep sadness at the misery and pain of so many victims of poverty, drought and warfare. Throughout his professional life in Australia, he had been cocooned, safe from the terrible plight of millions around the globe. His medicine had always been carried out in the most hygienic conditions, with the most sophisticated equipment and qualified support. The contrast with what he experienced in parts of Africa and the Palestinian territory, for instance, cast further doubt in his mind about his future as a doctor. Before he left for London he already had the dreadful concern about his ability to ever return to his work as a microsurgeon. He always prided himself on the fact that he was a perfectionist. Everybody who came into contact with his work encouraged him to think that way. However, the botched finger operation, his last before he turned to acting, shook him and undermined the feeling of infallibility he had in relation to his work.

The venture into a completely different world of medicine, would, he had hoped, provide a safety device for his lost confidence and an alternative way of practising his talent. But it didn't. The clarity that he'd hoped would come to guide him, just hadn't. What value was he to the teams? His real expertise was not generally needed. Could he adapt and perform more general medicine instead? He had a few months to come up with some solutions.

When he had discussed the possibilities with the supervising doctor of the medical teams, he promised he'd be back in touch after he'd finished his commitment to the television series back in Sydney. Dr McEnery had suggested that his reputation in microsurgery must be taken into consideration. He had told Henry that he didn't want to waste his acknowledged genius with the scalpel at the expense of those who could benefit from it, in order for him to practise general medicine in the field however worthy the cause. However, there was an alternative. Dr Pild could be included on a specialist roster and contacted if there was an emergency that could benefit from his skill. That way, whatever he was doing in his home country would only be interrupted occasionally and for short spells.

Henry had plenty to cogitate on, but within days, he really had to throw away the persona of a real man of medicine and affect the character of a pretend one for the cameras. First though, he wanted to follow up on the disturbing news about Veronica's mother and father that his own parents had told him. They also told him of the demise of Becker Clayton, but that didn't disturb him too much at all. The only thing that he found disquieting about the passing of that man was the fact that he had been given a state funeral. Like most people, Henry knew that Clayton, one of the country's richest men, was infamous for his boast that he had no intention of paying any money to the tax office if he could avoid it. His accountants, of course, made sure he could. Avoid it, that is.

Veronica was thrilled and relieved when Henry rang her. They had plenty to talk about and learn from each other. Their first meeting took place in the home she had inherited. The apartment brought back mixed feelings for the man who as a young student had really upset Goldie Milstein.

"She never forgave you, you know?" Veronica smiled. "But a lot of her anger was pure theatrics. Anyway, I'm sure she sees you in a different light now. At least I hope so, wherever she is."

Henry assured Veronica that he never really felt any animosity towards her mother and could well understand her reaction to his clumsiness. "I am a bit clumsy at times, as you well know, but something you don't really want to talk about. Sorry, I know you have other more important things on your mind, but perhaps one day..."

When his hostess reacted to what he started to pursue again, Henry realised their *tête à tête* could be over very quickly, so he changed his tack and congratulated her on gaining her medical degree and on the fact that she was very soon to be opened and would become a member of the spiritual brotherhood.

"You do realise, of course that once you do join up, you will be my sister. My spiritual sister. That's right. But don't worry, it won't preclude us from having a different relationship". Veronica took a very subtle double take.

"Did I hear you right? What sort of relationship?"

If Henry was full of doubts about his medical future, he was certain about one thing. Now that he had met up with her again, he wanted more than ever to really get close to the woman he had ignored for so many years. He wanted to express his feelings to her, but he had to be sure that she felt the same.

"Well, the sort of relationship where a man and a woman get to know each other and where they both know, deep inside, that the feelings they have are real. I'm pretty sure that's what I want, what about you?"

"What I want?" Part of her wanted to yell 'Of course, of course it's what I want, have wanted and always will want.' But another part, that part of her consciousness that was so affected by what Henry had talked about at the lunch, months ago, hesitated. He'd talked about staining your soul or taking on other people's baggage when you indulge in sex, simply for the sake of fornication. His words still echoed in her mind. It might seem unreasonable, but she had felt dirty then and she wanted more than anything to expunge the feeling and the effect, if it was possible. Just as this same man had suggested for himself, she hoped that a return to abstinence and the action of the *latihan* once she was opened would cleanse her. She had to be sincere but diplomatic when she answered. "What I want, well, what I want, is for you to know that yes, I want, I mean my feelings are like yours, but, listen, I really want to be able to say, I… that my want is right, and that I am right, I mean that I am the person you want me to be and for me to be that, I have to clear away any part of me that I am not happy about… in my past I mean. Does that make sense? I want the *latihan* to make me what you really want. You know, like you said. Though, I don't know, yes, I want that relationship. Very, very much." They could easily have fallen into each others arms and then into bed at this point. But Henry broke the spell and smiling broadly he leapt up from where he'd been sitting and said: "Great, how about dinner, then?"

★ ★ ★

The next few months seemed to pass very quickly for the couple. He started work on the second series of **The Specialist** and once again had the services of Bert to shuttle him to and from work and the keen eyes of security checking both him and his car inside and out.

    The first series had been such a resounding success in all ways, that producer, director and production staff had all been retained. Missing was Sandy the acting coach, now apparently redundant on this project, as everyone agreed that the 'star' of the show was so natural in the part of the specialist that he needed no extra advice for his performance.

In accordance with the contract, Henry had been closely consulted on the scripts and had given the final ok for each one well before rehearsals started.

The new head of the television channel had been appointed and he had a reputation as a tough guy who always got his way in his many television posts both in Australia and overseas. However, he knew a good thing when he saw it and the production that had raised the ratings for the channel was guaranteed the support and freedom that no other program received.

Veronica was opened to the *latihan* soon after she and Henry had virtually become a pair. She also started her internship and was happy to rejoin her old hospital, the King Abdullah Free Hospital, in this new role. She still had many friends on the staff there, so while young interns straight from university found the sudden introduction to working in a real hospital situation hard, if not stressful, the former nurse felt completely at home.

Meanwhile, whilst they both focussed on their separate roles, they managed to see each other fairly regularly and the relationship grew stronger and stronger. Particularly since Henry seemed to have given up the quest to find out the whole truth about his last operation. The subject was raised again just the once, but not in a probing way, when halfway through the production of **The Specialist,** the untimely death of the unfortunate cricketer occurred. The rumour and innuendo surrounding Wayne Carroll's loss of form, that in the tabloid press had been ascribed to his loss of something else, never came to Henry's notice. Or Veronica's. However, they both noted his passing. The newly appointed Superintendent of the King Abdullah Free had contacted Henry and suggested that he might like to attend the funeral for the man who had been so generous to the hospital in gratitude for Dr Pild's work on his finger.

The former surgeon, totally embarrassed by the reminder of his work and the still unanswered question it posed for him, declined, saying that his production schedule precluded his attendance however much he would have liked to have been there to represent the hospital. When he next saw her, he suggested that Veronica might like to go in his place, but like him, she also very quickly found a reason that prevented her from going. She also wanted to change the subject.

"Have you heard any funny clicking sounds when you're on the phone? You know, in the background?"

He had, and so had his father and mother.

"Of course. Actually I meant to tell you about it. I've been well aware that my phone has been sporadically tapped. That's what it is. So subtle. But try complaining about it and you'll get the 'you must be imagining things' routine. Fact is that it started after I got back from my trip and Sam and Kerrin heard those sounds on their phone shortly after the funeral for Rizal. We were all noted by the shadowy people. Don't worry, though, just don't plan any terrorist activities over the phone, or arrange to meet any suspicious men of middle-eastern appearance. Mind you, I'd want to know about them if you do. If you know any Yiddish curses, you might like to throw those down the line when you hear the clicks."

The phone tapping, camera surveillance on just about every road and public building and the ID cards created a background of fear and an erosion of the free-spirited culture that Australia, his country, used to enjoy. Who you were and what you did was now monitored and registered on data banks controlled by the police and the so-called security service. Not that this ethos was peculiar to this former antipodean paradise alone. Most, if not all, governments of the "democracies" in the world recognised the value in controlling and manipulating a society by inducing a climate of fear. They always had of course through tools like unemployment, but things were getting worse. The answer for Henry, for all those who had access to it, was the spiritual exercise. By turning to one's inner, where the real self resided and where the strength to sustain that self could be called on, was, he realised, the way to minimise the worst effect of the material world on the psyche of a person.

★ ★ ★

When the second series of **The Specialist** had been completed and the first program screened, Henry had survived once again the rounds of photographs and interviews required by the publicity department and his agent Mercy and he now had to make some very clear decisions. Already there was an unusual reaction to the series. All the reviewers had noted that the formula which eschewed the portrayal of graphic sex still worked and drew a growing and appreciative audience. "A bold and brave venture" one critic had pronounced it. But this second series revealed something else. Television columnists and many viewers remarked that there seemed to be an unusual, almost ethereal quality in the acting of the star of **The Specialist**.

Mercy Cryer took advantage of all the good things she was hearing and reading and immediately took out an option with the television channel for a third series with a contract to be negotiated later. She then approached Henry with the news and also told him that the producer of the proposed film was really excited to talk to Henry about that project later in the year. He'd said he felt that the "actor" was now ready for the big screen. Mercy was holding a lot of cards in her hand, but they all meant absolutely nothing for her unless she could get Henry interested first of all in signing a new contract that would continue their association as agent and star. The old one was now finished. And so was their association as far as Dr Pild was concerned. He was now quite ready to take the money he'd earned from his foray into television acting and continue his life in a different direction. No doubt this woman of immense resource and cunning would be putting pressure on him and he knew that there would be an unpleasant showdown at some stage, but he put that time off by telling her that once again he needed some space and he'd be in touch.

With the break, though, came time for reflection. He knew without doubt that he no longer wanted to be a recognised, and in some cases idolised, figure through television or any other medium that promoted the superficial. For one thing, he was becoming increasingly fed up with having to disguise himself whenever he was in public. He looked forward, for instance, to being able to enter a restaurant without having to wear dark glasses and a baseball cap on backwards.

What he didn't know, was whether he should attempt to return to the specialised discipline that he had formerly practised so successfully, before what he called the "aberration" occurred in his life. For the first time, he had lost the tight control he'd always had on his morals and ethics and uncharacteristically allowed someone to dominate his senses and lead him in a direction he had never before even dreamed of. The result had been both an adventure and a massive learning curve. He had arrived at a point where he had found the strength to recover his old integrity; to realise the mistakes he had made in his relationships; and after discovering the international medical team, to learn first hand about the world of the underprivileged and the misery and pain of the victims of drought and conflict all over the globe. Then there was the real question mark that was constantly forcing itself upon his consciousness demanding an answer. Could he ever operate again, without knowing what had really happened to him in that operating theatre on that fatal last day at the King Abdullah Free Hospital. He knew that one day somehow he would discover what he so desperately wanted to know. What persisted in tormenting him. At the same time, he was also very aware that he didn't want to destroy the relationship he was building with Veronica by forcing her to tell him what she really knew. Perhaps one day she would volunteer the information and that would put the business to rest, along with his mind.

He decided once again to approach the local group helpers to assist him if they could by testing with him about his future direction. Unfortunately, just as before, they were unable to reach any kind of consensus in their receiving and once again, he assumed that the mixed messages that they were getting, was caused to some extent by each individual's attitude towards him. They were, after all, human beings and it obviously wasn't easy to be able fully to dismiss the fact that they were being asked to give advice to this person who had already reached fame as a doctor, before becoming a household name as an actor. Perhaps he had to accept that their minds were getting in the way of their ability to totally surrender to the *latihan* and receive in an un-muddied way. He thanked them anyway.

After this disappointment, Henry phoned his father to see what he could suggest, apart at this stage, from another attempt to get through to a higher authority by using the portal that Sam had talked of. He rang at the right time, it seems, as there was to be a meeting of all the national helpers - representatives from groups around the country, plus the promised attendance of the international helpers for the region Australia was in. It was to be in Melbourne in a couple of days and Sam told his son, that he'd contact one of their number and ask if they could do a special test for him. He warned him, though that of course, there was no reason that their receiving was of any better quality than the local helpers' group, as they just happened in their current roles to have different mandates to fulfil.

"However", he tried to assure Henry, "as they may not know you or your reputation, they might be able to stay a bit clearer in their testing, who knows? Worth trying though. Can you go down to Melbourne, just now?"

Henry was more than interested. "Yes, of course, just give me the times and the address and I'll be there."

As Sam had mentioned, Dr Pild was apparently known only slightly by some of the gathered and he was grateful for that. However, his gratitude ran out with that discovery, because the assembled helpers in Melbourne couldn't give Henry any clearer idea of what future direction he should follow. One even suggested that perhaps acting was his real talent. After the session was over and apologies were made about the lack of clarity in the receiving, Henry discovered that his television show, which was broadcast all over the nation, had in fact been shown the previous evening.

★ ★ ★

When he returned to Sydney, after reporting on the second failure to get any clear answers to his problem, Sam reminded him once again about the portal and how to access it. Henry followed the advice.

Within twenty-four earth hours of his success in contacting Master Control and relating to Calisthene his dilemma, he received a mysterious email communication. It read: "Submission and surrender and in *latihan* tonight, the portal will be open to you again. Trust me." That was it and it was unsigned. He checked the address for clues but saw only a provider's name: *space@coolmail.com*. When he sent a reply to confirm, his email was instantly returned by the postmaster with the message: no such address exists. Then as he attempted to file the original, it disappeared completely from his computer.

Henry rang his father and told him about the response he'd received. He asked him if he thought it was suggesting that he should join a general group *latihan* at the hall that night or do one on his own at home. Sam told him it was important for him to be alone when he was able to access the portal. To stand on his own feet, both literally and metaphorically, even metaphysically and he wished him good luck.

That evening, after completely quietening his heart and mind, Henry stood and asked for the *latihan* to begin. When he felt the vibration of the spiritual exercise in his body, he called the name of his spiritual guide and he found himself in that unique state and space that he experienced when he last sought access to the portal.

"Hello, Henry isn't it. We're expecting you. How are you today?" The voice came from all sides of his existence. Quadraphonic sound but no image. So looking in no particular direction, but seeing only soft blue light, the man in the portal answered: "Fine, I'm fine... what do I..."

"Just hold on a second brother. The council has met and we do have a message for you, but I'll let Calisthene, your advocate, tell you all about it. Oh, I'm Mysalam, by the way, I'll just get Cal." The welcoming voice was replaced by celestial music. About three earth minutes later, with the soft constant blue changing gently to waves and spirals, the voice of Calisthene came over the portal, again filling every space around Henry.

"Hello once again, Henry, sorry you can't see me, but I can see you very clearly on the monitor in front of me. Well, now, let's see. Whether to practise medicine again or not, that's the guts of it isn't it?"

"Well, I wouldn't have used that expression, but yes, I suppose that's the core issue that I can't seem to get resolved through testing." Henry was smiling and fascinated at the conversation.

"Oh, I picked that phrase up from someone here called Parapip, he has acquired some quaint terminology since he joined us. But, look, let's get down to your question. What are your own feelings about returning to medicine and leaving that acting stuff behind you?" Calisthene was adjusting his monitor and bringing up a montage of pictures of Dr Pild in the role of **The Specialist.**

"Well, I'm pretty well convinced that I should return to medicine in some form or another, but..." Henry was just on the point of revealing the cause of his real doubt. He had no idea just how much the Intergalactic Helpers knew about him.

"But. But what?" Calisthene was pushing.

"But, I have a problem, it's difficult to describe, it has to do with my work as a microsurgeon... my last operation... you see..." Henry was struggling.

Calisthene decided to speed things up. "Oh, you mean the finger, the cock-up with the cricketer's finger, while you had your mind on that Mercy woman. Well relax, don't give it another thought. It was a set up, brother. Tell you one thing though, you can thank Veronica for really saving your embarrassment" Henry was completely thrown. He started to open his mouth but was cut off before he could utter a sound.

"She hasn't told you has she? Well I will. You were so preoccupied with your infatuation with your seductress, that you actually replaced the poor man's finger the wrong way round."

"No, that's not right... it was off kilter, that's bad enough" Henry had to interrupt.

"Wrong, brother," said the voice all around him. "You put the finger on the wrong way round. The knuckle and nail were facing the wrong way. If you were here, I could show you on the videotape we have."

The doctor wondered if he was being fooled. "There was no videotape taken that night, on the orders of the patient."

"You're right there Henry, but I am referring to our own recording. You wouldn't even have known about it or where the camera was. But let's get on. The fact is that after you left the theatre, Veronica and the other nurse noticed the mistake and in order to save your humiliation and, she thought, your reputation, your head nurse, the woman who loved you so unselfishly, reversed your work and re-attached the finger herself. As you say, slightly off centre. However, neither you nor the good nurse were really acting spontaneously. You were both being directed from here. The preoccupation with Mercy was part of our plan. In fact the whole acting nonsense was. And the action that Veronica took happened because she had a visitor within. Don't bother to try to understand that one. The whole point is this Henry. You were and you are still a brilliant microsurgeon. But you made the great mistake of trying to convince yourself that you were always striving for perfection. That's right, ring a bell, does it? Well that ain't your province, brother. Perfection that is. True perfection is God's business. The perfection you were attempting is a manifestation of the ego and leads to little more than egocentricity. It's not a bad idea to sometimes say to yourself: If a thing's worth doing, it's worth doing badly. I joke of course, but it tempers the need to strive for that perfection that is just the massaging of your self or ego. It's not entirely your fault of course. You inherited the need, albeit in a different form, from both your father and your grandfather. Not everyone knows of course, but that Jock Pild was the cock o' the north in his younger days.

"However, the ego thing can be a real problem in the spiritual world or even in religious practice. I mean the powers that be here, can't understand why so many personalities seem to dominate the various religions and try to lead their flocks or followers by persuasion. Persuasion of their personal views, not God's Will. Most of the time the interpretation of the words in their holy books are subjected to a convenient spin. That's ego with a capital "E", brother and where that kind of ego appears, then the Almighty tends to disappear. Also, I have to tell you that pretty well everyone connected with Master Control has a hard time controlling spontaneous laughter when they see the leaders of the various religions and many of their acolytes still wearing strange hats and long robes – we call them dresses. And what about those folk who shave their heads, they're a real hoot. But I digress. Finally, the council has reviewed your actions towards others and on balance you treat your fellow beings well, very well. Mind you, we felt that you might have offered to buy Goldie Milstein a replacement dress for the one you ruined. But, I know, you were just a student. Anyway, as I said, on balance... in fact, though I shouldn't be telling you this, in fact, you got some glowing testimonials from some we questioned. Also we were all pleased at your recognition of how shabbily you had treated Veronica. She is your soul mate and she also had to suffer to make you aware of that reality. You've got something good there brother, don't spoil it. I know you won't. One very last thing, before you leave us and return to your given talent of medicine, ask your father if the name Danilda means anything to him. Goodbye." The voice trailed off echoing the farewell and the blue faded. Henry stood in the middle of his lounge, his eyes closed and tears rolling down his cheek.

Where had he been? The questions invaded. Had he been to the deepest realms of his own soul or had he been to a place outside his body, outside of his comprehension? Was there a difference, or were they both the same? Last time he'd had a taste, this time he'd been completely immersed. It was the most overwhelming and beautiful experience he'd ever known. He wanted to talk to someone. To his father and mother. To Veronica. But he would have to leave it for the next day, when he might be fully returned to his old self.

Next morning, there was an excitement in his soul that he couldn't restrain. He desperately wanted to see Veronica and he also wanted to share his experience with his father.

When he phoned the hospital and spoke to Veronica, he was greeted by an enthusiastic voice telling him that she knew he would call and that she had something to tell him. They arranged to meet for lunch.

Then he drove over to his parents' house. His mother was already out with her local painting group and as he related his experience of the previous evening to his father, the house seemed full of the same tranquil state that he had experienced throughout his conversation with Calisthene. Sam was touched by it and seemed to understand everything he was told as if he already knew. Then when he was asked if he recognised the name Danilda, his eyes seemed alight. He told his son that that was the first time he'd heard that name mentioned for more years than he cared to remember. He said his father, Rufus or Jock as he was known, had told him that his mother, Sam's grandmother, was given that very name. But neither Henry nor

Sam really understood the true significance of Calisthene's enquiry.

★ ★ ★

Lunch with Veronica was a fairly abbreviated meeting, because of her commitment in the hospital, but its content was profound. Henry had decided that this was going to be his opportunity to tell her that he was completely finished with acting and about to return to his practice and his consultancy in the hospital. He was also hoping that he could explain something of his experience, without overwhelming her at this stage of her development in the *latihan*. But more than anything, he wanted to ask her to marry him. All of this and more was ready to flow from his mouth just as soon as they sat down, despite the awareness that all eyes were on them in the hospital canteen.

However, before he could say a word, Veronica was fidgeting with an envelope which she was obviously anxious to reveal the contents of. "I've got something to tell you, and I'm really excited about it." She said.

"And I've something to say to you, to tell you and to ask you" Henry was uncharacteristically anxious, she thought, but she wanted to tell her story first.

"You know how important names are, you know, the right names to fit the real person, like you told me and … that's why you were given the name Henry and that… well, look, I've got a new name… it's here, in here, look" And she slid a small note out of the envelope and passed it to Henry. "What do you think about that name for me?"

Henry unfolded the note and read the typewritten message which said, "the correct name for you, the name in harmony with your soul, is….Danilda."